THE COMPLETE SHORT STORIES
OF D. H. LAWRENCE

VOL. I

ALSO BY D. H. LAWRENCE

COMPASS BOOKS

Selected Poems

Sons and Lovers

Etruscan Places

Sex, Literature, and Censorship

Psychoanalysis and the Unconscious *and*
Fantasia of the Unconscious

Women in Love

Kangaroo

The Rainbow

Aaron's Rod

Twilight in Italy

Sea and Sardinia

THE VIKING PORTABLE LIBRARY

The Portable D. H. Lawrence
Edited by Diana Trilling

D. H. LAWRENCE

The Complete
Short Stories

VOL. I

VIKING PRESS · NEW YORK

The Complete Short Stories of D. H. Lawrence

in Three Volumes

COMPASS BOOKS EDITION

Issued in 1961 by The Viking Press, Inc.

625 Madison Avenue, New York 22, N. Y.

Distributed in Canada by
The Macmillan Company of Canada Limited

Stories from *The Woman Who Rode Away* are reprinted by arrangement with Alfred A. Knopf, Inc.

Fourth printing February 1966

Printed in the U.S.A. by The Murray Printing Company

CONTENTS

Volume I

Volume II

Volume II
(continued)

Volume III

A MODERN LOVER

THE road was heavy with mud. It was labour to move along it. The old, wide way, forsaken and grown over with grass, used not to be so bad. The farm traffic from Coney Grey must have cut it up. The young man crossed carefully again to the strip of grass on the other side.

It was a dreary, out-of-doors track, saved only by low fragments of fence and occasional bushes from the desolation of the large spaces of arable and of grassland on either side, where only the unopposed wind and the great clouds mattered, where even the little grasses bent to one another indifferent of any traveller. The abandoned road used to seem clean and firm. Cyril Mersham stopped to look round and to bring back old winters to the scene, over the ribbed red land and the purple wood. The surface of the field seemed suddenly to lift and break. Something had startled the peewits, and the fallow flickered over with pink gleams of birds white-breasting the sunset. Then the plovers turned, and were gone in the dusk behind.

Darkness was issuing out of the earth, and clinging to the trunks of the elms which rose like weird statues, lessening down the wayside. Mersham laboured forwards, the earth sucking and smacking at his feet. In front the Coney Grey farm was piled in shadow on the road. He came near to it, and saw the turnips heaped in a fabulous heap up the side of the barn, a buttress that rose almost to the eaves, and stretched out towards the cart-ruts in the road. Also, the pale breasts of the turnips got the sunset, and they were innumerable orange glimmers piled in the dusk. The two labourers who were pulping at the foot of the mound stood shadow-like to watch as he passed, breathing the sharp scent of turnips.

It was all very wonderful and glamorous here, in the old places that had seemed so ordinary. Three-quarters of the scarlet sun was settling among the branches of the elm in front, right ahead where he would come soon. But when he arrived at the brow where the hill swooped downwards, where the broad road ended suddenly, the sun had vanished from the space before him, and the evening star was white where the night urged up against the retreating, rose-coloured billow of day. Mersham passed through the stile and sat upon the remnant of the thorn tree on the brink of the valley. All the wide space before him was full of a mist of rose, nearly to his feet. The large ponds where hidden, the farms, the fields, the far-off coal-mine, under the rosy outpouring of twilight. Between him and the spaces of Leicestershire and the hills of Derbyshire, between him and all the South Country which he had fled, was the splendid rose-red strand of sunset, and the white star keeping guard.

Here, on the lee-shore of day, was the only purple showing of the woods and the great hedge below him; and the roof of the farm below him, with a film of smoke rising up. Unreal, like a dream which wastes a sleep with unrest. was the South and its hurrying to and fro. Here, on the farther shore of the sunset, with the flushed tide at his feet, and the large star flashing with strange laughter, did he himself naked walk with lifted arms into the quiet flood of life.

What was it he wanted, sought in the slowly-lapsing tide of days? Two years he had been in the large city in the south. There always his soul had moved among the faces that swayed on the thousand currents in that node of tides, hovering and wheeling and flying low over the faces of the multitude like a sea-gull over the waters, stooping now and again, and taking a fragment of life—a look, a contour, a movement—to feed upon. Of many people, his friends, he had asked that they would kindle again the smouldering embers of their experience; he had blown the low fires gently with his breath, and had leaned his face towards their glow, and had breathed in the words that rose like fumes from the revived embers, till he was sick with the strong drug of sufferings and ecstasies and sensations, and the dreams that ensued. But most folk had choked out the fires of their fiercer experience with rubble of sentimentality and stupid fear, and rarely could he feel the hot destruction of Life fighting out its way.

Surely, surely somebody could give him enough of the philtre of life to stop the craving which tortured him hither and thither, enough to satisfy for a while, to intoxicate him till he could laugh the crystalline laughter of the star, and bathe in the retreating flood of twilight like a naked boy in the surf, clasping the waves and beating them and answering their wild clawings with laughter sometimes, and sometimes gasps of pain.

He rose and stretched himself. The mist was lying in the valley like a flock of folded sheep; Orion had strode into the sky, and the Twins were playing towards the West. He shivered, stumbled down the path, and crossed the orchard, passing among the dark trees as if among people he knew.

II

He came into the yard. It was exceedingly, painfully muddy. He felt a disgust of his own feet, which were cold, and numbed, and heavy.

The window of the house was uncurtained, and shone like a yellow moon, with only a large leaf or two of ivy, and a cord of honeysuckle hanging across it. There seemed a throng of figures moving about the fire. Another light gleamed mysteriously among the out-buildings. He heard a voice in the cow-shed, and the impatient movement of a cow, and the rhythm of milk in the bucket.

He hesitated in the darkness of the porch; then he entered without knocking. A girl was opposite him, coming out of the dairy doorway with a loaf of bread. She started, and they stood a moment looking at each other across the room. They advanced to each other; he took her hand, plunged overhead, as it were, for a moment in her great brown eyes. Then he let her go, and looked aside, saying some words of greeting. He had not kissed her; he realised that when he heard her voice:

"When did you come?"

She was bent over the table, cutting bread-and-butter. What was it in her bowed, submissive pose, in the dark, small head with its black hair twining and hiding her face, that made him wince and shrink and close over his soul that had been open like a foolhardy flower to the night? Perhaps it was her very submission, which trammelled him, throwing the responsibility of her wholly on him, making him shrink from the burden of her.

Her brothers were home from the pit. They were two well-built lads of twenty and twenty-one. The coal-dust over their faces was like a mask, making them inscrutable, hiding any glow of greeting, making them strangers. He could only see their eyes wake with a sudden smile, which sank almost immediately, and they turned aside. The mother was kneeling at a big brown stew-jar in front of the open oven. She did not rise, but gave him her hand, saying: "Cyril! How are you?" Her large dark eyes wavered and left him. She continued with the spoon in the jar.

His disappointment rose as water suddenly heaves up the side of a ship. A sense of dreariness revived, a feeling, too, of the cold wet mud that he had struggled through.

These were the people who, a few months before, would look up in one fine broad glow of welcome whenever he entered the door, even if he came daily. Three years before, their lives would draw together into one flame, and whole evenings long would flare with magnificent mirth, and with play. They had known each other's lightest and deepest feelings. Now, when he came back to them after a long absence, they withdrew, turned aside. He sat down on the sofa under the window, deeply chagrined. His heart closed tight like a fir-cone, which had been open and full of naked seeds when he came to them.

They asked him questions of the South. They were starved for news, they said, in that God-forsaken hole.

"It is such a treat to hear a bit of news from outside," said the mother.

News! He smiled, and talked, plucking for them the leaves from off his tree: leaves of easy speech. He smiled, rather bitterly, as he slowly reeled off his news, almost mechanically. Yet he knew—and that was the irony of it—that they did not want his 'records'; they wanted the timorous buds of his hopes, and the unknown fruits of his experience, full of the taste of tears and what sunshine of gladness had gone to their ripening. But they asked for his 'news', and, because of some subtle perversity, he gave them what they begged, not what they wanted, not what he desired most sincerely to give them.

Gradually he exhausted his store of talk, that he had thought was limitless. Muriel moved about all the time, laying the table and listening, only looking now and again across the barren garden of his talk into his windows. But he hardened his heart and turned his head from her. The boys had stripped to their waists, and had knelt on the hearth-rug and washed themselves in a large tin bowl, the mother sponging and drying their backs. Now they stood wiping themselves, the fire-light bright and rosy on their fine torsos, their heavy arms swelling and sinking with life. They seemed to cherish the fire-light on their bodies. Benjamin, the younger, leaned his breast to the warmth, and threw back his head, showing his teeth in a voluptuous little smile. Mersham watched them, as he had watched the peewits and the sunset.

Then they sat down to their dinners, and the room was dim with the steam of food. Presently the father and the eldest brother were in from the cow-sheds, and all assembled at table. The conversation went haltingly; a little badinage on Mersham's part, a few questions on politics from the father. Then there grew an acute, fine feeling of discord. Mersham, particularly sensitive, reacted. He became extremely atten-tive to the others at table, and to his own manner of eating. He used English that was exquisitely accurate, pronounced with the Southern accent, very different from the heavily-sounded speech of the home folk. His nicety contrasted the more with their rough, country habit. They became shy and awkward, fumbling for something to say. The boys ate their dinners hastily, shovelling up the mass as a man shovels gravel. The eldest son clambered roughly with a great hand at the plate of bread-and-butter. Mersham tried to shut his eyes. He kept up all the time a brilliant tea-talk that they failed to appreciate in that atmosphere. It was evident to him; without forming the idea, he felt how irrevocably he was removing them from him, though he had loved them. The irony of the situation appealed to him, and added brightness and subtlety to his wit. Muriel, who had studied him so thoroughly, con-fusedly understood. She hung her head over her plate, and ate little. Now and again she would look up at him, toying all the time with her knife—though it was a family for ugly hands—and would address him some barren question. He always answered the question, but he invariably disregarded her look of earnestness, lapped in his unbreakable armour of light irony. He acknowledged, however, her power in the flicker of irritation that accompanied his reply. She quickly hid her face again.

They did not linger at tea, as in the old days. The men rose, with an "Ah well!" and went about their farm-work. One of the lads lay sprawling for sleep on the sofa; the other lighted a cigarette and sat with his arms on his knees, blinking into the fire. Neither of them ever wore a coat in the house, and their shirt-sleeves and their thick bare necks irritated the stranger still further by accentuating his strangeness. The men came tramping in and out to the boiler. The kitchen was full of bustle, of the carrying of steaming water, and of draughts. It seemed like a place out of doors. Mersham shrank up in his corner, and pretended to read the *Daily News*. He was ignored, like an owl sitting in the stalls of cattle.

"Go in the parlour, Cyril. Why don't you? It's comfortable there."

Muriel turned to him with this reproach, this remonstrance, almost chiding him. She was keenly aware of his discomfort, and of his painful discord with his surroundings. He rose without a word and obeyed her.

III

The parlour was a long, low room with red colourings. A bunch of mistletoe hung from the beam, and thickly-berried holly was over the pictures—over the little gilt-blazed water-colours that he hated so much because he had done them in his 'teens, and nothing is so hateful as the self one has left. He dropped in the tapestried chair called the Countess, and thought of the changes which this room had seen in him. There, by that hearth, they had threshed the harvest of their youth's experience, gradually burning the chaff of sentimentality and false romance that covered the real grain of life. How infinitely far away, now, seemed *Jane Eyre* and George Eliot. These had marked the beginning. He smiled as he traced the graph onwards, plotting the points with Carlyle and Ruskin, Schopenhauer and Darwin and Huxley, Omar Khayyam, the Russians, Ibsen and Balzac; then Guy de Maupassant and *Madame Bovary*. They had parted in the midst of *Madame Bovary*. Since then had come only Nietzsche and William James. They had not done so badly, he thought, during those years which now he was apt to despise a little, because of their dreadful strenuousness, and because of their later deadly, unrelieved seriousness. He wanted her to come in and talk about the old times. He crossed to the other side of the fire and lay in the big horse-hair chair, which pricked the back of his head. He looked about, and stuffed behind him the limp green cushions that were always sweating down.

It was a week after Christmas. He guessed they had kept up the holly and mistletoe for him. The two photographs of himself still occupied the post of honour on the mantelpiece; but between them was a stranger. He wondered who the fellow could be; good-looking he seemed to be; but a bit of a clown beside the radiant, subtle photos of himself. He smiled broadly at his own arrogance. Then he remembered that Muriel and her people were leaving the farm come Lady-day. Immediately, in valediction, he began to call up the old days, when they had romped and played so boisterously, dances, and wild charades, and all mad games. He was just telling himself that those were the days, the days of unconscious, ecstatic fun, and he was smiling at himself over his information, when she entered.

She came in, hesitating. Seeing him sprawling in his old abandonment, she closed the door softly. For a moment or two she sat, her elbows on her knees, her chin in her hands, sucking her little finger, and withdrawing it from her lips with a little pop, looking all the while in the fire. She was waiting for him, knowing all the time he would not begin. She was trying to feel him, as it were. She wanted to assure herself of him after so many months. She dared not look at him directly. Like all brooding, constitutionally earnest souls, she gave herself away unwisely, and was defenceless when she found herself pushed back, rejected so often with contempt.

"Why didn't you tell me you were coming?" she asked at last.

"I wanted to have exactly one of the old tea-times, and evenings."

"Ay!" she answered with hopeless bitterness. She was a dreadful pessimist. People had handled her so brutally, and had cheaply thrown away her most sacred intimacies.

He laughed, and looked at her kindly.

"Ah, well, if I'd thought about it I should have known this was what to expect. It's my own fault."

"Nay," she answered, still bitterly; "it's not your fault. It's ours. You bring us to a certain point, and when you go away, we lose it all again, and receive you like creatures who have never known you."

"Never mind," he said easily. "If it is so, it is! How are you?"

She turned and looked full at him. She was very handsome;

heavily moulded, coloured richly. He looked back smiling into her big, brown, serious eyes.

"Oh, I'm very well," she answered, with puzzled irony. "How are you?"

"Me? You tell me. What do you think of me?"

"What do I think?" She laughed a little nervous laugh and shook her head. "I don't know. Why—you look well—and very much of a gentleman."

"Ah—and you are sorry?"

"No—No, I am not! No! Only your're different, you see."

"Ah, the pity! I shall never be as nice as I was at twenty-one, shall I?" He glanced at his photo on the mantelpiece, and smiled, gently chaffing her.

"Well—you're different—it isn't that you're not so nice, but different. I always think you're like that, really."

She too glanced at the photo, which had been called the portrait of an intellectual prig, but which was really that of a sensitive, alert, exquisite boy. The subject of the portrait lay smiling at her. Then he turned voluptuously, like a cat spread out in the chair.

"And this is the last of it all——!"

She looked up at him, startled and pitiful.

"Of this phase, I mean," he continued, indicating with his eyes the room, the surroundings. "Of Crossleigh Bank, I mean, and this part of our lives."

"Ay!" she said, bowing her head, and putting into the exclamation all her depth of sadness and regret. He laughed.

"Aren't you glad?" he asked.

She looked up, startled, a little shocked.

"Good-bye's a fine word," he explained. "It means you're going to have a change, and a change is what you, of all people, want."

Her expression altered as she listened.

"It's true," she said. "I do."

"So you ought to say to yourself, 'What a treat! I'm going to say good-bye directly to the most painful phase of my life.' You make up your mind it shall be the most painful, by re-fusing to be hurt so much in the future. There you are! 'Men at most times are masters of their fates,' etcetera."

She pondered his method of reasoning, and turned to him with a little laughter that was full of pleading and yearning.

"Well," he said, lying, amiably smiling, "isn't that so?—and aren't you glad?"

"Yes!" she nodded. "I am—very glad."

He twinkled playfully at her, and asked, in a soft voice: "Then what do you want?"

"Yes," she replied, a little breathlessly. "What do I?" She looked at him with a rash challenge that pricked him.

"Nay," he said, evading her, "do you even ask me that?"

She veiled her eyes, and said, meekly in excuse: "It's a long time since I asked you anything, isn't it?"

"Ay! I never thought of it. Whom have you asked in the interim?"

"Whom have I asked?"—she arched her brows and laughed a monosyllable of scorn.

"No one, of course!" he said, smiling. "The world asks questions of you, you ask questions of me, and I go to some oracle in the dark, don't I?"

She laughed with him.

"No!" he said, suddenly serious. "Supposing you must answer me a big question—something I can never find out by myself?"

He lay out indolently in the chair and began smiling again. She turned to look with intensity at him, her hair's fine foliage all loose round her face, her dark eyes haunted with doubt, her finger at her lips. A slight perplexity flickered over his eyes.

"At any rate," he said, "you have something to give me."

She continued to look at him with dark, absorbing eyes. He probed her with his regard. Then he seemed to withdraw, and his pupils dilated with thought.

"You see," he said, "life's no good but to live—and you can't live your life by yourself. You must have a flint and a steel, both, to make the spark fly. Supposing you be my flint, my white flint, to spurt out red fire for me?"

"But how do you mean?" she asked breathlessly.

"You see," he continued, thinking aloud as usual: "thought —that's not life. It's like washing and combing and carding and weaving the fleece that the year of life has produced. Now I think—we've carded and woven to the end of our bundle—nearly. We've got to begin again—you and me— living together, see? Not speculating and poetising together— see?"

She did not cease to gaze absorbedly at him.

"Yes?" she whispered, urging him on.

"You see—I've come back to you—to you——" He waited for her.

"But," she said huskily, "I don't understand."

He looked at her with aggressive frankness, putting aside all her confusions.

"Fibber!" he said gently.

"But——" she turned in her chair from him—"but not clearly."

He frowned slightly:

"Nay, you should be able by now to use the algebra of speech. Must I count up on your fingers for you what I mean, unit by unit, in bald arithmetic?"

"No—no!" she cried, justifying herself; "but how can I understand—the change in you? You used to say—you couldn't.—Quite opposite."

He lifted his head as if taking in her meaning.

"Ah, yes, I have changed. I forget. I suppose I must have changed in myself. I'm older—I'm twenty-six. I used to shrink from the thought of having to kiss you, didn't I?" He smiled very brightly, and added, in a soft voice: "Well—I don't, now."

She flushed darkly and hid her face from him.

"Not," he continued, with slow, brutal candour—"not that I know any more than I did then—what love is—as you know it—but—I think you're beautiful—and we know each other so well—as we know nobody else, don't we? And so we . . ."

His voice died away, and they sat in a tense silence, listening to the noise outside, for the dog was barking loudly. They heard a voice speaking and quieting him. Cyril Mersham listened. He heard the clatter of the barn door latch, and a slurring ring of a bicycle-bell brushing the wall.

"Who is it?" he asked, unsuspecting.

She looked at him, and confessed with her eyes, guiltily, beseeching. He understood immediately.

"Good Lord!—Him?" He looked at the photo on the mantelpiece. She nodded with her usual despair, her finger between her lips again. Mersham took some moments to adjust himself to the new situation.

"Well!—so *he's* in my place! Why didn't you tell me?"

"How could I?—he's not. Besides—you never would have a place." She hid her face.

"No," he drawled, thinking deeply. "I wouldn't. It's my fault, altogether." Then he smiled, and said whimsically: "But I thought you kept an old pair of my gloves in the chair beside you."

"So I did, so I did!" she justified herself again with extreme bitterness, "till you asked me for them. You told me to—to take another man—and I did as you told me—as usual."

"Did I tell you?—did I tell you? I suppose I must. I suppose I am a fool. And do you like him?"

She laughed aloud, with scorn and bitterness.

"He's very good—and he's very fond of me."

"Naturally!" said Mersham, smiling and becoming ironical. "And how firmly is he fixed?"

IV

She was mortified, and would not answer him. The question for him now was how much did this intruder count. He looked, and saw she wore no ring—but perhaps she had taken it off for his coming. He began diligently to calculate what attitude he might take. He had looked for many women to wake his love, but he had been always disappointed. So he had kept himself virtuous, and waited. Now he would wait no longer. No woman and he could ever understand each other so well as he and Muriel whom he had fiercely educated into womanhood along with his own struggling towards a manhood of independent outlook. They had breathed the same air of thought, they had been beaten with the same storms of doubt and disillusionment, they had expanded together in days of pure poetry. They had grown so; spiritually, or rather psychically, as he preferred to say, they were married; and now he found himself thinking of the way she moved about the house.

The outer door had opened and a man had entered the kitchen, greeting the family cordially, and without any formality. He had the throaty, penetrating voice of a tenor singer, and it came distinctly over the vibrating rumble of the men's talking. He spoke good, easy English. The boys asked him about the 'iron-men' and the electric haulage, and he answered them with rough technicalities, so Mersham concluded he was a working electrician in the mine. They con-

tinued to talk casually for some time, though there was a false
note of secondary interest in it all. Then Benjamin came
forward and broke the check, saying, with a dash of braggart
taunting:

"Muriel's in th' parlour, Tom, if you want her."

"Oh, is she? I saw a light in; I thought she might be." He
affected indifference, as if he were kept thus at every visit.
Then he added, with a touch of impatience, and of the pro-
prietor's interest: "What is she doing?"

"She's talking. Cyril Mersham's come from London."

"What!—is *he* here?"

Mersham sat listening, smiling. Muriel saw his eyelids lift.
She had run up her flag of challenge taut, but continually she
slackened towards him with tenderness. Now her flag flew
out bravely. She rose, and went to the door.

"Hello!" she said, greeting the stranger with a little song
of welcome in one word, such as girls use when they become
aware of the presence of their sweetheart.

"You've got a visitor, I hear," he answered.

"Yes. Come along, come in!"

She spoke softly, with much gentle caressing.

He was a handsome man, well set-up, rather shorter than
Mersham. The latter rose indolently, and held out his hand,
smiling curiously into the beautiful, generous blue eyes of
the other.

"Cyril—Mr. Vickers."

Tom Vickers crushed Mersham's hand, and answered his
steady, smiling regard with a warm expansion of feeling,
then bent his head, slightly confused.

"Sit here, will you?" said Mersham, languidly indicating
the arm-chair.

"No, no, thanks, I won't. I shall do here, thanks." Tom
Vickers took a chair and placed it in front of the fire. He was
confusedly charmed with Mersham's natural frankness and
courtesy.

"If I'm not intruding," he added, as he sat down.

"No, of course not!" said Muriel, in her wonderfully soft,
fond tones—the indulgent tone of a woman who will sacrifice
anything to love.

"Couldn't!" added Mersham lazily. "We're always a public
meeting, Muriel and I. Aren't we, Miel? We're discussing
affinities, that ancient topic. You'll do for an audience. We

agree so beastly well, we two. We always did. It's her fault. Does she treat you so badly?"

The other was rather bewildered. Out of it all he dimly gathered that he was suggested as the present lover of Muriel, while Mersham referred to himself as the one discarded. So he smiled, reassured.

"How—badly?" he asked.

"Agreeing with you on every point?"

"No, I can't say she does that," said Vickers, smiling, and looking with little warm glances at her.

"Why, we never disagree, you know!" she remonstrated, in the same deep indulgent tone.

"I see," Mersham said languidly, and yet keeping his wits keenly to the point. "*You* agree with everything *she* says. Lord, how interesting!"

Muriel arched her eyelids with a fine flare of intelligence across at him, and laughed.

"Something like that," answered the other man, also indulgently, as became a healthy male towards one who lay limply in a chair and said clever nothings in a lazy drawl. Mersham noted the fine limbs, the solid, large thighs, and the thick wrists. He was classifying his rival among the men of handsome, healthy animalism, and good intelligence, who are children in simplicity, who can add two and two, but never xy and yx. His contours, his movements, his repose were, strictly, lovable. "But," said Mersham to himself, "if I were blind, or sorrowful, or very tired, I should not want him. He is one of the men, as George Moore says, whom his wife would hate after a few years for the very way he walked across the floor. I can imagine him with a family of children, a fine father. But unless he had a domestic wife——"

Muriel had begun to make talk to him.

"Did you cycle?" she asked, in that irritating private tone so common to lovers, a tone that makes a third person an impertinence.

"Yes—I was rather late," he replied, in the same caressing manner. The sense did not matter, the caress was everything.

"Didn't you find it very muddy?"

"Well, I did—but not any worse than yesterday."

Mersham sprawled his length in the chair, his eyelids almost shut, his fine white hands hanging over the arms of the chair like dead-white stoats from a bough. He was wondering how long Muriel would endure to indulge her sweetheart thus. Soon she began to talk second-hand to Mersham. They were speaking of Tom's landlady.

"You don't care for her, do you?" she asked, laughing insinuatingly, since the shadow of his dislike for other women heightened the radiance of his affection for her.

"Well, I can't say that I love her."

"How is it you always fall out with your landladies after six months? You must be a wretch to live with."

"Nay, I don't know that I am. But they're all alike; they're jam and cakes at first, but after a bit they're dry bread."

He spoke with solemnity, as if he uttered a universal truth. Mersham's eyelids flickered now and again. Muriel turned to him :

"Mr. Vickers doesn't like lodgings," she said.

Mersham understood that Vickers therefore wanted to marry her; he also understood that as the pretendant tired of his land-ladies, so his wife and he would probably weary one another. He looked this intelligence at Muriel, and drawled:

"Doesn't he? Lodgings are ideal. A good lodger can always boss the show, and have his own way. It's the time of his life."

"I don't think!" laughed Vickers.

"It's true," drawled Mersham torpidly, giving his words the effect of droll irony. "You're evidently not a good lodger. You only need to sympathise with a landlady—against her husband generally—and she'll move heaven and earth for you."

"Ah!" laughed Muriel, glancing at Mersham. "Tom doesn't believe in sympathising with women—especially married women."

"I don't!" said Tom emphatically, "—it's dangerous."

"You leave it to the husband," said Mersham.

"I do that! I don't want 'em coming to me with their troubles. I should never know the end."

"Wise of you. Poor woman! So you'll broach your barrel of sympathy for your wife, eh, and for nobody else?"

"That's it. Isn't that right?"

"Oh, quite. Your wife will be a privileged person. Sort of home-brewed beer to drink *ad infinitum*? Quite all right, that!"

"There's nothing better," said Tom, laughing.

"Except a change," said Mersham. "Now, I'm like a cup of tea to a woman."

Muriel laughed aloud at this preposterous cynicism, and knitted her brows to bid him cease playing ball with bombs.

"A fresh cup each time. Women never weary of tea. Muriel, I can see you having a rich time. Sort of long after-supper drowse with a good husband."

"Very delightful!" said Muriel sarcastically.

"If she's got a good husband, what more can she want?" asked Tom, keeping the tone of banter, but really serious and somewhat resentful.

"A lodger—to make things interesting."

"Why," said Muriel, intervening, "do women like you so?"

Mersham looked up at her, quietly, smiling into her eyes. She was really perplexed. She wanted to know what he put in the pan to make the balance go down so heavily on his side. He had, as usual, to answer her seriously and truthfully, so he said: "Because I can make them believe that black is green or purple—which it is, in reality." Then, smiling broadly as she wakened again with admiration for him, he added: "But you're trying to make me conceited, Miel—to stain my virgin modesty."

Muriel glanced up at him with softness and understanding, and laughed low. Tom gave a guffaw at the notion of Mersham's virgin modesty. Muriel's brow wrinkled with irritation, and she turned from her sweetheart to look in the fire.

v

Mersham, all unconsciously, had now developed the situation to the climax he desired. He was sure that Vickers would not count seriously in Muriel's movement towards himself. So he turned away, uninterested.

The talk drifted for some time, after which he suddenly bethought himself:

"I say, Mr. Vickers, will you sing for us? You do sing, don't you?"

"Well—nothing to speak of," replied the other modestly, wondering at Mersham's sudden change of interest. He looked at Muriel.

"Very well," she answered him, indulging him now like a child. "But——" she turned to Mersham—"but do you, really?"

"Yes, of course. Play some of the old songs. Do you play any better?"

She began "Honour and Arms."

"No, not that!" cried Mersham. "Something quiet—'*Sois triste et sois belle*'." He smiled gently at her, suggestively. "Try '*Du bist wie eine Blume*,' or '*Pur dicesti*'."

Vickers sang well, though without much imagination. But the songs they sang were the old songs that Mersham had taught Muriel years before, and she played with one of his memories in her heart. At the end of the first song, she turned and found him looking at her, and they met again in the poetry of the past.

"Daffodils," he said softly, his eyes full of memories.

She dilated, quivered with emotion, in response. They had sat on the rim of the hill, where the wild daffodils stood up to the sky, and there he had taught her, singing line by line: "*Du bist wie eine Blume*." He had no voice, but a very accurate ear.

The evening wore on to ten o'clock. The lads came through the room on their way to bed. The house was asleep save the father, who sat alone in the kitchen, reading *The Octopus*. They went in to supper.

Mersham had roused himself and was talking well. Muriel stimulated him, always, and turned him to talk of art and philosophy—abstract things that she loved, of which only he had ever spoken to her, of which only he could speak, she believed, with such beauty. He used quaint turns of speech, contradicted himself waywardly, then said something sad and whimsical, all in a wistful, irresponsible manner so that even the men leaned indulgent and deferential to him.

"Life," he said, and he was always urging this on Muriel in one form or another, "life is beautiful, so long as it is consuming you. When it is rushing through you, destroying you, life is glorious. It is best to roar away, like a fire with a great draught, white-hot to the last bit. It's when you burn a slow fire and save fuel that life's not worth having."

"You believe in a short life and a merry," said the father.

"Needn't be either short or merry. Grief is part of the fire of life—and suffering—they're the root of the flame of joy, as they say. No! With life, we're like the man who was so anxious to provide for his old age that he died at thirty from inanition."

"That's what we're not likely to do," laughed Tom.

"Oh, I don't know. You live most intensely in human contact—and that's what we shrink from, poor timid creatures, from giving our souls to somebody to touch; for they, bungling fools, will generally paw it with dirty hands."

Muriel looked at him with dark eyes of grateful understanding. She herself had been much pawed, brutally, by her brothers. But, then, she had been foolish in offering herself.

"And," concluded Mersham, "you are washed with the whitest fire of life—when you take a woman you love—and understand."

Perhaps Mersham did not know what he was doing. Yet his whole talk lifted Muriel as in a net, like a sea-maiden out of the waters, and placed her in his arms, to breathe his thin, rare atmosphere. She looked at him, and was certain of his pure earnestness, and believed implicitly he could not do wrong.

Vickers believed otherwise. He would have expressed his opinion, whatever it might be, in an: "Oh, ay, he's got plenty to say, and he'll keep on saying it—but, hang it all . . . !"

For Vickers was an old-fashioned, inarticulate lover; such as has been found the brief joy and the unending disappointment of a woman's life. At last he found he must go, as Mersham would not precede him. Muriel did not kiss him good-bye, nor did she offer to go out with him to his bicycle. He was angry at this, but more angry with the girl than with the man. He felt that she was fooling about, 'showing off' before the stranger. Mersham was a stranger to him, and so, in his idea, to Muriel. Both young men went out of the house together, and down the rough brick track to the barn. Mersham made whimsical little jokes: "I wish my feet weren't so fastidious. They dither when they go in a soft spot like a girl who's touched a toad. Hark at that poor old wretch—she sounds as if she'd got whooping-cough."

"A cow is not coughing when she makes that row," said Vickers.

"Pretending, is she?—to get some Owbridge's? Don't blame her. I guess she's got chilblains, at any rate. Do cows have chilblains, poor devils?"

Vickers laughed and felt he must take this man into his protection. "Mind," he said, as they entered the barn, which was very dark. "Mind your forehead against this beam." He put one hand on the beam, and stretched out the other to feel for Mersham. "Thanks," said the latter gratefully. He knew the position of the beam to an inch, however dark the barn, but he allowed Vickers to guide him past it. He rather enjoyed being taken into Tom's protection.

Vickers carefully struck a match, bowing over the ruddy core of light and illuminating himself like some beautiful lantern in the midst of the high darkness of the barn. For some moments he bent over his bicycle-lamp, trimming and adjusting the wick, and his face, gathering all the light on its ruddy beauty, seemed luminous and wonderful. Mersham could see the down on his cheeks above the razor-line, and the full lips in shadow beneath the moustache, and the brush of the eyebrows between the light.

"After all," said Mersham, "he's very beautiful; she's a fool to give him up."

Tom shut the lamp with a snap, and carefully crushed the match under his foot. Then he took the pump from the bicycle, and crouched on his heels in the dimness, inflating the tyre. The swift, unerring, untiring stroke of the pump, the light balance and the fine elastic adjustment of the man's body to his movements pleased Mersham.

"She could have," he was saying to himself, "some glorious hours with this man—yet she'd rather have me, because I can make her sad and set her wondering."

But to the man he was saying:

"You know, love isn't the twin-soul business. With you, for instance, women are like apples on a tree. You can have one that you can reach. Those that look best are overhead, but it's no good bothering with them. So you stretch up, perhaps you pull down a bough and just get your fingers round a good one. Then it swings back and you feel wild and you say your heart's broken. But there are plenty of apples as good for you no higher than your chest."

Vickers smiled, and thought there was something in it— generally; but for himself, it was nothing.

They went out of the barn to the yard gate. He watched the young man swing over his saddle and vanish, calling "Good-night."

"*Sic transit*," he murmured—meaning Tom Vickers, and beautiful lustihood that is unconscious like a blossom.

Mersham went slowly in the house. Muriel was clearing

away the supper things, and laying the table again for the men's breakfasts. But she was waiting for him as clearly as if she had stood watching in the doorway. She looked up at him, and instinctively he lifted his face towards her as if to kiss her. They smiled, and she went on with her work.

The father rose, stretching his burly form, and yawning. Mersham put on his overcoat.

"You will come a little way with me?" he said. She answered him with her eyes. The father stood, large and silent, on the hearth-rug. His sleepy, mazed disapproval had no more effect than a little breeze which might blow against them. She smiled brightly at her lover, like a child, as she pinned on her hat.

It was very dark outside in the starlight. He groaned heavily, and swore with extravagance as he went ankle-deep in mud.

"See, you should follow me. Come here," she commanded, delighted to have him in charge.

"Give me your hand," he said, and they went hand-in-hand over the rough places. The fields were open, and the night went up to the magnificent stars. The wood was very dark, and wet; they leaned forward and stepped stealthily, and gripped each other's hands fast with a delightful sense of adventure. When they stood and looked up a moment, they did not know how the stars were scattered among the tree-tops till he found the three jewels of Orion right in front.

There was a strangeness everywhere, as if all things had ventured out alive to play in the night, as they do in fairy-tales; the trees, the many stars, the dark spaces, and the mysterious waters below uniting in some magnificent game.

They emerged from the wood on to the bare hillside. She came down from the wood-fence into his arms, and he kissed her, and they laughed low together. Then they went on across the wild meadows where there was no path.

"Why don't you like him?" he asked playfully.

"Need you ask?" she said simply.

"Yes. Because he's heaps nicer than I am."

She laughed a full laugh of amusement.

"He is! Look! He's like summer, brown and full of warmth. Think how splendid and fierce he'd be——"

"Why do you talk about him?" she said.

"Because I want you to know what you're losing—and you

won't till you see him in my terms. He is very desirable—I
should choose him in preference to me—for myself."

"Should you?" she laughed. "But," she added with soft
certainty, "you don't understand."

"No—I don't. I suppose it's love; your sort, which is beyond
me. I shall never be blindly in love, shall I?"

"I begin to think you never will," she answered, not very
sadly. "You won't be blindly anything."

"The voice of love!" he laughed; and then: "No, if you pull
your flowers to pieces, and find how they pollinate, and where
are the ovaries, you don't go in blind ecstasies over to them.
But they mean more to you; they are intimate, like friends of
your heart, not like wonderful, dazing fairies."

"Ay!" she assented, musing over it with the gladness of
understanding him. "And then?"

Softly, almost without words, she urged him to the point.

"Well," he said, "you think I'm a wonderful, magical person,
don't you?—and I'm not—I'm not as good, in the long run, as
your Tom, who thinks you are a wonderful, magical person."

She laughed and clung to him as they walked. He continued,
very carefully and gently: "Now, I don't imagine for a moment
that you are princessy or angelic or wonderful. You often
make me thundering mad because you're an ass . . ."

She laughed low with shame and humiliation.

"Nevertheless—I come from the south to you—because—
well, with you I can be just as I feel, conceited or idiotic, without being afraid to be myself . . ." He broke off suddenly. "I
don't think I've tried to make myself out to you—any bigger
or better than I am?" he asked her wistfully.

"No," she answered, in beautiful, deep assurance. "No!
That's where it is. You have always been so honest. You are
more honest than anybody ever——" She did not finish,
being deeply moved. He was silent for some time, then he
continued, as if he must see the question to the end with her:

"But, you know—I do like you not to wear corsets. I like
to see you move inside your dress."

She laughed, half shame, half pleasure.

"I wondered if you'd notice," she said.

"I did—directly." There was a space of silence, after which
he resumed: "You see—we would marry tomorrow—but I
can't keep myself. I am in debt——"

She came close to him, and took his arm.

"—And what's the good of letting the years go, and the beauty of one's youth——?"

"No," she admitted, very slowly and softly, shaking her head.

"So—well!—you understand, don't you? And if you're willing—you'll come to me, won't you?—just naturally, as you used to come and go to church with me?—and it won't be—it won't be me coaxing you—reluctant? Will it?"

They had halted in front of a stile which they would have to climb. She turned to him in silence, and put up her face to him. He took her in his arms, and kissed her, and felt the night mist with which his moustache was drenched, and he bent his head and rubbed his face on her shoulder, and then pressed his lips on her neck. For a while they stood in silence, clasped together. Then he heard her voice, muffled in his shoulder, saying:

"But—but, you know—it's much harder for the woman—it means something so different for a woman."

"One can be wise," he answered, slowly and gently. "One need not blunder into calamities."

She was silent for a time. Then she spoke again.

"Yes, but—if it should be—you see—I couldn't bear it."

He let her go, and they drew apart, and the embrace no longer choked them from speaking. He recognised the woman defensive, playing the coward against her own inclinations, and even against her knowledge.

"If—if!" he exclaimed sharply, so that she shrank with a little fear. "There need be no ifs—need there?"

"I don't know," she replied, reproachfully, very quietly.

"If I say so——" he said, angry with her mistrust. Then he climbed the stile, and she followed.

"But you *do* know," he exclaimed. "I have given you books——"

"Yes, but——"

"But what?" He was getting really angry.

"It's so different for a woman—you don't know."

He did not answer this. They stumbled together over the mole-hills, under the oak trees.

"And look—how we should have to be—creeping together in the dark——"

This stung him; at once, it was as if the glamour went out of life. It was as if she had tipped over the fine vessel that held the wine of his desire, and had emptied him of all his vitality. He had played a difficult, deeply-moving part all night, and now the lights suddenly switched out, and there was left only weariness. He was silent, tired, very tired, bodily and spiritually. They walked across the wide, dark meadow with sunken heads. Suddenly she caught his arm.

"Don't be cold with me!" she cried.

He bent and kissed in acknowledgment the lips she offered him for love.

"No," he said drearily; "no, it is not coldness—only—I have lost hold—for to-night." He spoke with difficulty. It was hard to find a word to say. They stood together, apart, under the old thorn tree for some minutes, neither speaking. Then he climbed the fence, and stood on the highway above the meadow.

At parting also he had not kissed her. He stood a moment and looked at her. The water in a little brook under the hedge was running, chuckling with extraordinary loudness: away on Nethermere they heard the sad, haunting cry of the wild-fowl from the North. The stars still twinkled intensely. He was too spent to think of anything to say; she was too overcome with grief and fear and a little resentment. He looked down at the pale blotch of her face upturned from the low meadow beyond the fence. The thorn boughs tangled above her, drooping behind her like the roof of a hut. Beyond was the great width of the darkness. He felt unable to gather his energy to say anything vital.

"Good-bye," he said. "I'm going back—on Saturday. But— you'll write to me. Good-bye."

He turned to go. He saw her white uplifted face vanish, and her dark form bend under the boughs of the tree, and go out into the great darkness. She did not say good-bye.

THE OLD ADAM

THE maid who opened the door was just developing into a handsome womanhood. Therefore she seemed to have the insolent pride of one newly come to an inheritance. She would be a splendid woman to look at, having just enough of Jewish blood to enrich her comeliness into beauty. At nineteen her fine grey eyes looked challenge, and her warm complexion, her black hair looped up slack, enforced the sensuous folding of her mouth.

She wore no cap nor apron, but a well-looking sleeved over-all such as even very ladies don.

The man she opened to was tall and thin, but graceful in his energy. He wore white flannels, carried a tennis-racket. With a light bow to the maid he stepped beside her on the threshold. He was one of those who attract by their movement, whose movement is watched unconsciously, as we watch the flight of a sea-bird waving its wing leisurely. Instead of entering the house, the young man stood beside the maid-servant and looked back into the blackish evening. When in repose, he had the diffident, ironic bearing so remarkable in the educated youth of to-day, the very reverse of that traditional aggressiveness of youth.

"It is going to thunder, Kate," he said.

"Yes, I think it is," she replied, on an even footing.

The young man stood a moment looking at the trees across the road, and on the oppressive twilight.

"Look," he said, "there's not a trace of colour in the atmosphere, though it's sunset; all a dark, lustrous grey; and those oaks kindle green like a low fire—see!"

"Yes," said Kate, rather awkwardly.

"A troublesome sort of evening; must be, because it's your last with us."

"Yes," said the girl, flushing and hardening.

There was another pause; then:

"Sorry you're going?" he asked, with a faint tang of irony.

"In some ways," she replied, rather haughtily.

23

He laughed, as if he understood what was not said, then, with an "Ah well!" he passed along the hall.

The maid stood for a few moments clenching her young fists, clenching her very breast in revolt. Then she closed the door.

Edward Severn went into the dining-room. It was eight o'clock, very dark for a June evening; on the dusk-blue walls only the gilt frames of the pictures glinted pale. The clock occupied the room with its delicate ticking.

The door opened into a tiny conservatory that was lined with a grape-vine. Severn could hear, from the garden beyond, the high prattling of a child. He went to the glass door.

Running down the grass by the flower-border was a little girl of three, dressed in white. She was very bonny, very quick and intent in her movements; she reminded him of a field-mouse which plays alone in the corn, for sheer joy. Severn lounged in the doorway, watching her. Suddenly she perceived him. She started, flashed into greeting, gave a little gay jump, and stood quite still again, as if pleading.

"Mr. Severn," she cried, in wonderfully coaxing tones: "Come and see this."

"What?" he asked.

"Com' and see it," she pleaded.

He laughed, knowing she only wanted to coax him into the garden; and he went.

"Look," she said, spreading out her plump little arm.

"What?" he asked.

The baby was not going to admit that she had tricked him thither for her amusement.

"All gone up to buds," she said, pointing to the closed marigolds. Then "See!" she shrieked, flinging herself at his legs, grasping the flannel of his trousers, and tugging at him wildly. She was a wild little Mænad. She flew shrieking like a revelling bird down the garden, glancing back to see if he were coming. He had not the heart to desist, but went swiftly after her. In the obscure garden, the two white figures darted through the flowering plants, the baby, with her full silk skirts, scudding like a ruffled bird, the man, lithe and fleet, snatching her up and smothering his face in hers. And all the time her piercing voice re-echoed from his low calls of warning and of triumph as he hunted her. Often she was really frightened of him; then she clung fast round his neck, and he laughed and mocked her in a low, stirring voice, whilst she protested.

The garden was large for a London suburb. It was shut in by a high, dark embankment, that rose above a row of black poplar trees. And over the spires of the trees, high up, slid by the golden-lighted trains, with the soft movement of caterpillars and a hoarse, subtle noise.

Mrs. Thomas stood in the dark doorway watching the night, the trains, the flash and run of the two white figures.

"And now we must go in," she heard Severn say.

"No," cried the baby, wild and defiant as a bacchanal. She clung to him like a wild-cat.

"Yes," he said. "Where's your mother?"

"Give me a swing," demanded the child.

He caught her up. She strangled him hard with her young arms.

"I said, where's your mother?" he persisted, half smothered.

"She's op'tairs," shouted the child. "Give me a swing."

"I don't think she is," said Severn.

"She is. Give me a swing, a swi-i-ing!"

He bent forward, so that she hung from his neck like a great pendant. Then he swung her, laughing low to himself while she shrieked with fear. As she slipped he caught her to his breast.

"Mary!" called Mrs. Thomas, in that low, songful tone of a woman when her heart is roused and happy.

"Mary!" she called, long and sweet.

"Oh, no!" cried the child quickly.

But Severn bore her off. Laughing, he bowed his head and offered to the mother the baby who clung round his neck.

"Come along here," said Mrs. Thomas roguishly, clasping the baby's waist with her hands.

"Oh, no," cried the child, tucking her head into the young man's neck.

"But it's bed-time," said the mother. She laughed as she drew at the child to pull her loose from Severn. The baby clung tighter, and laughed, feeling no determination in her mother's grip. Severn bent his head to loosen the child's hold, bowed, and swung the heavy baby on his neck. The child clung to him, bubbling with laughter; the mother drew at her baby, laughing low, while the man swung gracefully, giving little jerks of laughter.

"Let Mr. Severn undress me," said the child, hugging close to the young man, who had come to lodge with her parents when she was scarce a month old.

"You're in high favour to-night," said the mother to Severn. He laughed, and all three stood a moment watching the trains pass and re-pass in the sky beyond the garden-end. Then they went indoors, and Severn undressed the child.

She was a beautiful girl, a bacchanal with her wild, dull-gold hair tossing about like a loose chaplet, her hazel eyes shining daringly, her small, spaced teeth glistening in little passions of laughter within her red, small mouth. The young man loved her. She was such a little bright wave of wilfulness, so abandoned to her impulses, so white and smooth as she lay at rest, so startling as she flashed her naked limbs about. But she was growing too old for a young man to undress.

She sat on his knee in her high-waisted night-gown, eating her piece of bread-and-butter with savage little bites of resentment: she did not want to go to bed. But Severn made her repeat a Pater Noster. She lisped over the Latin, and Mrs. Thomas, listening, flushed with pleasure; although she was a Protestant, and although she deplored the unbelief of Severn, who had been a Catholic.

The mother took the baby to carry her to bed. Mrs. Thomas was thirty-four years old, full-bosomed and ripe. She had dark hair that twined lightly round her low, white brow. She had a clear complexion, and beautiful brows, and dark-blue eyes. The lower part of her face was heavy.

"Kiss me," said Severn to the child.

He raised his face as he sat in the rocking-chair. The mother stood beside, looking down at him, and holding the laughing rogue of a baby against her breast. The man's face was up-tilted, his heavy brows set back from the laughing tenderness of his eyes, which looked dark, because the pupil was dilated. He pursed up his handsome mouth, his thick close-cut moustache roused.

He was a man who gave tenderness, but who did not ask for it. All his own troubles he kept, laughingly, to himself. But his eyes were very sad when quiet, and he was too quick to understand sorrow, not to know it.

Mrs. Thomas watched his fine mouth lifted for kissing. She leaned forward, lowering the baby, and suddenly, by a quick change in his eyes, she knew he was aware of her heavy woman's breasts approaching down to him. The wild rogue of a baby bent her face to his, and then, instead of kissing him, suddenly licked his cheek with her wet, soft tongue. He started back in aversion, and his eyes and his teeth flashed with a dangerous laugh.

"No, no," he laughed, in low strangled tones. "No dog-lick, my dear, oh no!"

The baby chuckled with glee, gave one wicked jerk of laughter, that came out like a bubble escaping.

He put up his mouth again, and again his face was horizontal below the face of the young mother. She looked down on him as if by a kind of fascination.

"Kiss me, then," he said with thick throat.

The mother lowered the baby. She felt scarcely sure of her balance. Again the child, when near to his face, darted out her tongue to lick him. He swiftly averted his face, laughing in his throat.

Mrs. Thomas turned her face aside; she would see no more.

"Come then," she said to the child. "If you won't kiss Mr. Severn nicely——"

The child laughed over the mother's shoulder like a squirrel crouched there. She was carried to bed.

It was still not quite dark; the clouds had opened slightly. The young man flung himself into an arm-chair, with a volume of French verse. He read one lyric, then he lay still.

"What, all in the dark!" exclaimed Mrs. Thomas, coming in. "And reading by *this* light." She rebuked him with timid affectionateness. Then, glancing at his white-flannelled limbs sprawled out in the gloom, she went to the door. There she turned her back to him, looking out.

"Don't these flags smell strongly in the evening?" she said at length.

He replied with a few lines of the French he had been reading.

She did not understand. There was a peculiar silence.

"A peculiar, brutal, carnal scent, iris," he drawled at length. "Isn't it?"

She laughed shortly, saying: "Eh, I don't know about that."

"It is," he asserted calmly.

He rose from his chair, went to stand beside her at the door. There was a great sheaf of yellow iris near the window.

Farther off, in the last twilight, a gang of enormous poppies balanced and flapped their gold-scarlet, which even the darkness could not quite put out.

"We ought to be feeling very sad," she said after a while.

"Why?" he asked.

"Well—isn't it Kate's last night?" she said, slightly mocking.

"She's a tartar, Kate," he said.

"Oh, she's too rude, she is really! The way she criticises the things you do, and her insolence——"

"The things *I* do?" he asked.

"Oh no; you can't do anything wrong. It's the things *I* do." Mrs. Thomas sounded very much incensed.

"Poor Kate, she'll have to lower her key," said Severn.

"Indeed she will, and a good thing too."

There was silence again.

"It's lightning," he said at last.

"Where?" she asked, with a suddenness that surprised him. She turned, met his eyes for a second. He sank his head, abashed.

"Over there in the north-east," he said, keeping his face from her. She watched his hand rather than the sky.

"Oh," she said uninterestedly.

"The storm will wheel round, you'll see," he said.

"I hope it wheels the other way, then."

"Well, it won't. You don't like lightning, do you? You'd even have to take refuge with Kate if I weren't here."

She laughed quietly at his irony.

"No," she said, quite bitterly. "Mr. Thomas is never in when he's wanted."

"Well, as he won't be urgently required, we'll acquit him, eh?"

At that moment a white flash fell across the blackness. They looked at each other, laughing. The thunder came broken and hesitatingly.

"I think we'll shut the door," said Mrs. Thomas, in normal, sufficiently distant tones. A strong woman, she locked and bolted the stiff fastenings easily. Severn pressed on the light. Mrs. Thomas noticed the untidiness of the room. She rang, and presently Kate appeared.

"Will you clear baby's things away?" she said, in the contemptuous tone of a hostile woman. Without answering, and in her superb, unhastening way, Kate began to gather up the small garments. Both women were aware of the observant, white figure of the man standing on the hearth. Severn balanced with a fine, easy poise, and smiled to himself, exulting a little to see the two women in this state of hostility. Kate moved about with bowed defiant head. Severn watched her curiously; he could not understand her. And she was leaving to-morrow. When she had gone out of the room, he remained still standing, thinking. Something in his lithe, vigorous balance, so alert, and white, and independent, caused Mrs. Thomas to glance at him from her sewing.

"I will let the blinds down," he said, becoming aware that he was attracting attention.

"Thank you," she replied conventionally.

He let the lattice blinds down, then flung himself into his chair.

Mrs. Thomas sat at the table, near him, sewing. She was a good-looking woman, well made. She sat under the one light that was turned on. The lamp-shade was of red silk lined with yellow. She sat in the warm-gold light. There was established between the two a peculiar silence, like suspense, almost painful to each of them, yet which neither would break. Severn listened to the snap of her needle, looked from the movement of her hand to the window, where the lightning beat and fluttered through the lattice. The thunder was as yet far off.

"Look," he said, "at the lightning."

Mrs. Thomas started at the sound of his voice, and some of the colour went from her face. She turned to the window.

There, between the cracks of the venetian blinds, came the white flare of lightning, then the dark. Several storms were in the sky. Scarcely had one sudden glare fluttered and palpitated out, than another covered the window with white. It dropped, and another flew up, beat like a moth for a moment, then vanished. Thunder met and overlapped; two battles were fought together in the sky.

Mrs. Thomas went very pale. She tried not to look at the window, yet, when she felt the lightning blench the lamp-light, she watched, and each time a flash leaped on the window, she shuddered. Severn, all unconsciously, was smiling with roused eyes.

"You don't like it?" he said, at last, gently.

"Not much," she answered, and he laughed.

"Yet all the storms are a fair way off," he said. "Not one near enough to touch us."

"No, but," she replied, at last laying her hands in her lap, and turning to him, "it makes me feel worked up. You don't know how it makes me feel, as if I couldn't contain myself."

She made a helpless gesture with her hand. He was watching her closely. She seemed to him pathetically helpless and bewildered; she was eight years older than he. He smiled in a strange, alert fashion, like a man who feels in jeopardy. She bent over her work, stitching nervously. There was a silence in which neither of them could breathe freely.

Presently a bigger flash than usual whitened through the yellow lamplight. Both glanced at the window, then at each other. For a moment it was a look of greeting; then his eyes dilated to a smile, wide with recklessness. He felt her waver, lose her composure, become incoherent. Seeing the faint helplessness of coming tears, he felt his heart thud to a crisis. She had her face at her sewing.

Severn sank in his chair, half suffocated by the beating of his heart. Yet, time after time, as the flashes came, they looked at each other, till in the end they both were panting, and afraid, not of the lightning but of themselves and of each other.

He was so much moved that he became conscious of his perturbation. "What the deuce is up?" he asked himself, wondering. At twenty-seven, he was quite chaste. Being highly civilised, he prized women for their intuition, and because of the delicacy with which he could transfer to them his thoughts and feelings, without cumbrous argument. From this to a state of passion he could only proceed by fine gradations, and such a procedure he had never begun. Now he was startled, astonished, perturbed, yet still scarcely conscious of his whereabouts. There was a pain in his chest that made him pant, and an involuntary tension in his arms, as if he must press someone to his breast. But the idea that this someone was Mrs. Thomas would have shocked him too much had he formed it. His passion had run on subconsciously, till now it had come to such a pitch it must drag his conscious soul into allegiance. This, however, would probably never happen; he would not yield allegiance, and blind emotion, in this direction, could not carry him alone.

Towards eleven o'clock Mr. Thomas came in.

"I wonder you come home at all," Severn heard Mrs. Thomas say as her husband stepped indoors.

"I left the office at half-past ten," the voice of Thomas replied, disagreeably.

"Oh, don't try to tell me that old tale," the woman answered contemptuously.

"I didn't try anything at all, Gertie," he replied with sarcasm. "Your question was answered."

Severn imagined him bowing with affected, magisterial dignity, and he smiled. Mr. Thomas was something in the law.

Mrs. Thomas left her husband in the hall, came and sat down again at table, where she and Severn had just finished supper, both of them reading the while.

Thomas came in, flushed very red. He was of middle stature, a thickly-built man of forty, good-looking. But he had grown round-shouldered with thrusting forward his chin in order to look the aggressive, strong-jawed man. He *had* a good jaw; but his mouth was small and nervously pinched. His brown eyes were of the emotional, affectionate sort, lacking pride or any austerity.

He did not speak to Severn nor Severn to him. Although as a rule the two men were very friendly, there came these times when, for no reason whatever, they were sullenly hostile. Thomas sat down heavily, and reached his bottle of beer. His hands were thick, and in their movement rudimentary. Severn watched the thick fingers grasp the drinking-glass as if it were a treacherous enemy.

"Have you *had* supper, Gertie?" he asked, in tones that sounded like an insult. He could not bear that these two should sit reading as if he did not exist.

"Yes," she replied, looking up at him in impatient surprise. "It's late enough." Then she buried herself again in her book.

Severn ducked low and grinned. Thomas swallowed a mouthful of beer.

"I wish you could answer my questions, Gertie, without superfluous *de*-tail," he said nastily, thrusting out his chin at her as if cross-examining.

"Oh," she said indifferently, not looking up. "Wasn't my answer right, then?"

"Quite—I thank you," he answered, bowing with great sarcasm. It was utterly lost on his wife.

"Hm-hm!" she murmured in abstraction, continuing to read. Silence resumed. Severn was grinning to himself, chuckling.

"I *had* a compliment paid me to-night, Gertie," said Thomas, quite amicably, after a while. He still ignored Severn.

"Hm-hm!" murmured his wife. This was a well-known beginning. Thomas valiantly struggled on with his courtship of his wife, swallowing his spleen.

"Councillor Jarndyce, in full committee—Are you listening, Gertie?"

"Yes," she replied, looking up for a moment.

"You know Councillor Jarndyce's style," Thomas continued, in the tone of a man determined to be patient and affable: "—the courteous Old English Gentleman——"

"Hm-hm!" replied Mrs. Thomas.

"He was speaking in reply to . . ." Thomas gave innumerable wearisome details, which no one heeded.

"Then he bowed to me, then to the Chairman—'I am compelled to say, Mr. Chairman, that we have *one* cause for congratulation; we are inestimably fortunate in *one* member of our staff; there is one point of which we can always be sure— the point of *law;* and it is an important point, Mr. Chairman."

"He bowed to the Chairman, he bowed to me. And you should have heard the applause all round that Council Chamber —that great, horse-shoe table, you don't know how impressive it is. And every face turned to me, and all round the board: 'Hear—Hear!' You don't know what respect I command in *business*, Mrs. Thomas."

"Then let it suffice you," said Mrs. Thomas, calmly indifferent.

Mr. Thomas bit his bread-and-butter.

"The fat-head's had two drops of Scotch, so he's drawing on his imagination," thought Severn, chuckling deeply.

"I thought you said there was no meeting to-night," Mrs. Thomas suddenly and innocently remarked after a while.

"There was a meeting, *in camera*," replied her husband, drawing himself up with official dignity. His excessive and wounded dignity convulsed Severn; the lie disgusted Mrs. Thomas in spite of herself.

Presently Thomas, always courting his wife and insultingly overlooking Severn, raised a point of politics, passed a lordly opinion very offensive to the young man. Severn had risen, stretched himself, and laid down his book. He was leaning on the mantelpiece in an indifferent manner, as if he scarcely noticed the two talkers. But hearing Thomas pronounce like a boor upon the Woman's Bill, he roused himself, and coolly contradicted his landlord. Mrs. Thomas shot a look of joy at the white-clad young man who lounged so scornfully on the hearth. Thomas cracked his knuckles one after another, and lowered his brown eyes, which were full of hate. After a sufficient pause, for his timidity was stronger than his impulse, he replied with a phrase that sounded final. Severn flipped the sense out of it with a few words. In the argument Severn, more cultured and far more nimble-witted than his antagonist, who hauled up his answers with a lawyer's show of invincibility, but who had not any fineness of perception, merely spiked his opponent's pieces and smiled at him. Also the young man enjoyed himself by looking down scornfully, straight into the brown eyes of his senior all the time, so that Thomas writhed.

Mrs. Thomas, meantime, took her husband's side against women, without reserve. Severn was angry; he was scornfully angry with her. Mrs. Thomas glanced at him from time to time, a little ecstasy lighting her fine blue eyes. The irony of her part was delicious to her. If she had sided with Severn, that young man would have pitied the forlorn man, and been gentle with him.

The battle of words had got quieter and more intense. Mrs. Thomas made no move to check it. At last Severn was aware he and Thomas were both getting overheated. Thomas had doubled and dodged painfully, like a half-frenzied rabbit that will not realise it is trapped. Finally his efforts had moved even his opponent to pity. Mrs. Thomas was not pitiful. She scorned her husband's dexterity of argument, when his intellectual dishonesty was so evident to her. Severn uttered his last phrases, and would say no more. Then Thomas cracked his knuckles one after the other, turned aside, consumed with morbid humiliation, and there was silence.

"I will go to bed," said Severn. He would have spoken some conciliatory words to his landlord; he lingered with that purpose; but he could not bring his throat to utter his purpose.

"Oh, before you go, do you mind, Mr. Severn, helping Mr. Thomas down with Kate's box? You may be gone before he's up in the morning, and the cab comes at ten. Do you mind?"

"Why should I?" replied Severn.

"Are you ready, Joe?" she asked her husband.

Thomas rose with the air of a man who represses himself and is determined to be patient.

"Where is it?" he asked.

"On the top landing. I'll tell Kate, and then we shan't frighten her. She has gone to bed."

Mrs. Thomas was quite mistress of the situation; both men were humble before her. She led the way, with a candle, to the third floor. There on the little landing, outside the closed door, stood a large tin trunk. The three were silent because of the baby.

"Poor Kate," Severn thought. "It's a shame to kick her out into the world, and all for nothing." He felt an impulse of hate towards womankind.

"Shall I go first, Mr. Severn?" asked Thomas.

It was surprising how friendly the two men were, as soon as they had something to do together, or when Mrs. Thomas was absent. Then they were comrades, Thomas, the elder, the thick-set, playing the protector's part, though always deferential to the younger, whimsical man.

"I had better go first," said Thomas kindly. "And if you put this round the handle, it won't cut your fingers."

He offered the young man a little flexible book from his pocket. Severn had such small, fine hands that Thomas pitied them.

Severn raised one end of the trunk. Leaning back, and flashing a smile to Mrs. Thomas, who stood with the candle, he whispered: "Kate's got a lot more impediments than I have."

"I know it's heavy," laughed Mrs. Thomas.

Thomas, waiting at the brink of the stairs, saw the young man tilting his bare throat towards the smiling woman, and whispering words which pleased her.

"At your pleasure, sir," he said in his most grating and official tones.

"Sorry," Severn flung out scornfully.

The elder man retreated very cautiously, stiffly lowering himself down one stair, looking anxiously behind.

"Are you holding the light for *me*, Gertie?" he snapped sarcastically, when he had managed one stair. She lifted the candle with a swoop. He was in a bustle and a funk. Severn, always indifferent, smiled slightly, and lowered the box with negligent ease of movement. As a matter of fact, three-quarters of the heavy weight pressed on Thomas. Mrs. Thomas watched the two figures from above.

"If I slip now," thought Severn, as he noticed the anxious, red face of his landlord, "I should squash him like a shrimp," and he laughed to himself.

"Don't come yet," he called softly to Mrs. Thomas, whom he heard following. "If you slip, your husband's bottom-most under the smash. 'Beware the fearful avalanche!'"

He laughed, and Mrs. Thomas gave a little chuckle. Thomas, very red and flustered, glanced irritably back at them, but said nothing.

Near the bottom of the staircase there was a twist in the stairs. Severn was feeling particularly reckless. When he came to the turn, he chuckled to himself, feeling his house-slippers unsafe on the narrowed, triangular stairs. He loved a risk above all things, and a subconscious instinct made the risk doubly sweet when his rival was under the box. Though Severn would not knowingly have hurt a hair of his landlord's head.

When Thomas was beginning to sweat with relief, being only one step from the landing, Severn did slip, quite accidentally. The great box crashed as if in pain, Severn glissaded down the stairs, Thomas was flung backwards across the landing, and his head went thud against the bannister post. Severn, seeing no great harm done, was struggling to his feet, laughing and saying: "I'm awfully sorry——" when Thomas got up. The elder man was infuriated like a bull. He saw the laughing face of Severn and he went mad. His brown eyes flared.

"You——, you did it on purpose!" he shouted, and straight-way he fetched the young man two heavy blows, upon the jaw and ear. Thomas, a footballer and boxer in his youth, had been brought up among the roughs of Swansea; Severn in a religious college in France. The young man had never been struck in the face before. He instantly went white and mad with rage. Thomas stood on guard, fists up. But on the small, lumbered landing there was no room for fight. Moreover, Severn had no instinct of fisticuffs. With open, stiff fingers, the young man sprang on his adversary. In spite of the blow he received, but did not feel, he flung himself again forward, and then, catching Thomas's collar, brought him down with a crash. Instantly his exquisite hands were dug in the other's thick throat, the linen collar having been torn open. Thomas fought madly, with blind, brute strength. But the other lay

wrapped on him like a white steel, his rare intelligence concentrated, not scattered; concentrated on strangling Thomas
swiftly. He pressed forward, forcing his landlord's head over
the edge of the next flight of stairs. Thomas, stout and full-
blooded, lost every trace of self-possession; he struggled like
an animal at slaughter. The blood came out of his nose over
his face; he made horrid choking sounds as he struggled.

Suddenly Severn felt his face turned between two hands.
With a shock of real agony, he met the eyes of Kate. She bent
forward, she captured his eyes.

"What do you think you're doing?" she cried in frenzy of
indignation. She leaned over him in her night-dress, her two
black plaits hanging perpendicular. He hid his face, and took
his hands away. As he kneeled to rise, he glanced up the
stairs. Mrs. Thomas stood against the bannisters, motionless
in a trance of horror and remorse. He saw the remorse plainly.
Severn turned away his face, and was wild with shame. He
saw his landlord kneeling, his hands at his throat, choking,
rattling, and gasping. The young man's heart filled with
remorse and grief. He put his arms round the heavy man,
and raised him, saying tenderly :

"Let me help you up."

He had got Thomas up against the wall, when the choked
man began to slide down again in collapse, gasping all the time
pitifully.

"No, stand up; you're best standing up," commanded Severn
sharply, rearing his landlord up again. Thomas managed to
obey, stupidly. His nose still bled, he still held his throat and
gasped with a crowing sound. But his breathing was getting
deeper.

"Water, Kate—and sponge—cold," said Severn.

Kate was back in an instant. The young man bathed his
landlord's face and temples and throat. The bleeding ceased
directly, the stout man's breathing became a series of irregular,
jerky gasps, like a child that has been sobbing hard. At last he
took a long breath, and his breast settled into regular stroke,
with little fluttering interruptions. Still holding his hand to
his throat, he looked up with dazed, piteous brown eyes,
mutely wretched and appealing. He moved his tongue as if
to try it, put back his head a little, and moved the muscles of
his throat. Then he replaced his hands on the place that ached.

Severn was grief-stricken. He would willingly, at that

moment, have given his right hand for the man he had
hurt.

Mrs. Thomas, meanwhile, stood on the stairs, watching:
for a long time she dared not move, knowing she would sink
down. She watched. One of the crises of her life was passing.
Full of remorse, she passed over into the bitter land of
repentance. She must no longer allow herself to hope for
anything for herself. The rest of her life must be spent in
self-abnegation: she must seek for no sympathy, must ask for
no grace in love, no grace and harmony in living. Henceforward, as far as her own desires went, she was dead. She
took a fierce joy in the anguish of it.

"Do you feel better?" Severn asked of the sick man.
Thomas looked at the questioner with tragic brown eyes, in
which was no anger, only mute self-pity. He did not answer,
but looked like a wounded animal, very pitiable. Mrs. Thomas
quickly repressed an impulse of impatient scorn, replacing it
with a numb, abstract sense of duty, lofty and cold.

"Come," said Severn, full of pity, and gentle as a woman.
"Let me help you to bed."

Thomas, leaning heaviy on the young man, whose white
garments were dabbed with bood and water, stumbled forlornly
into his room. There Severn unlaced his boots and got off the
remnant of his collar. At this point Mrs. Thomas came in.
She had taken her part; she was weeping also.

"Thank you, Mr. Severn," she said coldly. Severn, dismissed, slunk out of the room. She went up to her husband,
took his pathetic head upon her bosom, and pressed it there.
As Severn went downstairs, he heard the few sobs of the
husband, among the quick sniffing of the wife's tears. And
he saw Kate, who had stood on the stairs to see all went well,
climb up to her room with cold, calm face.

He locked up the house, put everything in order. Then he
heated some water to bathe his face, which was swelling painfully. Having finished his fomentations, he sat thinking
bitterly, with a good deal of shame.

As he sat, Mrs. Thomas came down for something. Her
bearing was cold and hostile. She glanced round to see all
was safe. Then:

"You will put out the light when you go to bed, Mr.
Severn," she said, more formally than a landlady at the sea-
side would speak. He was insulted: any ordinary being would

turn off the light on retiring. Moreover, almost every night it was he who locked up the house, and came last to bed.

"I will, Mrs. Thomas," he answered. He bowed, his eyes flickering with irony, because he knew his face was swollen.

She returned again after having reached the landing.

"Perhaps you wouldn't mind helping *me* down with the box," she said, quietly and coldly. He did not reply, as he would have done an hour before, that he certainly should not help her, because it was a man's job, and she must not do it. Now, he rose bowed, and went upstairs with her. Taking the greater part of the weight, he came quickly downstairs with the load.

"Thank you; it's very good of you. Good-night," said Mrs. Thomas, and she retired.

In the morning Severn rose late. His face was considerably swollen. He went in his dressing-gown across to Thomas's room. The other man lay in bed, looking much the same as ever, but mournful in aspect, though pleased within himself at being coddled.

"How are you this morning?" Severn asked.

Thomas smiled, looked almost with tenderness up at his friend.

"Oh, I'm all right, thanks," he replied.

He looked at the other's swollen and bruised cheek, then again, affectionately, into Severn's eyes.

"I'm sorry"—with a glance of indication—"for that," he said simply. Severn smiled with his eyes, in his own winsome manner.

"I didn't know we were such essential brutes," he said. "I thought I was so civilised . . ."

Again he smiled, with a wry, stiff mouth. Thomas gave a deprecating little grunt of a laugh.

"Oh, I don't know," he said. "It shows a man's got some fight in him."

He looked up in the other's face appealingly. Severn smiled, with a touch of bitterness. The two men grasped hands.

To the end of their acquaintance, Severn and Thomas were close friends, with a gentleness in their bearing, one towards the other. On the other hand, Mrs. Thomas was only polite and formal with Severn, treating him as if he were a stranger.

Kate, her fate disposed of by her 'betters', passed out of their three lives.

HER TURN

She was his second wife, and so there was between them that truce which is never held between a man and his first woman.

He was one for the women, and as such, an exception among the colliers. In spite of their prudery, the neighbour women liked him; he was big, naïve, and very courteous with them; he was so, even to his second wife.

Being a large man of considerable strength and perfect health, he earned good money in the pit. His natural courtesy saved him from enemies, while his fresh interest in life made his presence always agreeable. So he went his own way, had always plenty of friends, always a good job down pit.

He gave his wife thirty-five shillings a week. He had two grown-up sons at home, and they paid twelve shillings each. There was only one child by the second marriage, so Radford considered his wife did well.

Eighteen months ago, Bryan and Wentworth's men were out on strike for eleven weeks. During that time, Mrs. Radford could neither cajole nor entreat nor nag the ten shillings strike-pay from her husband. So that when the second strike came on, she was prepared for action.

Radford was going, quite inconspicuously, to the publican's wife at the 'Golden Horn'. She is a large, easy-going lady of forty, and her husband is sixty-three, moreover crippled with rheumatism. She sits in the little bar-parlour of the wayside public-house, knitting for dear life, and sipping a very moderate glass of Scotch. When a decent man arrives at the three-foot width of bar, she rises, serves him, surveys him over, and, if she likes his looks, says:

"Won't you step inside, sir?"

If he steps inside, he will find not more than one or two men present. The room is warm, quite small. The landlady knits. She gives a few polite words to the stranger, then resumes her conversation with the man who interests her most. She is straight, highly-coloured, with indifferent brown eyes.

"What was that you asked me, Mr. Radford?"

"What is the difference between a donkey's tail and a rainbow?" asked Radford, who had a consuming passion for conundrums.

"All the difference in the world," replied the landlady.

"Yes, but what special difference?"

"I s'll have to give it up again. You'll think me a donkey's head, I'm afraid."

"Not likely. But just you consider now, wheer . . ."

The conundrum was still under weigh, when a girl entered. She was swarthy, a fine animal. After she had gone out:

"Do you know who that is?" asked the landlady.

"I can't say as I do," replied Radford.

"She's Frederick Pinnock's daughter, from Stony Ford. She's courting our Willy."

"And a fine lass, too."

"Yes, fine enough, as far as that goes. What sort of a wife'll she make him, think you?"

"You just let me consider a bit," said the man. He took out a pocket-book and a pencil. The landlady continued to talk to the other guests.

Radford was a big fellow, black-haired, with a brown moustache, and darkish blue eyes. His voice, naturally deep, was pitched in his throat, and had a peculiar, tenor quality, rather husky, and disturbing. He modulated it a good deal as he spoke, as men do who talk much with women. Always, there was a certain indolence in his carriage.

"Our mester's lazy," his wife said. "There's many a bit of a jab wants doin', but get him to do it if you can."

But she knew he was merely indifferent to the little jobs, and not lazy.

He sat writing for about ten minutes, at the end of which time, he read:

"I see a fine girl full of life.
I see her just ready for wedlock,
But there's jealousy between her eyebrows
And jealousy on her mouth.
I see trouble ahead.
Willy is delicate.
She would do him no good.
She would never see when he wasn't well,
She would only see what she wanted——"

So, in phrases, he got down his thoughts. He had to fumble

for expression, and therefore anything serious he wanted to say he wrote in 'poetry', as he called it.

Presently, the landlady rose, saying:

"Well, I s'll have to be looking after our mester. I s'll be in again before we close."

Radford sat quite comfortably on. In a while, he too bade the company good-night.

When he got home, at a quarter-past eleven, his sons were in bed, and his wife sat awaiting him. She was a woman of medium height, fat and sleek, a dumpling. Her black hair was parted smooth, her narrow-opened eyes were sly and satirical, she had a peculiar twang in her rather sleering voice.

"Our missis is a puss-puss," he said easily, of her. Her extraordinarily smooth, sleek face was remarkable. She was very healthy.

He never came in drunk. Having taken off his coat and his cap, he sat down to supper in his shirt-sleeves. Do as he might, she was fascinated by him. He had a strong neck, with the crisp hair growing low. Let her be angry as she would, yet she had a passion for that neck of his, particularly when she saw the great vein rib under the skin.

"I think, missis," he said, "I'd rather ha'e a smite o' cheese than this meat."

"Well, can't you get it yourself?"

"Yi, surely I can," he said, and went out to the pantry.

"I think, if yer comin' in at this time of night, you can wait on yourself," she justified herself.

She moved uneasily in her chair. There were several jam-tarts alongside the cheese on the dish he brought.

"Yi, Missis, them tan-tafflins'll go down very nicely," he said.

"Oh, will they! Then you'd better help to pay for them," she said, amiably, but determined.

"Now what art after?"

"What am I after? Why, can't you think?" she said sarcastically.

"I'm not for thinkin', missis."

"No, I know you're not. But wheer's my money? You've been paid the Union to-day. Wheer do I come in?"

"Tha's got money, an' tha mun use it."

"Thank yer. An' 'aven't you none, as well?"

"I hadna, not till we was paid, not a ha'p'ny."

"Then you ought to be ashamed of yourself to say so."

" 'Appen so."

"We'll go shares wi' th' Union money," she said. "That's nothing but what's right."

"We shonna. Tha's got plenty o' money as tha can use."

"Oh, all right," she said. "I will do."

She went to bed. It made her feel sharp that she could not get at him.

The next day, she was just as usual. But at eleven o'clock she took her purse and went up town. Trade was very slack. Men stood about in gangs, men were playing marbles everywhere in the streets. It was a sunny morning. Mrs. Radford went into the furnisher-and-upholsterer's shop.

"There's a few things," she said to Mr. Allcock, "as I'm wantin' for the house, and I might as well get them now, while the men's at home, and can shift me the furniture."

She put her fat purse on to the counter with a click. The man should know she was not wanting 'strap'. She bought linoleum for the kitchen, a new wringer, a breakfast-service, a spring mattress, and various other things, keeping a mere thirty shillings, which she tied in a corner of her handkerchief. In her purse was some loose silver.

Her husband was gardening in a desultory fashion when she got back home. The daffodils were aut. The colts in the field at the end of the garden were tossing their velvety brown necks.

"Sithee here, missis," called Radford, from the shed which stood half-way down the path. Two doves in a cage were cooing.

"What have you got?" asked the woman, as she approached. He held out to her in his big, earthy hand a tortoise. The reptile was very, very slowly issuing its head again to the warmth.

"He's wakkened up betimes," said Radford.

"He's like th' men, wakened up for a holiday," said the wife. Radford scratched the little beast's scaly head.

"We pleased to see him out," he said.

They had just finished dinner, when a man knocked at the door.

"From Allcock's!" he said.

The plump woman took up the clothes-basket containing the crockery she had bought.

"Whativer hast got theer?" asked her husband.

"We've been wantin' some breakfast-cups for ages, so I went up town an' got 'em this mornin'," she replied.

He watched her taking out the crockery.

"Hm!" he said. "Tha's been on th' spend, seemly."

Again there was a thud at the door. The man had put down a roll of linoleum. Mr. Radford went to look at it.

"They come rolling in!" he exclaimed.

"Who's grumbled more than you about the raggy oilcloth of this kitchen?" said the insidious, cat-like voice of the wife.

"It's all right, it's all right," said Radford.

The carter came up the entry with another roll, which he deposited with a grunt at the door.

"An' how much do you reckon this lot is?" he asked.

"Oh, they're all paid for, don't worry," replied the wife.

"Shall yer gi'e me a hand, mester?" asked the carter.

Radford followed him down the entry, in his easy, slouching way. His wife went after. His waistcoat was hanging loose over his shirt. She watched his easy movement of well-being as she followed him, and she laughed to herself.

The carter took hold of one end of the wire mattress, dragged it forth.

"Well, this is a corker!" said Radford, as he received the burden.

"Now the mangle!" said the carter.

"What dost reckon tha's been up to, missis?" asked the husband.

"I said to myself last wash-day, if I had to turn that mangle again, tha'd ha'e ter wash the clothes thyself."

Radford followed the carter down the entry again. In the street, women were standing watching, and dozens of men were lounging round the cart. One officiously helped with the wringer.

"Gi'e him thrippence," said Mrs. Radford.

"Gi'e him thysen," replied her husband.

"I've no change under half a crown."

Radford tipped the carter, and returned indoors. He surveyed the array of crockery, linoleum, mattress, mangle, and other goods crowding the house and the yard.

"Well, this is a winder!" he repeated.

"We stood in need of 'em enough," she replied.

"I hope tha's got plenty more from wheer they came from," he replied dangerously.

"That's just what I haven't." She opened her purse. "Two half-crowns, that's every copper I've got i' th' world."

He stood very still as he looked.

"It's right," she said.

There was a certain smug sense of satisfaction about her. A wave of anger came over him, blinding him. But he waited and waited. Suddenly his arm leapt up, the fist clenched, and his eyes blazed at her. She shrank away, pale and frightened. But he dropped his fist to his side, turned, and went out, muttering. He went down to the shed that stood in the middle of the garden. There he picked up the tortoise, and stood with bent head, rubbing its horny head.

She stood hesitating, watching him. Her heart was heavy, and yet there was a curious, cat-like look of satisfaction round her eyes. Then she went indoors and gazed at her new cups, admiringly.

The next week he handed her his half-sovereign without a word.

"You'll want some for yourself," she said, and she gave him a shilling. He accepted it.

STRIKE-PAY

STRIKE-MONEY is paid in the Primitive Methodist Chapel. The crier was round quite early on Wednesday morning to say that paying would begin at ten o'clock.

The Primitive Methodist Chapel is a big barn of a place, built, designed, and paid for by the colliers themselves. But it threatened to fall down from its first form, so that a professional architect had to be hired at last to pull the place together.

It stands in the Square. Forty years ago, when Bryan and Wentworth opened their pits, they put up the 'squares' of miners' dwellings. They are two great quadrangles of houses, enclosing a barren stretch of ground, littered with broken pots and rubbish, which forms a square, a great, sloping, lumpy playground for the children, a drying-ground for many women's washing.

Wednesday is still wash-day with some women. As the men clustered round the Chapel, they heard the thud-thud-thud of many pouches, women pounding away at the wash-tub with a wooden pestle. In the Square the white clothes were waving in the wind from a maze of clothes-lines, and here and there women were pegging out, calling to the miners, or to the children who dodged under the flapping sheets.

Ben Townsend, the Union agent, has a bad way of paying. He takes the men in order of his round, and calls them by name. A big, oratorical man with a grey beard, he sat at the table in the Primitive school-room, calling name after name. The room was crowded with colliers, and a great group pushed up outside. There was much confusion. Ben dodged from the Scargill Street list to the Queen Street. For this Queen Street men were not prepared. They were not to the fore.

"Joseph Grooby—Joseph Grooby! Now, Joe, where are you?"

"Hold on a bit, Sorry!" cried Joe from outside. "I'm shovin' up."

There was a great noise from the men.

"I'm takin' Queen Street. All you Queen Street men should be ready. Here you are, Joe," said the Union agent loudly.

"Five children!" said Joe, counting the money suspiciously.

"That's right, I think," came the mouthing voice. "Fifteen shillings, is it not?"

"A bob a kid," said the collier.

"Thomas Sedgwick—How are you, Tom? Missis better?"

"Ay, 'er's shapin' nicely. Tha'rt hard at work to-day, Ben." This was sarcasm on the idleness of a man who had given up the pit to become a Union agent.

"Yes. I rose at four to fetch the money."

"Dunna hurt thysen," was the retort, and the men laughed.

"No—John Merfin!"

But the colliers, tired with waiting, excited by the strike spirit, began to rag. Merfin was young and dandiacal. He was choir-master at the Wesleyan Chapel.

"Does your collar cut, John?" asked a sarcastic voice out of the crowd.

"Hymn Number Nine.

'Diddle-diddle dumpling, my son John
Went to bed with his best suit on,' "

came the solemn announcement.

Mr. Merfin, his white cuffs down to his knuckles, picked up his half-sovereign, and walked away loftily.

"Sam Coutts!" cried the paymaster.

"Now, lad, reckon it up," shouted the voice of the crowd, delighted.

Mr. Coutts was a straight-backed ne'er-do-well. He looked at his twelve shillings sheepishly.

"Another two bob—he had twins a-Monday night—get thy money, Sam, tha's earned it—tha's addled it, Sam; dunna go be-out it. Let him ha' the two bob for 'is twins, mister," came the clamour from the men around.

Sam Coutts stood grinning awkwardly.

"You should ha' given us notice, Sam," said the paymaster sauvely. "We can make it all right for you next week——"

"Nay, nay, nay," shouted a voice. "Pay on delivery—the goods is there right enough."

"Get thy money, Sam, tha's addled it," became the universal cry, and the Union agent had to hand over another florin, to prevent a disturbance. Sam Coutts grinned with satisfaction.

"Good shot, Sam," the men exclaimed.

"Ephraim Wharmby," shouted the pay-man.

A lad came forward.

"Gi' him sixpence for what's on t'road," said a sly voice.

"Nay, nay," replied Ben Townsend; "pay on delivery."

There was a roar of laughter. The miners were in high spirits.

In the town they stood about in gangs, talking and laughing. Many sat on their heels in the market-place. In and out of the public-houses they went, and on every bar the half-sovereigns clicked.

"Comin' ter Nottingham wi' us, Ephraim?" said Sam Courts to the slender, pale young fellow of about twenty-two.

"I'm non walkin' that far of a gleamy day like this."

"He has na got the strength," said somebody, and a laugh went up.

"How's that?" asked another pertinent voice.

"He's a married man, mind yer," said Chris Smitheringale, "an' it ta'es a bit o' keepin' up."

The youth was teased in this manner for some time.

"Come on ter Nottingham wi's; tha'll be safe for a bit," said Coutts.

A gang set off, although it was only eleven o'clock. It was a nine-mile walk. The road was crowded with colliers travelling on foot to see the match between Notts and Aston Villa. In Ephraim's gang were Sam Coutts, with his fine shoulders and his extra florin, Chris Smitheringale, fat and smiling, and John Wharmby, a remarkable man, tall, erect as a soldier, black-haired and proud; he could play any music instrument, he declared.

"I can play owt from a comb up'ards. If there's music to be got outer a thing, I back I'll get it. No matter what shape or form of instrument you set before me, it doesn't signify if I nivir clapped cyes on it before, I's warrant I'll have a tune out of it in five minutes."

He beguiled the first two miles so. It was true, he had caused a sensation by introducing the mandoline into the townlet, filling the hearts of his fellow-colliers with pride as he sat on the platform in evening dress, a fine soldierly man, bowing his black head, and scratching the mewing mandoline with hands that had only to grasp the 'instrument' to crush it entirely.

Chris stood a can round at the 'White Bull' at Gilt Brook. John Wharmby took his turn at Kimberley top.

"We wunna drink again," they decided, "till we're at Cinder Hill. We'll non stop i' Nuttall."

They swung along the high-road under the budding trees. In Nuttall churchyard the crocuses blazed with yellow at the brim of the balanced, black yews. White and purple crocuses clipt up over the graves, as if the churchyard were bursting out in tiny tongues of flame.

"Sithee," said Ephraim, who was an ostler down pit, "sithee, here comes the Colonel. Sithee at his 'osses how they pick their toes up, the beauties!"

The Colonel drove past the men, who took no notice of him.

"Hast heard, Sorry," said Sam, "as they're com'n out i' Germany, by the thousand, an' begun riotin'?"

"An' comin' out i' France simbitar," cried Chris.

The men all gave a chuckle.

"Sorry," shouted John Wharmby, much elated, "we oughtna ter go back under a twenty per cent rise."

"We should get it," said Chris.

"An' easy! They can do nowt bi-out us, we'n on'y ter stop out long enough."

"I'm willin'," said Sam, and there was a laugh. The colliers looked at one another. A thrill went through them as if an electric current passed.

"We'n on'y ter stick out, an' we s'll see who's gaffer."

"Us!" cried Sam. "Why, what can they do again' us, if we come out all over th' world?"

"Nowt!" said John Wharmby. "Th' mesters is bobbin' about like corks on a cassivoy a'ready." There was a large natural reservoir, like a lake, near Bestwood, and this supplied the simile.

Again there passed through the men that wave of elation, quickening their pulses. They chuckled in their throats. Beyond all consciousness was this sense of battle and triumph in the hearts of the working-men at this juncture.

It was suddenly suggested at Nuttall that they should go over the fields to Bulwell, and into Nottingham that way. They went single file across the fallow, past the wood, and over the railway, where now no trains were running. Two fields away was a troop of pit ponies. Of all colours, but chiefly of red or brown, they clustered thick in the field, scarcely moving, and the two lines of trodden earth patches showed where fodder was placed down the field.

"Theer's the pit 'osses," said Sam. "Let's run 'em."

"It's like a circus turned out. See them skewbawd 'uns—seven skewbawd," said Ephraim.

The ponies were inert, unused to freedom. Occasionally one walked round. But there they stood, two thick lines of ruddy brown and pie-bald and white, across the trampled field. It was a beautiful day, mild, pale blue, a 'growing day', as the men said, when there was the silence of swelling sap everywhere.

"Let's ha'e a ride," said Ephraim.

The younger men went up to the horses.

"Come on—co-oop, Taffy—co-oop, Ginger."

The horses tossed away. But having got over the excitement of being above-ground, the animals were feeling dazed and rather dreary. They missed the warmth and the life of the pit. They looked as if life were a blank to them.

Ephraim and Sam caught a couple of steeds, on whose backs they went careering round, driving the rest of the sluggish herd from end to end of the field. The horses were good specimens, on the whole, and in fine condition. But they were out of their element.

Performing too clever a feat, Ephraim went rolling from his mount. He was soon up again, chasing his horse. Again he was thrown. Then the men proceeded on their way.

They were drawing near to miserable Bulwell, when Ephraim, remembering his turn was coming to stand drinks, felt in his pocket for his beloved half-sovereign, his strike-pay. It was not there. Through all his pockets he went, his heart sinking like lead.

"Sam," he said, "I believe I'n lost that ha'ef a sovereign."

"Tha's got it somewheer about thee," said Chris.

They made him take off his coat and waistcoat. Chris examined the coat, Sam the waistcoat, whilst Ephraim searched his trousers.

"Well," said Chris, "I'n foraged this coat, an' it's non theer."

"An' I'll back my life as th' on'y bit a metal on this wa'scoat is the buttons," said Sam.

"An't it's non in my breeches," said Ephraim. He took off his boots and his stockings. The half-sovereign was not there. He had not another coin in his possession.

"Well," said Chris, "we mun go back an' look for it."

Back they went, four serious-hearted colliers, and searched the field, but in vain.

"Well," said Chris, "we s'll ha'e ter share wi' thee, that's a'."

"I'm willin'," said John Wharmby.

"An' me," said Sam.

"Two bob each," said Chris.

Ephraim, who was in the depths of despair, shamefully accepted their six shillings.

In Bulwell they called in a small public-house, which had one long room with a brick floor, scrubbed benches and scrubbed tables. The central space was open. The place was full of colliers, who were drinking. There was a great deal of drinking during the strike, but not a vast amount drunk. Two men were playing skittles, and the rest were betting. The seconds sat on either side the skittle-board, holding caps of money, sixpences and coppers, the wagers of the 'backers'.

Sam, Chris and John Wharmby immediately put money on the man who had their favour. In the end Sam declared himself willing to play against the victor. He was the Bestwood champion. Chris and John Wharmby backed him heavily, and even Ephraim the Unhappy ventured sixpence.

In the end, Sam had won half a crown, with which he promptly stood drinks and bread and cheese for his comrades. At half-past one they set off again.

It was a good match between Notts and Villa—no goals at half-time, two-none for Notts at the finish. The colliers were hugely delighted, especially as Flint, the forward for Notts, who was an Underwood man well known to the four comrades, did some handsome work, putting the two goals through.

Ephraim determined to go home as soon as the match was over. He knew John Wharmby would be playing the piano at the 'Punch Bowl', and Sam, who had a good tenor voice, singing, while Chris cut in with witticisms, until evening. So he bade them farewell, as he must get home. They, finding him somewhat of a damper on their spirits, let him go.

He was the sadder for having witnessed an accident near the football-ground. A navvy, working at some drainage, carting an iron tip-tub of mud and emptying it, had got with his horse on to the deep deposit of ooze which was crusted over. The crust had broken, the man had gone under the horse, and it was some time before the people had realised he had vanished. When they found his feet sticking out, and hauled him forth, he was dead, stifled dead in the mud. The horse was at length hauled out, after having its neck nearly pulled from the socket.

Ephraim went home vaguely impressed with a sense of death, and loss, and strife. Death was loss greater than his own, the strike was a battle greater than that he would presently have to fight.

He arrived home at seven o'clock, just when it had fallen dark. He lived in Queen Street with his young wife, to whom he had been married two months, and with his mother-in-law, a widow of sixty-four. Maud was the last child remaining unmarried, the last of eleven.

Ephraim went up the entry. The light was burning in the kitchen. His mother-in-law was a big, erect woman, with wrinkled, loose face, and cold blue eyes. His wife was also large, with very vigorous fair hair, frizzy like unravelled rope. She had a quiet way of stepping, a certain cat-like stealth, in spite of her large build. She was five months pregnant.

"Might we ask wheer you've been to?" inquired Mrs. Marriott, very erect, very dangerous. She was only polite when she was very angry.

"I'n bin ter th' match."

"Oh, indeed!" said the mother-in-law. "And why couldn't we be told as you thought of jaunting off?"

"I didna know mysen," he answered, sticking to his broad Derbyshire.

"I suppose it popped into your mind, an' so you darted off," said the mother-in-law dangerously.

"I didna. It wor Chris Smitheringale who exed me."

"An' did you take much invitin'?"

"I didna want ter goo."

"But wasn't there enough man beside your jacket to say no?"

He did not answer. Down at the bottom he hated her. But he was, to use his own words, all messed up with having lost his strike-pay and with knowing the man was dead. So he was more helpless before his mother-in-law, whom he feared.

His wife neither looked at him nor spoke, but kept her head bowed. He knew she was with her mother.

"Our Maud's been waitin' for some money, to get a few things," said the mother-in-law.

In silence, he put five-and-sixpence on the table.

"Take that up, Maud," said the mother.

Maud did so.

"You'll want it for us board, shan't you?" she asked, furtively, of her mother.

"Might I ask if there's nothing you want to buy yourself, first?"

"No, there's nothink I want," answered the daughter.

Mrs. Marriott took the silver and counted it.

"And do you," said the mother-in-law, towering upon the shrinking son, but speaking slowly and statelily, "do you think I'm going to keep you and your wife for five and sixpence a week?"

"It's a' I've got," he answered sulkily.

"You've had a good jaunt, my sirs, if it's cost four and six-pence. You've started your game early, haven't you?"

He did not answer.

"It's a nice thing! Here's our Maud an' me been sitting since eleven o'clock this morning! Dinner waiting and cleared away, tea waiting and washed up; then in he comes crawling with five and sixpence. Five and sixpence for a man an' wife's board for a week, if you please!"

Still he did not say anything.

"You must think something of yourself, Ephraim Wharmby!" said his mother-in-law. "You must think something of yourself. You suppose, do you, *I'm* going to keep you an' your wife, while you make a holiday, off on the nines to Nottingham, drink an' women."

"I've neither had drink nor women, as you know right well," he said.

"I'm glad we know summat about you. For you're that close, anybody'd think we was foreigners to you. You're a pretty little jockey, aren't you? Oh, it's a gala time for you, the strike is. That's all men strike for, indeed. They enjoy themselves, they do that. Ripping and racing and drinking, from morn till night, my sirs!"

"Is there on'y tea for me?" he asked, in a temper.

"Hark at him! Hark-ye! Should I ask you whose house

you think you're in? Kindly order me about, do. Oh, it makes
him big, the strike does. See him land home after being out on
the spree for hours, and give his orders, my sirs! Oh, strike
sets the men up, it does. Nothing have they to do but guzzle
and gallivant to Nottingham. Their wives'll keep them, oh
yes. So long as they get something to eat at home, what more
do they want! What more *should* they want, prithee?
Nothing! Let the women and children starve and scrape,
but fill the man's belly, and let him have his fling. My sirs,
indeed, I think so! Let tradesmen go—what do they matter!
Let rent go. Let children get what they can catch. Only the
man will see *he's* all right. But not here, though!"

"Are you goin' ter gi'e me ony bloody tea?"

His mother-in-law started up.

"If tha dares ter swear at me, I'll lay thee flat."

"Are yer—goin' ter—gi'e me—any blasted, rotten, còssed,
blòody tèa?" he bawled, in a fury, accenting every other word
deliberately.

"Maud!" said the mother-in-law, cold and stately, "If you
gi'e him any tea after that, you're a trollops." Whereupon she
sailed out to her other daughters.

Maud quietly got the tea ready.

"Shall y'ave your dinner warmed up?" she asked.

"Ay."

She attended to him. Not that she was really meek. But—
he was *her* man, not her mother's.

THE WITCH *A LA MODE*

WHEN Bernard Coutts alighted at East Croydon he knew he was tempting Providence.

"I may just as well," he said to himself, "stay the night here, where I am used to the place, as go to London. I can't get to Connie's forlorn spot to-night, and I'm tired to death, so why shouldn't I do what is easiest?"

He gave his luggage to a porter.

Again, as he faced the approaching tram-car: "I don't see why I shouldn't go down to Purley. I shall just be in time for tea."

Each of these concessions to his desires he made against his conscience. But beneath his sense of shame his spirit exulted.

It was an evening of March. In the dark hollow below Crown Hill the buildings accumulated, bearing the black bulk of the church tower up into the rolling and smoking sunset.

"I know it so well," he thought. "And love it," he confessed secretly in his heart.

The car ran on familiarly. The young man listened for the swish, watched for the striking of the blue splash overhead, at the bracket. The sudden fervour of the spark, splashed out of the mere wire, pleased him.

"Where does it come from?" he asked himself, and a spark struck bright again. He smiled a little, roused.

The day was dying out. One by one the arc lamps fluttered or leaped alight, the strand of copper overhead glistened against the dark sky that now was deepening to the colour of monkshood. The tram-car dipped as it ran, seeming to exult. As it came clear of the houses, the young man, looking west, saw the evening star advance, a bright thing approaching from a long way off, as if it had been bathing in the surf of the daylight, and now was walking shorewards to the night. He greeted the naked star with a bow of the head, his heart surging as the car leaped.

"It seems to be greeting me across the sky—the star," he said, amused by his own vanity.

Above the colouring of the afterglow the blade of the new moon hung sharp and keen. Something recoiled in him.

"It is like a knife to be used at a sacrifice," he said to himself. Then, secretly: "I wonder for whom?"

He refused to answer this question, but he had the sense of Constance, his betrothed, waiting for him in the Vicarage in the north. He closed his eyes.

Soon the car was running full-tilt from the shadow to the fume of yellow light at the terminus, where shop on shop and lamp beyond lamp heaped golden fire on the floor of the blue night. The car, like an eager dog, ran in home, sniffing with pleasure the fume of lights.

Coutts flung away uphill. He had forgotten he was tired. From the distance he could distinguish the house, by the broad white cloth of alyssum flowers that hung down the garden walls. He ran up the steep path to the door, smelling the hyacinths in the dark, watching for the pale fluttering of daffodils and the steadier show of white crocuses on the grassy banks.

Mrs. Braithwaite herself opened the door to him.

"There!" she exclaimed. "I expected you. I had your card saying you would cross from Dieppe to-day. You wouldn't make up your mind to come here, not till the last minute, would you? No—that's what I expected. You know where to put your things; I don't think we've altered anything in the last year."

Mrs. Braithwaite chattered on, laughing all the time. She was a young widow, whose husband had been dead two years. Of medium height, sanguine in complexion and temper, there was a rich oily glisten in her skin and in her black hair, suggesting the flesh of a nut. She was dressed for the evening in a long gown of soft, mole-coloured satin.

"Of course, I'm delighted you've come," she said at last, lapsing into conventional politeness, and then, seeing his eyes, she began to laugh at her attempt at formality.

She let Coutts into a small, very warm room that had a dark, foreign sheen, owing to the black of the curtains and hangings covered thick with glistening Indian embroidery, and to the sleekness of some Indian ware. A rosy old gentleman, with exquisite white hair and side-whiskers, got up shakily and stretched out his hand. His cordial expression of welcome was rendered strange by a puzzled, wondering look of old age, and by a certain stiffness of his countenance, which now would only render a few expressions. He wrung the newcomer's hand heartily, his manner contrasting pathetically with his bowed and trembling form.

"Oh, why—why, yes, it's Mr. Coutts! H'm—ay. Well, and how are you—h'm? Sit down, sit down." The old man rose again, bowing, waving the young man into a chair. "Ay! well, and how are you? . . . What? Have some tea—come on, come along; here's the tray. Laura, ring for fresh tea for Mr. Coutts. But I will do it." He suddenly remembered his old gallantry, forgot his age and uncertainty. Fumbling, he rose to go to the bell-pull.

"It's done, Peter—the tea will be in a minute," said his daughter in high, distinct tones. Mr. Cleveland sank with relief into his chair.

"You know, I'm beginning to be troubled with rheumatism," he explained in confidential tones. Mrs. Braithwaite glanced at the young man and smiled. The old gentleman babbled and chattered. He had no knowledge of his guest beyond the fact of his presence; Coutts might have been any other young man, for all his host was aware.

"You didn't tell us you were going away. Why didn't you?" asked Laura, in her distinct tones, between laughing and re-proach. Coutts looked at her ironically, so that she fidgeted with some crumbs on the cloth.

"I don't know," he said. "Why do we do things?"

"I'm sure I don't know. Why do we? Because we want to, I suppose," and she ended again with a little run of laughter. Things were so amusing, and she was so healthy.

"Why *do* we do things, Pater?" she suddenly asked in a loud voice, glancing with a little chuckle of laughter at Coutts.

"Ay—why do we do things? What things?" said the old man, beginning to laugh with his daughter.

"Why, any of the things that we do."

"Eh? Oh!" The old man was illuminated, and delighted. "Well, now, that's a difficult question. I remember, when I was a little younger, we used to discuss Free Will—got very hot about it . . ." He laughed, and Laura laughed, then said, in a high voice:

"Oh! Free Will! We shall really think you're *passé*, if you revive that, Pater."

Mr. Cleveland looked puzzled for a moment. Then, as if answering a conundrum, he repeated:

"Why do we do things? Now, why *do* we do things?"

"I suppose," he said, in all good faith, "it's because we can't help it—eh? What?"

Laura laughed. Coutts showed his teeth in a smile.

"That's what I think, Pater," she said loudly.

"And are you still engaged to your Constance?" she asked of Coutts, with a touch of mockery this time. Coutts nodded.

"And how is she?" asked the widow.

"I believe she is very well—unless my delay has upset her," said Coutts, his tongue between his teeth. It hurt him to give pain to his fiancée, and yet he did it wilfully.

"Do you know, she always reminds me of a Bunbury—I call her your Miss Bunbury," Laura laughed.

Coutts did not answer.

"We missed you *so* much when you first went away," Laura began, re-establishing the proprieties.

"Thank you," he said. She began to laugh wickedly.

"On Friday evenings," she said, adding quickly: "Oh, and this is Friday evening, and Winifred is coming just as she used to—how long ago?—ten months?"

"Ten months," Coutts corroborated.

"Did you quarrel with Winifred?" she asked suddenly.

"Winifred never quarrels," he answered.

"I don't believe she does. Then why *did* you go away? You are such a puzzle to me, you know—and I shall never rest till I have had it out of you. Do you mind?"

"I like it," he said, quietly, flashing a laugh at her.

She laughed, then settled herself in a dignified, serious way.

"No, I can't make you out at all—nor can I Winifred. You *are* a pair! But it's you who are the real wonder. When are you going to be married?"

"I don't know—When I am sufficiently well off."

"I *asked* Winifred to come to-night," Laura confessed. The eyes of the man and woman met.

"Why is she so ironic to me?—does she really like me?" Coutts asked of himself. But Laura looked too bonny and jolly to be fretted by love.

"And Winifred won't tell me a word," she said.

"There is nothing to tell," he replied.

Laura looked at him closely for a few moments. Then she rose and left the room.

Presently there arrived a German lady with whom Coutts was slightly acquainted. At about half-past seven came Winifred Varley. Coutts heard the courtly old gentleman welcoming her in the hall, heard her low voice in answer. When she entered, and saw him, he knew it was a shock to her, though she hid it as well as she could. He suffered too. After hesitating for a second in the doorway, she came forward, shook hands without speaking, only looking at him with rather frightened blue eyes. She was of medium height, sturdy in build. Her face was white and impassive, without the least trace of a smile. She was a blonde of twenty-eight, dressed in a white gown just short enough not to touch the ground. Her throat was solid and strong, her arms heavy and white and beautiful, her blue eyes heavy with unacknowledged passion. When she had turned away from Coutts, she flushed vividly. He could see the pink in her arms and throat, and he flushed in answer.

"That blush would hurt her," he said to himself, wincing.

"I did not expect to see you," she said, with a reedy timbre of voice, as if her throat were half-closed. It made his nerves tingle.

"No—nor I you. At least . . ." He ended indefinitely.

"You have come down from Yorkshire?" she asked. Apparently she was cold and self-possessed. Yorkshire meant the Rectory where his fiancée lived; he felt the sting of sarcasm.

"No," he answered. "I am on my way there."

There was a moment's pause. Unable to resolve the situation, she turned abruptly to her hostess.

"Shall we play, then?"

They adjourned to the drawing-room. It was a large room upholstered in dull yellow. The chimney-piece took Coutts' attention. He knew it perfectly well, but this evening it had a new, lustrous fascination. Over the mellow marble of the mantel rose an immense mirror, very translucent and deep, like deep grey water. Before this mirror, shining white as moons on a soft grey sky, was a pair of statues in alabaster, two feet high. Both were nude figures. They glistened under the side lamps, rose clean and distinct from their pedestals. The Venus leaned slightly forward, as if

anticipating someone's coming. Her attitude of suspense made
the young man stiffen. He could see the clean suavity of her
shoulders and waist reflected white on the deep mirror. She
shone, catching, as she leaned forward, the glow of the lamp
on her lustrous marble loins.

Laura played Brahms; the delicate, winsome German lady
played Chopin; Winifred played on her violin a Grieg sonata,
to Laura's accompaniment. After having sung twice, Coutts
listened to the music. Unable to criticise, he listened till he
was intoxicated. Winifred, as she played, swayed slightly. He
watched the strong forward thrust of her neck, the powerful
and angry striking of her arm. He could see the outline of her
figure; she wore no corsets; and he found her of resolute independent build. Again he glanced at the Venus bending in
suspense. Winifred was blonde with a solid whiteness, an
isolated woman.

All the evening, little was said, save by Laura. Miss Syfurt
exclaimed continually: "Oh, that is fine! You play gra-and,
Miss Varley, don't you know. If I could play the violin—ah!
the violin!"

It was not later than ten o'clock when Winifred and
Miss Syfurt rose to go, the former to Croydon. the latter
to Ewell.

"We can go by car together to West Croydon," said the
German lady, gleefully, as if she were a child. She was a frail,
excitable little woman of forty, naïve and innocent. She gazed
with bright brown eyes of admiration on Coutts.

"Yes, I am glad," he answered.

He took up Winifred's violin, and the three proceeded downhill to the tram-terminus. There a car was on the point of
departure. They hurried forward. Miss Syfurt mounted the
step. Coutts waited for Winifred. The conductor called:

"Come along, please, if you're going."

"No," said Winifred. "I prefer to walk this stage."

"We can walk from West Croydon," said Coutts.

The conductor rang the bell.

"Aren't you coming?" cried the frail, excitable little lady,
from the footboard. "Aren't you coming?—Oh!"

"I walk from West Croydon every day; I prefer to walk
here, in the quiet," said Winifred.

"Aw! aren't you coming with me?" cried the little lady,
quite frightened. She stepped back, in supplication, towards

the footboard. The conductor impatiently buzzed the bell. The car started forward, Miss Syfurt staggered, was caught by the conductor.

"Aw!" she cried, holding her hand out to the two who stood on the road, and breaking almost into tears of disappointment. As the tram darted forward she clutched at her hat. In a moment she was out of sight.

Coutts stood wounded to the quick by this pain given to the frail, child-like lady.

"We may as well," said Winifred, "walk over the hill to 'The Swan'." Her note had that intense reedy quality which always set the man on edge; it was the note of her anger, or, more often, of her tortured sense of discord. The two turned away, to climb the hill again. He carried the violin; for a long time neither spoke.

"Ah, how I hate her, how I hate her!" he repeated in his heart. He winced repeatedly at the thought of Miss Syfurt's little cry of supplication. He was in a position where he was not himself, and he hated her for putting him there, forgetting that it was he who had come, like a moth to the candle. For half a mile he walked on, his head carried stiffly, his face set, his heart twisted with painful emotion. And all the time, as she plodded, head down, beside him, his blood beat with hate of her, drawn to her, repelled by her.

At last, on the high-up, naked down, they came upon those meaningless pavements that run through the grass, waiting for the houses to line them. The two were thrust up into the night above the little flowering of the lamps in the valley. In front was the daze of light from London, rising midway to the zenith, just fainter than the stars. Across the valley, on the blackness of the opposite hill, little groups of lights like gnats seemed to be floating in the darkness. Orion was heeled over the West. Below, in a cleft in the night, the long, low garland of arc lamps strung down the Brighton Road, where now and then the golden tram-cars flew along the track, passing each other with a faint, angry sound.

"It is a year last Monday since we came over here," said Winifred, as they stopped to look about them.

"I remember—but I didn't know it was then," he said. There was a touch of hardness in his voice. "I don't remember our dates."

After a wait, she said in very low, passionate tones:

"It *is* a beautiful night."

"The moon has set, and the evening star," he answered; "both were out as I came down."

She glanced swiftly at him to see if this speech was a bit of symbolism. He was looking across the valley with a set face. Very slightly, by an inch or two, she nestled towards him.

"Yes," she said, half-stubborn, half-pleading. "But the night is a very fine one, for all that."

"Yes," he replied, unwillingly.

Thus, after months of separation, they dove-tailed into the same love and hate.

"You are staying down here?" she asked at length, in a forced voice. She never intruded a hair's-breadth on the most trifling privacy; in which she was Laura's antithesis; so that this question was almost an impertinence for her. He felt her shrink.

"Till the morning—then Yorkshire," he said cruelly

He hated it that she could not bear outspokenness.

At that moment a train across the valley threaded the opposite darkness with its gold thread. The valley re-echoed with vague threat. The two watched the express, like a gold-and-black snake, curve and dive seawards into the night. He turned, saw her full, fine face tilted up to him. It showed pale, distinct and firm, very near to him. He shut his eyes and shivered.

"I hate trains," he said, impulsively.

"Why?" she asked, with a curious, tender little smile that caressed, as it were, his emotion towards her.

"I don't know; they pitch one about here and there . . ."

"I thought," she said, with faint irony, "that you preferred change."

"I do like life. But now I should like to be nailed to something, if it were only a cross."

She laughed sharply, and said, with keen sarcasm:

"Is it so difficult, then, to let yourself be nailed to a cross? I thought the difficulty lay in getting free."

He ignored her sarcasm on his engagement.

"There is nothing now that matters," he said, adding quickly, to forestall her: "Of course I'm wild when dinner's late, and so on; but . . . apart from those things . . . nothing seems to matter."

She was silent.

"One goes on—remains in office, so to speak; and life's all right—only, it doesn't seem to matter."

"This does sound like complaining of trouble because you've got none," she laughed.

"Trouble . . ." he repeated. "No, I don't suppose I've got any. Vexation, which most folk call trouble; but something I really grieve about in my soul—no, nothing. I wish I had."

She laughed again sharply; but he perceived in her laughter a little keen despair.

"I find a lucky pebble. I think, now I'll throw it over my left shoulder, and wish. So I spit over my little finger, and throw the white pebble behind me, and then, when I want to wish, I'm done. I say to myself: 'Wish,' and myself says back: 'I don't wan't anything.' I say again: 'Wish, you fool,' but I'm as dumb of wishes as a newt. And then, because it rather frightens me, I say in a hurry: 'A million of money.' Do *you* know what to wish for when you see the new moon?"

She laughed quickly.

"I think so," she said. "But my wish varies."

"I wish mine did," he said, whimsically lugubrious.

She took his hand in a little impulse of love.

They walked hand in hand on the ridge of the down, bunches of lights shining below, the big radiance of London advancing like a wonder in front.

"You know . . ." he began, then stopped.

"I don't . . ." she ironically urged.

"Do you want to?" he laughed.

"Yes; one is never at peace with oneself till one understands."

"Understands what?" he asked brutally. He knew she meant that she wanted to understand the situation he and she were in.

"How to resolve the discord," she said, balking the issue. He would have liked her to say: "What you want of me."

"Your foggy weather of symbolism, as usual," he said.

"The fog is not of symbols," she replied, in her metallic voice of displeasure. "It may be symbols are candles in a fog."

"I prefer my fog without candles. I'm the fog, eh? Then I'll blow out your candle, and you'll see me better. Your candles of speech, symbols and so forth, only lead you more wrong. I'm going to wander blind, and go by instinct, like a moth that flies and settles on the wooden box his mate is shut up in."

"Isn't it an *ignis fatuus* you are flying after, at that rate?" she said.

"Maybe, for if I breathe outwards, in the positive movement towards you, you move off. If I draw in a vacant sigh of soulfulness, you flow nearly to my lips."

"This is a very interesting symbol," she said, with sharp sarcasm.

He hated her, truly. She hated him. Yet they held hands fast as they walked.

"We are just the same as we were a year ago," he laughed. But he hated her, for all his laughter.

When, at the "Swan and Sugar-Loaf", they mounted the car, she climbed to the top, in spite of the sharp night. They nestled side by side, shoulders caressing, and all the time that they ran under the round lamps neither spoke.

At the gate of a small house in a dark tree-lined street, both waited a moment. From her garden leaned an almond tree whose buds, early this year, glistened in the light of the street lamp, with theatrical effect. He broke of a twig.

"I always remember this tree," he said; "how I used to feel sorry for it when it was full out, and so lively, at midnight in the lamplight. I thought it must be tired."

"Will you come in?" she asked tenderly.

"I did get a room in town," he answered, following her.

She opened the door with her latch-key, showing him, as usual, into the drawing-room. Everything was just the same; cold in colouring, warm in appointment; ivory-coloured walls, blond, polished floor, with thick ivory-coloured rugs; three deep arm-chairs in pale amber, with large cushions; a big black piano, a violin-stand beside it; and the room very warm with a clear red fire, the brass shining hot. Coutts, according to his habit, lit the piano-candles and lowered the blinds.

"I say," he said; "this is a variation from your line!"

He pointed to a bowl of magnificent scarlet anemones that stood on the piano.

"Why?" she asked, pausing in arranging her hair at the small mirror.

"On the *piano*!" he admonished.

"Only while the table was in use," she smiled, glancing at the litter of papers that covered her table.

"And then—*red* flowers!" he said.

"Oh, I thought they were such a fine piece of colour," she replied.

"I would have wagered you would buy freesias," he said.

"Why?" she smiled. He pleased her thus.

"Well—for their cream and gold and restrained, bruised purple, and their scent. I can't believe you bought scentless flowers!"

"What!" She went forward, bent over the flowers.

"I had not noticed," she said, smiling curiously, "that they were scentless."

She touched the velvet black centres.

"Would you have bought them had you noticed?" he asked.

She thought for a moment, curiously.

"I don't know . . . probably I should not."

"You would never buy scentless flowers," he averred. "Any more than you'd love a man because he was handsome."

"I did not know," she smiled. She was pleased.

The housekeeper entered with a lamp, which she set on a stand.

"You will illuminate me?" he said to Winifred. It was her habit to talk to him by candle-light.

"I have thought about you—now I will look at you," she said quietly, smiling.

"I see—To confirm your conclusions?" he asked.

Her eyes lifted quickly in acknowledgment of his guess.

"That is so," she replied.

"Then," he said, "I'll wash my hands."

He ran upstairs. The sense of freedom, of intimacy, was very fascinating. As he washed, the little everyday action of twining his hands in the lather set him suddenly considering his other love. At her house he was always polite and formal; gentlemanly, in short. With Connie he felt the old, manly superiority; he was the knight, strong and tender, she was the beautiful maiden with a touch of God on her brow. He kissed her, he softened and selected his speech for her, he forbore from being the greater part of himself. She was his betrothed, his wife, his queen, whom he loved to idealise, and for whom he carefully modified himself. She should rule him later on— that part of him which was hers. But he loved her, too, with a pitying, tender love. He thought of her tears upon her pillow in the northern Rectory, and he bit his lip, held his breath under the strain of the situation. Vaguely he knew she would bore him. And Winifred fascinated him. He and she really played with fire. In her house, he was roused and keen. But she was not, and never could be, frank. So he was not frank, even to himself. Saying nothing, betraying nothing, immediately they were together they began the same game. Each shuddered, each defenceless and exposed, hated the other by turns. Yet they came together again. Coutts felt a vague fear of Winifred. She was intense and unnatural—and he became unnatural and intense, beside her.

When he came downstairs she was fingering the piano from the score of "Walküre".

"First wash in England," he announced, looking at his hands. She laughed swiftly. Impatient herself of the slightest soil, his indifference to temporary grubbiness amused her.

He was a tall, bony man, with small hands and feet. His features were rough and rather ugly, but his smile was taking. She was always fascinated by the changes in him. His eyes, particularly, seemed quite different at times; sometimes hard, insolent, blue; sometimes dark, full of warmth and tenderness; sometimes flaring like an animal's.

He sank wearily into a chair.

"My chair," he said, as if to himself.

She bowed her head. Of compact physique, uncorsetted, her figure bowed richly to the piano. He watched the shallow concave between her shoulders, marvelling at its rich solidity. She let one arm fall loose, he looked at the shadows in the dimples of her elbow. Slowly smiling a look of brooding affection, of acknowledgment upon him for a forgetful moment, she said:

"And what have you done lately?"

"Simply nothing," he replied quietly. "For all that these months have been so full of variety, I think they will sink out of my life; they will evaporate and leave no result; I shall forget them."

Her blue eyes were dark and heavy upon him, watching. She did not answer. He smiled faintly at her.

"And you?" he said, at length.

"With me it is different," she said quietly.

"You sit with your crystal," he laughed.

"While you tilt . . ." She hung on her ending.

He laughed, sighed, and they were quiet awhile.

"I've got such a skinful of heavy visions, they come sweating through my dreams," he said.

"Whom have you read?" She smiled.

"Meredith. Very healthy," he laughed.

She laughed quickly at being caught.

"Now, have you found out all you want?" he asked.

"Oh, no," she cried with full throat.

"Well, finish, at any rate. I'm not diseased. How are you?"

"But . . . but . . ." she stumbled on doggedly. "What *do* you intend to do?"

He hardened the line of his mouth and eyes, only to retort with immediate lightness:

"Just go on."

This was their battlefield: she could not understand how he could marry: it seemed almost monstrous to her; she fought against his marriage. She looked up at him, witch-like, from under bent brows. Her eyes were dark blue and heavy. He shivered, shrank with pain. She was so cruel to that other, common, everyday part of him.

"I wonder you dare go on like it," she said.

"Why dare?" he replied. "What's the odds?"

"I don't know," she answered, in deep, bitter displeasure.

"And I don't care," he said.

"But . . ." she continued, slowly, gravely pressing the point: "You know what you intend to do."

"Marry—settle—be a good husband, good father, partner in the business; get fat, be an amiable gentleman—Q.E.F."

"Very good," she said, deep and final.

"Thank you."

"I did not congratulate you," she said.

"Ah!" His voice tailed off into sadness and self-mistrust. Meanwhile she watched him heavily. He did not mind being scrutinised: it flattered him.

"Yes, it is, or may be, very good," she began; "but *why* all this?—*why*?"

"And why not? And why?—Because I want to."

He could not leave it thus flippantly.

"You know, Winifred, we should only drive each other into insanity, you and I: become abnormal."

"Well," she said, "and even so, why the other?"

"My marriage?—I don't know. Instinct."

"One has so many instincts," she laughed bitterly.

That was a new idea to him.

She raised her arms, stretched them above her head, in a weary gesture. They were fine, strong arms. They reminded Coutts of Euripides' "Bacchae": white, round arms, long arms. The lifting of her arms lifted her breasts. She dropped suddenly as if inert, lolling her arms against the cushions.

"I really don't see why you should be," she said drearily, though always with a touch of a sneer, "why we should always—be fighting."

"Oh, yes, you do," he replied. It was a deadlock which he could not sustain.

"Besides," he laughed, "it's your fault."

"Am I so bad" she sneered.

"Worse," he said.

"But"—she moved irritably—"is this to the point?"

"What point?" he answered; then, smiling: "You know you only like a wild-goose chase."

"I do," she answered plaintively. "I miss you very much. You snatch things from the Kobolds for me."

"Exactly," he said in a biting tone. "Exactly! That's what you want me for. I am to be your crystal, your 'genius'. My length of blood and bone you don't care a rap for. Ah, yes, you like me for a crystal-glass, to see things in: to hold up to the light. I'm a blessed Lady-of-Shalott looking-glass for you."

"You talk to me," she said, dashing his fervour, "of my fog of symbols!"

"Ah, well, if so, 'tis your own asking."

"I did not know it." She looked at him coldly. She was angry.

"No," he said.

Again, they hated each other.

"The old ancients," he laughed, "gave the gods the suet and intestines: at least, I believe so. They ate the rest. You shouldn't be a goddess."

"I wonder, among your rectory acquaintances, you haven't learned better manners," she answered in cold contempt. He closed his eyes, lying back in his chair, his legs sprawled towards her.

"I suppose we're civilised savages," he said sadly. All was silent.

At last, opening his eyes again, he said: "I shall have to be going directly, Winifred; it is past eleven . . ." Then the appeal in his voice changed to laughter. "Though I know I shall be winding through all the *Addios* in 'Traviata' before you can set me travelling." He smiled gently at her, then closed his eyes once more, conscious of deep, but vague, suffering. She lay in her chair, her face averted, rosily, towards the fire. Without glancing at her he was aware of the white approach of her throat towards her breast. He seemed to perceive her with another, unknown sense that acted all over his body. She lay perfectly still and warm in the fire-glow. He was dimly aware that he suffered.

"Yes," she said at length; "if we were linked together we should only destroy each other."

He started, hearing her admit, for the first time, this point of which he was so sure.

"You should never *marry* anyone," he said.

"And you," she asked in irony, "must offer your head to harness and be bridled and driven?"

"There's the makings of quite a good, respectable trotter in me," he laughed. "Don't you see it's what I *want* to be?"

"I'm not sure," she laughed in return.

"I think so."

They were silent for a time. The white lamp burned steadily as moonlight, the red fire like sunset; there was no stir or flicker.

"And what of you?" he asked.

She crooned a faint, tired laugh.

"If you are jetsam, as you say you are," she answered, "I am flotsam. I shall lie stranded."

"Nay," he pleaded. "When were you wrecked?"

She laughed quickly, with a sound like a tinkle of tears.

"Oh, dear Winifred!" he cried despairingly.

She lifted her arms towards him, hiding her face between them, looking up through the white closure with dark, uncanny eyes, like an invocation. His breast lifted towards her uptilted arms. He shuddered, shut his eyes, held himself rigid. He heard her drop her arms heavily.

"I must go," he said in a dull voice.

The rapidly-chasing quivers that ran in tremors down the front of his body and limbs made him stretch himself, stretch hard.

"Yes," she assented gravely; "you must go."

He turned to her. Again looking up darkly, from under her

lowered brows, she lifted her hands like small white orchids towards him. Without knowing, he gripped her wrists with a grasp that circled his blood-red nails with white rims.

"Good-bye," he said, looking down at her. She made a small, moaning noise in her throat, lifting her face so that it came open and near to him like a suddenly-risen flower, borne on a strong white stalk. She seemed to extend, to fill the world, to become atmosphere and all. He did not know what he was doing. He was bending forward, his mouth on hers, her arms round his neck, and his own hands, still fastened on to her wrists, almost bursting the blood under his nails with the intensity of their grip. They remained for a few moments thus, rigid. Then, weary of the strain, she relaxed. She turned her face, offered him her throat, white, hard, and rich, below the ear. Stooping still lower, so that he quivered in every fibre at the strain, he laid his mouth to the kiss. In the intense silence, he heard the deep, dull pulsing of her blood, and a minute click of a spark within the lamp.

Then he drew her from the chair up to him. She came, arms always round his neck, till at last she lay along his breast as he stood, feet planted wide, clasping her tight, his mouth on her neck. She turned suddenly to meet his full, red mouth in a kiss. He felt his moustache prick back into his lips. It was the first kiss she had genuinely given. Dazed, he was conscious of the throb of one great pulse, as if his whole body were a heart that contracted in throbs. He felt, with an intolerable ache, as if he, the heart, were setting the pulse in her, in the very night, so that everything beat from the throb of his overstrained, bursting body.

The hurt became so great it brought him out of the reeling stage to distinct consciousness. She clipped her lips, drew them away, leaving him her throat. Already she had had enough. He opened his eyes as he bent with his mouth on her neck, and was startled; there stood the objects of the room, stark; there, close below his eyes, were the half-sunk lashes of the woman, swooning on her unnatural ebb of passion. He saw her thus, knew that she wanted no more of him than that kiss. And the heavy form of this woman hung upon him. His whole body ached like a swollen vein, with heavy intensity, while his heart grew dead with misery and despair. This woman gave him anguish and a cutting-short like death; to the other woman he was false. As he shivered with suffering, he opened his eyes again, and caught sight of the pure ivory of the lamp. His heart flashed with rage.

A sudden involuntary blow of his foot, and he sent the lamp-stand spinning. The lamp leaped off, fell with a smash on the fair, polished floor. Instantly a bluish hedge of flame quivered, leaped up before them. She had lightened her hold round his neck, and buried her face against his throat. The flame veered at her, blue, with a yellow tongue that licked her dress and her arm. Convulsive, she clutched him, almost strangled him, though she made no sound.

He gathered her up and bore her heavily out of the room. Slipping from her clasp, he brought his arms down her form, crushing the starting blaze of her dress. His face was singed. Staring at her, he could scarcely see her.

"I am not hurt," she cried. "But you?"

The housekeeper was coming; the flames were sinking and waving up in the drawing-room. He broke away from Winifred, threw one of the great woollen rugs on to the flame, then stood a moment looking at the darkness.

Winifred caught at him as he passed her.

"No, no," he answered, as he fumbled for the latch. "I'm not hurt. Clumsy fool I am—clumsy fool!"

In another instant he was gone, running with burning-red hands held out blindly, down the street.

NEW EVE AND OLD ADAM

I

"AFTER all," she said, with a little laugh, "I can't see it was so wonderful of you to hurry home to me, if you are so cross when you do come."

"You would rather I stayed away?" he asked.

"I wouldn't mind."

"You would rather I had stayed a day or two in Paris—or a night or two."

She burst into a jeering "pouf!" of laughter.

"You!" she cried. "You and Parisian Nights' Entertainment! What a fool you would look."

"Still," he said, "I could try."

"You *would!*" she mocked. "You would go dribbling up to a woman. 'Please take me—my wife is so unkind to me!'"

He drank his tea in silence. They had been married a year. They had married quickly, for love. And during the last three months there had gone on almost continuously that battle between them which so many married people fight, without knowing why. Now it had begun again. He felt the physical sickness rising in him. Somewhere down in his belly the big, feverish pulse began to beat, where was the inflamed place caused by the conflict between them.

She was a beautiful woman of about thirty, fair, luxuriant, with proud shoulders and a face borne up by a fierce, native vitality. Her green eyes had a curiously puzzled contraction just now. She sat leaning on the table against the tea-tray, absorbed. It was as if she battled with herself in him. Her green dress reflected in the silver, against the red of the fire-light. Leaning abstractedly forward, she pulled some primroses from the bowl, and threaded them at intervals in the plait which bound round her head in the peasant fashion. So, with her little starred fillet of flowers, there was something of the Gretchen about her. But her eyes retained the curious half-smile.

Suddenly her face lowered gloomily. She sank her beautiful

71

arms, laying them on the table. Then she sat almost sullenly, as if she would not give in. He was looking away out of the window. With a quick movement she glanced down at her hands. She took off her wedding-ring, reached to the bowl for a long flower-stalk, and shook the ring glittering round and round upon it, regarding the spinning gold, and spinning it as if she would spurn it. Yet there was something about her of a fretful, naughty child as she did so.

The man sat by the fire, tired, but tense. His body seemed so utterly still because of the tension in which it was held. His limbs, thin and vigorous, lay braced like a listening thing, always vivid for action, yet held perfectly still. His face was set and expressionless. The wife was all the time, in spite of herself, conscious of him, as if the cheek that was turned towards him had a sense which perceived him. They were both rendered elemental, like impersonal forces, by the battle and the suffering.

She rose and went to the window. Their flat was the fourth, the top storey of a large house. Above the high-ridged, handsome red roof opposite was an assembly of telegraph wires, a square, squat framework, towards which hosts of wires sped from four directions, arriving in darkly-stretched lines out of the white sky. High up, at a great height, a seagull sailed. There was a noise of traffic from the town beyond.

Then, from behind the ridge of the house-roof opposite a man climbed up into the tower of wires, belted himself amid the netted sky, and began to work, absorbedly. Another man, half-hidden by the roof-ridge, stretched up to him with a wire. The man in the sky reached down to receive it. The other, having delivered, sank out of sight. The solitary man worked absorbedly. Then he seemed drawn away from his task. He looked round almost furtively, from his lonely height, the space pressing on him. His eyes met those of the beautiful woman who stood in her afternoon-gown, with flowers in her hair, at the window.

"I like you," she said, in her normal voice.

Her husband, in the room with her, looked round slowly and asked:

"Whom do you like?"

Receiving no answer, he resumed his tense stillness.

She remained watching at the window, above the small, quiet street of large houses. The man, suspended there in the sky, looked across at her and she at him. The city was far below. Her eyes and his met across the lofty space. Then, crouching together again into his forgetfulness, he hid himself in his work. He would not look again. Presently he climbed down, and the tower of wires was empty against the sky.

The woman glanced at the little park at the end of the clear, grey street. The diminished, dark-blue form of a soldier was seen passing between the green stretches of grass, his spurs giving the faintest glitter to his walk.

Then she turned hesitating from the window, as if drawn by her husband. He was sitting still motionless, and detached from her, hard; held absolutely away from her by his will. She wavered, then went and crouched on the hearth-rug at his feet, laying her head on his knee.

"Don't be horrid with me!" she pleaded, in a caressing, languid, impersonal voice. He shut his teeth hard, and his lips parted slightly with pain.

"You know you love me," she continued, in the same heavy, sing-song way. He breathed hard, but kept still.

"Don't you?" she said, slowly, and she put her arms round his waist, under his coat, drawing him to her. It was as if flames of fire were running under his skin.

"I have never denied it," he said woodenly.

"Yes," she pleaded, in the same heavy, toneless voice. "Yes. You are always trying to deny it." She was rubbing her cheek against his knee, softly. Then she gave a little laugh, and shook her head. "But it's no good." She looked up at him. There was a curious light in his eyes, of subtle victory. "It's no good, my love, is it?"

His heart ran hot. He knew it was no good trying to deny he loved her. But he saw her eyes, and his will remained set and hard. She looked away into the fire.

"You hate it that you have to love me," she said, in a pensive voice through which the triumph flickered faintly. "You hate it that you love me—and it is petty and mean of you. You hate it that you had to hurry back to me from Paris."

Her voice had become again quite impersonal, as if she were talking to herself.

"At any rate," he said, "it is your triumph."

She gave a sudden, bitter-contemptuous laugh.

"Ha!" she said. "What is triumph to me, you fool? You

can have your triumph. I should be only too glad to give it you."

"And I to take it."

"Then take it," she cried, in hostility. "I offer it you often enough."

"But you never mean to part with it."

"It is a lie. It is you, you, who are too paltry to take a woman. How often do I fling myself at you——"

"Then don't—don't."

"Ha!—and if I don't—I get nothing out of you. Self! self! that is all you are."

His face remained set and expressionless. She looked up at him. Suddenly she drew him to her again, and hid her face against him.

"Don't kick me off, Pietro, when I come to you," she pleaded.

"You *don't* come to me," he answered stubbornly.

She lifted her head a few inches away from him and seemed to listen, or to think.

"What do I do, then" she asked, for the first time quietly.

"You treat me as if I were a piece of cake, for you to eat when you wanted."

She rose from him with a mocking cry of scorn, that yet had something hollow in its sound.

"Treat you like a piece of cake, do I!" she cried. "I, who have done all I have for you!"

There was a knock, and the maid entered with a telegram. He tore it open.

"No answer," he said, and the maid softly closed the door.

"I suppose it is for you," he said, bitingly, rising and handing her the slip of paper. She read it, laughed, then read it again, aloud:

" 'Meet me Marble Arch 7.30—theatre—Richard.' Who is Richard?" she asked, looking at her husband rather interested. He shook his head.

"Nobody of mine," he said. "Who is he?"

"I haven't the faintest notion," she said, flippantly.

"But," and his eyes went bullying, "you *must* know."

She suddenly became quiet, and jeering, took up his challenge.

"Why must I know?" she asked.

"Because it isn't for me, therefore it must be for you."

"And couldn't it be for anybody else?" she sneered.

" 'Moest, 14 Merrilies Street,' " he read, decisively.

For a second she was puzzled into earnestness.

"Pah, you fool," she said, turning aside. "Think of your own friends," and she flung the telegram away.

"It is not for me," he said, stiffly and finally.

"Then it is for the man in the moon—I should think *his* name is Moest," she added, with a pouf of laughter against him.

"Do you mean to say you know nothing about it?" he asked.

"Do you mean to say," she mocked, mouthing the words, and sneering; "Yes, I do mean to say, poor little man."

He suddenly went hard with disgust.

"Then I simply don't believe you," he said coldly.

"Oh—don't you believe me!" she jeered, mocking the touch of sententiousness in his voice. "What a calamity. The poor man doesn't believe!"

"It couldn't possibly be any acquaintance of mine," he said slowly.

"Then hold your tongue!" she cried harshly. "I've heard enough of it."

He was silent, and soon she went out of the room. In a few minutes he heard her in the drawing-room, improvising furiously. It was a sound that maddened him: something yearning, yearning, striving, and something perverse, that counteracted the yearning. Her music was always working up towards a certain culmination, but never reaching it, falling away in a jangle. How he hated it. He lit a cigarette, and went across to the sideboard for a whisky and soda. Then she began to sing. She had a good voice, but she could not keep time. As a rule it made his heart warm with tenderness for her, hearing her ramble through the songs in her own fashion, making Brahms sound so different by altering his time. But to-day he hated her for it. Why the devil couldn't she submit to the natural laws of the stuff!

In about fifteen minutes she entered, laughing. She laughed as she closed the door, and as she came to him where he sat.

"Oh," she said, "you silly thing, you silly thing! Aren't you a stupid clown?"

She crouched between his knees and put her arms round him. She was smiling into his face, her green eyes looking into

his, were bright and wide. But somewhere in them, as he
looked back, was a little twist that could not come loose to
him, a little cast, that was like an aversion from him, a
strain of hate for him. The hot waves of blood flushed
over his body, and his heart seemed to dissolve under her
caresses. But at last, after many months, he knew her well
enough. He knew that curious little strain in her eyes, which
was waiting for him to submit to her, and then would spurn
him again. He resisted her while ever it was there.

"Why don't you let yourself love me?" she asked, pleading,
but a touch of mockery in her voice. His jaw set hard.

"Is it because you are afraid?"

He heard the slight sneer.

"Of what?" he asked.

"Afraid to trust yourself?"

There was silence. It made him furious that she could sit
there caressing him and yet sneer at him.

"What *have* I done with myself?" he asked.

"Carefully saved yourself from giving all to me, for fear
you might lose something."

"Why should I lose anything?" he asked.

And they were both silent. She rose at last and went away
from him to get a cigarette. The silver box flashed red with
firelight in her hands. She struck a match, bungled, threw the
stick aside, lit another.

"What did you come running back for?" she asked,
insolently, talking with half-shut lips because of the cigarette.
"I told you I wanted peace. I've had none for a year. And
for the last three months you've done nothing but try to
destroy me."

"You have not gone frail on it," he answered sarcastically.

"Nevertheless," she said, "I am ill inside me. I am sick of
you—sick. You make an eternal demand, and you give nothing
back. You leave one empty." She puffed the cigarette in
feminine fashion, then suddenly she struck her forehead with
a wild gesture. "I have a ghastly, empty feeling in my head,"
she said. "I feel I simply *must* have rest—I must."

The rage went through his veins like flame.

"From your labours?" he asked, sarcastically, suppressing
himself.

"From you—from *you*?" she cried, thrusting forward her
head at him. "You, who use a woman's soul up, with your

rotten life. I suppose it is partly your health, and you can't help it," she added, more mildly. "But I simply can't stick it— I simply can't, and that is all."

She shook her cigarette carelessly in the direction of the fire. The ash fell on the beautiful Asiatic rug. She glanced at it, but did not trouble. He sat, hard with rage.

"May I ask how I use you up, as you say?" he asked.

She was silent a moment, trying to get her feeling into words. Then she shook her hand at him passionately, and took the cigarette from her mouth.

"By—by following me about—by not leaving me *alone*. You give me no peace—*I* don't know what you do, but it is something ghastly."

Again the hard stroke of rage went down his mind.

"It is very vague," he said.

"I know," she cried, "I can't put it into words—but there it is. You—you don't love. I pour myself out to you, and then—there's nothing there—you simply aren't there."

He was silent for some time. His jaw had set hard with fury and hate.

"We have come to the incomprehensible," he said. "And now, what about Richard?"

It had grown nearly dark in the room. She sat silent for a moment. Then she took the cigarette from her mouth and looked at it.

"I'm going to meet him," her voice, mocking, answered out of the twilight.

His head went molten, and he could scarcely breathe.

"Who is he?" he asked, though he did not believe the affair to be anything at all, even if there were a Richard.

"I'll introduce him to you when I know him a little better," she said. He waited.

"But who is he?"

"I tell you, I'll introduce him to you later."

There was a pause.

"Shall I come with you?"

"It would be like you," she answered, with a sneer.

The maid came in, softly, to draw the curtains and turn on the light. The husband and wife sat silent.

"I suppose," he said, when the door was closed again, "you are wanting a Richard for a rest?"

She took his sarcasm simply as a statement.

"I am," she said. "A simple, warm man who would love me without all these reservation and difficulties. That is just what I do want."

"Well, you have your own independence," he said.

"Ha," she laughed. "You needn't tell me that. It would take more than you to rob me of my independence."

"I meant your own income," he answered quietly, while his heart was plunging with bitterness and rage.

"Well," she said, "I will go and dress."

He remained without moving, in his chair. The pain of this was almost too much. For some moments the great, inflamed pulse struck through his body. It died gradually down, and he went dull. He had not wanted to separate from her at this point of their union they would probably, if they parted in such a crisis, never come together again. But if she insisted, well then, it would have to be. He would go away for a month. He could easily make business in Italy. And when he came back, they could patch up some sort of domestic arrangement, as most other folk had to do.

He felt dull and heavy inside, and without the energy for anything. The thought of having to pack and take a train to Milan appalled him; it would mean such an effort of will. But it would have to be done, and so he must do it. It was no use his waiting at home. He might stay in town a night, at his brother-in-law's, and go away the next day. It were better to give her a little time to come to herself. She was really impulsive. And he did not really want to go away from her.

He was still sitting thinking, when she came downstairs. She was in costume and furs and toque. There was a radiant, half-wistful, half-perverse look about her. She was a beautiful woman, her bright, fair face set among the black furs.

"Will you give me some money?" she said. "There isn't any."

He took two sovereigns, which she put in her little black purse. She would go without a word of reconciliation. It made his heart set hard again.

"You would like me to go away for a month?" he said, calmly.

"Yes," she answered, stubbornly.

"All right, then, I will. I must stop in town for to-morrow, but I will sleep at Edmund's."

"You could do that, couldn't you?" she said, accepting his suggestion, a little bit hesitating.

"If you want me to."

"I'm so *tired*!" she lamented.

But there was exasperation and hate in the last word, too.

"Very well," he answered.

She finished buttoning her glove.

"You'll go, then?" she said suddenly, brightly, turning to depart. "Good-bye."

He hated her for the flippant insult of her leave-taking.

"I shall be at Edmund's to-morrow," he said.

"You will write to me from Italy, won't you?"

He would not answer the unnecessary question.

"Have you taken the dead primroses out of your hair?" he asked.

"I haven't," she said.

And she unpinned her hat.

"Richard *would* think me cracked," she said, picking out the crumpled, creamy fragments. She strewed the withered flowers carelessly on the table, set her hat straight.

"Do you *want* me to go?" he asked, again, rather yearning.

She knitted her brows. It irked her to resist the appeal. Yet she had in her breast a hard, repellent feeling for him. She had loved him, too. She had loved him dearly. And—he had not seemed to realise her. So that now she *did* want to be free of him for a while. Yet the love, the passion she had had for him clung about her. But she did want, first and primarily, to be free of him again.

"Yes," she said, half pleading.

"Very well," he answered.

She came across to him, and put her arms round his neck. Her hat-pin caught his head, but he moved, and she did not notice.

"You don't mind very much, do you, my love?" she said caressingly.

"I mind all the world, and all I am," he said.

She rose from him, fretted, miserable, and yet determined.

"I *must* have some rest," she repeated.

He knew that cry. She had had it, on occasions, for two months now. He had cursed her, and refused either to go away or to let her go. Now he knew it was no use.

"All right," he said. "Go and get it from Richard."

"Yes." She hesitated. "Good-bye," she called, and was gone.

He heard her cab whirr away. He had no idea whither she was gone—but probably to Madge, her friend.

He went upstairs to pack. Their bedroom made him suffer. She used to say, at first, that she would give up anything rather than her sleeping with him. And still they were always together. A kind of blind helplessness drove them to one another, even when, after he had taken her, they only felt more apart than ever. It had seemed to her that he had been mechanical and barren with her. She felt a horrible feeling of aversion from him, inside her, even while physically she still desired him. His body had always a kind of fascination for her. But had hers for him? He seemed, often, just to have served her, or to have obeyed some impersonal instinct for which she was the only outlet, in his loving her. So at last she rose against him, to cast him off. He seemed to follow her so, to draw her life into his. It made her feel she would go mad. For he seemed to do it just blindly, without having any notion of her herself. It was as if she were sucked out of herself by some non-human force. As for him, he seemed only like an instrument for his work, his business, not like a person at all. Sometimes she thought he was a big fountain-pen which was always sucking at her blood for ink.

He could not understand anything of this. He loved her—he could not bear to be away from her. He tried to realise her and to give her what she wanted. But he could not understand. He could not understand her accusations against him. Physically, he knew, she loved him, or had loved him, and was satisfied by him. He also knew that she would have loved another man nearly as well. And for the rest, he was only himself. He could not understand what she said about his using her and giving her nothing in return. Perhaps he did not thing of her, as a separate person from himself, sufficiently. But then he did not see, he could not see that she had any real personal life, separate from himself. He tried to think of her in every possible way, and to give her what she wanted. But it was no good; she was never at peace. And lately there had been growing a breach between them. They had never come together without his realising it, afterwards. Now he must submit, and go away.

And her quilted dressing-gown—it was a little bit torn, like most of her things—and her pearl-backed mirror, with one of the pieces of pearl missing—all her untidy, flimsy, lovable things hurt him as he went about the bedroom, and made his heart go hard with hate, in the midst of his love.

II

Instead of going to his brother-in-law's, he went to an hotel for the night. It was not till he stood in the lift, with the attendant at his side, that he began to realise that he was only a mile or so away from his own home, and yet farther away than any miles could make him. It was about nine o'clock. He hated his bedroom. It was comfortable, and not ostentatious; its only fault was the neutrality necessary to an hotel apartment. He looked round. There was one semi-erotic Florentine picture of a lady with cat's eyes, over the bed. It was not bad. The only other ornament on the walls was the notice of hours and prices of meals and rooms. The couch sat correctly before the correct little table, on which the writing-sachet and inkstand stood mechanically. Down below, the quiet street was half illuminated, the people passed sparsely, like stunted shadows. And of all times of the night, it was a quarter-past nine. He thought he would go to bed. Then he looked at the white-and-glazed doors which shut him off from the bath. He would bath, to pass the time away. In the bath-closet everything was so comfortable and white and warm—too warm; the level, unvarying heat of the atmosphere, from which there was no escape anywhere, seemed so hideously hotel-like; this central-heating forced a unity into the great building, making it more than ever like an enormous box with incubating cells. He loathed it. But at any rate the bath-closet was human, white and business-like and luxurious.

He was trying, with the voluptuous warm water, and the exciting thrill of the shower-bath, to bring back the life into his dazed body. Since she had begun to hate him, he had gradually lost that physical pride and pleasure in his own physique which the first months of married life had given him. His body had gone meaningless to him again, almost as if it were not there. It had wakened up, there had been the physical glow and satisfaction about his movements of a creature which rejoices in itself; a glow which comes on a man who loves and is loved passionately and successfully. Now this was going again. All the life was accumulating in his mental

consciousness, and his body felt like a piece of waste. He was
not aware of this. It was instinct which made him want to
bathe. But that, too, was a failure. He went under the shower-
spray with his mind occupied by business, or some care of
affairs, taking the tingling water almost without knowing it,
stepping out mechanically, as a man going through a barren
routine. He was dry again, and looking out of the window,
without having experienced anything during the last hour.

Then he remembered that she did not know his address. He
scribbled a note and rang to have it posted.

As soon as he had turned out the light, and there was
nothing left for his mental consciousness to flourish amongst,
it dropped, and it was dark inside him as without. It was his
blood, and the elemental male in it, that now rose from him;
unknown instincts suffocated him, and he could not bear it,
that he was shut in this great, warm building. He wanted to
be outside, with space springing from him. But, again, the
reasonable being in him knew it was ridiculous, and he
remained staring at the dark, having the horrible sensation of
a roof low down over him; whilst that dark, unknown being,
which lived below all his consciousness in the eternal gloom of
his blood, heaved and raged blindly against him.

It was not his thoughts that represented him. They spun
like straws or the iridescence of oil on a dark stream. He
thought of her, sketchily, spending an evening of light amusement with the symbolical Richard. That did not mean much
to him. He did not really speculate about Richard. He had
the dark, powerful sense of her, how she wanted to get away
from him and from the deep, underneath intimacy which had
gradually come between them, back to the easy, everyday life
where one knows nothing of the underneath, so that it takes
its way apart from the consciousness. She did not want to
have the deeper part of herself in direct contact with or under
the influence of any other intrinsic being. She wanted, in the
deepest sense, to be free of him. She could not bear the close,
basic intimacy into which she had been drawn. She wanted
her life for herself. It was true, her strongest desire had been
previously to know the contact through the whole of her
being, down to the very bottom. Now it troubled her. She
wanted to disengage his roots. Above, in the open, she would
live. But she must live perfectly free of herself, and not, at
her source, be connected with anybody. She was using this

symbolical Richard as a spade to dig him away from her. And he felt like a thing whose roots are all straining on their hold, and whose elemental life, that blind source, surges backwards and forwards darkly, in a chaos, like something which is threatened with spilling out of its own vessel.

This tremendous swaying of the most elemental part of him continued through the hours, accomplishing his being, whilst superficially he thought of the journey, of the Italian he would speak, how he had left his coat in the train, and the rascally official interpreter had tried to give him twenty lire for a sovereign—how the man in the hat-shop in the Strand had given him the wrong change—of the new shape in hats, and the new felt—and so on. Underneath it all, like the sea under a pleasure pier, his elemental, physical soul was heaving in great waves through his blood and his tissue, the sob, the silent lift, the slightly-washing fall away again. So his blood, out of whose darkness everything rose, being moved to its depth by her revulsion, heaved and swung towards its own rest, surging blindly to its own re-settling.

Without knowing it, he suffered that night almost more than he had ever suffered during his life. But it was all below his consciousness. It was his life itself at storm, not his mind and his will engaged at all.

In the morning he got up, thin and quiet, without much movement anywhere, only with some of the clearing after-storm. His body felt like a clean, empty shell. His mind was limpidly clear. He went through the businesss of the toilet with a certain accuracy, and at breakfast, in the restaurant, there was about him that air of neutral correctness which makes men seem so unreal.

At lunch, there was a telegram for him. It was like her to telegraph.

"Come to tea, my dear love."

As he read it, there was a great heave of resistance in him. But then he faltered. With his consciousness, he remembered how impulsive and eager she was when she dashed off her telegram, and he relaxed. It went without saying that he would go.

III

When he stood in the lift going up to his own flat, he was
almost blind with the hurt of it all. They had loved each other
so much in his first home. The parlour-maid opened to him,
and he smiled at her affectionately. In the golden-brown and
cream-coloured hall—Paula would have nothing heavy or
sombre about her—a bush of rose-coloured azaleas shone, and
a little tub of lilies twinkled naïvely.

She did not come out to meet him.

"Tea is in the drawing-room," the maid said, and he went
in while she was hanging up his coat. It was a big room,
with a sense of space, and a spread of whitey carpet almost
the colour of unpolished marble—and grey and pink border;
of pink roses on big white cushions, pretty Dresden china, and
deep chintz-covered chairs and sofas which looked as if they
were used freely. It was a room where one could roll in soft,
fresh-comfort, a room which had not much breakable in it,
and which seemed, in the dusky spring evening, fuller of light
than the streets outside.

Paula rose, looking queenly and rather radiant, as she held
out her hand. A young man whom Peter scarcely noticed rose
on the other side of the hearth.

"I expected you an hour ago," she said, looking into her
husband's eyes. But though she looked at him, she did not
see him. And he sank his head.

"This is another Moest," she said, presenting the stranger.
"He knows Richard, too."

The young man, a German of about thirty, with a clean-
shaven æsthetic face, long black hair brushed back a little
wearily or bewildered from his brow, and inclined to fall in
an odd loose strand again, so that he nervously put it back
with his fine hand, looked at Moest and bowed. He had a
finely-cut face, but his dark-blue eyes were strained, as if he
did not quite know where he was. He sat down again, and his
pleasant figure took a self-conscious attitude, of a man whose
business it was to say things that should be listened to. He
was not conceited or affected—naturally sensitive and rather
naïve; but he could only move in an atmosphere of literature
and literary ideas; yet he seemed to know there was something
else, vaguely, and he felt rather at a loss. He waited for the

conversation to move his way, as, inert, an insect waits for
the sun to set it flying.

"Another Moest," Paula was pronouncing emphatically.
"Actually another Moest, of whom we have never heard, and
under the same roof with us."

The stranger laughed, his lips moving nervously over his
teeth.

"You are in this house?" Peter asked, surprised.

The young man shifted in his chair, dropped his head,
looked up again.

"Yes," he said, meeting Moest's eyes as if he were somewhat dazzled. "I am staying with the Lauriers, on the second
floor."

He spoke English slowly, with a quaint, musical quality in
his voice, and a certain rhythmic enunciation.

"I see; and the telegram was for you?" said the host.

"Yes," replied the stranger, with a nervous little laugh.

"My husband," broke in Paula, evidently repeating to the
German what she had said before, for Peter's benefit this time,
"was quite convinced I had an *affaire*"—she pronounced it in
the French fashion—"with this terrible Richard."

The German gave his little laugh, and moved, painfully self-
conscious, in his chair.

"Yes," he said, glancing at Moest.

"Did you spend a night of virtuous indignation?" Paula
laughed to her husband, "imagining my perfidy?"

"I did not," said her husband. "Were you at Madge's?"

"No," she said. Then, turning to her guest: "Who is Richard,
Mr. Moest?"

"Richard," began the German, word by word, "is my
cousin." He glanced quickly at Paula, to see if he were understood. She rustled her skirts, and arranged herself comfortably,
lying, or almost squatting, on the sofa by the fire. "He lives
in Hampstead."

"And what is he like?" she asked, with eager interest.

The German gave his little laugh. Then he moved his fingers
across his brow, in his dazed fashion. Then he looked, with
his beautiful blue eyes, at his beautiful hostess.

"I——" He laughed again nervously. "He is a man whose
parts—are not very much—very well known to me. You see,"
he broke forth, and it was evident he was now conversing to
an imaginary audience—"I cannot easily express myself in

English. I—I never have talked it. I shall speak, because I know nothing of modern England, a kind of Renaissance English."

"How lovely!" cried Paula. "But if you would rather, speak German. We shall understand sufficiently."

"I would rather hear some Renaissance English," said Moest.

Paula was quite happy with the new stranger. She listened to descriptions of Richard, shifting animatedly on her sofa. She wore a new dress, of a rich red-tile colour, glossy and long and soft, and she had threaded daisies, like buttons, in the braided plait of her hair. Her husband hated her for these familiarities. But she was beautiful too, and warm-hearted. Only, through all her warmth and kindliness, lay, he said, at the bottom, an almost feline selfishness, a coldness.

She was playing to the stranger—nay, she was not playing, she was really occupied by him. The young man was the favourite disciple of the most famous present-day German poet and *Meister*. He himself was occupied in translating Shakespeare. Having been always a poetic disciple, he had never come into touch with life save through literature, and for him, since he was a rather fine-hearted young man, with a human need to live, this was a tragedy. Paula was not long in discovering what ailed him, and she was eager to come to his rescue.

It pleased her, nevertheless, to have her husband sitting by, watching her. She forgot to give tea to anyone. Moest and the German both helped themselves, and the former attended also to his wife's cup. He sat rather in the background, listening, and waiting. She had made a fool of him with her talk to this stranger of "Richard;" lightly and flippantly she had made a fool of him. He minded, but was used to it. Now she had absorbed herself in this dazed, starved, literature-bewildered young German, who was, moreover, really lovable, evidently a gentleman. And she was seeing in him her mission— "just as," said Moest bitterly to himself, "she saw her mission in me, a year ago. She is no woman. She's got a big heart for everybody, but it must be like a common-room; she's got no private, sacred heart, except perhaps for herself, where there's no room for a man in it."

At length the stranger rose to go, promising to come again.

"Isn't he adorable?" cried Paula, as her husband returned to the drawing-room. "I think he is simply adorable."

"Yes!" said Moest.

"He called this morning to ask about the telegram. But, poor devil, isn't it a shame what they've done to him?"

"What who have done to him?" her husband asked coldly, jealous.

"Those literary creatures. They take a young fellow like that, and stick him up among the literary gods, like a mantelpiece ornament, and there he has to sit, being a minor ornament, while all his youth is gone. It is criminal."

"He should get off the mantelpiece, then," said Moest.

But inside him his heart was black with rage against her. What had she, after all, to do with this young man, when he himself was being smashed up by her? He loathed her pity and her kindliness, which was like a charitable institution. There was no core to the woman. She was full of generosity and bigness and kindness, but there was no heart in her, no security, no place for one single man. He began to understand now sirens and sphinxes and the other Greek fabulous female things. They had not been created by fancy, but out of bitter necessity of the man's human heart to express itself.

"Ha!" she laughed, half contemptuous. "Did *you* get off your miserable, starved isolation by yourself?—you didn't. You had to be fetched down, and I had to do it."

"Out of your usual charity," he said.

"But you can sneer at another man's difficulties," she said.

"Your name ought to be Panacea, not Paula," he replied.

He felt furious and dead against her. He could even look at her without the tenderness coming. And he was glad. He hated her. She seemed unaware. Very well; let her be so.

"Oh, but he makes me so miserable, to see him!" she cried. "Self-conscious, can't get into contact with anybody, living a false literary life like a man who takes poetry as a drug.—One *ought* to help him."

She was really earnest and distressed.

"Out of the frying-pan into the fire," he said.

"I'd rather be in the fire any day, than in a frying-pan," she said, abstractedly, with a little shudder. She never troubled to see the meaning of her husband's sarcasms.

They remained silent. The maid came in for the tray, and to ask him if he would be in to dinner. He waited for his wife to answer. She sat with her chin in her hands, brooding over the young German, and did not hear. The rage flashed up in his heart. He would have liked to smash her out of this false absorption.

"No," he said to the maid. "I think not. Are you at home for dinner, Paula?"

"Yes," she said.

And he knew by her tone, easy and abstracted, that she intended him to stay, too. But she did not trouble to say anything.

At last, after some time, she asked:

"What did you do?"

"Nothing—went to bed early," he replied.

"Did you sleep well?"

"Yes, thank you."

And he recognised the ludicrous civilities of married people, and he wanted to go. She was silent for a time. Then she asked, and her voice had gone still and grave:

"Why don't you ask me what I did?"

"Because I don't care—you just went to somebody's for dinner."

"Why don't you care what I do? Isn't it your place to care?"

"About the things you do to spite me?—no!"

"Ha!" she mocked. "I did nothing to spite you. I was in deadly earnest."

"Even with your Richard?"

"Yes," she cried. "There *might* have been a Richard. What did you care!"

"In that case you'd have been a liar and worse, so why should I care about you then?"

"You *don't* care about me," she said, sullenly.

"You say what you please," he answered.

She was silent for some time.

"And did you do absolutely nothing last night?" she asked.

"I had a bath and went to bed."

Then she pondered.

"No," she said, "you don't care for me."

He did not trouble to answer. Softly, a little china clock rang six.

"I shall go to Italy in the morning," he said.

"Yes."

"And," he said, slowly, forcing the words out, "I shall stay at the Aquila Nera at Milan—you know my address."

"Yes," she answered.

"I shall be away about a month. Meanwhile you can rest."

"Yes," she said, in her throat, with a little contempt of him and his stiffness. He, in spite of himself, was breathing heavily. He knew that this parting was the real separation of their souls, marked the point beyond which they could go no farther, but accepted the marriage as a comparative failure. And he had built all his life on his marriage. She accused him of not loving her. He gripped the arms of his chair. Was there something in it? Did he only want the attributes which went along with her, the peace of heart which a man has in living to one woman, even if the love between them be not complete; the singleness and unity in his life that made it easy; the fixed establishment of himself as a married man with a home; the feeling that he belonged somewhere, that one woman existed —not was paid but *existed*—really to take care of him; was it these things he wanted, and not her? But he wanted her for these purposes—her, and nobody else. But was that not enough for her? Perhaps he wronged her—it was possible. What she said against him was in earnest. And what she said in earnest he had to believe, in the long run, since it was the utterance of her being. He felt miserable and tired.

When he looked at her, across the gathering twilight of the room, she was staring into the fire and biting her finger-nail, restlessly, restlessly, without knowing. And all his limbs went suddenly weak, as he realised that she suffered too, that something was gnawing at her. Something in the look of her, the crouching, dogged, wondering look made him faint with tenderness for her.

"Don't bite your finger-nails," he said quietly, and, obediently, she took her hand from her mouth. His heart was beating quickly. He could feel the atmosphere of the room changing. It had stood aloof, the room, like something placed round him, like a great box. Now everything got softer, as if it partook of the atmosphere, of which he partook himself, and they were all one.

His mind reverted to her accusations, and his heart beat like a caged thing against what he could not understand. She said he did not love her. But he knew that in his way, he did. In his way—but was his way wrong? His way was himself, he thought, struggling. Was there something wrong, something missing in his nature, that he could not love? He struggled

madly, as if he were in a mesh, and could not get out. He
did not want to believe that he was deficient in his nature.
Wherein was he deficient? It was nothing physical. She said
he would not come out of himself, that he was no good to
her, because he could not get outside himself. What did she
mean? Not outside himself! It seemed like some acrobatic
feat, some slippery, contortionist trick. No, he could not
understand. His heart flashed hot with resentment. She did
nothing but find fault with him. What did she care about
him, really, when she could taunt him with not being able
to take a light woman when he was in Paris? Though his
heart, forced to do her justice, knew that for this she loved
him, really.

But it was too complicated and difficult, and already, as they
sat thinking, it had gone wrong between them and things felt
twisted, horribly twisted, so that he could not breathe. He
must go. He could dine at the hotel and go to the theatre.

"Well," he said casually, "I must go. I think I shall go and
see 'The Black Sheep'."

She did not answer. Then she turned and looked at him
with a queer, half-bewildered, half-perverse smile that seemed
conscious of pain. Her eyes, shining rather dilated and
triumphant, and yet with something heavily yearning behind
them, looked at him. He could not understand, and, between
her appeal and her defiant triumph, he felt as if his chest was
crushed so that he could not breathe.

"My love," she said, in a little singing, abstract fashion, her
lips somehow sipping towards him, her eyes shining dilated;
and yet he felt as if he were not in it, himself.

His heart was a flame that prevented his breathing. He
gripped the chair like a man who is going to be put under
torture.

"What?" he said, staring back at her.

"Oh, my love!" she said softly, with a little, intense laugh
on her face, that made him pant. And she slipped from her
sofa and came across to him quickly, and put her hand
hesitating on his hair. The blood struck like flame across his
consciousness, and the hurt was keen like joy, like the releas-
ing of something that hurts as the pressure is relaxed and the
movement comes, before the peace. Afraid, his fingers touched
her hand, and she sank swiftly between his knees, and put her
face on his breast. He held her head hard against his chest,

and again and again the flame went down his blood, as he
felt her round, small, nut of a head between his hands pressing into his chest where the hurt had been bruised in so deep.
His wrists quivered as he pressed her head to him, as he felt
the deadness going out of him; the real life released, flowing
into his body again. How hard he had shut it off, against her,
when she hated him. He was breathing heavily with relief,
blindly pressing her head against him. He believed in her
again.

She looked up, laughing, childish, inviting him with her
lips. He bent to kiss her, and as his eyes closed, he saw hers
were shut. The feeling of restoration was almost unbearable.

"Do you love me?" she whispered, in a little ecstasy.

He did not answer, except with the quick tightening of his
arms, clutching her a little closer against him. And he loved
the silkiness of her hair, and its natural scent. And it hurt him
that the daisies she had threaded in should begin to wither.
He resented their hurting her by their dying.

He had not understood. But the trouble had gone off. He
was quiet, and he watched her from out of his sensitive stillness, a little bit dimly, unable to recover. She was loving to
him, protective, and bright, laughing like a glad child too.

"We must tell Maud I shall be in to dinner," he said.

That was like him—always aware of the practical side of
the case, and the appearances. She laughed a little bit ironically. Why should she have to take her arm from round him,
just to tell Maud he would be in to dinner?

"I'll go," she said.

He drew the curtains and turned on the light in the big
lamp that stood in a corner. The room was dim, and palely
warm. He loved it dearly.

His wife, when she came back, as soon as she had closed
the door, lifted her arms to him in a little ecstasy, coming to
him. They clasped each other closer, body to body. And the
intensity of his feeling was so fierce, he felt himself going dim,
fusing into something soft and plastic between her hands. And
this connection with her was bigger than life or death. And at
the bottom of his heart was a sob.

She was gay and winsome at the dinner. Like lovers, they
were just deliciously waiting for the night to come up. But
there remained in him always the slightly broken feeling
which the night before had left.

"And you won't go to Italy," she said, as if it were an understood thing.

She gave him the best things to eat, and was solicitous for his welfare—which was not usual with her. It gave him deep, shy pleasure. He remembered a verse she was often quoting as one she loved. He did not know it for himself:

"On my breasts I warm thy foot-soles;
Wine I pour, and dress thy meats;
Humbly, when my lord disposes,
Lie with him on perfumed sheets."

She said it to him sometimes, looking up at him from the pillow. But it never seemed real to him. She might, in her sudden passion, put his feet between her breasts. But he never felt like a lord, never more pained and insignificant than at those times. As a little girl, she must have subjected herself before her dolls. And he was something like her lordliest plaything. He liked that too. If only . . .

Then, seeing some frightened little way of looking at him which she had, the pure pain came back. He loved her, and it would never be peace between them; she would never belong to him, as a wife. She would take him and reject him, like a mistress. And perhaps for that reason he would love her all the more; it might be so.

But then, he forgot. Whatever was or was not, now she loved him. And whatever came after, this evening he was the lord. What matter if he were deposed to-morrow, and she hated him!

Her eyes, wide and candid, were staring at him a little bit wondering, a little bit forlorn. She knew he had not quite come back. He held her close to him.

"My love," she murmured consolingly. "My love."

And she put her fingers through his hair, arranging it in little, loose curves, playing with it and forgetting everything else. He loved that dearly, to feel the light lift and touch— touch of her finger-tips making his hair, as she said, like an Apollo's. She lifted his face to see how he looked, and, with a little laugh of love, kissed him. And he loved to be made much of by her. But he had the dim, hurting sense that she would not love him to-morrow, that it was only her great need to love that exalted him to-night. He *knew* he was no

king; he did not feel a king, even when she was crowning and
kissing him.

"Do you love me?" she asked, playfully whispering.

He held her fast and kissed her, while the blood hurt in his
heart-chambers.

"You know," he answered, with a struggle.

Later, when he lay holding her with a passion intense like
pain, the words blurted from him:

"Flesh of my flesh. Paula!—Will you——?"

"Yes, my love," she answered consolingly.

He bit his mouth with pain. For him it was almost an agony
of appeal.

"But, Paula—I mean it—flesh of my flesh—a wife?"

She tightened her arms round him without answering. And
he knew, and she knew, that she put him off like that.

IV

Two months later, she was writing to him in Italy: "Your
idea of your woman is that she is an expansion, no, a *rib* of
yourself, without any existence of her own. That I am a being
by myself is more than you can grasp. I wish I could absolutely
submerge myself in a man—and *so I do*. I *always* loved
you . . .

"You will say 'I was patient.' Do you call that patient,
hanging on for your needs, as you have done? The innermost life you have *always* had of me, and you held yourself
aloof because you were afraid.

"The unpardonable thing was you told me you loved me.—
Your *feelings* have hated me these three months, which did
not prevent you from taking my love and every breath from
me.—Underneath you undermined me, in some subtle, corrupt
way that I did not see because I believed you, when you told
me you loved me . . .

"The insult of the way you took me these last three months
I shall never forgive you. I honestly *did* give myself, and
always in vain and rebuffed. The strain of it all has driven
me quite mad.

"You say I am a tragédienne, but I don't do any of your
perverse undermining tricks. You are always luring one into
the open like a clever enemy, but you keep safely under cover
all the time.

"This practically means, for me, that life is over, my belief in life—I hope it will recover, but it never could do so with you . . ."

To which he answered; "If I kept under cover it is funny, for there isn't any cover now.—And you can hope, pretty easily, for your own recovery apart from me. For my side, without you, I am done . . . But you lie to yourself. You *wouldn't* love *me*, and you won't be able to love anybody else —except yourself."

THE PRUSSIAN OFFICER

I

THEY had marched more than thirty kilometres since dawn, along the white, hot road where occasional thickets of trees threw a moment of shade, then out into the glare again. On either hand, the valley, wide and shallow, glittered with heat; dark-green patches of rye, pale young corn, fallow and meadow and black pine woods spread in a dull, hot diagram under a glistening sky. But right in front the mountains ranged across, pale blue and very still, snow gleaming gently out of the deep atmosphere. And towards the mountains, on and on, the regiment marched between the rye-fields and the meadows, between the scraggy fruit trees set regularly on either side the high road. The burnished, dark-green rye threw off a suffocating heat, the mountains drew gradually nearer and more distinct. While the feet of the soldiers grew hotter, sweat ran through their hair under their helmets, and their knapsacks could burn no more in contact with their shoulders, but seemed instead to give off a cold, prickly sensation.

He walked on and on in silence, staring at the mountains ahead, that rose sheer out of the land, and stood fold behind fold, half earth, half heaven, the heaven, the barrier with slits of soft snow, in the pale, bluish peaks.

He could now walk almost without pain. At the start, he had determined not to limp. It had made him sick to take the first steps, and during the first mile or so, he had compressed his breath, and the cold drops of sweat had stood on his forehead. But he had walked it off. What were they after all but bruises! He had looked at them, as he was getting up: deep bruises on the backs of his thighs. And since he had made his first step in the morning, he had been conscious of them, till now he had a tight, hot place in his chest, with suppressing the pain, and holding himself in. There seemed no air when he breathed. But he walked almost lightly.

The Captain's hand had trembled at taking his coffee at dawn: his orderly saw it again. And he saw the fine figure of the Captain wheeling on horseback at the farmhouse ahead, a handsome figure in pale-blue uniform with facings of scarlet, and the metal gleaming on the black helmet and the sword-scabbard, and dark streaks of sweat coming on the silky bay horse. The orderly felt he was connected with that figure moving so suddenly on horseback: he followed it like a shadow, mute and inevitable and damned by it. And the officer was always aware of the tramp of the company behind, the march of his orderly among the men.

The Captain was a tall man of about forty, grey at the temples. He had a handsome, finely-knit figure, and was one of the best horsemen in the West. His orderly, having to rub him down, admired the amazing riding-muscles of his loins.

For the rest, the orderly scarcely noticed the officer any more than he noticed himself. It was rarely he saw his master's face: he did not look at it. The Captain had reddish-brown, stiff hair, that he wore short upon his skull. His moustache was also cut short and bristly over a full, brutal mouth. His face was rather rugged, the cheeks thin. Perhaps the man was the more handsome for the deep lines in his face, the irritable tension of his brow, which gave him the look of a man who fights with life. His fair eyebrows stood bushy over light-blue eyes that were always flashing with cold fire.

He was a Prussian aristocrat, haughty and overbearing. But his mother had been a Polish countess. Having made too many gambling debts when he was young, he had ruined his prospects in the Army, and remained an infantry captain. He had never married: his position did not allow of it, and no woman had ever moved him to it. His time he spent riding—occasionally he rode one of his own horses at the races—and at the officers' club. Now and then he took himself a mistress. But after such an event, he returned to duty with his brow still more tense, his eyes still more hostile and irritable. With the men, however, he was merely impersonal, though a devil when roused; so that, on the whole, they feared him, but had no great aversion from him. They accepted him as the inevitable.

To his orderly he was at first cold and just and indifferent: he did not fuss over trifles. So that his servant knew practically nothing about him, except just what orders he would give, and how he wanted them obeyed. That was quite simple. Then the change gradually came.

The orderly was a youth of about twenty-two, of medium

height, and well built. He had strong, heavy limbs, was swarthy, with a soft, black, young moustache. There was something altogether warm and young about him. He had firmly marked eyebrows over dark, expressionless eyes, that seemed never to have thought, only to have received life direct through his senses, and acted straight from instinct.

Gradually the officer had become aware of his servant's young vigorous, unconscious presence about him. He could not get away from the sense of the youth's person, while he was in attendance. It was like a warm flame upon the older man's tense, rigid body, that had become almost unliving, fixed. There was something so free and self-contained about him, and something in the young fellow's movement, that made the officer aware of him. And this irritated the Prussian. He did not choose to be touched into life by his servant. He might easily have changed his man, but he did not. He now very rarely looked direct at his orderly, but kept his face averted, as if to avoid seeing him. And yet as the young soldier moved unthinking about the apartment, the elder watched him, and would notice the movement of his strong young shoulders under the blue cloth, the bend of his neck. And it irritated him. To see the soldier's young, brown, shapely peasant's hand grasp the loaf or the wine-bottle sent a flash of hate or of anger through the elder man's blood. It was not that the youth was clumsy: it was rather the blind, instinctive sureness of movement of an unhampered young animal that irritated the officer to such a degree.

Once, when a bottle of wine had gone over, and the red gushed out on to the tablecloth, the officer had started up with an oath, and his eyes, bluey like fire, had held those of the confused youth for a moment. It was a shock for the young soldier. He felt something sink deeper, deeper into his soul, where nothing had ever gone before. It left him rather blank and wondering. Some of his natural completeness in himself was gone, a little uneasiness took its place. And from that time an undiscovered feeling had held between the two men.

Henceforward the orderly was afraid of really meeting his master. His subconsciousness remembered those steely blue eyes and the harsh brows, and did not intend to meet them again. So he always stared past his master, and avoided him. Also, in a little anxiety, he waited for the three months to have gone, when his time would be up. He began to feel a constraint in the Captain's presence, and the soldier even more than the officer wanted to be left alone, in his neutrality as servant.

He had served the Captain for more than a year, and knew his duty. This he performed easily, as if it were natural to him. The officer and his commands he took for granted, as he took the sun and the rain, and he served as a matter of course. It did not implicate him personally.

But now if he were going to be forced into a personal interchange with his master he would be like a wild thing caught, he felt he must get away.

But the influence of the young soldier's being had penetrated through the officer's stiffened discipline, and perturbed the man in him. He, however, was a gentleman, with long, fine hands and cultivated movements, and was not going to allow such a thing as the stirring of his innate self. He was a man of passionate temper, who had always kept himself suppressed. Occasionally there had been a duel, an outburst before the soldiers. He knew himself to be always on the point of breaking out. But he kept himself hard to the idea of the Service. Whereas the young soldier seemed to live out his warm, full nature, to give it off in his very movements, which had a certain zest, such as wild animals have in free movement. And this irritated the officer more and more.

In spite of himself, the Captain could not regain his neutrality of feeling towards his orderly. Nor could he leave the man alone. In spite of himself, he watched him, gave him sharp orders, tried to take up as much of his time as possible. Sometimes he flew into a rage with the young soldier, and bullied him. Then the orderly shut himself off, as it were out of earshot, and waited, with sullen, flushed face, for the end of the noise. The words never pierced to his intelligence, he made himself, protectively, impervious to the feelings of his master.

He had a scar on his left thumb, a deep seam going across the knuckle. The officer had long suffered from it, and wanted to do something to it. Still it was there, ugly and brutal on the young, brown hand. At last the Captain's reserve gave way. One day, as the orderly was smoothing out the tablecloth, the officer pinned down his thumb with a pencil, asking:

"How did you come by that?"

The young man winced and drew back at attention.

"A wood axe, Herr Hauptmann," he answered.

The officer waited for further explanation. None came. The orderly went about his duties. The elder man was sullenly angry. His servant avoided him. And the next day he had to use all his will-power to avoid seeing the scarred thumb. He wanted to get hold of it and—— A hot flame ran in his blood.

He knew his servant would soon be free, and would be glad. As yet, the soldier had held himself off from the elder man. The Captain grew madly irritable. He could not rest when the soldier was away, and when he was present, he glared at him with tormented eyes. He hated those fine, black brows over the unmeaning, dark eyes, he was infuriated by the free movement of the handsome limbs, which no military discipline could make stiff. And he became harsh and cruelly bullying, using contempt and satire. The young soldier only grew more mute and expressionless.

"What cattle were you bred by, that you can't keep straight eyes? Look me in the eyes when I speak to you."

And the soldier turned his dark eyes to the other's face, but there was no sight in them: he stared with the slightest possible cast, holding back his sight, perceiving the blue of his master's eyes, but receiving no look from them. And the elder man went pale, and his reddish eyebrows twitched. He gave his order, barrenly.

Once he flung a heavy military glove into the young soldier's face. Then he had the satisfaction of seeing the black eyes flare up into his own, like a blaze when straw is thrown on a fire. And he had laughed with a little tremor and a sneer.

But there were only two months more. The youth instinctively tried to keep himself intact: he tried to serve the officer as if the latter were an abstract authority and not a man. All his instinct was to avoid personal contact, even definite hate. But in spite of himself the hate grew, responsive to the officer's passion. However, he put it in the background. When he had left the Army he could dare acknowledge it. By nature he was active, and had many friends. He thought what amazing good fellows they were. But, without knowing it, he was alone. Now this solitariness was intensified. It would carry him through his term. But the officer seemed to be going irritably insane, and the youth was deeply frightened.

The soldier had a sweetheart, a girl from the mountains, independent and primitive. The two walked together, rather silently. He went with her, not to talk, but to have his arm round her, and for the physical contact. This eased him, made it easier for him to ignore the Captain; for he could rest with her held fast against his chest. And she, in some unspoken fashion, was there for him. They loved each other.

The Captain perceived it, and was mad with irritation. He kept the young man engaged all the evenings long, and took pleasure in the dark look that came on his face. Occasionally, the eyes of the two men met, those of the younger sullen and dark, doggedly unalterable, those of the elder sneering with restless contempt.

The officer tried hard not to admit the passion that had got hold of him. He would not know that his feeling for his orderly was anything but that of a man incensed by his stupid, perverse servant. So, keeping quite justified and conventional in his consciousness, he let the other thing run on. His nerves, however, were suffering. At last he slung the end of a belt in his servant's face. When he saw the youth start back, the pain-tears in his eyes and the blood on his mouth, he had felt at once a thrill of deep pleasure and of shame.

But this, he acknowledged to himself, was a thing he had never done before. The fellow was too exasperating. His own nerves must be going to pieces. He went away for some days with a woman.

It was a mockery of pleasure. He simply did not want the woman. But he stayed on for his time. At the end of it, he came back in an agony of irritation, torment, and misery. He rode all the evening, then came straight in to supper. His orderly was out. The officer sat with his long, fine hands lying on the table, perfectly still, and all his blood seemed to be corroding.

At last his servant entered. He watched the strong, easy young figure, the fine eyebrows, the thick black hair. In a week's time the youth had got back his old well-being. The hands of the officer twitched and seemed to be full of mad flame. The young man stood at attention, unmoving, shut off.

The meal went in silence. But the orderly seemed eager. He made a clatter with the dishes.

"Are you in a hurry?" asked the officer, watching the intent, warm face of his servant. The other did not reply.

"Will you answer my question?" said the Captain.

"Yes, sir," replier the orderly, standing with his pile of deep Army plates. The Captain waited, looked at him, then asked again:

"Are you in a hurry?"

"Yes, sir," came the answer, that sent a flash through the listener.

"For what?"

"I was going out, sir."

"I want you this evening."

There was a moment's hesitation. The officer had a curious stiffness of countenance.

"Yes, sir," replied the servant, in his throat.

"I want you to-morrow evening also—in fact you may consider your evenings occupied, unless I give you leave."

The mouth with the young moustache set close.

"Yes, sir," answered the orderly, loosening his lips for a moment.

He again turned to the door.

"And why have you a piece of pencil in your ear?"

The orderly hesitated, then continued on his way without answering. He set the plates in a pile outside the door, took the stump of pencil from his ear, and put it in his pocket. He had been copying a verse for his sweetheart's birthday card. He returned to finish clearing the table. The officer's eyes were dancing, he had a little, eager smile.

"Why have you a piece of pencil in your ear?" he asked.

The orderly took his hands full of dishes. His master was standing near the great green stove, a little smile on his face, his chin thrust forward. When the young soldier saw him his heart suddenly ran hot. He felt blind. Instead of answering, he turned dazedly to the door. As he was crouching to set down the dishes, he was pitched forward by a kick from behind. The pots went in a stream down the stairs, he clung to the pillar of the banisters. And as he was rising he was kicked heavily again and again, so that he clung sickly to the post for some moments. His master had gone swiftly into the room and closed the door. The maid-servant downstairs looked up the staircase and made a mocking face at the crockery disaster.

The officer's heart was plunging. He poured himself a glass of wine, part of which he spilled on the floor, and gulped the remainder, leaning against the cool, green stove. He heard his

man collecting the dishes from the stairs. Pale, as if intoxicated, he waited. The servant entered again. The Captain's
heart gave a pang, as of pleasure, seeing the young fellow
bewildered and uncertain on his feet with pain.

"Schöner!" he said.

The soldier was a little slower in coming to attention.

"Yes, sir!"

The youth stood before him, with pathetic young moustache,
and fine eyebrows very distinct on his forehead of dark
marble.

"I asked you a question."

"Yes, sir."

The officer's tone bit like acid.

"Why had you a pencil in your ear?"

Again the servant's heart ran hot, and he could not breathe.
With dark, strained eyes, he looked at the officer, as if
fascinated. And he stood there sturdily planted, unconscious.
The withering smile came into the Captain's eyes, and he
lifted his foot.

"I forgot it—sir," panted the soldier, his dark eyes fixed on
the other man's dancing blue ones.

"What was it doing there?"

He saw the young man's breast heaving as he made an effort
for words.

"I had been writing."

"Writing what?"

Again the soldier looked him up and down. The officer
could hear him panting. The smile came into the blue eyes.
The soldier worked his dry throat, but could not speak. Suddenly the smile lit like a flame on the officer's face, and a
kick came heavily against the orderly's thigh. The youth
moved sideways. His face went dead, with two black, staring
eyes.

"Well?" said the officer.

The orderly's mouth had gone dry, and his tongue rubbed
in it as on dry brown-paper. He worked his throat. The officer
raised his foot. The servant went stiff.

"Some poetry, sir," came the crackling, unrecognisable
sound of his voice.

"Poetry, what poetry?" asked the Captain, with a sickly
smile.

Again there was the working in the throat. The Captain's

heart had suddenly gone down heavily, and he stood sick and tired.

"For my girl, sir," he heard the dry, inhuman sound.

"Oh!" he said, turning away. "Clear the table."

"Click!" went the soldier's throat; then again, "click!" and then the half-articulate:

"Yes, sir."

The young soldier was gone, looking old, and walking heavily.

The officer, left alone, held himself rigid, to prevent himself from thinking. His instinct warned him that he must not think. Deep inside him was the intense gratification of his passion, still working powerfully. Then there was a counter-action, a horrible breaking down of something inside him, a whole agony of reaction. He stood there for an hour motion-less, a chaos of sensations, but rigid with a will to keep blank his consciousness, to prevent his mind grasping. And he held himself so until the worst of the stress had passed, when he began to drink, drank himself to an intoxication, till he slept obliterated. When he woke in the morning he was shaken to the base of his nature. But he had fought off the realisation of what he had done. He had prevented his mind from taking it in, had suppressed it along with his instincts, and the conscious man had nothing to do with it. He felt only as after a bout of intoxication, weak, but the affair itself all dim and not to be recovered. Of the drunkenness of his passion he successfully refused remembrance. And when his orderly appeared with coffee, the officer assumed the same self he had had the morning before. He refused the event of the past night—denied it had ever been—and was successful in his denial. He had not done any such thing—not he himself. Whatever there might be lay at the door of a stupid insub-ordinate servant.

The orderly had gone about in a stupor all the evening. He drank some beer because he was parched, but not much, the alcohol made his feeling come back, and he could not bear it. He was dulled, as if nine-tenths of the ordinary man in him were inert. He crawled about disfigured. Still, when he thought of the kicks, he went sick, and when he thought of the threat of more kicking, in the room afterwards, his heart went hot and faint, and he panted, remembering the one that had come. He had been forced to say: "For my girl." He was much too done even to want to cry. His mouth hung slightly open, like an idiot's. He felt vacant, and wasted. So, he wandered at his work, painfully, and very slowly and clumsily, fumbling blindly with the brushes, and finding it difficult, when he sat down, to summon the energy to move again. His limbs, his jaw, were slack and nerveless. But he was very tired. He got to bed at last, and slept inert, relaxed, in a sleep that was rather stupor than slumber, a dead night of stupefaction shot through with gleams of anguish.

In the morning were the manœuvres. But he woke even before the bugle sounded. The painful ache in his chest, the dryness of his throat, the awful steady feeling of misery made his eyes come awake and dreary at once. He knew, without thinking, what had happened. And he knew that the day had come again, when he must go on with his round. The last bit of darkness was being pushed out of the room. He would have to move his inert body and go on. He was so young, and had known so little trouble, that he was bewildered. He only wished it would stay night, so that he could lie still, covered up by the darkness. And yet nothing would prevent the day from coming, nothing would save him from having to get up and saddle the Captain's horse, and make the Captain's coffee. It was there, inevitable. And then, he thought, it was impossible. Yet they would not leave him free. He must go and take the coffee to the Captain. He was too stunned to understand it. He only knew it was inevitable—inevitable, however long he lay inert.

At last, after heaving at himself, for he seemed to be a mass of inertia, he got up. But he had to force every one of his movements from behind, with his will. He felt lost, and dazed, and helpless. Then he clutched hold of the bed, the pain was so keen. And looking at his thighs he saw the darker bruises on his swarthy flesh, and he knew that if he pressed one of his fingers on one of the bruises, he should faint. But he did not want to faint—he did not want anybody to know. No one should ever know. It was between him and the Captain. There were only the two people in the world now —himself and the Captain.

Slowly, economically, he got dressed and forced himself to walk. Everything was obscure, except just what he had his hands on. But he managed to get through his work. The very pain revived his dull senses. The worst remained yet. He took the tray and went up to the Captain's room. The officer, pale and heavy, sat at the table. The orderly, as he saluted, felt himself put out of existence. He stood still for a moment submitting to his own nullification—then he gathered himself, seemed to regain himself, and then the Captain began to grow vague, unreal, and the younger soldier's heart beat up. He clung to this situation—that the Captain did not exist—so that he himself might live. But when he saw his officer's hand tremble as he took the coffee, he felt everything falling shattered. And he went away, feeling as if he himself were coming to pieces, disintegrated. And when the Captain was there on horseback, giving orders, while he himself stood, with rifle and knapsack, sick with pain, he felt as if he must shut his eyes—as if he must shut his eyes on everything. It was only the long agony of marching with a parched throat that filled him with one single, sleep-heavy intention: to save himself.

II

He was getting used even to his parched throat. That the snowy peaks were radiant among the sky, that the whity-green glacier-river twisted through its pale shoals, in the valley below, seemed almost supernatural. But he was going mad with fever and thirst. He plodded on uncomplaining. He did not want to speak, not to anybody. There were two gulls, like flakes of water and snow, over the river. The scent of green rye soaked in sunshine came like a sickness. And the march continued, monotonously, almost like a bad sleep.

At the next farmhouse, which stood low and broad near the high road, tubs of water had been put out. The soldiers clustered round to drink. They took off their helmets, and the steam mounted from their wet hair. The Captain sat on horseback, watching. He needed to see his orderly. His helmet threw a dark shadow over his light, fierce eyes, but his moustache and mouth and chin were distinct in the sunshine. The orderly must move under the presence of the figure of the horseman. It was not that he was afraid, or cowed. It was as if he was disembowelled, made empty, like an empty shell. He felt himself as nothing, a shadow creeping under the sunshine. And, thirsty as he was, he could scarcely drink, feeling the Captain near him. He would not take off his helmet to wipe his wet hair. He wanted to stay in shadow, not to be forced into consciousness. Starting, he saw the light heel of the officer prick the belly of the horse; the Captain cantered away, and he himself could relapse into vacancy.

Nothing, however, could give him back his living place in the hot, bright morning. He felt like a gap among it all. Whereas the Captain was prouder, overriding. A hot flash went through the young servant's body. The Captain was firmer and prouder with life, he himself was empty as a shadow. Again the flash went through him, dazing him out. But his heart ran a little firmer.

The company turned up the hill, to make a loop for the return. Below, from among the trees, the farm-bell clanged. He saw the labourers, mowing bare-foot at the thick grass, leave off their work and go downhill, their scythes hanging over their shoulders, like long, bright claws curving down behind them. They seemed like dream-people, as if they had no relation to himself. He felt as in a blackish dream: as if all the other things were there and had form, but he himself was only a consciousness, a gap that could think and perceive.

The soldiers were tramping silently up the glaring hill-side. Gradually his head began to revolve, slowly, rhythmically. Sometimes it was dark before his eyes, as if he saw this world through a smoked glass, frail shadows and unreal. It gave him a pain in his head to walk.

The air was too scented, it gave no breath. All the lush green-stuff seemed to be issuing its sap, till the air was deathly, sickly with the smell of greenness. There was the perfume of clover, like pure honey and bees. Then there grew a faint acrid tang—they were near the beeches; and then a queer clattering noise, and a suffocating, hideous smell; they were passing a flock of sheep, a shepherd in a black smock, holding his crook. Why should the sheep huddle together under this fierce sun? He felt that the shepherd would not see him, though he could see the shepherd.

At last there was the halt. They stacked rifles in a conical stack, put down their kit in a scattered circle around it, and dispersed a little, sitting on a small knoll high on the hill-side. The chatter began. The soldiers were steaming with heat, but were lively. He sat still, seeing the blue mountains rising upon the land, twenty kilometres away. There was a blue fold in the ranges, then out of that, at the foot, the broad, pale bed of the river, stretches of whity-green water between pinkish-grey shoals among the dark pine woods. There it was, spread out a long way off. And it seemed to come downhill, the river. There was a raft being steered, a mile away. It was a strange country. Nearer, a red-roofed, broad farm with white base and square dots of windows crouched beside the wall of beech foliage on the wood's edge. There were long strips of rye and clover and pale green corn. And just at his feet, below the knoll, was a darkish bog, where globe flowers stood breathless still on their slim stalks. And some of the pale gold bubbles were burst, and a broken fragment hung in the air. He thought he was going to sleep.

Suddenly something moved into this coloured mirage before his eyes. The Captain, a small, light-blue and scarlet figure, was trotting evenly between the strips of corn, along the level brow of the hill. And the man making flag-signals was coming on. Proud and sure moved the horseman's figure, the quick, bright thing, in which was concentrated all the light of this morning, which for the rest lay fragile, shining shadow. Submissive, apathetic, the young soldier sat and stared. But as the horse slowed to a walk, coming up the last steep path, the great flash flared over the body and soul of the orderly. He sat waiting. The back of his head felt as if it were weighted with a heavy piece of fire. He did not want to eat. His hands trembled slightly as he moved them. Meanwhile the officer on horseback was approaching slowly and proudly. The tension grew in the orderly's soul. Then again, seeing the Captain ease himself on the saddle, the flash blazed through him.

The Captain looked at the patch of light blue and scarlet, and dark head, scattered closely on the hill-side. It pleased him. The command pleased him. And he was feeling proud. His orderly was among them in common subjection. The officer rose a little on his stirrups to look. The young soldier sat with averted, dumb face. The Captain relaxed on his seat. His slim-legged, beautiful horse, brown as a beech nut, walked proudly uphill. The Captain passed into the zone of the company's atmosphere: a hot smell of men, of sweat, of leather. He knew it very well. After a word with the lieutenant, he went a few paces higher, and sat there, a dominant figure, his sweat-marked horse swishing its tail, while he looked down on his men, on his orderly, a nonentity among the crowd.

The young soldier's heart was like fire in his chest, and he breathed with difficulty. The officer, looking downhill, saw three of the young soldiers, two pails of water between them, staggering across a sunny green field. A table had been set up under a tree, and there the slim lieutenant stood, importantly busy. Then the Captain summoned himself to an act of courage. He called his orderly.

The flame leapt into the young soldier's throat as he heard the command, and he rose blindly, stifled. He saluted, standing below the officer. He did not look up. But there was the flicker in the Captain's voice.

"Go to the inn and fetch me . . ." the officer gave his commands. "Quick!" he added.

At the last word, the heart of the servant leapt with a flash, and he felt the strength come over his body. But he turned in mechanical obedience, and set off at a heavy run downhill, looking almost like a bear, his trousers bagging over his military boots. And the officer watched this blind, plunging run all the way.

But it was only the outside of the orderly's body that was obeying so humbly and mechanically. Inside had gradually accumulated a core into which all the energy of that young life was compact and concentrated. He executed his commission, and plodded quickly back uphill. There was a pain in his head as he walked that made him twist his features unknowingly. But hard there in the centre of his chest was himself, himself, firm, and not to be plucked to pieces.

The Captain had gone up into the wood. The orderly plodded through the hot, powerfully smelling zone of the company's atmosphere. He had a curious mass of energy inside him now. The Captain was less real than himself. He approached the green entrance to the wood. There, in the half-shade, he saw the horse standing, the sunshine and the flickering shadow of leaves dancing over his brown body. There was a clearing where timber had lately been felled. Here, in the gold-green shade beside the brilliant cup of sunshine, stood two figures, blue and pink, the bits of pink showing out plainly. The Captain was talking to his lieutenant.

The orderly stood on the edge of the bright clearing, where great trunks of trees, stripped and glistening, lay stretched like naked, brown-skinned bodies. Chips of wood littered the trampled floor, like splashed light, and the bases of the felled trees stood here and there, with their raw, level tops. Beyond was the brilliant, sunlit green of a beech.

"Then I will ride forward," the orderly heard his Captain say. The lieutenant saluted and strode away. He himself went forward. At hot flash passed through his belly, as he tramped towards his officer.

The Captain watched the rather heavy figure of the young soldier stumble forward, and his veins, too, ran hot. This was to be man to man between them. He yielded before the solid, stumbling figure with bent head. The orderly stooped and put the food on a level-sawn tree-base. The Captain watched the glistening, sun-inflamed, naked hands. He wanted to speak to the young soldier, but could not. The servant propped a bottle against his thigh, pressed open the cork, and poured out the beer into the mug. He kept his head bent. The Captain accepted the mug.

"Hot!" he said, as if amiably.

The flame sprang out of the orderly's heart, nearly suffocating him.

"Yes, sir," he replied, between shut teeth.

And he heard the sound of the Captain's drinking, and he clenched his fists, such a strong torment came into his wrists. Then came the faint clang of the closing of the pot-lid. He looked up. The Captain was watching him. He glanced swiftly away. Then he saw the officer stoop and take a piece of bread from the tree-base. Again the flash of flame went through the young soldier, seeing the stiff body stoop beneath him, and his hands jerked. He looked away. He could feel the officer was nervous. The bread fell as it was being broken. The officer ate the other piece. The two men stood tense and still, the master laboriously chewing his bread, the servant staring with averted face, his fist clenched.

Then the young soldier started. The officer had pressed open the lid of the mug again. The orderly watched the lip of the mug, and the white hand that clenched the handle, as if he were fascinated. It was raised. The youth followed it with his eyes. And then he saw the thin, strong throat of the elder man moving up and down as he drank, the strong jaw working. And the instinct which had been jerking at the young man's wrists suddenly jerked free. He jumped, feeling as if it were rent in two by a strong flame.

The spur of the officer caught in a tree root, he went down

backwards with a crash, the middle of his back thudding sick-
eningly against a sharp-edged tree-base, the pot flying away.
And in a second the orderly, with serious, earnest young face,
and underlip between his teeth, had got his knee in the officer's
chest and was pressing the chin backward over the farther
edge of the tree-stump, pressing, with all his heart behind in
a passion of relief, the tension of his wrists exquisite with
relief. And with the base of his palms he shoved at the chin,
with all his might. And it was pleasant, too, to have that chin
that hard jaw already slightly rough with beard, in his hands.
He did not relax one hair's breadth, but, all the force of all
his blood exulting in his thrust, he shoved back the head of
the other man, till there was a little "cluck" and a crunching
sensation. Then he felt as if his head went to vapour. Heavy
convulsions shook the body of the officer, frightening and
horrifying the young soldier. Yet it pleased him, too, to repress
them. It pleased him to keep his hands pressing back the chin,
to feel the chest of the other man yield in expiration to the
weight of his strong, young knees, to feel the hard twitchings
of the prostrate body jerking his own whole frame, which was
pressed down on it.

But it went still. He could look into the nostrils of the other
man, the eyes he could scarcely see. How curiously the mouth
was pushed out, exaggerating the full lips, and the moustache
bristling up from them. Then, with a start, he noticed the
nostrils gradually filled with blood. The red brimmed,
hesitated, ran over, and went in a thin trickle down the face
to the eyes.

It shocked and distressed him. Slowly, he got up. The body
twitched and sprawled there, inert. He stood and looked at it
in silence. It was a pity *it* was broken. It represented more
than the thing which had kicked and bullied him. He was
afraid to look at the eyes. They were hideous now, only the
whites showing, and the blood running to them. The face of
the orderly was drawn with horror at the sight. Well, it was
so. In his heart he was satisfied. He had hated the face of the
Captain. It was extinguished now. There was a heavy relief
in the orderly's soul. That was as it should be. But he could
not bear to see the long, military body lying broken over the
tree-base, the fine fingers crisped. He wanted to hide it away.

Quickly, busily, he gathered it up and pushed it under the
felled tree trunks, which rested their beautiful, smooth length

either end on the logs. The face was horrible with blood. He covered it with the helmet. Then he pushed the limbs straight and decent, and brushed the dead leaves off the fine cloth of the uniform. So, it lay quite still in the shadow under there. A little strip of sunshine ran along the breast, from a chink between the logs. The orderly sat by it for a few moments. Here his own life also ended.

Then, through his daze, he heard the lieutentant, in a loud voice, explaining to the men outside the wood, that they were to suppose the bridge on the river below was held by the enemy. Now they were to march to the attack in such and such a manner. The lieutenant had no gift of expression. The orderly, listening from habit, got muddled. And when the lieutenant began it all again he ceased to hear.

He knew he must go. He stood up. It surprised him that the leaves were glittering in the sun, and the chips of wood reflecting white from the ground. For him a change had come over the world. But for the rest it had not—all seemed the same. Only he had left it. And he could not go back. It was his duty to return with the beer-pot and the bottle. He could not. He had left all that. The lieutenant was still hoarsely explaining. He must go, or they would overtake him. And he could not bear contact with anyone now.

He drew his fingers over his eyes, trying to find out where he was. Then he turned away. He saw the horse standing in the path. He went up to it and mounted. It hurt him to sit in the saddle. The pain of keeping his seat occupied him as they cantered through the wood. He would not have minded anything, but he could not get away from the sense of being divided from the others. The path led out of the trees. On the edge of the wood he pulled up and stood watching. There in the spacious sunshine of the valley soldiers were moving in a little swarm. Every now and then, a man harrowing on a strip of fallow shouted to his oxen, at the turn. The village and the white-towered church was small in the sunshine. And he no longer belonged to it—he sat there, beyond, like a man outside in the dark. He had gone out from everyday life into the unknown and he could not, he even did not want to go back.

Turning from the sun-blazing valley, he rode deep into the wood. Tree trunks, like people standing grey and still, took no notice as he went. A doe, herself a moving bit of sunshine and shadow, went running through the flecked shade. There were bright green rents in the foliage. Then it was all pine wood, dark and cool. And he was sick with pain, and had an intolerable great pulse in his head, and he was sick. He had never been ill in his life. He felt lost, quite dazed with all this.

Trying to get down from the horse, he fell, astonished at the pain and his lack of balance. The horse shifted uneasily. He jerked its bridle and sent it cantering jerkily away. It was his last connection with the rest of things.

But he only wanted to lie down and not be disturbed. Stumbling through the trees, he came on a quiet place where beeches and pine trees grew on a slope. Immediately he had lain down and closed his eyes, his consciousness went racing on without him. A big pulse of sickness beat in him as if it throbbed through the whole earth. He was burning with dry heat. But he was too busy, too tearingly active in the incoherent race of delirium to observe.

III

He came to with a start. His mouth was dry and hard, his heart beat heavily, but he had not the energy to get up. His heart beat heavily. Where was he?—the barracks—at home? There was something knocking. And, making an effort, he looked round—trees, and litter of greenery, and reddish, bright, still pieces of sunshine on the floor. He did not believe he was himself, he did not believe what he saw. Something was knocking. He made a struggle towards consciousness, but relapsed. Then he struggled again. And gradually his surroundings fell into relationship with himself. He knew, and a great pang of fear went through his heart. Somebody was knocking. He could see the heavy, black rags of a fir tree overhead. Then everything went black. Yet he did not believe he had closed his eyes. He had not. Out of the blackness sight slowly emerged again. And someone was knocking. Quickly, he saw the blood-disfigured face of his Captain, which he hated. And he held himself still with horror. Yet, deep inside him, he knew that it was so, the Captain should be dead. But the physical delirium got hold of him. Someone was knocking. He lay perfectly still, as if dead, with fear. And he went unconscious.

When he opened his eyes again he started, seeing some-

thing creeping swiftly up a tree trunk. It was a little bird.
And the bird was whistling overhead. Tap-tap-tap—it was the
small, quick bird rapping the tree trunk with its beak, as if its
head were a little round hammer. He watched it curiously. It
shifted sharply, in its creeping fashion. Then, like a mouse, it
slid down the bare trunk. Its swift creeping sent a flash of
revulsion through him. He raised his head. It felt a great
weight. Then, the little bird ran out of the shadow across a
still patch of sunshine, its little head bobbing swiftly, its white
legs twinkling brightly for a moment. How neat it was in its
build, so compact, with piece of white on its wings. There
were several of them. They were so pretty—but they crept
like swift, erratic mice, running here and there among the
beech-mast.

He lay down again exhausted, and his consciousness lapsed.
He had a horror of the little creeping birds. All his blood
seemed to be darting and creeping in his head. And yet he
could not move.

He came to with a further ache of exhaustion. There was
the pain in his head, and the horrible sickness, and his in-
ability to move. He had never been ill in his life. He did
not know where he was or what he was. Probably he had got
sunstroke. Or what else?—he had silenced the Captain for
ever—some time ago—oh, a long time ago. There had been
blood on his face, and his eyes had turned upwards. It was
all right, somehow. It was peace. But now he had got beyond
himself. He had never been here before. Was it life, or not
life? He was by himself. They were in a big, bright place,
those others, and he was outside. The town, all the country,
a big bright place of light: and he was outside, here, in the
darkened open beyond, where each thing existed alone. But
they would all have to come out there sometime, those others.
Little, and left behind him, they all were. There had been
father and mother and sweetheart. What did they all matter?
This was the open land.

He sat up. Something scuffled. It was a little brown squirrel
running in lovely undulating bounds over the floor, its red tail
completing the undulation of its body—and then, as it sat up,
furling and unfurling. He watched it, pleased. It ran on again,
friskily, enjoying itself. It flew wildly at another squirrel, and
they were chasing each other, and making little scolding,
chattering noises. The soldier wanted to speak to them. But

only a hoarse sound came out of his throat. The squirrels burst away—they flew up the trees. And then he saw the one peeping round at him, half-way up a tree trunk. A start of fear went through him, though in so far as he was conscious, he was amused. It still stayed, its little keen face staring at him half-way up the tree trunk, its little ears pricked up, its clawey little hands clinging to the bark, its white breast reared. He started from it in panic.

Struggling to his feet, he lurched away. He went on walking, walking, looking for something—for a drink. His brain felt hot and inflamed for want of water. He stumbled on. Then he did not know anything. He went unconscious as he walked. Yet he stumbled on, his mouth open.

When, to his dumb wonder, he opened his eyes on the world again, he no longer tried to remember what it was. There was thick, golden light behind golden-green glitterings, and tall, grey-purple shafts, and darknesses farther off, surrounding him, growing deeper. He was conscious of a sense of arrival. He was amid the reality, on the real, dark bottom. But there was the thirst burning in his brain. He felt lighter, not so heavy. He supposed it was newness. The air was muttering with thunder. He thought he was walking wonderfully swiftly and was coming straight to relief—or was it to water?

Suddenly he stood still with fear. There was a tremendous flare of gold, immense—just a few dark trunks like bars between him and it. All the young level wheat was burnished gold glaring on its silky green. A woman, full-skirted, a black cloth on her head for head-dress, was passing like a block of shadow through the glistening, green corn, into the full glare. There was a farm, too, pale blue in shadow, and the timber black. And there was a church spire, nearly fused away in the gold. The woman moved on, away from him. He had no language with which to speak to her. She was the bright, solid unreality. She would make a noise of words that would confuse him, and her eyes would look at him without seeing him. She was crossing there to the other side. He stood against a tree.

When at last he turned, looking down the long, bare grove whose flat bed was already filling dark, he saw the mountains in a wonder-light, not far away, and radiant. Behind the soft, grey ridge of the nearest range the farther mountains stood golden and pale grey, the snow all radiant like pure, soft gold.

So still, gleaming in the sky, fashioned pure out of the ore of the sky, they shone in their silence. He stood and looked at them, his face illuminated. And like the golden, lustrous gleaming of the snow he felt his own thirst bright in him. He stood and gazed, leaning against a tree. And then everything slid away into space.

During the night the lightning fluttered perpetually, making the whole sky white. He must have walked again. The world hung livid round him for moments, fields a level sheen of grey-green light, trees in dark bulk, and the range of clouds black across a white sky. Then the darkness fell like a shutter, and the night was whole. A faint flutter of a half-revealed world, that could not quite leap out of the darkness!—Then there again stood a sweep of pallor for the land, dark shapes looming, a range of clouds hanging overhead. The world was a ghostly shadow, thrown for a moment upon the pure darkness, which returned ever whole and complete.

And the mere delirium of sickness and fever went on inside him—his brain opening and shutting like the night—then sometimes convulsions of terror from something with great eyes that stared round a tree—then the long agony of the march, and the sun decomposing his blood—then the pang of hate for the Captain, followed by a pang of tenderness and ease. But everything was distorted, born of an ache and resolving into an ache.

In the morning he came definitely awake. Then his brain flamed with the sole horror or thirstiness! The sun was on his face, the dew was steaming from his wet clothes. Like one possessed, he got up. There, straight in front of him, blue and cool and tender, the mountains ranged across the pale edge of the morning sky. He wanted them—he wanted them alone—he wanted to leave himself and be identified with them. They did not move, they were still and soft, with white, gentle markings of snow. He stood still, mad with suffering, his hands crisping and clutching. Then he was twisting in a paroxysm on the grass.

He lay still, in a kind of dream of anguish. His thirst seemed to have separated itself from him, and to stand apart, a single demand. Then the pain he felt was another single self. Then there was the clog of his body, another separate thing. He was divided among all kinds of separate things. There was some strange, agonised connection between them, but they were drawing farther apart. Then they would all split. The sun, drilling down on him, was drilling through the bond. Then they would all fall, fall through the everlasting lapse of space. Then again, his consciousness reasserted itself. He roused on to his elbow and stared at the gleaming mountains. There they ranked, all still and wonderful between earth and heaven. He stared till his eyes went black, and the mountains, as they stood in their beauty, so clean and cool, seemed to have it, that which was lost in him.

IV

When the soldiers found him, three hours later, he was lying with his face over his arm, his black hair giving off heat under the sun. But he was still alive. Seeing the open, black mouth the young soldiers dropped him in horror.

He died in the hospital at night, without having seen again.

The doctors saw the bruises on his legs, behind, and were silent.

The bodies of the two men lay together, side by side, in the mortuary, the one white and slender, but laid rigidly at rest, the other looking as if every moment it must rouse into life again, so young and unused, from a slumber.

THE THORN IN THE FLESH

I

A WIND was running, so that occasionally the poplars whitened as if a flame flew up them. The sky was broken and blue among moving clouds. Patches of sunshine lay on the level fields, and shadows on the rye and the vineyards. In the distance, very blue, the cathedral bristled against the sky, and the houses of the city of Metz clustered vaguely below, like a hill.

Among the fields by the lime trees stood the barracks, upon bare, dry ground, a collection of round-roofed huts of corrugated iron, where the soldiers' nasturtiums climbed brilliantly. There was a tract of vegetable garden at the side, with the soldiers' yellowish lettuces in rows, and at the back the big, hard drilling-yard surrounded by a wire fence.

At this time in the afternoon, the huts were deserted, all the beds pushed up, the soldiers were lounging about under the lime trees waiting for the call to drill. Bachmann sat on a bench in the shade that smelled sickly with blossom. Pale green, wrecked lime flowers were scattered on the ground. He was writing his weekly post card to his mother. He was a fair, long, limber youth, good-looking. He sat very still indeed, trying to write his post card. His blue uniform, sagging on him as he sat bent over the card, disfigured his youthful shape. His sunburnt hand waited motionless for the words to come. "Dear mother"—was all he had written. Then he scribbled mechanically: "Many thanks for your letter with what you sent. Everything is all right with me. We are just off to drill on the fortifications——" Here he broke off and sat suspended, oblivious of everything, held in some definite suspense. He looked again at the card. But he could write no more. Out of the knot of his consciousness no word would come. He signed himself, and looked up, as a man looks to see if anyone has noticed him in his privacy.

There was a self-conscious strain in his blue eyes, and a pallor about his mouth, where the young, fair moustache glistened. He was almost girlish in his good looks and his grace.

But he had something of military consciousness, as if he believed in the discipline for himself, and found satisfaction in delivering himself to his duty. There was also a trace of youthful swagger and dare-devilry about his mouth and his limber body, but this was in suppression now.

He put the post card in the pocket of his tunic, and went to join a group of his comrades who were lounging in the shade, laughing and talking grossly. Today he was out of it. He only stood near to them for the warmth of the association. In his own consciousness something held him down.

Presently they were summoned to ranks. The sergeant came out to take command. He was a strongly built, rather heavy man of forty. His head was thrust forward, sunk a little between his powerful shoulders, and the strong jaw was pushed out aggressively. But the eyes were smouldering, the face hung slack and sodden with drink.

He gave his orders in brutal, barking shouts, and the little company moved forward, out of the wire-fenced yard to the open road, marching rhythmically, raising the dust. Bachmann, one of the inner file of four deep, marched in the airless ranks, half suffocated with heat and dust and enclosure. Through the moving of his comrades' bodies, he could see the small vines dusty by the roadside, the poppies among the tares fluttering and blown to pieces, the distant spaces of sky and fields all free with air and sunshine. But he was bound in a very dark enclosure of anxiety within himself.

He marched with his usual ease, being healthy and well adjusted. But his body went on by itself. His spirit was clenched apart. And ever the few soldiers drew nearer and nearer the town, ever the consciousness of the youth became more gripped and separate, his body worked by a kind of mechanical intelligence, a mere presence of mind.

They diverged from the high road and passed in single file down a path among trees. All was silent and green and mysterious, with shadow of foliage and long, green, undisturbed grass. Then they came out in the sunshine on a moat of water, which wound silently between the long, flowery grass, at the foot of the earthworks, that rose in front in terraces walled smooth on the face, but all soft with long grass at the top. Marguerite daisies and lady's-slipper glimmered white and gold in the lush grass, preserved here in the intense peace of the fortifications. Thickets of trees stood round about. Occasion-

ally a puff of mysterious wind made the flowers and the long
grass that crested the earthworks above bow and shake as with
signals of oncoming alarm.

The group of soldiers stood at the end of the moat, in their
light blue and scarlet uniforms, very bright. The sergeant was
giving them instruction, and his shout came sharp and alarm-
ing in the intense, untouched stillness of the place. They
listened, finding it difficult to make the effort of understanding.

Then it was over, and the men were moving to make preparations. On the other side of the moat the ramparts rose
smooth and clear in the sun, sloping slightly back. Along the
summit grass grew and tall daisies stood ledged high, like
magic, against the dark green of the tree-tops behind. The
noise of the town, the running of tram-cars, was heard
distinctly, but it seemed not to penetrate this still place.

The water of the moat was motionless. In silence the
practice began. One of the soldiers took a scaling-ladder, and
passing along the narrow ledge at the foot of the earthworks,
with the water of the moat just behind him, tried to get a
fixture on the slightly sloping wall-face. There he stood, small
and isolated, at the foot of the wall, trying to get his ladder
settled. At last it held, and the clumsy, groping figure in the
baggy blue uniform began to clamber up. The rest of the
soldiers stood and watched. Occasionally the sergeant barked
a command. Slowly the clumsy blue figure clambered higher
up the wall-face. Bachmann stood with his bowels turned
to water. The figure of the climbing soldier scrambled out
on to the terrace up above, and moved, blue and distinct,
among the bright green grass. The officer shouted from below.
The soldier tramped along, fixed the ladder in another spot,
and carefully lowered himself on to the rungs. Bachmann
watched the blind foot groping in space for the ladder, and
he felt the world fall away beneath him. The figure of the
soldier clung cringing against the face of the wall, cleaving,
groping downwards like some unsure insect working its way
lower and lower, fearing every movement. At last, sweating
and with a strained face, the figure had landed safely and
turned to the group of soldiers. But still it had a stiffness and
a blank mechanical look, was something less than human.

Bachmann stood there heavy and condemned, waiting for
his own turn and betrayal. Some of the men went up easily
enough, and without fear. That only showed it could be done

lightly, and made Bachmann's case more bitter. If only he could do it lightly, like that.

His turn came. He knew intuitively that nobody knew his condition. The officer just saw him as a mechanical thing. He tried to keep it up, to carry it through on the face of things. His inside gripped tight, as yet under control, he took the ladder and went along under the wall. He placed his ladder with quick success, and wild, quivering hope possessed him. Then blindly he began to climb. But the ladder was not very firm; and at every hitch a great, sick melting feeling took hold of him. He clung on fast. If only he could keep that grip on himself, he would get through. He knew this, in agony. What he could not understand was the blind gush of white-hot fear, that came with great force whenever the ladder swerved, and which almost melted his belly and all his joints, and left him powerless. If once it melted all his joints and his belly, he was done. He clung desperately to himself. He knew the fear, he knew what it did when it came, he knew he had only to keep a firm hold. He knew all this. Yet, when the ladder swerved and his foot missed, there was the great blast of fear blowing on his heart and bowels, and he was melting weaker and weaker, in a horror of fear and lack of control, melting to fall.

Yet he groped slowly higher and higher, always staring upwards with desperate face, and always conscious of the space below. But all of him, body and soul, was growing hot to fusion point. He would have to let go for very relief's sake. Suddenly his heart began to lurch. It gave a great, sickly swoop, rose, and again plunged in a swoop of horror. He lay against the wall inert as if dead, inert, at peace, save for one deep core of anxiety, which knew that it was *not* all over, that he was still high in space against the wall. But the chief effort of will was gone.

There came into his consciousness a small, foreign sensation. He woke up a little. What was it? Then slowly it penetrated him. His water had run down his leg. He lay there, clinging, still with shame, half conscious of the echo of the sergeant's voice thundering from below. He waited, in depth of shame beginning to recover himself. He had been shamed so deeply. Then he could go on, for his fear for himself was conquered. His shame was known and published. He must go on.

Slowly he began to grope for the rung above, when a great

shock shook through him. His wrists were grasped from above,
he was being hauled out of himself up, up to the safe ground.
Like a sack he was dragged over the edge of the earthworks
by large hands, and landed there on his knees, grovelling in
the grass to recover command of himself, to rise up on his
feet.

Shame, blind, deep shame and ignominy overthrew his spirit
and left it writhing. He stood there shrunk over himself,
trying to obliterate himself.

Then the presence of the officer who had hauled him up
made itself felt upon him. He heard the panting of the elder
man, and then the voice came down on his veins like a fierce
whip. He shrank in tension of shame.

"Put up your head—eyes front," shouted the enraged
sergeant, and mechanically the soldier obeyed the command,
forced to look into the eyes of the sergeant. The brutal, hanging face of the officer violated the youth. He hardened himself
with all his might from seeing it. The tearing noise of the
sergeant's voice continued to lacerate his body.

Suddenly he set back his head, rigid, and his heart leapt to
burst. The face had suddenly thrust itself close, all distorted
and showing the teeth, the eyes smouldering into him. The
breath of the barking words was on his nose and mouth. He
stepped aside in revulsion. With a scream the face was upon
him again. He raised his arm, involuntarily, in self-defence.
A shock of horror went through him, as he felt his forearm
hit the face of the officer a brutal blow. The latter staggered,
swerved back, and with a curious cry, reeled backwards over
the ramparts, his hands clutching the air. There was a second
of silence, then a crash to water.

Bachmann, rigid, looked out of his inner silence upon the
scene. Soldiers were running.

"You'd better clear," said one young, excited voice to him.
And with immediate instinctive decision he started to walk
away from the spot. He went down the tree-hidden path to
the high road where the trams ran to and from the town. In
his heart was a sense of vindication, of escape. He was leaving
it all, the military world, the shame. He was walking away
from it.

Officers on horseback rode sauntering down the street,
soldiers passed along the pavement. Coming to the bridge,
Bachmann crossed over to the town that heaped before him,

rising from the flat, picturesque French houses down below at the water's edge, up a jumble of roofs and chasms of streets, to the lovely dark cathedral with its myriad pinnacles making points at the sky.

He felt for the moment quite at peace, relieved from a great strain. So he turned along by the river to the public gardens. Beautiful were the heaped, purple lilac trees upon the green grass, and wonderful the walls of the horse-chestnut trees, lighted like an altar with white flowers on every ledge. Officers went by, elegant and all coloured, women and girls sauntered in the chequered shade. Beautiful it was, he walked in a vision, free.

II

But where was he going? He began to come out of his trance of delight and liberty. Deep within him he felt the steady burning of shame in the flesh. As yet he could not bear to think of it. But there it was, submerged beneath his attention, the raw, steady-burning shame.

It behoved him to be intelligent. As yet he dared not remember what he had done. He only knew the need to get away, away from everything he had been in contact with.

But how? A great pang of fear went through him. He could not bear his shamed flesh to be put again between the hands of authority. Already the hands had been laid upon him, brutally upon his nakedness, ripping open his shame and making him maimed, crippled in his own control.

Fear became an anguish. Almost blindly he was turning in the direction of the barracks. He could not take the responsibility of himself. He must give himself up to someone. Then his heart, obstinate in hope, became obsessed with the idea of his sweetheart. He would make himself her responsibility.

Blenching as he took courage, he mounted the small, quick-hurrying tram that ran out of the town in the direction of the barracks. He sat motionless and composed, static.

He got out at the terminus and went down the road. A wind was still running. He could hear the faint whisper of the rye, and the stronger swish as a sudden gust was upon it. No one was about. Feeling detached and impersonal, he went down a field-path between the low vines. Many little vine trees rose up in spires, holding out tender pink shoots, waving their tendrils. He saw them distinctly, and wondered over them. In a field a little way off, men and women were taking up the hay. The bullock-wagon stood by on the path, the men in their blue shirts, the women with white cloths over their heads carried hay in their arms to the cart, all brilliant and distinct upon the shorn, glowing green acres. He felt himself looking out of darkness on to the glamorous, brilliant beauty of the world around him, outside him.

The Baron's house, where Emilie was maid-servant, stood square and mellow among trees and garden and fields. It was an old French grange. The barracks was quite near. Bachmann walked, drawn by a single purpose, towards the courtyard. He entered the spacious, shadowy, sun-swept place. The dog, seeing a soldier, only jumped and whined for greeting. The pump stood peacefully in a corner, under a lime tree, in the shade.

The kitchen door was open. He hesitated, then walked in, speaking shyly and smiling involuntarily. The two women started, but with pleasure. Emile was preparing the tray for afternoon coffee. She stood beyond the table, drawn up, startled, and challenging, and glad. She had the proud, timid eyes of some wild animal, some proud animal. Her black hair was closely banded, her grey eyes watched steadily. She wore a peasant dress of blue cotton sprigged with little red roses, that buttoned tight over her strong maiden breasts.

At the table sat another young woman, the nursery governess, who was picking cherries from a huge heap, and dropping them into a bowl. She was young, pretty, freckled.

"Good day!" she said pleasantly. "The unexpected."

Emile did not speak. The flush came in her dark cheek. She still stood watching, between fear and a desire to escape, and on the other hand joy that kept her in his presence.

"Yes," he said, bashful and strained, while the eyes of the two women were upon him. "I've got myself in a mess this time."

"What?" asked the nursery governess, dropping her hands in her lap. Emilie stood rigid.

Bachmann could not raise his head. He looked sideways at the glistening, ruddy cherries. He could not recover the normal world.

"I knocked Sergeant Huber over the fortifications down into the moat," he said. "It was accident—but——"

And he grasped at the cherries, and began to eat them, unknowing, hearing only Emilie's little exclamation.

"You knocked him over the fortifications!" echoed Fräulein Hesse in horror. "How?"

Spitting the cherry-stones into his hand, mechanically, absorbedly, he told them.

"Ach!" exclaimed Emilie sharply.

"And how did you get here?" asked Fräulein Hesse.

"I ran off," he said.

There was a dead silence. He stood, putting himself at the mercy of the women. There came a hissing from the stove, and a stronger smell of coffee. Emilie turned swiftly away. He saw her flat, straight back and her strong loins, as she bent over the stove.

"But what are you going to do?" said Fräulein Hesse, aghast.

"I don't know," he said, grasping at more cherries. He had come to an end.

"You'd better go to the barracks," she said. "We'll get the Herr Baron to come and see about it."

Emilie was swiftly and quietly preparing the tray. She picked it up, and stood with the glittering china and silver before her, impassive, waiting for his reply. Bachmann remained with his head dropped, pale and obstinate. He could not bear to go back.

"I'm going to try to get into France," he said.

"Yes, but they'll catch you," said Fräulein Hesse.

Emilie watched with steady, watchful grey eyes.

"I can have a try, if I could hide till to-night," he said.

Both women knew what he wanted. And they all knew it was no good. Emilie picked up the tray, and went out. Bachmann stood with his head dropped. Within himself he felt the dross of shame and incapacity.

"You'd never get away," said the governess.

"I can try," he said.

To-day he could not put himself between the hands of the military. Let them do as they liked with him to-morrow, if he escaped to-day.

They were silent. He ate cherries. The colour flushed bright into the cheeks of the young governess.

Emilie returned to prepare another tray.

"He could hide in your room," the governess said to her.

The girl drew herself away. She could not bear the intrusion.

"That is all I can think of that is safe from the children," said Fräulein Hesse.

Emilie gave no answer. Bachmann stood waiting for the two women. Emilie did not want the close contact with him.

"You could sleep with me," Fräulein Hesse said to her.

Emilie lifted her eyes and looked at the young man, direct, clear, reserving herself.

"Do you want that?" she asked, her strong virginity proof against him.

"Yes—yes——" he said uncertainly, destroyed by shame.

She put back her head.

"Yes," she murmured to herself.

Quickly she filled the tray, and went out.

"But you can't walk over the frontier in a night," said Fräulein Hesse.

"I can cycle," he said.

Emilie returned, a restraint, a neutrality in her bearing.

"I'll see if it's all right," said the governess.

In a moment or two Bachmann was following Emilie through the square hall, where hung large maps on the walls. He noticed a child's blue coat with brass buttons on the peg, and it reminded him of Emilie walking holding the hand of the youngest child, whilst he watched, sitting under the lime tree. Already this was a long way off. That was a sort of freedom he had lost, changed for a new, immediate anxiety.

They went quickly, fearfully up the stairs and down a long corridor. Emilie opened her door, and he entered, ashamed, into her room.

"I must go down," she murmured, and she departed, closing the door softly.

It was a small, bare, neat room. There was a little dish for holy water, a picture of the Sacred Heart, a crucifix, and a prie-Dieu. The small bed lay white and untouched, the wash-hand bowl of red earth stood on a bare table, there was a little mirror and a small chest of drawers. That was all.

Feeling safe, in sanctuary, he went to the window, looking over the courtyard at the shimmering, afternoon country. He was going to leave this land, this life. Already he was in the unknown.

He drew away into the room. The curious simplicity and severity of the little Roman Catholic bedroom was foreign but restoring to him. He looked at the crucifix. It was a long, lean, peasant Christ carved by a peasant in the Black Forest. For the first time in his life Bachmann saw the figure as a human thing. It represented a man hanging there in helpless torture. He stared at it, closely, as if for new knowledge.

Within his own flesh burned and smouldered the restless shame. He could not gather himself together. There was a gap in his soul. The shame within him seemed to displace his strength and his manhood.

He sat down on his chair. The shame, the roused feeling of exposure acted on his brain, made him heavy, unutterably heavy.

Mechanically, his wits all gone, he took off his boots, his belt, his tunic, put them aside, and lay down, heavy, and fell into a kind of drugged sleep.

Emilie came in a little while, and looked at him. But he was sunk in sleep. She saw him lying there inert, and terribly still, and she was afraid. His shirt was unfastened at the throat. She saw his pure white flesh, very clean and beautiful. And he slept inert. His legs, in the blue uniform trousers, his feet in the coarse stockings, lay foreign on her bed. She went away.

III

She was uneasy, perturbed, to her last fibre. She wanted to remain clear, with no touch on her. A wild instinct made her shrink away from any hands which might be laid on her.

She was a foundling, probably of some gipsy race, brought up in a Roman Catholic Rescue Home. A naïve, paganly religious being, she was attached to the Baroness, with whom she had served for seven years, since she was fourteen.

She came into contact with no one, unless it were with Ida Hesse, the governess. Ida was a calculating, good-natured, not very straightforward flirt. She was the daughter of a poor country doctor. Having gradually come into connection with Emilie, more an alliance than an attachment, she put no distinction of grade between the two of them. They worked together, sang together, walked together, and went together to the rooms of Franz Brand, Ida's sweetheart. There the three talked and laughed together, or the women listened to Franz, who was a forester, playing on his violin.

In all this alliance there was no personal intimacy between the young women. Emilie was naturally secluded in herself, of a reserved, native race. Ida used her as a kind of weight to balance her own flighty movement. But the quick, shifty governess, occupied always in her dealings with admirers, did all she could to move the violent nature of Emilie towards some connection with men.

But the dark girl, primitive yet sensitive to a high degree, was fiercely virgin. Her blood flamed with rage when the common soldiers made the long, sucking, kissing noise behind her as she passed. She hated them for their almost jeering offers. She was well protected by the Baroness.

And her contempt of the common men in general was ineffable. But she loved the Baroness, and she revered the Baron, and she was at her ease when she was doing something for the service of a gentleman. Her whole nature was at peace in the service of real masters or mistresses. For her, a gentleman had some mystic quality that left her free and proud in service. The common soldiers were brutes, merely nothing. Her desire was to serve.

She held herself aloof. When, on Sunday afternoon, she had looked through the windows of the Reichshalle in passing, and had seen the soldiers dancing with the common girls, a cold revulsion and anger had possessed her. She could not bear to see the soldiers taking off their belts and pulling open their tunics, dancing with their shirts showing through the open, sagging tunic, their movements gross, their faces transfigured and sweaty, their coarse hands holding their coarse girls under the arm-pits, drawing the female up to their breasts. She hated to see them clutched breast to breast, the legs of the men moving grossly in the dance.

At evening, when she had been in the garden, and heard on the other side of the hedge the sexual, inarticulate cries of the girls in the embraces of the soldiers, her anger had been too much for her, and she had cried, loud and cold:

"What are you doing there, in the hedge?"

She would have had them whipped.

But Bachmann was not quite a common soldier. Fräulein Hesse had found out about him, and had drawn him and Emilie together. For he was a handsome, blond youth, erect and

walking with a kind of pride, unconscious yet clear. Moreover, he came of a rich farming stock, rich for many genera-
tions. His father was dead, his mother controlled the moneys
for the time being. But if Bachmann wanted a hundred pounds
at any moment, he could have them. By trade he, with one of
his brothers, was a wagon-builder. The family had the farming, smithy, and wagon-building of their village. They worked
because that was the form of life they knew. If they had
chosen, they could have lived independent upon their means.

In this way, he was a gentleman in sensibility, though his
intellect was not developed. He could afford to pay freely for
things. He had, moveover, his native, fine breeding. Emilie
wavered uncertainly before him. So he became her sweetheart, and she hungered after him. But she was virgin, and
shy, and needed to be in subjection, because she was primitive
and had no grasp on civilised forms of living, nor on civilised
purposes.

IV

At six o'clock came the inquiry of the soldiers: Had anything been seen of Bachmann? Fräulein Hesse answered,
pleased to be playing a rôle:

"No, I've not seen him since Sunday—have you, Emilie?"

"No, I haven't seen him," said Emilie, and her awkwardness
was construed as bashfulness. Ida Hesse, stimulated, asked
questions, and played her part.

"But it hasn't killed Sergeant Huber?" she cried in con-
sternation.

"No. He fell into the water. But it gave him a bad shock,
and smashed his foot on the side of the moat. He's in hospital.
It's a bad look-out for Bachmann."

Emilie, implicated and captive, stood looking on. She was
no longer free, working with all this regulated system which
she could not understand and which was almost god-like to
her. She was put out of her place. Bachmann was in her
room, she was no longer the faithful in service serving with
religious surety.

Her situation was intolerable to her. All evening long the
burden was upon her, she could not live. The children must
be fed and put to sleep. The Baron and Baroness were going
out, she must give them light refreshment. The man-servant

was coming in to supper after returning with the carriage. And all the while she had the insupportable feeling of being out of the order, self-responsible, bewildered. The control of her life should come from those above her, and she should move within that control. But now she was out of it, uncontrolled and troubled. More than that, the man, the lover, Bachmann, who was he, what was he? He alone of all men contained for her the unknown quality which terrified her beyond her service. Oh, she had wanted him as a distant sweetheart, not close, like this, casting her out of her world.

When the Baron and Baroness had departed, and the young man-servant had gone out to enjoy himself, she went upstairs to Bachmann. He had wakened up, and sat dimly in the room. Out in the open he heard the soldiers, his comrades, singing the sentimental songs of the nightfall, the drone of the concertina rising in accompaniment.

*"Wenn ich zu mei . . . nem Kinde geh' . . .
In seinem Au . . . g die Mutter seh'. . . ."*

But he himself was removed from it now. Only the sentimental cry of young, unsatisfied desire in the soldiers' singing penetrated his blood and stirred him subtly. He let his head hang; he had become gradually roused: and he waited in concentration, in another world.

The moment she entered the room where the man sat alone, waiting intensely, the thrill passed through her, she died in terror, and after the death, a great flame gushed up, obliterating her. He sat in trousers and shirt on the side of the bed. He looked up as she came in, and she shrank from his face. She could not bear it. Yet she entered near to him.

"Do you want anything to eat?" she said.

"Yes," he answered, and she stood in the twilight of the room with him, he could only hear his heart beat heavily. He saw her apron just level with his face. She stood silent, a little distance off, as if she would be there for ever. He suffered.

As if in a spell she waited, standing motionless and looming there, he sat rather crouching on the side of the bed. A second will in him was powerful and dominating. She drew gradually nearer to him, coming up slowly, as if unconscious. His heart beat up swiftly. He was going to move.

As she came quite close, almost invisibly he lifted his arms and put them round her waist, drawing her with his will and desire. He buried his face into her apron, into the terrible softness of her belly. And he was a flame of passion intense about her. He had forgotten. Shame and memory were gone in a whole, furious flame of passion.

She was quite helpless. Her hands leapt, fluttered, and closed over his head, pressing it deeper into her belly, vibrating as she did so. And his arms tightened on her, his hands spread over her loins, warm as flame on her loveliness. In was intense anguish of bliss for her, and she lost consciousness.

When she recovered, she lay translated in the peace of satisfaction.

It was what she had had no inkling of, never known could be. She was strong with eternal gratitude. And he was there with her. Instinctively with an instinct of reverence and gratitude, her arms tightened in a little embrace upon him who held her thoroughly embraced.

And he was restored and completed, close to her. That little, twitching, momentary clasp of acknowledgment that she gave him in her satisfaction, roused his pride unconquerable. They loved each other, and all was whole. She loved him, he had taken her, she was given to him. It was right. He was given to her, and they were one, complete.

Warm, with a glow in their hearts and faces, they rose again, modest, but transfigured with happiness.

"I will get you something to eat," she said, and in joy and security of service again, she left him, making a curious little homage of departure. He sat on the side of the bed, escaped, liberated, wondering, and happy.

v

Soon she came again with the tray, followed by Fräulein Hesse. The two women watched him eat, watching the pride and wonder of his being, as he sat there blond and naïve again. Emilie felt rich and complete. Ida was a lesser thing than herself.

"And what are you going to do?" asked Fräulein Hesse, jealous.

"I must get away," he said.

But words had no meaning for him. What did it matter?
He had the inner satisfaction and liberty.

"But you'll want a bicycle," said Ida Hesse.

"Yes," he said.

Emilie sat silent, removed and yet with him, connected
with him in passion. She looked from this talk of bicycles
and escape.

They discussed plans. But in two of them was the one will,
that Bachmann should stay with Emilie. Ida Hesse was an
outsider.

It was arranged, however, that Ida's lover should put out
his bicycle, leave it at the hut where he sometimes watched.
Bachmann should fetch it in the night, and ride into France.
The hearts of all three beat hot in suspense, driven to thought.
They sat in a fire of agitation.

Then Bachmann would get away to America, and Emilie
would come and join him. They would be in a fine land then.
The tale burned up again.

Emilie and Ida had to go round to Franz Brand's lodging.
They departed with slight leave-taking. Bachmann sat in the
dark, hearing the bugle for retreat sound out of the night.
Then he remembered his post card to his mother. He slipped
out after Emilie, gave it her to post. His manner was careless
and victorious, hers shining and trustful. He slipped back to
shelter.

There he sat on the side of the bed, thinking. Again he went
over the events of the afternoon, remembering his own anguish
of apprehension because he had known he could not climb the
wall without fainting with fear. Still, a flush of shame came
alight in him at the memory. But he said to himself: "What
does it matter?—I can't help it, well then I can't. If I go up
a height, I get absolutely weak, and can't help myself." Again
memory came over him, and a gush of shame, like fire. But
he sat and endured it. It had to be endured, admitted, and
accepted. "I'm not a coward, for all that," he continued. "I'm
not afraid of danger. If I'm made that way, that heights melt
me and make me let go my water"—it was torture for him to
pluck at this truth—"if I'm made like that, I shall have to
abide by it, that's all. It isn't all of me." He thought of Emilie,
and was satisfied. "What I am, I am; and let it be enough,"
he thought.

Having accepted his own defect, he sat thinking, waiting for

Emilie, to tell her. She came at length, saying that Franz could not arrange about his bicycle this night. It was broken. Bachmann would have to stay over another day.

They were both happy. Emilie, confused before Ida, who was excited and prurient, came again to the young man. She was stiff and dignified with an agony of unusedness. But he took her between his hands, and uncovered her, and enjoyed almost like madness her helpless, virgin body that suffered so strongly, and that took its joy so deeply. While the moisture of torment and modesty was still in her eyes, she clasped him closer, and closer, to the victory and the deep satisfaction of both of them. And they slept together, he in repose still satisfied and peaceful, and she lying close in her static reality.

VI

In the morning, when the bugle sounded from the barracks they rose and looked out of the window. She loved his body that was proud and blond and able to take command. And he loved her body that was soft and eternal. They looked at the faint grey vapour of summer steaming off from the greenness and ripeness of the fields. There was no town anywhere, their look ended in the haze of the summer morning. Their bodies rested together, their minds tranquil. Then a little anxiety stirred in both of them from the sound of the bugle. She was called back to her old position, to realise the world of authority she did not understand but had wanted to serve. But this call died away again from her. She had all.

She went downstairs to her work, curiously changed. She was in a new world of her own, that she had never even imagined, and which was the land of promise for all that. In this she moved and had her being. And she extended it to her duties. She was curiously happy and absorbed. She had not to strive out of herself to do her work. The doing came from within her without call or command. It was a delicious outflow, like sunshine, the activity that flowed from her and put her tasks to rights.

Bachmann sat busily thinking. He would have to get all his plans ready. He must write to his mother, and she must send him money to Paris. He would go to Paris, and from thence, quickly, to America. It had to be done. He must make all preparations. The dangerous part was the getting into France. He thrilled in anticipation. During the day he would need a time-table of the trains going to Paris—he would need to think. It gave him delicious pleasure, using all his wits. It seemed such an adventure.

This one day, and he would escape then into freedom. What an agony of need he had for absolute, imperious freedom. He had won to his own being, in himself and Emilie, he had drawn the stigma from his shame, he was beginning to be himself. And now he wanted madly to be free to go on. A home, his work, and absolute freedom to move and to be, in her, with her, this was his passionate desire. He thought in a kind of ecstasy, living an hour of painful intensity.

Suddenly he heard voices, and a tramping of feet. His heart gave a great leap, then went still. He was taken. He had known all along. A complete silence filled his body and soul, a silence like death, a suspension of life and sound. He stood motionless in the bedroom, in perfect suspension.

Emilie was busy passing swiftly about the kitchen preparing the children's breakfasts when she heard the tramp of feet and the voice of the Baron. The latter had come in from the garden, and was wearing an old green linen suit. He was a man of middle stature, quick, finely made, and of whimsical charm. His right hand had been shot in the Franco-Prussian war, and now, as always when he was much agitated, he shook it down at his side, as if it hurt. He was talking rapidly to a young, stiff ober-leutnant. Two private soldiers stood bearishly in the doorway.

Emilie, shocked out of herself, stood pale and erect, recoiling.

"Yes, if you think so, we can look," the Baron was hastily and irascibly saying.

"Emilie," he said, turning to the girl, "did you put a post card to the mother of this Bachmann in the box last evening?"

Emilie stood erect and did not answer.

"Yes?" said the Baron sharply.

"Yes, Herr Baron," replied Emilie, neutral.

The Baron's wounded hand shook rapidly in exasperation. The lieutenant drew himself up still more stiffly. He was right.

"And do you know anything of the fellow?" asked the Baron looking at her with his blazing, greyish-golden eyes. The girl looked back at him steadily, dumb, but her whole soul naked before him. For two seconds he looked at her in silence. Then in silence, ashamed and furious, he turned away.

"Go up!" he said, with his fierce, peremptory command, to the young officer.

The lieutenant gave his order, in military cold confidence, to the soldiers. They all tramped across the hall. Emilie stood motionless, her life suspended.

The Baron marched swiftly upstairs and down the corridor, the lieutenant and the common soldiers followed. The Baron flung open the door of Emilie's room, and looked at Bachmann, who stood watching, standing in shirt and trousers beside the bed, fronting the door. He was perfectly still. His eyes met the furious, blazing look of the Baron. The latter shook his wounded hand, and then went still. He looked into the eyes of the soldier, steadily. He saw the same naked soul exposed, as if he looked really into the *man*. And the man was helpless, the more helpless for his singular nakedness.

"Ha!" he exclaimed impatiently, turning to the approaching lieutenant.

The latter appeared in the doorway. Quickly his eyes travelled over the bare-footed youth. He recognised him as his object. He gave the brief command to dress.

Bachmann turned round for his clothes. He was very still, silent in himself. He was in an abstract, motionless world. That the two gentlemen and the two soldiers stood watching him, he scarcely realised. They could not see him.

Soon he was ready. He stood at attention. But only the shell of his body was at attention. A curious silence, a blankness, like something eternal, possessed him. He remained true to himself.

The lieutenant gave the order to march. The little procession went down the stairs with careful, respectful tread, and passed through the hall to the kitchen. There Emilie stood with her face uplifted, motionless and expressionless. Bachmann did not look at her. They knew each other. They were themselves. Then the little file of men passed out into the courtyard.

The Baron stood in the doorway watching the four figures in uniform pass through the chequered shadows under the lime trees. Bachmann was walking neutralised, as if he were not there. The lieutenant went brittle and long, the two soldiers lumbered beside. They passed out into the sunny morning, growing smaller, going towards the barracks.

The Baron turned into the kitchen. Emilie was cutting bread.

"So he stayed the night here?" he said.

The girl looked at him, scarcely seeing. She was too much herself. The Baron saw the dark, naked soul of her body in her unseeing eyes.

"What were you going to do?" he asked.

"He was going to America," she replied, in a still voice.

"Pah! You should have sent him straight back," fired the Baron.

Emilie stood at his bidding, untouched.

"He's done for now," he said.

But he could not bear the dark, deep nakedness of her eyes, that scarcely changed under this suffering.

"Nothing but a fool," he repeated, going away in agitation, and preparing himself for what he could do.

DAUGHTERS OF THE VICAR

I

MR. LINDLEY was first vicar of Aldecross. The cottages of this tiny hamlet had nestled in peace since their beginning, and the country folk had crossed the lanes and farm-land, two or three miles, to the parish church at Greymeed, on the bright Sunday mornings.

But when the pits were sunk, blank rows of dwellings started up beside the high roads, and a new population, skimmed from the floating scum of workmen, was filled in, the cottages and the country people almost obliterated.

To suit the convenience of these new collier-inhabitants, a church must be built at Aldecross. There was not too much money. And so the little building crouched like a humped stone-and-mortar mouse, with two little turrets at the west corners for ears, in the fields near the cottages and the apple trees, as far as possible from the dwellings down the high road. It had an uncertain, timid look about it. And so they planted big-leaved ivy, to hide its shrinking newness. So that now the little church stands buried in its greenery, stranded and sleeping among the fields, while the brick houses elbow nearer and nearer, threatening to crush it down. It is already obsolete.

The Reverend Ernest Lindley, aged twenty-seven, and newly married, came from his curacy in Suffolk to take charge of his church. He was just an ordinary young man, who had been to Cambridge and taken orders. His wife was a self-assured young woman, daughter of a Cambridgeshire rector. Her father had spent the whole of his thousand a year, so that Mrs. Lindley had nothing of her own. Thus the young married people came to Aldecross to live on a stipend of about a hundred and twenty pounds, and to keep up a superior position.

They were not very well received by the new, raw, dis-affected population of colliers. Being accustomed to farm labourers, Mr. Lindley had considered himself as belonging indisputably to the upper or ordering classes. He had to be humble to the county families, but still, he was of their kind, whilst the common people were something different. He had no doubts of himself.

He found, however, that the collier population refused to accept this arrangement. They had no use for him in their lives, and they told him so, callously. The women merely said: "they were throng," or else: "Oh, it's no good you coming here, we're Chapel." The men were quite good-humoured so long as he did not touch them too nigh, they were cheerfully contemptuous of him, with a preconceived contempt he was powerless against.

At last, passing from indignation to silent resentment, even, if he dared have acknowledged it, to conscious hatred of the majority of his flock, and unconscious hatred of himself, he confined his activities to a narrow round of cottages, and he had to submit. He had no particular character, having always depended on his position in society to give him position among men. Now he was so poor, he had no social standing even among the common vulgar tradespeople of the district, and he had not the nature nor the wish to make his society agree-able to them, nor the strength to impose himself where he would have liked to be recognised. He dragged on, pale and miserable and neutral.

At first his wife raged with mortification. She took on airs and used a high hand. But her income was too small, the wrestling with tradesmen's bills was too pitiful, she only met with general, callous ridicule when she tried to be impressive.

Wounded to the quick of her pride, she found herself isolated in an indifferent, callous population. She raged in-doors and out. But soon she learned that she must pay too heavily for her outdoor rages, and then she only raged within the walls of the rectory. There her feeling was so strong that she frightened herself. She saw herself hating her husband, and she knew that, unless she were careful, she would smash her form of life and bring catastrophe upon him and upon herself. So in very fear she went quiet. She hid, bitter and beaten by fear, behind the only shelter she had in the world, her gloomy, poor parsonage.

Children were born one every year; almost mechanically, she continued to perform her maternal duty, which was forced upon her. Gradually, broken by the suppressing of her violent anger and misery and disgust, she became an invalid and took to her couch.

The children grew up healthy, but unwarmed and rather rigid. Their father and mother educated them at home, made them very proud and very genteel, put them definitely and cruelly in the upper classes, apart from the vulgar around them. So they lived quite isolated. They were good-looking, and had that curiously clean, semi-transparent look of the genteel, isolated and poor.

Gradually Mr. and Mrs. Lindley lost all hold on life, and spent their hours, weeks and years merely haggling to make ends meet, and bitterly repressing and pruning their children into gentility, urging them to ambition, weighting them with duty. On Sunday morning the whole family, except the mother, went down the lane to church, the long-legged girls in skimpy frocks, the boys in black coats and long, grey, un-fitting trousers. They passed by their father's parishioners with mute clear faces, childish mouths closed in pride that was like a doom to them, and childish eyes already unseeing. Miss Mary, the eldest, was the leader. She was a long, slim thing with a fine profile and a proud, pure look of submission to a high fate. Miss Louisa, the second, was short and plump and obstinate-looking. She had more enemies than ideals. She looked after the lesser children, Miss Mary after the elder. The collier children watched the pale, distinguished procession of the vicar's family pass mutely by, and they were impressed by the air of gentility and distance, they made mock of the trousers of the small sons, they felt inferior in themselves, and hate stirred their hearts.

In her time, Miss Mary received as governess a few little daughters of tradesmen; Miss Louisa managed the house and went among her father's church-goers, giving lessons on the piano to the colliers' daughters at thirteen shillings for twenty-six lessons.

II

One winter morning, when his daughter Mary was about twenty years old, Mr. Lindley, a thin, unobtrusive figure in his black overcoat and his wideawake, went down into Aldecross with a packet of white papers under his arm. He was delivering the parish almanacs.

A rather pale, neutral man of middle age, he waited while the train thumped over the level-crossing, going up to the pit which rattled busily just along the line. A wooden-legged man hobbled to open the gate, Mr. Lindley passed on. Just at his left hand, below the road and the railway, was the red roof of a cottage, showing through the bare twigs of apple trees. Mr. Lindley passed round the low wall, and descended the worn steps that led from the highway down to the cottage which crouched darkly and quietly away below the rumble of passing trains and the clank of coal-carts, in a quiet little underworld of its own. Snowdrops with tight-shut buds were hanging very still under the bare currant bushes.

The clergyman was just going to knock when he heard a clinking noise, and turning saw through the open door of a black shed just behind him an elderly woman in a black lace cap stooping among reddish big cans, pouring a very bright liquid into a tundish. There was a smell of paraffin. The woman put down her can, took the tundish and laid it on a shelf, then rose with a tin bottle. Her eyes met those of the clergyman.

"Oh, is it you, Mr. Lin'ley!" she said, in a complaining tone. "Go in."

The minister entered the house. In the hot kitchen sat a big, elderly man with a great grey beard, taking snuff. He grunted in a deep, muttering voice, telling the minister to sit down, and then took no more notice of him, but stared vacantly into the fire. Mr. Lindley waited.

The woman came in, the ribbons of her black lace cap, or bonnet, hanging on her shawl. She was of medium stature, everything about her was tidy. She went up a step out of the kitchen, carrying the paraffin-tin. Feet were heard entering the room up the step. It was a little haberdashery shop, with parcels on the shelves of the walls, a big, old-fashioned sewing-machine with tailor's work lying round it, in the open space. The woman went behind the counter, gave the child who had entered the paraffin-bottle, and took from her a jug.

"My mother says shall yer put it down," said the child, and she was gone. The woman wrote in a book, then came into the kitchen with her jug. The husband, a very large man, rose and brought more coal to the already hot fire. He moved slowly and sluggishly. Already he was going dead; being a tailor, his large form had become an encumbrance to him. In his youth he had been a great dancer and boxer. Now he was taciturn, and inert. The minister had nothing to say, so he sought for his phrases. But John Durant took no notice, existing silent and dull.

Mrs. Durant spread the cloth. Her husband poured himself beer into a mug, and began to smoke and drink.

"Shall you have some?" he growled through his beard at the clergyman, looking slowly from the man to the jug, capable of this one idea.

"No, thank you," replied Mr. Lindley, though he would have liked some beer. He must set the example in a drinking parish.

"We need a drop to keep us going," said Mrs. Durant.

She had rather a complaining manner. The clergyman sat on uncomfortably while she laid the table for the half-past ten lunch. Her husband drew up to eat. She remained in her little round arm-chair by the fire.

She was a woman who would have liked to be easy in her life, but to whose lot had fallen a rough and turbulent family, and a slothful husband who did not care what became of himself or anybody. So, her rather good-looking square face was peevish, she had that air of having been compelled all her life to serve unwillingly, and to control where she did not want to control. There was about her, too, that masterful aplomb of a woman who has brought up and ruled her sons: but even them she had ruled unwillingly. She had enjoyed managing her little haberdanshery shop, riding in the carrier's cart to Nottingham, going through the big warehouses to buy her goods. But the fret of managing her sons she did not like. Only she loved her youngest boy, because he was her last, and she saw herself free.

This was one of the houses the clergyman visited occasionally. Mrs. Durant, as part of her regulation, had brought up all her sons in the Church. Not that she had any religion. Only, it was what she was used to. Mr. Durant was without religion. He read the fervently evangelical *Life of John Wesley* with a curious pleasure, getting from it a satisfaction as from the warmth of the fire, or a glass of brandy. But he cared no more about John Wesley, in fact, than about John Milton, of whom he had never heard.

Mrs. Durant took her chair to the table.

"I don't feel like eating," she sighed.

"Why—aren't you well?" asked the clergyman, patronising.

"It isn't that," she sighed. She sat with shut, straight mouth. "I don't know what's going to become of us."

But the clergyman had ground himself down so long that he could not easily sympathise.

"Have you any trouble?" he asked.

"Ay, have I any trouble!" cried the elderly woman. "I shall end my days in the workhouse."

The minister waited unmoved. What could she know of poverty in her little house of plenty!

"I hope not," he said.

"And the one lad as I wanted to keep by me——" she lamented.

The minister listened without sympathy, quite neutral.

"And the lad as would have been a support to my old age! What is going to become of us?" she said.

The clergyman, justly, did not believe in the cry of poverty, but wondered what had become of the son.

"Has anything happened to Alfred?" he asked.

"We've got word he's gone for a Queen's sailor," she said sharply.

"He has joined the Navy!" exclaimed Mr. Lindley. "I think he could scarcely have done better—to serve his Queen and country on the sea . . ."

"He is wanted to serve *me*," she cried. "And I wanted my lad at home."

Alfred was her baby, her last, whom she had allowed herself the luxury of spoiling.

"You will miss him," said Mr. Lindley, "that is certain. But this is no regrettable step for him to have taken—on the contrary."

"That's easy for you to say, Mr. Lindley," she replied tartly. "Do you think I want my lad climbing ropes at another man's bidding, like a monkey——"

"There is no *dishonour*, surely, in serving in the Navy?"

"Dishonour this dishonour that," cried the angry old woman. "He goes and makes a slave of himself, and he'll rue it."

Her angry, scornful impatience nettled the clergyman, and silenced him for some moments.

"I do not see," he retorted at last, white at the gills and inadequate, "that the Queen's service is any more to be called slavery than working in a mine."

"At home he was at home, and his own master. *I* know he'll find a difference."

"It may be the making of him," said the clergyman. "It will take him away from bad companionship and drink."

Some of the Durants' sons were notorious drinkers, and Alfred was not quite steady.

"And why indeed shouldn't he have his glass?" cried the mother. "He picks no man's pocket to pay for it!"

The clergyman stiffened at what he thought was an allusion to his own profession, and his unpaid bills.

"With all due consideration, I am glad to hear he has joined the Navy," he said.

"Me with my old age coming on, and his father working very little! I'd thank you to be glad about something else besides that, Mr. Lindley."

The woman began to cry. Her husband, quite impassive, finished his lunch of meat-pie, and drank some beer. Then he turned to the fire, as if there were no one in the room but himself.

"I shall respect all men who serve God and their country on the sea, Mrs. Durant," said the clergyman stubbornly.

"That is very well, when they're not your sons who are doing the dirty work. It makes a difference," she replied tartly.

"I should be proud if one of my sons were to enter the Navy."

"Ay—well—we're not all of us made alike——"

The minister rose. He put down a large folded paper.

"I've brought the almanac," he said.

Mrs. Durant unfolded it.

"I do like a bit of colour in things," she said, petulantly.

The clergyman did not reply.

"There's that envelope for the organist's fund——" said the old woman, and rising, she took the thing from the mantelpiece, went into the shop, and returned sealing it up.

"Which is all I can afford," she said.

Mr. Lindley took his departure, in his pocket the envelope containing Mrs. Durant's offering for Miss Louisa's services. He went from door to door delivering the almanacs, in dull routine. Jaded with the monotony of the business, and with the repeated effort of greeting half-known people, he felt barren and rather irritable. At last he returned home.

In the dining-room was a small fire. Mrs. Lindley, growing

very stout, lay on her couch. The vicar carved the cold mutton: Miss Louisa, short and plump and rather flushed, came in from the kitchen; Miss Mary, dark, with a beautiful white brow and grey eyes, served the vegetables; the children chattered a little, but not exuberantly. The very air seemed starved.

"I went to the Durants," said the vicar, as he served out small portions of mutton; "it appears Alfred has run away to join the Navy."

"Do him good," came the rough voice of the invalid.

Miss Louisa, attending to the youngest child, looked up in protest.

"Why has he done that?" asked Mary's low, musical voice.

"He wanted some excitement, I suppose," said the vicar. "Shall we say grace?"

The children were arranged, all bent their heads, grace was pronounced, at the last word every face was being raised to go on with the interesting subject.

"He's just done the right thing, for once," came the rather deep voice of the mother; "save him from becoming a drunken sot, like the rest of them."

"They're not *all* drunken, mama," said Miss Louisa, stubbornly.

"It's no fault of their upbringing if they're not. Walter Durant is a standing disgrace."

"As I told Mrs. Durant," said the vicar, eating hungrily, "it is the best thing he could have done. It will take him away from temptation during the most dangerous years of his life— how old is he—nineteen?"

"Twenty," said Miss Louisa.

"Twenty!" repeated the vicar. "It will give him wholesome discipline and set before him some sort of standard of duty and honour—nothing could have been better for him. But——"

"We shall miss him from the choir," said Miss Louisa, as if taking opposite sides to her parents.

"That is as it may be," said the vicar. "I prefer to know he is safe in the Navy than running the risk of getting into bad ways here."

"Was he getting into bad ways?" asked the stubborn Miss Louisa.

"You know, Louisa, he wasn't quite what he used to be,"

said Miss Mary gently and steadily. Miss Louisa shut her rather heavy jaw sulkily. She wanted to deny it, but she knew it was true.

For her he had been a laughing, warm lad, with something kindly and something rich about him. He had made her feel warm. It seemed the days would be colder since he had gone.

"Quite the best thing he could do," said the mother with emphasis.

"I think so," said the vicar. "But his mother was almost abusive because I suggested it."

He spoke in an injured tone.

"What does she care for her children's welfare?" said the invalid. "Their wages is all her concern."

"I suppose she wanted him at home with her," said Miss Louisa.

"Yes, she did—at the expense of his learning to be a drunkard like the rest of them," retorted her mother.

"George Durant doesn't drink," defended her daughter.

"Because he got burned so badly when he was nineteen—in the pit—and that frightened him. The Navy is a better remedy than that, at least."

"Certainly," said the vicar. "Certainly."

And to this Miss Louisa agreed. Yet she could not but feel angry that he had gone away for so many years. She herself was only nineteen.

III

It happened when Miss Mary was twenty-three years old that Mr. Lindley was very ill. The family was exceedingly poor at the time, such a lot of money was needed, so little was forthcoming. Neither Miss Mary nor Miss Louisa had suitors. What chance had they? They met no eligible young men in Aldecross. And what they earned was a mere drop in a void. The girls' hearts were chilled and hardened with fear of this perpetual, cold penury, this narrow struggle, this horrible nothingness of their lives.

A clergyman had to be found for the church work. It so happened the son of an old friend of Mr. Lindley's was waiting three months before taking up his duties. He would come and officiate, for nothing. The young clergyman was keenly expected. He was not more than twenty-seven, a Master of

Arts of Oxford, had written his thesis on Roman Law. He came of an old Cambridgeshire family, had some private means, was going to take a church in Northamptonshire with a good stipend, and was not married. Mrs. Lindley incurred new debts, and scarcely regretted her husband's illness.

But when Mr. Massy came there was a shock of disappointment in the house. They had expected a young man with a pipe and a deep voice, but with better manners than Sidney, the eldest of the Lindleys. There arrived instead a small, *chétif* man, scarcely larger than a boy of twelve, spectacled, timid in the extreme, without a word to utter at first; yet with a certain inhuman self-sureness.

"What a little abortion!" was Mrs. Lindley's exclamation to herself on first seeing him, in his buttoned-up clerical coat. And for the first time for many days she was profoundly thankful to God that all her children were decent specimens.

He had not normal powers of perception. They soon saw that he lacked the full range of human feelings, but had rather a strong philosophical mind, from which he lived. His body was almost unthinkable, in intellect he was something definite. The conversation at once took a balanced, abstract tone when he participated. There was no spontaneous exclamation, no violent assertion or expression of personal conviction, but all cold, reasonable assertion. This was very hard on Mrs. Lindley. The little man would look at her, after one of her pronouncements, and then give, in his thin voice, his own calculated version, so that she felt as if she were tumbling into thin air through a hole in the flimsy floor on which their conversation stood. It was she who felt a fool. Soon she was reduced to a hardy silence.

Still, at the back of her mind, she remembered that he was an unattached gentleman, who would shortly have an income altogether of six or seven hundred a year. What did the man matter, if there were pecuniary ease! The man was a trifle thrown in. After twenty-two years her sentimentality was ground away, and only the millstone of poverty mattered to her. So she supported the little man as a representative of a decent income.

His most irritating habit was that of a sneering little giggle, all on his own, which came when he perceived or related some illogical absurdity on the part of another person. It was the only form of humour he had. Stupidity in thinking seemed to him exquisitely funny. But any novel was unintelligibly meaningless and dull, and to an Irish sort of humour he listened curiously, examining it like mathematics, or else simply not hearing. In normal human relationship he was not there. Quite unable to take part in simple everyday talk, he padded silently round the house, or sat in the dining-room looking nervously from side to side, always apart in a cold, rarefied little world of his own. Sometimes he made an ironic remark, that did not seem humanly relevant, or he gave his little laugh, like a sneer. He had to defend himself and his own insufficiency. And he answered questions grudgingly, with a yes or no, because he did not see their import and was nervous. It seemed to Miss Louisa he scarcely distinguished one person from another, but that he liked to be near to her, or to Miss Mary, for some sort of contact which stimulated him unknown.

Apart from all this, he was the most admirable workman. He was unremittingly shy, but perfect in his sense of duty: as far as he could conceive Christianity, he was a perfect Christian. Nothing that he realised he could do for anyone did he leave undone, although he was so incapable of coming into contact with another being that he could not proffer help. Now he attended assiduously to the sick man, investigated all the affairs of the parish or the church which Mr. Lindley had in control, straightened out accounts, made lists of the sick and needy, padded round with help and to see what he could do. He heard of Mrs. Lindley's anxiety about her sons, and began to investigate means of sending them to Cambridge. His kindness almost frightened Miss Mary. She honoured it so, and yet she shrank from it. For, in it all Mr. Massy seemed to have no sense of any person, any human being whom he was helping: he only realised a kind of mathematical working out, solving of given situations, a calculated well-doing. And it was as if he had accepted the Christian tenents as axioms. His religion consisted in what his scrupulous, abstract mind approved of.

Seeing his acts, Miss Mary must respect and honour him. In consequence she must serve him. To this she had to force herself, shuddering and yet desirous, but he did not perceive it. She accompanied him on his visiting in the parish, and whilst she was cold with admiration for him, often she was touched with pity for the little padding figure with bent shoulders, buttoned up to the chin in his overcoat. She was a handsome, calm girl, tall, with a beautiful repose. Her clothes were poor, and she wore a black silk scarf, having no furs. But she was a lady. As the people saw her walking down Aldecross beside Mr. Massy they said:

"My word, Miss Mary's got a catch. Did you ever see such a sickly little shrimp!"

She knew they were talking so, and it made her heart grow hot against them, and she drew herself as it were protectively towards the little man beside her. At any rate, she could see and give honour to his genuine goodness.

He could not walk fast, or far.

"You have not been well?" she asked, in her dignified way.

"I have an internal trouble."

He was not aware of her slight shudder. There was silence, whilst she bowed to recover her composure, to resume her gentle manner towards him.

He was fond of Miss Mary. She had made it a rule of hospitality that he should always be escorted by herself or by her sister on his visits in the parish, which were not many. But some mornings she was engaged. Then Miss Louisa took her place. It was no good Miss Louisa's trying to adopt to Mr. Massy an attitude of queenly service. She was unable to regard him save with aversion. When she saw him from behind, thin and bent-shouldered, looking like sickly lad of thirteen, she disliked him exceedingly, and felt a desire to put him out of existence. And yet a deeper justice in Mary made Louisa humble before her sister.

They were going to see Mr. Durant, who was paralysed and not expected to live. Miss Louisa was crudely ashamed at being admitted to the cottage in company with the little clergyman.

Mrs. Durant was, however, much quieter in the face of her real trouble.

"How is Mr. Durant?" asked Louisa.

"He is no different—and we don't expect him to be," was the reply. The little clergyman stood looking on.

They went upstairs. The three stood for some time looking at the bed, at the grey head of the old man on the pillow, the grey beard over the sheet. Miss Louisa was shocked and afraid.

"It is so dreadful," she said, with a shudder.

"It is how I always thought it would be," replied Mrs. Durant.

Then Miss Louisa was afraid of her. The two women were uneasy, waiting for Mr. Massy to say something. He stood, small and bent, too nervous to speak.

"Has he any understanding?" he asked at length.

"Maybe," said Mrs. Durant. "Can you hear, John?" she asked loudly. The dull blue eye of the inert man looked at her feebly.

"Yes, he understands," said Mrs. Durant to Mr. Massy. Except for the dull look in his eyes, the sick man lay as if dead. The three stood in silence. Miss Louisa was obstinate but heavy-hearted under the load of unlivingness. It was Mr. Massy who kept her there in discipline. His non-human will dominated them all.

Then they heard a sound below, a man's footsteps, and a man's voice called subduedly:

"Are you upstairs, mother?"

Mrs. Durant started and moved to the door. But already a quick, firm step was running up the stairs.

"I'm a bit early, mother," a troubled voice said, and on the landing they saw the form of the sailor. His mother came and clung to him. She was suddenly aware that she needed something to hold on to. He put his arms round her, and bent over her, kissing her.

"He's not gone, mother?" he asked anxiously, struggling to control his voice.

Miss Louisa looked away from the mother and son who stood together in the gloom on the landing. She could not bear it that she and Mr. Massy should be there. The latter stood nervously, as if ill at ease before the emotion that was running. He was a witness nervous, unwilling, but dispassionate. To Miss Louisa's hot heart it seemed all, all wrong that they should be there.

Mrs. Durant entered the bedroom, her face wet.

"There's Miss Louisa and the vicar," she said, out of voice and quavering.

Her son, red-faced and slender, drew himself up to salute. But Miss Louisa held out her hand. Then she saw his hazel eyes recognise her for a moment, and his small white teeth showed in a glimpse of the greeting she used to love. She was covered with confusion. He went round to the bed; his boots clicked on the plaster floor, he bowed with dignity.

"How are you, dad?" he said, laying his hand on the sheet, faltering. But the old man stared fixedly and unseeing. The son stood perfectly still for a few minutes, then slowly recoiled. Miss Louisa saw the fine outline of his breast, under the sailor's blue blouse, as his chest began to heave.

"He doesn't know me," he said, turning to his mother. He gradually went white.

"No, my boy!" cried the mother, pitiful, lifting her face. And suddenly she put her face against his shoulder, he was stooping down to her, holding her against him, and she cried aloud for a moment or two. Miss Louisa saw his sides heaving, and heard the sharp hiss of his breath. She turned away, tears streaming down her face. The father lay inert upon the white bed, Mr. Massy looked queer and obliterated, so little now that the sailor with his sun-burned skin was in the room. He stood waiting. Miss Louisa wanted to die, she wanted to have done. She dared not turn round again to look.

"Shall I offer a prayer?" came the frail voice of the clergyman, and all kneeled down.

Miss Louisa was frightened of the inert man upon the bed. Then she felt a flash of fear of Mr. Massy, hearing his thin, detached voice. And then, calmed, she looked up. On the far side of the bed were the head of the mother and son, the one in the black lace cap, with the small white nape of the neck beneath, the other, with brown, sun-scorched hair too close and wiry to allow of a parting, and neck tanned firm, bowed as if unwillingly. The great grey beard of the old man did not move, the prayer continued. Mr. Massy prayed with a pure lucidity that they all might conform to the higher Will. He was like something that dominated the bowed heads, something dispassionate that governed them inexorably. Miss Louisa was afraid of him. And she was bound, during the course of the prayer, to have a little reverence for him. It was like a foretaste of inexorable, cold death, a taste of pure justice.

That evening she talked to Mary of the visit. Her heart, her veins were possessed by the thought of Alfred Durant as he held his mother in his arms; then the break in his voice, as she remembered it again and again, was like a flame through her; and she wanted to see his face more distinctly in her mind, ruddy with the sun, and his golden-brown eyes, kind and careless, strained now with a natural fear, the fine nose tanned hard by the sun, the mouth that could not help smiling at her. And it went through her with pride, to think of his figure, a fine jet of life.

"He is a handsome lad," said she to Miss Mary, as if he had not been a year older than herself. Underneath was the deeper dread, almost hatred, of the inhuman being of Mr. Massy. She felt she must protect herself and Alfred from him.

"When I felt Mr. Massy there," she said, "I almost hated him. What right had he to be there!"

"Surely he has all right," said Miss Mary after a pause. "He is *really* a Christian."

"He seems to me nearly an imbecile," said Miss Louisa.

Miss Mary, quiet and beautiful, was silent for a moment:

"Oh, no," she said. "Not *imbecile*——"

"Well then—he reminds me of a six months' child—or a five months' child—as if he didn't have time to get developed enough before he was born."

"Yes," said Miss Mary, slowly. "There is something lacking. But there is something wonderful in him: and he is really *good*——"

"Yes," said Miss Louisa, "it doesn't seem right that he should be. What right has *that* to be called goodness!"

"But it *is* goodness," persisted Mary. Then she added, with a laugh: "And come, you wouldn't deny that as well."

There was a doggedness in her voice. She went about very quietly. In her soul, she knew what was going to happen. She knew that Mr. Massy was stronger than she, and that she must submit to what he was. Her physical self was prouder, stronger than he, her physical self disliked and despised him. But she was in the grip of his moral, mental being. And she felt the days allotted out to her. And her family watched.

IV

A few days after, old Mr. Durant died. Miss Louisa saw Alfred once more, but he was stiff before her now, treating her not like a person, but as if she were some sort of will in command and he a separate, distinct will waiting in front of her. She had never felt such utter steel-plate separation from anyone. It puzzled her and frightened her. What had become of him? And she hated the military discipline—she was antagonistic to it. Now he was not himself. He was the will which obeys set over against the will which commands. She hesitated over accepting this. He had put himself out of her range. He had ranked himself inferior, subordinate to her. And that was how he could get away from her, that was how he would avoid all connection with her: by fronting her impersonally from the opposite camp, by taking up the abstract position of an inferior.

She went brooding steadily and sullenly over this, brooding and brooding. Her fierce, obstinate heart could not give way. It clung to its own rights. Sometimes she dismissed him. Why should he, her inferior, trouble her?

Then she relapsed to him, and almost hated him. It was his way of getting out of it. She felt the cowardice of it, his calmly placing her in a superior class, and placing himself inaccessibly apart, in an inferior, as if she, the sentient woman who was fond of him, did not count. But she was not going to submit. Dogged in her heart she held on to him.

V

In six months' time Miss Mary had married Mr. Massy. There had been no love-making, nobody had made any remark. But everybody was tense and callous with expectation. When one day Mr. Massy asked for Mary's hand, Mr. Lindley started and trembled from the thin, abstract voice of the little man. Mr. Massy was very nervous, but so curiously absolute.

"I shall be very glad," said the vicar, "but of course the decision lies with Mary herself." And his still feeble hand shook as he moved a Bible on his desk.

The small man, keeping fixedly to his idea, padded out of the room to find Miss Mary. He sat a long time by her, while she made some conversation, before he had readiness to speak. She was afraid of what was coming, and sat stiff in apprehension. She felt as if her body would rise and fling him aside. But her spirit quivered and waited. Almost in expectation she waited, almost wanting him. And then she knew he would speak.

"I have already asked Mr. Lindley," said the clergyman, while suddenly she looked with aversion at his little knees, "if he would consent to my proposal." He was aware of his own disadvantage, but his will was set.

She went cold as she sat, and impervious, almost as if she had become stone. He waited a moment nervously. He would not persuade her. He himself never even heard persuasion, but pursued his own course. He looked at her, sure of himself, unsure of her, and said:

"Will you become my wife, Mary?"

Still her heart was hard and cold. She sat proudly.

"I should like to speak to mama first," she said.

"Very well," replied Mr. Massy. And in a moment he padded away.

Mary went to her mother. She was cold and reserved.

"Mr. Massy has asked me to marry him, mama," she said. Mrs. Lindley went on staring at her book. She was cramped in her feeling.

"Well, and what did you say?"

They were both keeping calm and cold.

"I said I would speak to you before answering him."

This was equivalent to a question. Mrs. Lindley did not want to reply to it. She shifted her heavy form irritably on the couch. Miss Mary sat calm and straight, with closed mouth.

"Your father thinks it would not be a bad match," said the mother, as if casually.

Nothing more was said. Everybody remained cold and shut-off. Miss Mary did not speak to Miss Louisa, the Reverend Ernest Lindley kept out of sight.

At evening Miss Mary accepted Mr. Massy.

"Yes, I will marry you," she said, with even a little movement of tenderness towards him. He was embarrassed, but satisfied. She could see him making some movement towards her, could feel the male in him, something cold and triumphant, asserting itself. She sat rigid, and waited.

When Miss Louisa knew, she was silent with bitter anger against everybody, even against Mary. She felt her faith wounded. Did the real things to her not matter after all? She wanted to get away. She thought of Mr. Massy. He had some curious power, some unanswerable right. He was a will that they could not controvert. Suddenly a flush started in her. If he had come to her she would have flipped him out of the room. He was never going to touch *her*. And she was glad. She was glad that her blood would rise and exterminate the little man, if he came too near to her, no matter how her judgment was paralysed by him, no matter how he moved in abstract goodness. She thought she was perverse to be glad, but glad she was. "I would just flip him out of the room," she said, and she derived great satisfaction from the open statement. Nevertheless, perhaps she ought still to feel that Mary, on her plane, was a higher being than herself. But then Mary was Mary, and she was Louisa, and that also was inalterable.

Mary, in marrying him, tried to become a pure reason such as he was, without feeling or impulse. She shut herself up, she shut herself rigid against the agonies of shame and the terror of violation which came at first. She would not feel, and she would not feel. She was a pure will acquiescing to him. She elected a certain kind of fate. She would be good and purely just, she would live in a higher freedom than she had ever known, she would be free of mundane care, she was a pure will towards right. She had sold herself, but she had a new freedom. She had got rid of her body. She had sold a lower thing, her body, for a higher thing, her freedom from material things. She considered that she paid for all she got from her husband. So, in kind of independence, she moved proud and free. She had paid with her body: that was henceforward out of consideration. She was glad to be rid of it. She had bought her position in the world—that henceforth was taken for granted. There remained only the direction of her activity towards charity and high-minded living.

She could scarcely bear other people to be present with her and her husband. Her private life was her shame. But then, she could keep it hidden. She lived almost isolated in the rectory of the tiny village miles from the railway. She suffered as if it were an insult to her own flesh, seeing the repulsion which some people felt for her husband, or the special maner they had of treating him, as if he were a "case". But most people were uneasy before him, which restored her pride.

If she had let herself, she would have hated him, hated his padding round the house, his thin voice devoid of human understanding, his bent little shoulders and rather incomplete face that reminded her of an abortion. But rigorously she kept her position. She took care of him and was just to him. There was also a deep, craven fear of him, something slave-like.

There was not much fault to be found with his behaviour. He was scrupulously just and kind according to his lights. But the male in him was cold and self-complete, and utterly domineering. Weak, insufficient little thing as he was, she had not expected this of him. It was something in the bargain she had not understood. It made her hold her head, to keep still. She knew, vaguely, that she was murdering herself. After all, her body was not quite so easy to get rid of. And this manner of disposing of it—ah, sometimes she felt she must rise and bring about death, lift her hand for utter denial of everything, by a general destruction.

He was almost unaware of the conditions about him. He did not fuss in the domestic way, she did as she liked in the house. Indeed, she was a great deal free of him. He would sit obliterated for hours. He was kind, and almost anxiously considerate. But when he considered he was right, his will was just blindly male, like a cold machine. And on most points he was logically right, or he had with him the right of the creed they both accepted. It was so. There was nothing for her to go against.

Then she found herself with child, and felt for the first time horror, afraid before God and man. This also she had to go through—it was the right. When the child arrived, it was a bonny, healthy lad. Her heart hurt in her body, as she took the baby between her hands. The flesh that was trampled and silent in her must speak again in the boy. After all, she had to live—it was not so simple after all. Nothing was finished completely. She looked and looked at the baby, and almost hated it, and suffered an anguish of love for it. She hated it because it made her live again in the flesh, when she *could* not live in the flesh, she could not. She wanted to trample her flesh down, down, extinct, to live in the mind. And now there was this child. It was too cruel, too racking. For she must love the child. Her purpose was broken in two again. She had to become amorphous, purposeless, without real being. As a mother, she was a fragmentary, ignoble thing.

Mr. Massy, blind to everything else in the way of human feeling, became obsessed by the idea of his child. When it arrived, suddenly it filled the whole world of feeling for him. It was his obsession, his terror was for its safety and well-being. It was something new, as if he himself had been born a naked infant, conscious of his own exposure, and full of apprehension. He who had never been aware of anyone else, all his life, now was aware of nothing but the child. Not that he ever played with it, or kissed it, or tended it. He did nothing for it. But it dominated him, it filled, and at the same time emptied his mind. The world was all baby for him.

This his wife must also bear, his question: "What is the reason that he cries?"—his reminder, at the first sound: "Mary, that is the child,"—his restlessness if the feeding-time were five minutes past. She had bargained for this—now she must stand by her bargain.

VI

Miss Louisa, at home in the dingy vicarage, had suffered a great deal over his sister's wedding. Having once begun to cry out against it, during the engagement, she had been silenced by Mary's quiet: "I don't agree with you about him, Louisa, I *want* to marry him." Then Miss Louisa had been angry deep in her heart, and therefore silent. This dangerous state started the change in her. Her own revulsion made her recoil from the hitherto undoubted Mary.

"I'd beg the streets barefoot first," said Miss Louisa, thinking of Mr. Massy.

But evidently Mary could perform a different heroism. So she, Louisa the practical, suddenly felt that Mary, her ideal, was questionable after all. How could she be pure—one cannot be dirty in act and spiritual in being. Louisa distrusted Mary's high spirituality. It was no longer genuine for her. And if Mary were spiritual and misguided, why did not her father protect her? Because of the money. He disliked the whole affair, but he backed away, because of the money. And the mother frankly did not care: her daughters could do as they liked. Her mother's pronouncement:

"Whatever happens to *him*, Mary is safe for life,"—so evidently and shallowly a calculation, incensed Louisa.

"I'd rather be safe in the workhouse," she cried.

"Your father will see to that," replied her mother brutally. This speech, in its directness, so injured Miss Louisa that she hated her mother deep, deep in her heart, and almost hated herself. It was a long time resolving itself out, this hate. But it worked and worked, and at last the young woman said:

"They are wrong—they are all wrong. They have ground out their souls for what isn't worth anything, and there isn't a grain of love in them anywhere. And I *will* have love. They

want us to deny it. They've never found it, so they want to
say it doesn't exist. But I *will* have it. I *will* love—it is my
birthright. I will love the man I marry—that is all I care
about."

So Miss Louisa stood isolated from everybody. She and
Mary had parted over Mr. Massy. In Louisa's eyes, Mary was
degraded, married to Mr. Massy. She could not bear to think
of her lofty, spiritual sister degraded in the body like this.
Mary was wrong, wrong, wrong: she was not superior, she
was flawed, incomplete. The two sisters stood apart. They
still loved each other, they would love each other as long as
they lived. But they had parted ways. A new solitariness
came over the obstinate Louisa, and her heavy jaw set stubbornly. She was going on her own way. But which way? She
was quite alone, with a blank world before her. How could
she be said to have any way? Yet she had her fixed will to
love, to have the man she loved.

VII

When her boy was three years old, Mary had another baby,
a girl. The three years had gone by monotonously. They might
have been an eternity, they might have been brief as a sleep.
She did not know. Only, there was always a weight on top of
her, something that pressed down her life. The only thing
that had happened was that Mr. Massy had had an operation.
He was always exceedingly fragile. His wife had soon learned
to attend to him mechanically, as part of her duty.

But this third year, after the baby girl had been born, Mary
felt oppressed and depressed. Christmas drew near: the
gloomy, unleavened Christmas of the rectory, where all the
days were of the same dark fabric. And Mary was afraid. It
was as if the darkness were coming upon her.

"Edward, I should like to go home for Christmas," she said,
and a certain terror filled her as she spoke.

"But you can't leave baby," said her husband, blinking.

"We can all go."

He thought, and stared in his collective fashion.

"Why do you wish to go?" he asked.

"Because I need a change. A change would do me good, and
it would be good for the milk."

He heard the will in his wife's voice. and was at a loss.

Her language was unintelligible to hm. But somehow he felt
that Mary was set upon it. And while she was breeding, either
about to have a child, or nursing, he regarded her as a special
sort of being.

"Wouldn't it hurt baby to take her by the train?" he said.

"No," replied the mother, "why should it?"

They went. When they were in the train it began to snow.
From the window of his first-class carriage the little clergyman watched the big flakes sweep by, like a blind drawn
across the country. He was obsessed by thought of the baby,
and afraid of the draughts of the carriage.

"Sit right in the corner," he said to his wife, "and hold baby
close back."

She moved at his bidding, and stared out of the window.
His eternal presence was like an iron weight on her brain.
But she was going partially to escape for a few days.

"Sit on the other side, Jack," said the father. "It is less
draughty. Come to this window."

He watched the boy in anxiety. But his children were the
only beings in the world who took not the slightest notice of
him.

"Look, mother, look!" cried the boy. "They fly right in my
face"—he meant the snowflakes.

"Come into this corner," repeated his father, out of another
world.

"He's jumped on this one's back, mother, an' they're riding
to the bottom!" cried the boy, jumping with glee.

"Tell him to come on this side," the little man bade his
wife.

"Jack, kneel on this cushion," said the mother, putting her
white hand on the place.

They boy slid over in silence to the place she indicated,
waited still for a moment, then almost deliberately, stridently
cried:

"Look at all those in the corner, mother, making a heap,"
and he pointed to the cluster of snowflakes with finger pressed
dramatically on the pane, and he turned to his mother a bit
ostentatiously.

"All in a heap!" she said.

He had seen her face, and had her response, and he was
somewhat assured. Vaguely uneasy, he was reassured if he
could win her attention.

They arrived at the vicarage at half-past two, not having had lunch.

"How are you, Edward?" said Mr. Lindley, trying on his side to be fatherly. But he was always in a false position with his son-in-law, frustrated before him, therefore, as much as possible, he shut his eyes and ears to him. The vicar was looking thin and pale and ill-nourished. He had gone quite grey. He was, however, still haughty; but, since the growing-up of his children, it was a brittle haughtiness, that might break at any moment and leave the vicar only an impoverished, pitiable figure. Mrs. Lindley took all the notice of her daughter, and of the children. She ignored her son-in-law. Miss Louisa was clucking and laughing and rejoicing over the baby. Mr. Massy stood aside, a bent, persistent little figure.

"Oh a pretty!—a little pretty! oh a cold little pretty come in a railway train!" Miss Louisa was cooing to the infant, crouching on the hearth-rug, opening the white woollen wraps and exposing the child to the fireglow.

"Mary," said the little clergyman, "I think it would be better to give baby a warm bath; she may take cold."

"I think it is not necessary," said the mother, coming and closing her hand judiciously over the rosy feet and hands of the mite. "She is not chilly."

"Not a bit," cried Miss Louisa. "She's not caught cold."

"I'll go and bring her flannels," said Mr. Massy, with one idea.

"I can bath her in the kitchen then," said Mary, in an altered, cold tone.

"You can't, the girl is scrubbing there," said Miss Louisa. "Besides, she doesn't want a bath at this time of day."

"She'd better have one," said Mary, quietly, out of submission. Miss Louisa's gorge rose, and she was silent. When the little man padded down with the flannels on his arm, Mrs. Lindley asked:

"Hadn't *you* better take a hot bath, Edward?"

But the sarcasm was lost on the little clergyman. He was absorbed in the preparations round the baby.

The room was dull and threadbare, and the snow outside seemed fairy-like by comparision, so white on the lawn and tufted on the bushes. Indoors the heavy pictures hung obscurely on the walls, everything was dingy with gloom.

Except in the fireglow, where they had laid the bath on the

hearth. Mrs. Massy, her black hair always smoothly coiled and queenly, kneeled by the bath, wearing a rubber apron, and holding the kicking child. Her husband stood holding the towels and the flannels to warm. Louisa, too cross to share in the joy of the baby's bath, was laying the table. The boy was hanging on the door-knob, wrestling with it to get out. His father looked round.

"Come away from the door, Jack," he said ineffectually. Jack tugged harder at the knob as if he did not hear. Mr. Massy blinked at him.

"He must come away from the door, Mary," he said. "There will be a draught if it is opened."

"Jack, come away from the door, dear," said the mother, dexterously turning the shiny wet baby on to her towelled knee, then glancing round: "Go and tell Auntie Louisa about the train."

Louisa, also afraid to open the door, was watching the scene on the hearth. Mr. Massy stood holding the baby's flannel, as if assisting at some ceremonial. If everybody had not been subduedly angry, it would have been ridiculous.

"I want to see out of the window," Jack said. His father turned hastily.

"Do *you* mind lifting him on to a chair, Louisa," said Mary hastily. The father was too delicate.

When the baby was flannelled, Mr. Massy went upstairs and returned with four pillows, which he set in the fender to warm. Then he stood watching the mother feed her child, obsessed by the idea of his infant.

Louisa went on with her preparations for the meal. She could not have told why she was so sullenly angry. Mrs. Lindley, as usual, lay silently watching.

Mary carried her child upstairs, followed by her husband with the pillows. After a while he came down again.

"What is Mary doing? Why doesn't she come down to eat?" asked Mrs. Lindley.

"She is staying with baby. The room is rather cold. I will ask the girl to put in a fire." He was going absorbedly to the door.

"But Mary has had nothing to eat. It is *she* who will catch cold," said the mother, exasperated.

Mr. Massy seemed as if he did not hear. Yet he looked at his mother-in-law, and answered:

"I will take her something."

He went out. Mrs. Lindley shifted on her couch with anger. Miss Louisa glowered. But no one said anything, because of the money that came to the vicarage from Mr. Massy.

Louisa went upstairs. Her sister was sitting by the bed, reading a scrap of paper.

"Won't you come down and eat?" the younger asked.

"In a moment or two," Mary replied, in a quiet, reserved voice, that forbade anyone to approach her.

It was this that made Miss Louisa most furious. She went downstairs, and announced to her mother:

"I am going out. I may not be home to tea."

VIII

No one remarked on her exit. She put on her fur hat, that the village people knew so well, and the old Norfolk jacket. Louisa was short and plump and plain. She had her mother's heavy jaw, her father's proud brow, and her own grey, brooding eyes that were very beautiful when she smiled. It was true, as the people said, that she looked sulky. Her chief attraction was her glistening, heavy, deep-blonde hair, which shone and gleamed with a richness that was not entirely foreign to her.

"Where am I going?" she said to herself, when she got outside in the snow. She did not hesitate, however, but by mechanical walking found herself descending the hill towards Old Aldecross. In the valley that was black with trees, the colliery breathed in stertorous pants, sending out high conical columns of steam that remained upright, whiter than the snow on the hills, yet shadowy, in the dead air. Louisa would not acknowledge to herself whither she was making her way, till she came to the railway crossing. Then the bunches of snow in the twigs of the apple tree that leaned towards the fence told her she must go and see Mrs. Durant. The tree was in Mrs. Durant's garden.

Alfred was now at home again, living with his mother in the cottage below the road. From the highway hedge, by the railway crossing, the snowy garden sheered down steeply, like the side of a hole, then dropped straight in a wall. In this depth the house was snug, its chimney just level with the road. Miss Louisa descended the stone stairs, and stood below in the little back-yard, in the dimness and the semi-secrecy. A big tree leaned overhead, above the paraffin-hut. Louisa felt secure from all the world down there. She knocked at the open door, then looked round. The tongue of garden narrowing in from the quarry bed was white with snow: she thought of the thick fringes of snowdrops it would show beneath the currant bushes in a month's time. The ragged fringe of pinks hanging over the garden brim behind her was whitened now with snowflakes, that in summer held white blossom to Louisa's face. It was pleasant, she thought, to gather flowers that stooped to one's face from above.

She knocked again. Peeping in, she saw the scarlet glow of the kitchen, red firelight falling on the brick floor and on the bright chintz cushions. It was alive and bright as a peep-show. She crossed the scullery, where still an almanac hung. There was no one about. "Mrs. Durant," called Louisa softly, "Mrs. Durant."

She went up the brick step into the front room, that still had its little shop counter and its bundles of goods, and she called from the stair-foot. Then she knew Mrs. Durant was out.

She went into the yard, to follow the old woman's footsteps up the garden path.

She emerged from the bushes and raspberry canes. There was the whole quarry bed, a wide garden white and dimmed, brindled with dark bushes, lying half submerged. On the left, overhead, the little colliery train rumbled by. Right away at the back was a mass of trees.

Louisa followed the open path, looking from right to left, and then she gave a cry of concern. The old woman was sitting rocking slightly among the ragged snowy cabbages. Louisa ran to her, found her whimpering with little, involuntary cries.

"Whatever have you done?" cried Louisa, kneeling in the snow.

"I've—I've— I was pulling a brussel-sprout stalk—and—oh-h!—something tore inside me. I've had a pain," the old woman wept from shock and suffering, gasping between her whimpers,—"I've had a pain there—a long time—and now—oh—oh!" She panted, pressed her hand on her side, leaned as if she would faint, looking yellow against the snow. Louisa supported her.

"Do you think you could walk now?" she asked.

"Yes," gasped the old woman.

Louisa helped her to her feet.

"Get the cabbage—I want it for Alfred's dinner," panted Mrs. Durant. Louisa picked up the stalk of brussel-sprouts, and with difficulty got the old woman indoors. She gave her brandy, laid her on the couch, saying:

"I'm going to send for a doctor—wait just a minute."

The young woman ran up the steps to the public-house a few yards away. The landlady was astonished to see Miss Louisa.

"Will you send for a doctor at once to Mrs. Durant," she said, with some of her father in her commanding tone.

"Is something the matter?" fluttered the landlady in concern.

Louisa, glancing out up the road, saw the grocer's cart driving to Eastwood. She ran and stopped the man, and told him.

Mrs. Durant lay on the sofa, her face turned away, when the young woman came back.

"Let me put you to bed," Louisa said. Mrs. Durant did not resist.

Louisa knew the ways of the working people. In the bottom drawer of the dresser she found dusters and flannels. With the old pit-flannel she snatched out the oven shelves, wrapped them up, and put them in the bed. From the son's bed she took a blanket, and, running down, set it before the fire. Having undressed the little old woman, Louisa carried her upstairs.

"You'll drop me, you'll drop me!" cried Mrs. Durant.

Louisa did not answer, but bore her burden quickly. She could not light a fire, because there was no fire-place in the bedroom. And the floor was plaster. So she fetched the lamp, and stood it lighted in one corner.

"It will air the room," she said.

"Yes," moaned the old woman.

Louisa ran with more hot flannels, replacing those from the oven shelves. Then she made a bran-bag and laid it on the woman's side. There was a big lump on the side of the abdomen.

"I've felt it coming a long time," moaned the old lady, when the pain was easier, "but I've not said anything; I didn't want to upset our Alfred."

Louisa did not see why "our Alfred" should be spared.

"What time is it?" came the plaintive voice.

"A quarter to four."

"Oh!" wailed the old lady, "he'll be here in half an hour, and no dinner ready for him."

"Let me do it?" said Louisa, gently.

"There's that cabbage—and you'll find the meat in the pantry—and there's an apple-pie you can hot up. But *don't you* do it——!"

"Who will, then?" asked Louisa.

"I don't know," moaned the sick woman, unable to consider.

Louisa did it. The doctor came and gave serious examination. He looked very grave.

"What is it, doctor?" asked the old lady, looking up at him with old, pathetic eyes in which already hope was dead.

"I think you've torn the skin in which a tumour hangs," he replied.

"Ay!" she murmured, and she turned away.

"You see, she may die any minute—and it *may* be swaled away," said the old doctor to Louisa.

The young woman went upstairs again.

"He says the lump may be swaled away, and you may get quite well again," she said.

"Ay!" murmured the old lady. It did not deceive her. Presently she asked:

"Is there a good fire?"

"I think so," answered Louisa.

"He'll want a good fire," the mother said. Louisa attended to it.

Since the death of Durant, the widow had come to church occasionally, and Louisa had been friendly to her. In the girl's heart the purpose was fixed. No man had affected her as Alfred Durant had done, and to that she kept. In her heart, she adhered to him. A natural sympathy existed between her and his rather hard, materialistic mother.

Alfred was the most lovable of the old woman's sons. He had grown up like the rest, however, headstrong and blind to everything but his own will. Like the other boys, he had insisted on going into the pit as soon as he left school, because that was the only way speedily to become a man, level with all the other men. This was a great chagrin to his mother, who would have liked to have this last of her sons a gentleman.

But still he remained constant to her. His feeling for her

was deep and unexpressed. He noticed when she was tired, or when she had a new night-cap. And he bought little things for her occasionally. She was not wise enough to see how much he lived by her.

At the bottom he did not satisfy her, he did not seem manly enough. He liked to read books occasionally, and better still he liked to play the piccolo. It amused her to see his head nod over the instrument as he made an effort to get the right note. It made her fond of him, with tenderness, almost pity, but not with respect. She wanted a man to be fixed, going his own way without knowledge of women. Whereas she knew Alfred depended on her. He sang in the choir because he liked singing. In the summer he worked in the garden, attended to the fowls and pigs. He kept pigeons. He played on Saturday in the cricket or football team. But to her he did not seem the man, the independent man her other boys had been. He was her baby—and whilst she loved him for it, she was a little bit contemptuous of him.

There grew up a little hostility between them. Then he began to drink, as the others had done; but not in their blind, oblivious way. He was a little self-conscious over it. She saw this, and she pitied it in him. She loved him most, but she was not satisfied with him because he was not free of her. He could not quite go his own way.

Then at twenty he ran away and served his time in the Navy. This had made a man of him. He had hated it bitterly, the service, the subordination. For years he fought with himself under the military discipline, for his own self-respect, struggling through blind anger and shame and a cramping sense of inferiority. Out of humiliation and self-hatred he rose into a sort of inner freedom. And his love for his mother, whom he idealised, remained the fact of hope and of belief.

He came home again, nearly thirty years old, but naïve and inexperienced as a boy, only with a silence about him that was new: a sort of dumb humility before life, a fear of living. He was almost quite chaste. A strong sensitiveness had kept him from women. Sexual talk was all very well among men, but somehow it had no application to living women. There were two things for him, the *idea* of women, with which he sometimes debauched himself, and real women, before whom he felt a deep uneasiness, and a need to draw away. He shrank and defended himself from the approach of any woman. And then he felt ashamed. In his innermost soul he felt he was not a man, he was less than the normal man. In Genoa he went with an under-officer to a drinking-house were the cheaper sort of girl came in to look for lovers. He sat there with his glass, the girls looked at him, but they never came to him. He knew that if they did come he could only pay for food and drink for them, because he felt a pity for them, and was anxious lest they lacked good necessities. He could not have gone with one of them; he knew it, and was ashamed, looking with curious envy at the swaggering, easy-passionate Italian whose body went to a woman by instinctive impersonal attraction. They were men, he was not a man. He sat feeling short, feeling like a leper. And he went away imagining sexual scenes between himself and a woman, walking wrapt in this indulgence. But when the ready woman presented herself, the very fact that she was a palpable woman made it impossible for him to touch her. And this incapacity was like a core of rottenness in him.

So several times he went, drunk, with his companions, to the licensed prostitute-houses abroad. But the sordid insignificance of the experience appalled him. It had not been anything really: it meant nothing. He felt as if he were, not physically, but spiritually impotent: not actually impotent, but intrinsically so.

He came home with this secret, never changing burden of his unknown, unbestowed self torturing him. His Navy training left him in perfect physical condition. He was sensible of, and proud of his body. He bathed and used dumb-bells, and kept himself fit. He played cricket and football. He read books and began to hold fixed ideas which he got from the Fabians. He played his piccolo, and was considered an expert. But at the bottom of his soul was always this canker of shame and incompleteness: he was miserable beneath all his healthy cheerfulness, he was uneasy and felt despicable among all his confidence and superiority of ideas. He would have changed with any mere brute, just to be free of himself, to be free of this shame of self-consciousness. He saw some collier lurching straight forward without misgiving, pursuing his own satisfactions, and he envied him. Anything, he would have given for this spontaneity and this blind stupidity which went to its own satisfaction direct.

IX

He was not unhappy in the pit. He was admired by the men, and well enough liked. It was only he himself who felt the difference between himself and the others. He seemed to hide his own stigma. But he was never sure that the others did not really despise him for a ninny, as being less a man than they were. Only he pretended to be more manly, and was surprised by the ease with which they were deceived. And, being naturally cheerful, he was happy at work. He was sure of himself there. Naked to the waist, hot and grimy with labour, they squatted on their heels for a few minutes and talked, seeing each other dimly by the light of the safety lamps, while the black coal rose jutting round them, and the props of wood stood like little pillars in the low, black, very dark temple. Then the pony came and the gang-lad with a message from Number 7, or with a bottle of water from the horse-trough or some news of the world above. The day passed pleasantly enough. There was an ease, a go-as-you-please about the day underground, a delightful camaraderie of men shut off alone from the rest of the world, in a dangerous place, and a variety of labour, holing, loading, timbering, and a glamour of mystery and adventure in the atmosphere, that made the pit not unattractive to him when he had again got over his anguish of desire for the open air and the sea.

This day there was much to do and Durant was not in humour to talk. He went on working in silence through the afternoon.

"Loose-all" came, and they tramped to the bottom. The white-washed underground office shone brightly. Men were putting out their lamps. They sat in dozens round the bottom of the shaft, down which black, heavy drops of water fell continuously into the sump. The electric lights shone away down the main underground road.

"Is it raining?" asked Durant.

"Snowing," said an old man, and the younger was pleased. He liked to go up when it was snowing.

"It'll just come right for Christmas?" said the old man.

"Ay," replied Durant.

"A green Christmas, a fat churchyard," said the other sententiously.

Durant laughed, showing his small, rather pointed teeth.

The cage came down, a dozen men lined on. Durant noticed tufts of snow on the perforated, arched roof of the chain, and he was pleased. He wondered how it liked its excursion underground. But already it was getting soppy with black water.

He liked things about him. There was a little smile on his face. But underlying it was the curious consciousness he felt in himself.

The upper world came almost with a flash, because of the glimmer of snow. Hurrying along the bank, giving up his lamp at the office, he smiled to feel the open about him again, all glimmering round him with snow. The hills on either hand were pale blue in the dusk, and the hedges looked savage and dark. The snow was trampled between the railway lines. But far ahead, beyond the black figures of miners moving home, it became smooth again, spreading right up to the dark wall of the coppice.

To the west there was a pinkness, and a big star hovered half revealed. Below, the lights of the pit came out crisp and yellow among the darkness of the buildings, and the lights of Old Aldecross twinkled in rows down the bluish twilight.

Durant walked glad with life among the miners, who were all talking animatedly because of the snow. He liked their company, he liked the white dusky world. It gave him a little thrill to stop at the garden gate and see the light of home down below, shining on the silent blue snow.

X

By the big gate of the railway, in the fence, was a little gate, that he kept locked. As he unfastened it, he watched the kitchen light that shone on to the bushes and the snow outside. It was a candle burning till night set in, he thought to himself. He slid down the steep path to the level below. He liked making the first marks in the smooth snow. Then he came through the bushes to the house. The two women heard his heavy boots ring outside on the scraper, and his voice as he opened the door:

"How much worth of oil do you reckon to save by that candle, mother?" He liked a good light from the lamp.

He had just put down his bottle and snap-bag and was hanging his coat behind the scullery door, when Miss Louisa came upon him. He was startled, but he smiled.

His eyes began to laugh—then his face went suddenly straight, and he was afraid.

"Your mother's had an accident," she said.

"How?" he exclaimed.

"In the garden," she answered. He hesitated with his coat in his hands. Then he hung it up and turned to the kitchen.

"Is she in bed?" he asked.

"Yes," said Miss Louisa, who found it hard to deceive him. He was silent. He went into the kitchen, sat down heavily in his father's old chair, and began to pull off his boots. His head was small, rather finely shapen. His brown hair, close and crisp, would look jolly whatever happened. He wore heavy, moleskin trousers that gave off the stale, exhausted scent of the pit. Having put on his slippers, he carried his boots into the scullery.

"What is it?" he asked, afraid.

"Something internal," she replied.

He went upstairs. His mother kept herself calm for his coming. Louisa felt his tread shake the plaster floor of the bedroom above.

"What have you done?" he asked.

"It's nothing, my lad," said the old woman, rather hard. "It's nothing. You needn't fret, my boy, it's nothing more the matter with me than I had yesterday, or last week. The doctor said I'd done nothing serious."

"What were you doing?" asked her son.

"I was pulling up a cabbage, and I suppose I pulled too hard; for, oh—there was such a pain——"

Her son looked at her quickly. She hardened herself.

"But who doesn't have a sudden pain sometimes, my boy? We all do."

"And what's it done?"

"I don't know," she said, "but I don't suppose it's anything."

The big lamp in the corner was screened with a dark green screen, so that he could scarcely see her face. He was strung tight with apprehension and many emotions. Then his brow knitted.

"What did you go pulling your inside out at cabbages for," he asked, "and the ground frozen? You'd go on dragging and dragging, if you killed yourself."

"Somebody's got to get them," she said.

"You needn't do yourself harm."

But they had reached futility.

Miss Louisa could hear plainly downstairs. Her heart sank. It seemed so hopeless between them.

"Are you sure it's nothing much, mother?" he asked, appealing, after a little silence.

"Ay, it's nothing," said the old woman, rather bitter.

"I don't want you to—to—to be badly—you know."

"Go an' get your dinner," she said. She knew she was going to die: moreover, the pain was torture just then. "They're only cosseting me up a bit because I'm an old woman. Miss Louisa's *very* good—and she'll have got your dinner ready, so you'd better go and eat it."

He felt stupid and ashamed. His mother put him off. He had to turn away. The pain burned in his bowels. He went downstairs. The mother was glad he was gone, so that she could moan with pain.

He had resumed the old habit of eating before he washed himself. Miss Louisa served his dinner. It was strange and exciting to her. She was strung up tense, trying to understand him and his mother. She watched him as he sat. He was turned away from his food, looking in the fire. Her soul watched him, trying to see what he was. His black face and arms were uncouth, he was foreign. His face was masked black with coal-dust. She could not see him, she could not know him. The brown eyebrows, the steady eyes, the coarse, small moustache above the closed mouth—these were the only familiar indications. What was he, as he sat there in his pit-dirt? She could not see him, and it hurt her.

She ran upstairs, presently coming down with flannels and the bran-bag, to heat them, because the pain was on again.

He was half-way through his dinner. He put down the fork, suddenly nauseated.

"They will soothe the wrench," she said. He watched, useless and left out.

"Is she bad?" he asked.

"I think she is," she answered.

It was useless for him to stir or comment. Louisa was busy. She went upstairs. The poor old woman was in a white, cold sweat of pain. Louisa's face was sullen with suffering as she went about to relieve her. Then she sat and waited. The pain passed gradually, the old woman sank into a state of coma. Louisa still sat silent by the bed. She heard the sound of water downstairs. Then came the voice of the old mother, faint but unrelaxing:

"Alfred's washing himself—he'll want his back washing——"

Louisa listened anxiously, wondering what the sick woman wanted.

"He can't bear if his back isn't washed——" the old woman persisted, in a cruel attention to his needs. Louisa rose and wiped the sweat from the yellowish brow.

"I will go down," she said soothingly.

"If you would," murmured the sick woman.

Louisa waited a moment. Mrs. Durant closed her eyes, having discharged her duty. The young woman went downstair. Herself, or the man, what did they matter? Only the suffering woman must be considered.

Alfred was kneeling on the hearth-rug, stripped to the waist, washing himself in a large panchion of earthenware. He did so every evening, when he had eaten his dinner; his brothers had done so before him. But Miss Louisa was strange in the house.

He was mechanically rubbing the white lather on his head, with a repeated, unconscious movement, his hand every now and then passing over his neck. Louisa watched. She had to brace herself to this also. He bent his head into the water, washed it free of soap, and pressed the water out of his eyes.

"Your mother said you would want your back washing," she said.

Curious how it hurt her to take part in their fixed routine of life! Louisa felt the almost repulsive intimacy being forced upon her. It was all so common, so like herding. She lost her own distinctness.

He ducked his face round, looking up at her in what was a very comical way. She had to harden herself.

"How funny he looks with his face upside down," she thought. After all, there was a difference between her and the common people. The water in which his arms were plunged was quite black, the soap-froth was darkish. She could scarcely conceive him as human. Mechanically, under the influence of habit, he groped in the black water, fished out soap and flannel, and handed them backward to Louisa.

Then he remained rigid and submissive, his two arms thrust straight in the panchion, supporting the weight of his shoulders. His skin was beautifully white and unblemished, of an opaque, solid whiteness. Gradually Louisa saw it: this also was what he was. It fascinated her. Her feelings of separateness passed away: she ceased to draw back from contact with him and his mother. There was this living centre. Her heart ran hot. She had reached some goal in this beautiful, clear, male body. She loved him in a white, impersonal heat. But the sun-burnt, reddish neck and ears: they were more personal, more curious. A tenderness rose in her, she loved even his queer ears. A person—an intimate being he was to her. She put down the towel and went upstairs again, troubled in her heart. She had only seen one human being in her life—and that was Mary. All the rest were strangers. Now her soul was going to open, she was going to see another. She felt strange and pregnant.

"He'll be more comfortable," murmured the sick woman abstractedly, as Louisa entered the room. The latter did not answer. Her own heart was heavy with its own responsibility. Mrs. Durant lay silent awhile, then she murmured plaintively:

"You mustn't mind, Miss Louisa."

"Why should I?" replied Louisa, deeply moved.

"It's what we're used to," said the old woman.

And Louisa felt herself excluded again from their life. She sat in pain, with the tears of disappointment distilling in her heart. Was that all?

Alfred came upstairs. He was clean, and in his shirt-sleeves. He looked a workman now. Louisa felt that she and he were foreigners, moving in different lives. It dulled her again. Oh, if she could only find some fixed relations, something sure and abiding.

"How do you feel?" he said to his mother.

"It's a bit better," she replied wearily, impersonally. This strange putting herself aside, this abstracting herself and answering him only what she thought good for him to hear, made the relations between mother and son poignant and cramping to Miss Louisa. It made the man so ineffectual, so nothing. Louisa groped as if she had lost him. The mother was real and positive—he was not very actual. It puzzled and chilled the young woman.

"I'd better fetch Mrs. Harrison?" he said, waiting for his mother to decide.

"I suppose we shall have to have somebody," she replied.

Miss Louisa stood by, afraid to interfere in their business. They did not include her in their lives, they felt she had nothing to do with them, except as a help from outside. She was quite external to them. She felt hurt and powerless against this unconscious difference. But something patient and un-yielding in her made her say:

"I will stay and do the nursing: you can't be left."

The other two were shy, and at a loss for an answer.

"We s'll manage to get somebody," said the old woman wearily. She did not care very much what happened, now.

"I will stay until to-morrow, in any case," said Louisa. "Then we can see."

"I'm sure you've no right to trouble yourself," moaned the old woman. But she must leave herself in my hands.

Miss Louisa felt glad that she was admitted, even in an official capacity. She wanted to share their lives. At home they would need her, now Mary had come. But they must manage without her.

"I must write a note to the vicarage," she said.

Alfred Durant looked at her inquiringly, for her service. He had always that intelligent readiness to serve, since he had been in the Navy. But there was a simple independence in his willingness, which she loved. She felt nevertheless it was hard to get at him. He was so deferential, quick to take the slightest suggestion of an order from her, implicitly, that she could not get at the man in him.

He looked at her very keenly. She noticed his eyes were golden brown, with a very small pupil, the kind of eyes that can see a long way off. He stood alert, at military attention. His face was still rather weather-reddened.

"Do you want pen and paper?" he asked, with deferential suggestion to a superior, which was more difficult for her than reserve.

"Yes, please," she said.

He turned and went downstairs. He seemed to her so self-contained, so utterly sure in his movement. How was she to approach him? For he would take not one step towards her. He would only put himself entirely and impersonally at her service, glad to serve her, but keeping himself quite removed from her. She could see he felt real joy in doing anything for her, but any recognition would confuse him and hurt him. Strange it was to her, to have a man going about the house in his shirt-sleeves, his waistcoat unbuttoned, his throat bare, waiting on her. He moved well, as if he had plenty of life to spare. She was attracted by his completeness. And yet, when all was ready, and there was nothing more for him to do, she quivered, meeting his questioning look.

As she sat writing, he placed another candle near her. The rather dense light fell in two places on the overfoldings of her hair till it glistened heavy and bright, like a dense golden plumage folded up. Then the nape of her neck was very white, with fine down and pointed wisps of gold. He watched it as it it were a vision, losing himself. She was all that was beyond him, of revelation and exquisiteness. All that was ideal and beyond him, she was that—and he was lost to himself in looking at her. She had no connection with him. He did not approach her. She was there like a wonderful distance. But it was a treat, having her in the house. Even with this anguish for his mother tightening about him, he was sensible of the wonder of living this evening. The candles glistened on her hair, and seemed to fascinate him. He felt a little awe of her, and a sense of uplifting, that he and she and his mother should be together for a time, in the strange, unknown atmosphere. And, when he got out of the house, he was afraid. He saw the stars above ringing with fine brightness, the snow beneath just visible, and a new night was gathering round him. He was afraid almost with obliteration. What was this new night ringing about him, and what was he? He could not recognise himself nor any of his surroundings. He was afraid to think of his mother. And yet his chest was conscious of her, and of what was happening to her. He could not escape from her, she carried him with her into an unformed, unknown chaos.

XI

He went up the road in an agony, not knowing what it was all about, but feeling as if a red-hot iron were gripped round his chest. Without thinking, he shook two or three tears on to the snow. Yet in his mind he did not believe his mother would die. He was in the grip of some greater consciousness. As he sat in the hall of the vicarage, waiting whilst Mary put things for Louisa into a bag, he wondered why he had been so upset. He felt abashed and humbled by the big house, he felt again as if he were one of the rank and file. When Miss Mary spoke to him, he almost saluted.

"An honest man," thought Mary. And the patronage was applied as salve to her own sickness. She had station, so she could patronise: it was almost all that was left to her. But she could not have lived without having a certain position She could never have trusted heself outside a definite place, nor respected heself except as a woman of superior class.

As Alfred came to the latch-gate, he felt the grief at his heart again, and saw the new heavens. He stood a moment looking northward to the Plough climbing up the night, and at the far glimmer of snow in distant fields. Then his grief came on like physical pain. He held tight to the gate, biting his mouth, whispering "Mother!" It was a fierce, cutting, physical pain of grief, that came on in bouts, as his mother's pain came on in bouts, and was so acute he could scarcely keep erect. He did not know where it came from, the pain, nor why. It had nothing to do with his thoughts. Almost it had nothing to do with him. Only it gripped him and he must submit. The whole tide of his soul, gathering in its unknown towards this expansion into death, carried him with it helplessly, all the fritter of his thought and consciousness caught up as nothing, the heave passing on towards its breaking, taking him farther than he had ever been. When the young man had regained himself, he went indoors, and there he was almost gay. It seemed to excite him. He felt in high spirits: he made whimsical fun of things. He sat on one side of his mother's bed, Louisa on the other, and a certain gaiety seized them all. But the night and the dread was coming on.

Alfred kissed his mother and went to bed. When he was half undressed the knowledge of his mother came upon him, and the suffering seized him in its grip like two hands, in agony. He lay on the bed screwed up tight. It lasted so long, and exhausted him so much, that he fell asleep, without having the energy to get up and finish undressing. He awoke after midnight to find himself stone cold. He undressed and got into bed, and was soon asleep again.

At a quarter to six he woke, and instantly remembered. Having pulled on his trousers and lighted a candle, he went into his mother's room. He put his hand before the candle flame so that no light fell on the bed.

"Mother!" he whispered.

"Yes," was the reply.

There was a hesitation.

"Should I go to work?"

He waited, his heart was beating heavily.

"I think I'd go, my lad."

His heart went down in a kind of despair.

"You want me to?"

He let his hand down from the candle flame. The light fell on the bed. There he saw Louisa lying looking up at him. Her eyes were upon him. She quickly shut her eyes and half buried her face in the pillow, her back turned to him. He saw the rough hair like bright vapour about her round head, and the two plaits flung coiled among the bedclothes. It gave him a shock. He stood almost himself, determined. Louisa cowered down. He looked, and met his mother's eyes. Then he gave way again, and ceased to be sure, ceased to be himself.

"Yes, go to work, my boy," said the mother.

"All right," replied he, kissing her. His heart was down at despair, and bitter. He went away.

"Alfred!" cried his mother faintly.

He came back with beating heart.

"What, mother?"

"You'll always do what's right, Alfred?" the mother asked, beside herself in terror now he was leaving her. He was too terrified and bewildered to know what she meant.

"Yes," he said.

She turned her cheek to him. He kissed her, then went away in bitter despair. He went to work.

XII

By midday his mother was dead. The word met him at the pit-mouth. As he had known, inwardly, it was not a shock to him, and yet he trembled. He went home quite calmly, feeling only heavy in his breathing.

Miss Louisa was still at the house. She had seen to everything possible. Very succinctly, she informed him of what he needed to know. But there was one point of anxiety for her.

"You *did* half expect it—it's not come as a blow to you?" she asked, looking up at him. Her eyes were dark and calm and searching. She too felt lost. He was so dark and inchoate.

"I suppose—yes," he said stupidly. He looked aside, unable to endure her eyes on him.

"I could not bear to think you might not have guessed," she said.

He did not answer.

He felt it a great strain to have her near him at this time. He wanted to be alone. As soon as the relatives began to arrive, Louisa departed and came no more. While everything was arranging, and a crowd was in the house, whilst he had business to settle, he went well enough, with only those uncontrollable paroxysms of grief. For the rest, he was superficial. By himself, he endured the fierce, almost insane bursts of grief which passed again and left him calm, almost clear, just wondering. He had not known before that everything could break down, that he himself could break down, and all be a great chaos, very vast and wonderful. It seemed as if life in him had burst its bounds, and he was lost in a great, bewildering flood, immense and unpeopled. He himself was broken and spilled out amid it all. He could only breathe panting in silence. Then the anguish came on again.

When all the people had gone from the Quarry Cottage, leaving the young man alone with an elderly housekeeper, then the long trial began. The snow had thawed and frozen, a fresh fall had whitened the grey, this then began to thaw. The world was a place of loose grey slosh. Alfred had nothing to do in the evenings. He was a man whose life had been filled up with small activities. Without knowing it, he had been centralised, polarised in his mother. It was she who had kept him. Even now, when the old housekeeper had left him, he might still have gone on in his old way. But the force and balance of his life was lacking. He sat pretending to read, all the time holding his fists clenched, and holding himself in, enduring he did not know what. He walked the black and sodden miles of field-paths, till he was tired out: but all this was only running away from whence he must return. At work he was all right. If it had been summer he might have escaped by working in the garden till bedtime. But now, there was no escape, no relief, no help. He, perhaps, was made for action rather than for understanding; for doing than for being. He was shocked out of his activities, like a swimmer who forgets to swim.

For a week, he had the force to endure this suffocation and struggle, then he began to get exhausted, and knew it must come out. The instinct of self-preservation became strongest. But there was the question: Where was he to go? The public-house really meant nothing to him, it was no good going there. He began to think of emigration. In another country he would be all right. He wrote to the emigration offices.

On the Sunday after the funeral, when all the Durant people had attended church, Alfred had seen Miss Louisa, impassive and reserved, sitting with Miss Mary, who was proud and very distant, and with the other Lindleys, who were people removed. Alfred saw them as people remote. He did not think about it. They had nothing to do with his life. After service Louisa had come to him and shaken hands.

"My sister would like you to come to supper one evening, if you would be so good."

He looked at Miss Mary, who bowed. Out of kindness, Mary had proposed this to Louisa, disapproving of her even as she did so. But she did not examine herself closely.

"Yes," said Durant awkwardly, "I'll come if you want me." But he vaguely felt that it was misplaced.

"You'll come to-morrow evening, then, about half-past six."

He went. Miss Louisa was very kind to him. There could be no music, because of the babies. He sat with his fists clenched on his thighs, very quiet and unmoved, lapsing, among all those people, into a kind of muse or daze. There was nothing between him and them. They knew it as well as he. But he remained very steady in himself, and the evening passed slowly. Mrs. Lindley called him "young man".

"Will you sit here, young man?"

He sat there. One name was as good as another. What had they to do with him?

Mr. Lindley kept a special tone for him, kind, indulgent, but patronising. Durant took it all without criticism or offence, just submitting. But he did not want to eat—that troubled him, to have to eat in their presence. He knew he was out of place. But it was his duty to stay yet awhile. He answered precisely, in monosyllables.

When he left he winced with confusion. He was glad it was

finished. He got away as quickly as possible. And he wanted still more intensely to go right away, to Canada.

Miss Louisa suffered in her soul, indignant with all of them, with him too, but quite unable to say why she was indignant.

XIII

Two evenings after, Louisa tapped at the door of the Quarry Cottage, at half-past six. He had finished dinner, the woman had washed up and gone away, but still he sat in his pit-dirt. He was going later to the New Inn. He had begun to go there because he must go somewhere. The mere contact with other men was necessary to him, the noise, the warmth, the forgetful flight of the hours. But still he did not move. He sat alone in the empty house till it began to grow on him like something unnatural.

He was in his pit-dirt when he opened the door.

"I have been wanting to call—I thought I would," she said, and she went to the sofa. He wondered why she wouldn't use his mother's round arm-chair. Yet something stirred in him, like anger, when the housekeeper placed herself in it.

"I ought to have been washed by now," he said, glancing at the clock, which was adorned with butterflies and cherries, and the name of "T. Brooks, Mansfield". He laid his black hands along his mottled dirty arms. Louisa looked at him. There was the reserve, and the simple neutrality towards her, which she dreaded in him. It made it impossible for her to approach him.

"I am afraid," she said, "that I wasn't kind in asking you to supper."

"I'm not used to it," he said, smiling with his mouth, showing the interspaced white teeth. His eyes, however, were steady and unseeing.

"It's not *that*," she said hastily. Her repose was exquisite and her dark grey eyes rich with understanding. He felt afraid of her as she sat there, as he began to grow conscious of her.

"How do you get on alone?" she asked.

He glanced away to the fire.

"Oh——" he answered, shifting uneasily, not finishing his answer.

Her face settled heavily.

"How close it is in this room. You have such immense fires. I will take off my coat," she said.

He watched her take off her hat and coat. She wore a cream cashmir blouse embroidered with gold silks. It seemed to him a very fine garment, fitting her throat and wrists close. It gave him a feeling of pleasure and cleanness and relief from himself.

"What were you thinking about, that you didn't get washed?" she asked, half intimately. He laughed, turning aside his head. The whites of his eyes showed very distinct his black face.

"Oh," he said, "I couldn't tell you."

There was a pause.

"Are you going to keep this house on?" she asked.

He stirred in his chair, under the question.

"I hardly know," he said. "I'm very likely going to Canada."

Her spirit became very quiet and attentive.

"What for?" she asked.

Again he shifted restlessly on his seat.

"Well,"—he said slowly—"to try the life."

"But which life?"

"There's various things—farming or lumbering or mining. I don't mind much what it is."

"And is that what you want?"

He did not think in these times, so he could not answer.

"I don't know," he said, "till I've tried."

She saw him drawing away from her for ever.

"Aren't you sorry to leave this house and garden?" she asked.

"I don't know," he answered reluctantly. "I suppose our Fred would come in—that's what he's wanting."

"You don't want to settle down?" she asked.

He was leaning forward on the arms of his chair. He turned to her. Her face was pale and set. It looked heavy and impassive, her hair shone richer as she grew white. She was to him something steady and immovable and eternal presented to him. His heart was hot in an anguish of suspense. Sharp twitches of fear and pain were in his limbs. He turned his whole body away from her. The silence was unendurable. He could not bear her to sit there any more. It made his heart got hot and stifled in his breast.

"Were you going out to-night?" she asked.

"Only to the New Inn," he said.

Again there was silence.

She reached for her hat. Nothing else was suggested to her. She *had* to go. He sat waiting for her to be gone, for relief. And she knew that if she went out of that house as she was, she went out a failure. Yet she continued to pin on her hat; in a moment she would have to go. Something was carrying her.

Then suddenly a sharp pang, like lightning, seared her from head to foot, and she was beyond herself.

"Do you want me to go?" she asked, controlled, yet speaking out of a fiery anguish, as if the words were spoken from her without her intervention.

He went white under his dirt.

"Why?" he asked, turning to her in fear, compelled.

"Do you want me to go?" she repeated.

"Why?" he asked again.

"Because I wanted to stay with you," she said, suffocated, with her lungs full of fire.

His face worked, he hung forward a little, suspended, staring straight into her eyes, in torment, in an agony of chaos, unable to collect himself. And as if turned to stone, she looked back into his eyes. The souls were exposed bare for a few moments. It was agony. They could not bear it. He dropped his head, whilst his body jerked with little sharp twitchings.

She turned away for her coat. Her soul had gone dead in her. Her hands trembled, but she could not feel any more. She drew on her coat. There was a cruel suspense in the room. The moment had come for her to go. He lifted his head. His eyes were like agate, expressionless, save for the black points of torture. They held her, she had no will, no life any more. She felt broken.

"Don't you want me?" she said helplessly.

A spasm of torture crossed his eyes, which held her fixed.

"I—I——" he began, but he could not speak. Something drew him from his chair to her. She stood motionless, spellbound, like a creature given up as prey. He put his hand tentatively, uncertainly, on her arm. The expression of his face was strange and inhuman. She stood utterly motionless. Then clumsily he put his arms round her, and took her, cruelly, blindly, straining her till she nearly lost consciousness, till he himself had almost fallen.

Then, gradually, as he held her gripped, and his brain reeled round, and he felt himself falling, falling from himself, and whilst she, yielded up, swooned to a kind of death of herself, a moment of utter darkness came over him, and they began to wake up again as if from a long sleep. He was himself.

After a while his arms slackened, she loosened herself a little, and put her arms round him, as he held her. So they held each other close, and hid each against the other for assurance, helpless in speech. And it was ever her hands that trembled more closely upon him, drawing him nearer into her, with love.

And at last she drew back her face and looked up at him, her eyes wet, and shining with light. His heart, which saw, was silent with fear. He was with her. She saw his face all sombre and inscrutable, and he seemed eternal to her. And all the echo of pain came back into the rarity of bliss, and all her tears came up.

"I love you," she said, her lips drawn to sobbing. He put down his head against her, unable to hear her, unable to bear the sudden coming of the peace and passion that almost broke his heart. They stood together in silence whilst the thing moved away a little.

At last she wanted to see him. She looked up. His eyes were strange and glowing, with a tiny black pupil. Strange, they were, and powerful over her. And his mouth came to hers, and slowly her eyelids closed, as his mouth sought hers closer and closer, and took possession of her.

They were silent for a long time, too much mixed up with passion and grief and death to do anything but hold each other in pain and kiss with long, hurting kisses wherein fear was transfused into desire. At last she disengaged herself. He felt as if his heart were hurt, but glad, and he scarcely dared look at her.

"I'm glad," she said also.

He held her hands in passionate gratitude and desire. He had not yet the presence of mind to say anything. He was dazed with relief.

"I ought to go," she said.

He looked at her. He could not grasp the thought of her going, he knew he could never be separated from her any more. Yet he dared not assert himself. He held her hands tight.

"Your face is black," she said.

He laughed.

"Yours is a bit smudged," he said.

They were afraid of each other, afraid to talk. He could only keep her near to him. After a while she wanted to wash her face. He brought her some warm water, standing by and watching her. There was something he wanted to say, that he dared not. He watched her wiping her face, and making tidy her hair.

"They'll see your blouse is dirty," he said.

She looked at her sleeves and laughed for joy.

He was sharp with pride.

"What shall you do?" he asked.

"How?" she said.

He was awkward at a reply.

"About me," he said.

"What do you want me to do?" she laughed.

He put his hand out slowly to her. What did it matter!

"But make yourself clean," she said.

XIV

As they went up the hill, the night seemed dense with the unknown. They kept close together, feeling as if the darkness were alive and full of knowledge, all around them. In silence they walked up the hill. At first the street lamps went their way. Several people passed them. He was more shy than she, and would have let her go had she loosened in the least. But she held firm.

Then they came into the true darkness, between the fields. They did not want to speak, feeling closer together in silence. So they arrived at the vicarage gate. They stood under the naked horse-chestnut tree.

"I wish you didn't have to go," he said.

She laughed a quick little laugh.

"Come to-morrow," she said, in a low tone, "and ask father,"

She felt his hand close on hers.

She gave the same sorrowful little laugh of sympathy. Then she kissed him, sending him home.

At home, the old grief came on in another paroxysm, obliterating Louisa, obliterating even his mother for whom the stress was raging like a burst of fever in a wound. But something was sound in his heart.

XV

The next evening he dressed to go to the vicarage, feeling it was to be done, not imagining what it would be like. He would not take this seriously. He was sure of Louisa, and this marriage was like fate to him. It filled him also with a blessed feeling of fatality. He was not responsible, neither had her people anything really to do with it.

They ushered him into the little study, which was fireless. By and by the vicar came in. His voice was cold and hostile as he said:

"What can I do for you, young man?"

He knew already, without asking.

Durant looked up at him, again like a sailor before a superior. He had the subordinate manner. Yet his spirit was clear.

"I wanted, Mr. Lindley——" he began respectfully, then all the colour suddenly left his face. It seemed now a violation to say what he had to say. What was he doing there? But he stood on, because it had to be done. He held firmly to his own independence and self-respect. He must not be indecisive. He must put himself aside: the matter was bigger than just his personal self. He must not feel. This was his highest duty.

"You wanted——" said the vicar.

Durant's mouth was dry, but he answered with steadiness:

"Miss Louisa—Louisa—promised to marry me——"

"You asked Miss Louisa if she would marry you—yes——" corrected the vicar. Durant reflected he had not asked her this:

"If she would marry me, sir. I hope you—don't mind."

He smiled. He was a good-looking man, and the vicar could not help seeing it.

"And my daughter was willing to marry you?" said Mr. Lindley.

"Yes," said Durant seriously. It was pain to him, nevertheless. He felt the natural hostility between himself and the elder man.

"Will you come this way?" said the vicar. He led into the dining-room, where were Mary, Louisa, and Mrs. Lindley. Mr. Massy sat in a corner with a lamp.

"This young man has come on your account, Louisa?" said Mr. Lindley.

"Yes," said Louisa, her eyes on Durant, who stood erect, in discipline. He dared not look at her, but he was aware of her.

"You don't want to marry a collier, you little fool," cried Mrs. Lindley harshly. She lay obese and helpless upon the couch, swathed in a loose dove-grey gown.

"Oh, hush, Mother," cried Mary, with quiet intensity and pride.

"What means have you to· support a wife?" demanded the vicar's wife roughly.

"I!" Durant replied, starting. "I think I can earn enough."

"Well, and how much?" came the rough voice.

"Seven and six a day," replied the young man.

"And will it get to be any more?"

"I hope so."

"And are you going to live in that poky little house?"

"I think so," said Durant, "if it's all right."

He took small offence, only was upset, because they would not think him good enough. He knew that, in their sense, he was not.

"Then she's a fool, I tell you, if she marries you," cried the mother roughly, casting her decision.

"After all, mama, it is Louisa's affair," said Mary distinctly, "and we must remember——"

"As she makes her bed, she must lie—but she'll repent it," interrupted Mrs. Lindley.

"And after all," said Mr. Lindley, "Louisa cannot quite hold herself free to act entirely without consideration for her family."

"What do you want, Papa?" asked Louisa sharply.

"I mean that if you marry this man, it will make my position very difficult for me, particularly if you stay in this parish. If you were moving quite away, it would be simpler. But living here in a collier's cottage, under my nose, as it were—it would be almost unseemly. I have my position to maintain, and a position which may not be taken lightly."

"Come over here, young man," cried the mother, in her rough voice, "and let us look at you."

Durant, flushing, went over and stood—not quite at attention, so that he did not know what to do with his hands. Miss

Louisa was angry to see him standing there, obedient and acquiescent. He ought to show himself a man.

"Can't you take her away and live out of sight?" said the mother. "You'd both of you be better off."

"Yes, we can go away," he said.

"Do you want to?" asked Miss Mary clearly.

He faced round. Mary looked very stately and impressive. He flushed.

"I do if it's going to be a trouble to anybody," he said.

"For yourself, you would rather stay?" said Mary.

"It's my home," he said, "and that's the house I was born in."

"Then"—Mary turned clearly to her parents, "I really don't see how you can make the conditions, papa. He has his own rights, and if Louisa wants to marry him——"

"Louisa, Louisa!" cried the father impatiently. "I cannot understand why Louisa should not behave in the normal way. I cannot see why she should only think of herself, and leave her family out of count. The thing is enough in itself, and she ought to try to ameliorate it as much as possible. And if——"

"But I love the man, papa," said Louisa.

"And I hope you love your parents, and I hope you want to spare them as much of the—the loss of prestige as possible."

"We *can* go away to live," said Louisa, her face breaking to tears. At last she was really hurt.

"Oh yes, easily," Durant replied hastily, pale, distressed.

There was dead silence in the room.

"I think it would really be better," murmured the vicar, mollified.

"Very likely it would," said the rough-voiced invalid.

"Though I think we ought to apologise for asking such a thing," said Mary haughtily.

"No," said Durant. "It will be best all round." He was glad there was no more bother.

"And shall we put up the banns here or go to the registrar?" he asked clearly, like a challenge.

"We will go to the registrar," replied Louis decidedly.

Again there was a dead silence in the room.

"Well, if you will have your own way, you must go your own way," said the mother emphatically.

All the time Mr. Massy had sat obscure and unnoticed in a

corner of the room. At this juncture he got up, saying:

"There is baby, Mary."

Mary rose and went out of the room, stately; her little husband padded after her. Durant watched the fragile, small man go, wondering.

"And where," asked the vicar, almost genial, "do you think you will go when you are married?"

Durant started.

"I was thinking of emigrating," he said.

"To Canada? Or where?"

"I think to Canada."

"Yes, that would be very good."

Again there was a pause.

"We shan't see much of you then, as a son-in-law," said the mother, roughly but amicably.

"Not much," he said.

Then he took his leave. Louisa went with him to the gate. She stood before him in distress.

"You won't mind them, will you?" she said humbly.

"I don't mind them, if they don't mind me!" he said. Then he stooped and kissed her.

"Let us be married soon," she murmured, in tears.

"All right," he said. "I'll go to-morrow to Barford."

A FRAGMENT OF STAINED GLASS

BEAUVALE is, or was, the largest parish in England. It is thinly
populated, only just netting the stragglers from shoals of
houses in three large mining villages. For the rest, it holds a
great tract of woodland, fragment of old Sherwood, a few hills
of pasture and arable land, three collieries, and, finally, the
ruins of a Cistercian abbey. These ruins lie in a still rich
meadow at the foot of the last fall of woodland, through
whose oaks shines a blue of hyacinths, like water, in May-
time. Of the abbey, there remains only the east wall of the
chancel standing, a wild thick mass of ivy weighting one
shoulder, while pigeons perch in the tracery of the lofty
window. This is the window in question.

The vicar of Beauvale is a bachelor of forty-two years. Quite
early in life some illness caused a slight paralysis of his right
side, so that he drags a little, and so that the right corner of his
mouth is twisted up into his cheek with a constant grimace,
unhidden by a heavy moustache. There is something pathetic
about this twist on the vicar's countenance: his eyes are so
shrewd and sad. It would be hard to get near to Mr. Colbran.
Indeed, now, his soul has some of the twist to his face, so that,
when he is not ironical, he is satiric. Yet a man of more complete tolerance and generosity scarcely exists. Let the boors
mock him, he merely smiles on the other side, and there is no
malice in his eyes, only a quiet expression of waiting till they
have finished. His people do not like him, yet none could
bring forth an accusation against him, save that "You never
can tell when he's having you."

I dined the other evening with the vicar in his study. The
room scandalises the neighbourhood because of the statuary
which adorns it: a Laocoön and other classic copies, with
bronze and silver Italian Renaissance works. For the rest, it
is all dark and tawny.

Mr. Colbran is an archæologist. He does not take himself
seriously, however, in his hobby, so that nobody knows the
worth of his opinions on the subject.

"Here you are," he said to me after dinner, "I've found
another paragraph for my great work."

"What's that?" I asked.

"Haven't I told you I was compiling a Bible of the English people—the Bible of their hearts—their exclamations in presence of the unknown? I've found a fragment at home, a jump at God from Beauvale."

"Where?" I asked, startled.

The vicar closed his eyes whilst looking at me.

"Only on parchment," he said.

Then, slowly, he reached for a yellow book, and read, translating as he went:

"Then, while we chanted, came a crackling at the window, at the great east window, where hung our Lord on the Cross. It was a malicious coveitous Devil wrathed by us, rended the lovely image of the glasse. We saw the iron clutches of the fiend pick the window, and a face flaming red like fire in a basket did glower down on us. Our hearts melted away, our legs broke, we thought to die. The breath of the wretch filled the chapel.

"But our dear Saint, etc., etc., came hastening down heaven to defend us. The fiend began to groan and bray—he was daunted and beat off.

"When the sun up-rose, and it was morning, some went out in dread upon the thin snow. There the figure of our Saint was broken and thrown down, whilst in the window was a wicked hole as from the Holy Wounds the Blessed Blood was run out at the touch of the Fiend, and on the snow was the Blood, sparkling like gold. Some gathered it up for the joy of this House. . . ."

"Interesting," I said. "Where's it from?"

"Beauvale records—fifteenth century."

"Beauvale Abbey," I said; "they were only very few, the monks. What frightened them, I wonder."

"I wonder," he repeated.

"Somebody climbed up," I supposed, "and attempted to get in."

"What?" he exclaimed, smiling.

"Well, what do you think?"

"Pretty much the same," he replied. "I glossed it out for my book."

"Your great work? Tell me."

He put a shade over the lamp so that the room was almost in darkness.

"Am I more than a voice?" he asked.

"I can see your hand," I replied. He moved entirely from the circle of light. Then his voice began, sing-song, sardonic:

"I was a serf at Rollestoun's, Newthorpe Manor, master of the stables, I was. One day a horse bit me as I was grooming him. He was an old enemy of mine. I fetched him a blow across the nose. Then, when he got a chance, he lashed out at me and caught me a gash over the mouth. I snatched at a hatchet and cut his head. He yelled, fiend as he was, and strained for me with all his teeth bare. I brought him down.

"For killing him they flogged me till they thought I was dead. I was sturdy, because we horse-serfs got plenty to eat. I was sturdy, but they flogged me till I did not move. The next night I set fire to the stables, and the stables set fire to the house. I watched and saw the red flame rise and look out of the window, I saw the folk running, each for himself, master no more than one of a frightened party. It was freezing, but the heat made me sweat. I saw them all turn again to watch, all rimmed with red. They cried, all of them, when the roof went in, when the sparks splashed up at rebound. They cried then like dogs at the bagpipes howling. Master cursed me, till I laughed as I lay under a bush quite near.

"As the fire went down I got frightened. I ran for the woods with fire blazing in my eyes and crackling in my ears. For hours I was all fire. Then I went to sleep under the bracken. When I woke it was evening. I had no mantle, was frozen stiff. I was afraid to move, lest all the sores of my back should be broken like thin ice. I lay still until I could bear my hunger no longer. I moved then to get used to the pain of movement, when I began to hunt for food. There was nothing to be found but hips.

"After wandering about till I was faint I dropped again in the bracken. The boughs above me creaked with frost. I started and looked round. The branches were like hair among the starlight. My heart stood still. Again there was a creak, creak, and suddenly a whoop, that whistled in fading. I fell down in the bracken like dead wood. Yet, by the peculiar whistling sound at the end, I knew it was only the ice bending or tightening in the frost. I was in the woods above the lake, only two miles from the Manor. And yet, when the lake whooped hollowly again, I clutched the frozen soil, every one of my muscles as stiff as the stiff earth. So all the night long I dare not move my face, but pressed it flat down, and taut I lay as if pegged down and braced.

"When morning came still I did not move, I lay still in a dream. By afternoon my ache was such it enlivened me. I cried, rocking my breath in the ache of moving. Then again I became fierce. I beat my hands on the rough bark to hurt them, so that I should not ache so much. In such a rage I was I swung my limbs to torture till I fell sick with pain. Yet I fought the hurt, fought it and fought by twisting and flinging myself, until it was overcome. Then the evening began to draw on. All day the sun had not loosened the frost. I felt the sky chill again towards afternoon. Then I knew the night was coming, and, remembering the great space I had just come through, horrible so that it seemed to have made me another man, I fled across the wood.

"But in my running I came upon the oak where hanged five bodies. There they must hang, bar-stiff, night after night. It was a terror worse than any. Turning, blundering through the forest, I came out where the trees thinned, where only hawthorns, ragged and shaggy, went down to the lake's edge.

"The sky across was red, the ice on the water glistened as if it were warm. A few wild geese sat out like stones on the sheet of ice. I thought of Martha. She was the daughter of the miller at the upper end of the lake. Her hair was red like beech leaves in a wind. When I had gone often to the mill with the horses she had brought me food.

" 'I thought,' said I to her, ' 'twas a squirrel sat on your shoulder. 'Tis your hair fallen loose.'

" 'They call me the fox,' she said.

" 'Would I were your dog,' said I. She would bring me bacon and good bread, when I called at the mill with the horses. The thought of cakes of bread and of bacon made me reel as if drunk. I had torn at the rabbit-holes, I had chewed wood all day. In such a dimness was my head that I felt neither the soreness of my wounds nor the cuts of thorns on my knees, but stumbled towards the mill, almost past fear of man and death, panting with fear of the darkness that crept behind me from trunk to trunk.

"Coming to the gap in the wood, below which lay the pond, I heard no sound. Always I knew the place filled with the buzz of water, but now it was silent. In fear of this stillness I ran forward, forgetting myself, forgetting the frost. The

wood seemed to pursue me. I fell, just in time, down by a
shed wherein were housed the few wintry pigs. The miller
came riding in on his horse, and the barking of dogs was for
him. I heard him curse the day, curse his servant, curse me,
whom he had been out to hunt, in his rage of wasted labour,
curse all. As I lay I heard inside the shed a sucking. Then I
knew that the sow was there, and that the most of her sucking pigs would be already killed for to-morrow's Christmas.
The miller, from forethought to have young at that time,
made profit by his sucking pigs that were sold for the mid-
winter feast.

"When in a moment all was silent in the dusk, I broke the
bar and came into the shed. The sow grunted, but did not
come forth to discover me. By and by I crept in towards her
warmth. She had but three young left, which now angered
her, she being too full of milk. Every now and again she
slashed at them and they squealed. Busy as she was with
them, I in the darkness advanced towards her. I trembled so
that scarce dared I trust myself near her, for long dared not
put my naked face towards her. Shuddering with hunger and
fear, I at last fed of her, guarding my face with my arm. Her
own full young tumbled squealing against me, but she, feeling her ease, lay grunting. At last, I, too, lay drunk, swooning.

"I was roused by the shouting of the miller. He, angered by
his daughter who wept, abused her, driving her from the house
to feed the swine. She came, bowing under a yoke, to the door
of the shed. Finding the pin broken she stood afraid, then, as
the sow grunted, she came cautiously in. I took her with my
arm, my hand over her mouth. As she struggled against my
breast my heart began to beat loudly. At last she knew it was
I. I clasped her. She hung in my arms, turning away her face,
so that I kissed her throat. The tears blinded my eyes, I know
not why, unless it were the hurt of my mouth, wounded by
the horse, was keen.

" 'They will kill you,' she whispered.

" 'No,' I answered.

"And she wept softly. She took my head in her arms and
kissed me, wetting me with her tears, brushing me with her
keen hair, warming me through.

" 'I will not go away from here,' I said. 'Bring me a knife,
and I will defend myself.'

" 'No,' she wept. 'Ah, no!'

"When she went I lay down, pressing my chest where she had rested on the earth, lest being alone were worse emptiness than hunger.

"Later she came again. I saw her bend in the doorway, a lanthorn hanging in front. As she peered under the redness of her falling hair, I was afraid of her. But she came with food. We sat together in the dull light. Sometimes still I shivered and my throat would not swallow.

" 'If,' said I, 'I eat all this you have brought me, I shall sleep till somebody finds me.'

"Then she took away the rest of the meat.

" 'Why,' said I, 'should I not eat?' She looked at me in tears of fear.

" 'What?' I said, but still she had no answer. I kissed her, and the hurt of my wounded mouth angered me.

" 'Now there is my blood,' said I, 'on your mouth.' Wiping her smooth hand over her lips, she looked thereat, then at me.

" 'Leave me,' I said, 'I am tired.' She rose to leave me.

" 'But bring a knife,' I said. Then she held the lanthorn near my face, looking as at a picture.

" 'You look to me,' she said, 'like a stirk that is roped for the axe. Your eyes are dark, but they are wide open.'

" 'Then I will sleep,' said I, 'but will not wake too late.'

" 'Do not stay here,' she said.

" 'I will not sleep in the wood,' I answered, and it was my heart that spoke, 'for I am afraid. I had better be afraid of the voice of man and dogs, than the sounds in the woods. Bring me a knife, and in the morning I will go. Alone will I not go now.'

"The searchers will take you,' she said.

" 'Bring me a knife,' I answered.

" 'Ah, go,' she wept.

" 'Not now—I will not——'

"With that she lifted the lanthorn, lit up her own face and mine. Her blue eyes dried of tears. Then I took her to myself, knowing she was mine.

" 'I will come again,' she said.

"She went, and I folded my arms, lay down and slept.

"When I woke, she was rocking me wildly to rouse me.

" 'I dreamed,' said I, 'that a great heap, as if it were a hill, lay on me and above me.'

"She put a cloak over me, gave me a hunting-knife and a

wallet of food, and other things I did not note. Then under her own cloak she hid the lanthorn.

" 'Let us go,' she said, and blindly I followed her.

"When I came out into the cold someone touched my face and my hair.

" 'Ha!' I cried, 'who now——?' Then she swiftly clung to me, hushed me.

" 'Someone has touched me,' I said aloud, still dazed with sleep.

" 'Oh, hush!' she wept. ' 'Tis snowing.' The dogs within the house began to bark. She fled forward, I after her. Coming to the ford of the stream she ran swiftly over, but I broke through the ice. Then I knew where I was. Snowflakes, fine and rapid, were biting at my face. In the wood there was no wind nor snow.

" 'Listen,' said I to her, 'listen, for I am locked up with sleep.'

" 'I hear roaring overhead,' she answered. 'I hear in the trees like great bats squeaking.'

" 'Give me your hand,' said I.

"We heard many noises as we passed. Once as there uprose a whiteness before us, she cried aloud.

" 'Nay,' said I, 'do not untie thy hand from mine,' and soon we were crossing fallen snow. But ever and again she started back from fear.

" 'When you draw back my arm,' I said, angry, 'you loosen a weal on my shoulder.'

"Thereafter she ran by my side like a fawn beside its mother.

" 'We will cross the valley and gain the stream,' I said. 'That will lead us on its ice as on a path deep into the forest. There we can join the outlaws. The wolves are driven from this part. They have followed the driven deer.'

"We came directly on a large gleam that shaped itself up among flying grains of snow.

" 'Ah!' she cried, and she stood amazed.

"Then I thought we had gone through the bounds into faery realm, and I was no more a man. How did I know what eyes were gleaming at me between the snow, what cunning spirits in the draughts of air? So I waited for what would happen, and I forgot her, that she was there. Only I could feel the spirits whirling and blowing about me.

"Whereupon she clung upon me, kissing me lavishly, and,

were dogs or men or demons come upon us at that moment, she had let us be stricken down, nor heeded not. So we moved forward to the shadow that shone in colours upon the passing snow. We found ourselves under a door of light which shed its colours mixed with snow. This Martha had never seen, nor I, this door open for a red and brave issuing like fires. We wondered.

" 'It is faery," she said, and after a while, 'Could one catch such—— Ah, no!'

"Through the snow shone bushes of red and blue.

" 'Could one have such a little light like a red flower—only a little, like a rose-berry scarlet on one's breast!—then one were singled out as Our Lady.'

"I flung off my cloak and my burden to climb up the face of the shadow. Standing on rims of stone, then in pockets of snow, I reached upward. My hand was red and blue, but I could not take the stuff. Like colour of a moth's wing it was on my hand, it flew on the increasing snow. I stood higher on the head of a frozen man, reached higher my hand. Then I felt the bright stuff cold. I could not pluck it off. Down below she cried to me to come again to her. I felt a rib that yielded, I struck at it with my knife. There came a gap in the redness. Looking through, I saw below as it were white stunted angels, with sad faces lifted in fear. Two faces they had each, and round rings of hair. I was afraid. I grasped the shining red, I pulled. Then the cold man under me sank, so I fell as if broken on to the snow.

"Soon I was risen again, and we were running downwards towards the stream. We felt ourselves eased when the smooth road of ice was beneath us. For a while it was resting, to travel thus evenly. But the wind blew round us, the snow hung upon us, we leaned us this way and that, towards the storm. I drew her along, for she came as a bird that stems lifting and swaying against the wind. By and by the snow came smaller, there was no wind in the wood. Then I felt nor labour, nor cold. Only I knew the darkness drifted by on either side, that overhead was a lane of paleness where a moon fled us before. Still, I can feel the moon fleeing from me, can feel the trees passing round me in slow dizzy reel, can feel the hurt of my shoulder and my straight arm torn with holding her. I was following the moon and the stream, for I knew where the water peeped from its burrow in the ground there were shelters of the outlaw. But she fell, without sound or sign.

"I gathered her up and climbed the bank. There all round me hissed the larchwood, dry beneath, and laced with its dry-fretted cords. For a little way I carried her into the trees. Then I laid her down till I cut flat hairy boughs. I put her in my bosom on this dry bed, so we swooned together through the night. I laced her round and covered her with myself, so she lay like a nut within its shell.

"Again, when morning came, it was pain of cold that woke me. I groaned, but my heart was warm as I saw the heap of red hair in my arms. As I looked at her, her eyes opened into mine. She smiled—from out of her smile came fear. As if in a trap she pressed back her head.

" 'We have no flint,' said I.

" 'Yes—in the wallet, flint and steel and tinder-box,' she answered.

" 'God yield you blessing,' I said.

"In a place a little open I kindled a fire of larch boughs. She was afraid of me, hovering near, yet never crossing a space.

"Come,' said I, 'let us eat this food.'

" 'Your face,' she said, 'is smeared with blood.'

"I opened out my cloak.

" But come,' said I, 'you are frosted with cold.'

"I took a handful of snow in my hand, wiping my face with it, which then I dried on my cloak.

" 'My face is no longer painted with blood. You are no longer afraid of me. Come here then, sit by me while we eat.'

"But as I cut the cold bread for her, she clasped me suddenly, kissing me. She fell before me, clasped my knees to her breast, weeping. She laid her face down to my feet, so that her hair spread like a fire before me. I wondered at the woman. 'Nay,' I crid. At that she lifted her face to me from below. 'Nay,' I cried, feeling my tears fall. With her head on my breast, my own tears rose from their source, wetting my cheek and her hair, which was wet with the rain of my eyes.

"Then I remembered and took from my bosom the coloured light of that night before. I saw it was black and rough.

" 'Ah,' said I, 'this is magic.'

" 'The black stone!' she wondered.

" 'It is magic,' she answered.

" 'Shall I throw it?' said I, lifting the stone, 'shall I throw it away, for fear?'

" 'It shines!' she cried, looking up, 'it shines like the eye of a creature at night, the eye of a wolf in the doorway.'

" ' 'Tis magic,' I said, 'let me throw it from us.' But nay, she held my arm.

" 'It is red and shining,' she cried.

" 'It is a bloodstone,' I answered. 'It will hurt us, we shall die in blood.'

" 'But give it to me,' she answered.

" 'It is red of blood,' I said.

" 'Ah, give it to me,' she called.

" 'It is my blood,' I said.

" 'Give it,' she commanded, low.

" 'It is my life-stone,' I said.

" 'Give it me,' she pleaded.

"I gave it her. She held it up, she smiled, she smiled in my face, lifting her arms to me. I took her with my mouth, her mouth, her white throat. Nor she ever shrank, but trembled with happiness.

"What woke us, when the woods were filling again with shadow, when the fire was out, when we opened our eyes and looked up as if drowned, into the light which stood bright and thick on the tree-tops, what woke us was the sound of wolves. . . ."

"Nay," said the vicar, suddenly rising, "they lived happily ever after."

"No," I said.

THE SHADES OF SPRING

I

It was a mile nearer through the wood. Mechanically, Syson turned up by the forge and lifted the field-gate. The blacksmith and his mate stood still, watching the trespasser. But Syson looked too much a gentleman to be accosted. They let him go on in silence across the small field to the wood.

There was not the least difference between this morning and those of the bright springs, six or eight years back. White and sandy-gold fowls still scratched round the gate, littering the earth and the field with feathers and scratched-up rubbish. Between the two thick holly bushes in the wood-hedge was the hidden gap, whose fence one climbed to get into the wood; the bars were scored just the same by the keeper's boots. He was back in the eternal.

Syson was extraordinarily glad. Like an uneasy spirit he had returned to the country of his past, and he found it waiting for him, unaltered. The hazel still spread glad little hands downwards, the bluebells here were still wan and few, among the lush grass and in shade of the bushes.

The path through the wood, on the very brow of a slope, ran winding easily for a time. All around were twiggy oaks, just issuing their gold, and floor spaces diapered with woodruff, with patches of dog-mercury and tufts of hyacinth. Two fallen trees still lay across the track. Syson jolted down a steep, rough slope, and came again upon the open land, this time looking north as through a great window in the wood. He stayed to gaze over the level fields of the hill-top, at the village which strewed the bare upland as if it had tumbled off the passing wagons of industry, and been forsaken. There was a stiff, modern, grey little church, and blocks and rows of red dwellings lying at random; at the back, the twinkling headstocks of the pit, and the looming pit-hill. All was naked and out-of-doors, not a tree! It was quite unaltered.

Syson turned, satisfied, to follow the path that sheered downhill into the wood. He was curiously elated, feeling himself back in an enduring vision. He started. A keeper was standing a few yards in front, barring the way.

"Where might you be going this road, sir?" asked the man. The tone of his question had a challenging twang. Syson looked at the fellow with an impersonal, observant gaze. It was a young man of four- or five-and-twenty, ruddy and well favoured. His dark blue eyes now stared aggressively at the intruder. His black moustache, very thick, was cropped short over a small, rather soft mouth. In every other respect the fellow was manly and good-looking. He stood just above middle height; the strong forward thrust of his chest, and the perfect ease of his erect, self-sufficient body, gave one the feeling that he was taut with animal life, like the thick jet of a fountain balanced in itself. He stood with the butt of his gun on the ground, looking uncertainly and questioningly at Syson. The dark, restless eyes of the trespasser, examining the man and penetrating into him without heeding his office, troubled the keeper and made him flush.

"Where is Naylor? Have you got his job?" Syson asked.

"You're not from the House, are you?" inquired the keeper. It could not be, since everyone was away.

"No, I'm not from the House," the other replied. It seemed to amuse him.

"Then might I ask where you were making for?" said the keeper, nettled.

"Where I am making for?" Syson repeated. "I am going to Willey-Water Farm."

"This isn't the road."

"I think so. Down this path, past the well, and out by the white gate."

"But that's not the public road."

"I suppose not. I used to come so often, in Naylor's time, I had forgotten. Where is he, by the way?"

"Crippled with rheumatism," the keeper answered reluctantly.

"Is he?" Syson exclaimed in pain.

"And who might you be?" asked the keeper, with a new intonation.

"John Adderley Syson; I used to live in Cordy Lane."

"Used to court Hilda Millership?"

Syson's eyes opened with a pained smile. He nodded. There was an awkward silence.

"And you—who are you?" asked Syson.

"Arthur Pilbeam—Naylor's my uncle," said the other.

"You live here in Nuttall?"

"I'm lodgin' at my uncle's—at Naylor's."

"I see!"

"Did you say you was goin' down to Willey-Water?" asked the keeper.

"Yes."

There was a pause of some moments, before the keeper blurted: "*I'm* courtin' Hilda Millership."

The young fellow looked at the intruder with a stubborn defiance, almost pathetic. Syson opened new eyes.

"Are you?" he said, astonished. The keeper flushed dark.

"She and me are keeping company," he said.

"I didn't know!" said Syson. The other man waited uncomfortably.

"What, is the thing settled?" asked the intruder.

"How, settled?" retorted the other sulkily.

"Are you going to get married soon, and all that?"

The keeper stared in silence for some moments, impotent.

"I suppose so," he said, full of resentment.

"Ah!" Syson watched closely.

"I'm married myself," he added, after a time.

"You are?" said the other incredulously.

Syson laughed in his brilliant, unhappy way.

"This last fifteen months," he said.

The keeper gazed at him with wide, wondering eyes, apparently thinking back, and trying to make things out.

"Why, didn't you know?" asked Syson.

"No, I didn't," said the other sulkily.

There was silence for a moment.

"Ah well!" said Syson, "I will go on. I suppose I may."

The keeper stood in silent opposition. The two men hesitated in the open, grassy space, set round with small sheaves of sturdy bluebells; a little open platform on the brow of the hill. Syson took a few indecisive steps forward, then stopped.

"I say, how beautiful!" he cried.

He had come in full view of the downslope. The wide path ran from his feet like a river, and it was full of bluebells, save for a green winding thread down the centre, where the keeper walked. Like a stream the path opened into azure shallows at the levels, and there were pools of bluebells, with still the green thread winding through, like a thin current of ice-water through blue lakes. And from under the twig-purple of the bushes swam the shadowed blue, as if the flowers lay in flood water over the woodland.

"Ah, isn't it lovely!" Syson exclaimed; this was his past, the country he had abandoned, and it hurt him to see it so beautiful. Wood-pigeons cooed overhead, and the air was full of the brightness of birds singing.

"If you're married, what do you keep writing to her for, and sending her poetry books and things?" asked the keeper. Syson stared at him, taken aback and humiliated. Then he began to smile.

"Well," he said, "I did not know about you . . ."

Again the keeper flushed darkly.

"But if you are married——" he charged.

"I am," answered the other cynically.

Then, looking down the blue, beautiful path, Syson felt his own humiliation. "What right *have* I to hang on to her?" he thought, bitterly self-contemptuous.

"She knows I'm married and all that," he said.

"But you keep sending her books," challenged the keeper.

Syson, silenced, looked at the other man quizzically, half pitying. Then he turned.

"Good day," he said, and was gone. Now, everything irritated him : the two sallows, one all gold and perfume and murmur, one silver-green and bristly, reminded him that here he had taught her about pollination. What a fool he was! What god-forsaken folly it all was!

"Ah well," he said to himself; "the poor devil seems to have a grudge against me. I'll do my best for him." He grinned to himself, in a very bad temper.

II

The farm was less than a hundred yards from the wood's edge. The wall of trees formed the fourth side to the open quadrangle. The house faced the wood. With tangled emotions, Syson noted the plum blossom falling on the profuse, coloured primroses, which he himself had brought here and set. How they had increased! There were thick tufts of scarlet, and pink, and pale purple primroses under the plum trees. He saw somebody glance at him through the kitchen window, heard men's voices.

The door opened suddenly: very womanly she had grown! He felt himself going pale.

"You?—Addy!" she exclaimed, and stood motionless.

"Who?" called the farmer's voice. Men's low voices answerered. Those low voices, curious and almost jeering, roused the tormented spirit in the visitor. Smiling brilliantly at her, he waited.

"Myself—why not?" he said.

The flush burned very deep on her cheek and throat.

"We are just finishing dinner," she said.

"Then I will stay outside." He made a motion to show that he would sit on the red earthenware pipkin that stood near the door among the daffodils, and contained the drinking-water.

"Oh no, come in," she said hurriedly. He followed her. In the doorway, he glanced swiftly over the family, and bowed. Everyone was confused. The farmer, his wife, and the four sons sat at the coarsely laid dinner-table, the men with arms bare to the elbows.

"I am sorry I come at lunch-time," said Syson.

"Hello, Addy!" said the farmer, assuming the old form of address, but his tone cold. "How are you?"

And he shook hands.

"Shall you have a bit?" he invited the young visitor, but taking for granted the offer would be refused. He assumed that Syson was become too refined to eat so roughly. The young man winced at the imputation.

"Have you had any dinner?" asked the daughter.

"No," replied Syson. "It is too early. I shall be back at half-past one."

"You call it lunch, don't you?" asked the eldest son, almost ironical. He had once been an intimate friend of this young man.

"We'll give Addy something when we've finished," said the mother, an invalid, deprecating.

"No—don't trouble. I don't want to give you any trouble," said Syson.

"You could allus live on fresh air an' scenery," laughed the youngest son, a lad of nineteen.

Syson went round the buildings, and into the orchard at the

back of the house, where daffodils all along the hedgerow swung like yellow, ruffled birds on their perches. He loved the place extraordinarily, the hills ranging round, with bear-skin woods covering their giant shoulders, and small red farms like brooches clasping their garments; the blue streak of water in the valley, the bareness of the home pasture, the sound of myriad-threaded bird-singing, which went mostly unheard. To his last day, he would dream of this place, when he felt the sun on his face, or saw the small handfuls of snow between the winter twigs, or smelt the coming of spring.

Hilda was very womanly. In her presence he felt constrained. She was twenty-nine, as he was, but she seemed to him much older. He felt foolish, almost unreal beside her. She was so static. As he was fingering some shed plum blossom on a low bough, she came to the back door to shake the tablecloth. Fowls raced from the stack-yard, birds rustled from the trees. Her dark hair was gathered up in a coil like a crown on her head. She was very straight, distant in her bearing. As she folded the cloth, she looked away over the hills.

Presently Syson returned indoors. She had prepared eggs and curd cheese, stewed gooseberries and cream.

"Since you will dine to-night," she said, "I have only given you a light lunch."

"It is awfully nice," he said. "You keep a real idyllic atmosphere—your belt of straw and ivy buds."

Still they hurt each other.

He was uneasy before her. Her brief, sure speech, her distant bearing, were unfamiliar to him. He admired again her grey-black eyebrows, and her lashes. Their eyes met. He saw, in the beautiful grey and black of her glance, tears and a strange light, and at the back of all, calm acceptance of herself, and triumph over him.

He felt himself shrinking. With an effort he kept up the ironic manner.

She sent him into the parlour while she washed the dishes. The long low room was refurnished from the Abbey sale, with chairs upholstered in claret-coloured rep, many years old, and an oval table of polished walnut, and another piano, handsome, though still antique. In spite of the strangeness, he was pleased. Opening a high cupboard let into the thickness of the wall, he found it full of his books, his old lesson-books, and volumes of verse he had sent her, English and German. The daffodils in the white window-bottoms shone across the room, he could almost feel their rays. The old glamour caught him again. His youthful water-colours on the wall no longer made him grin; he remembered how fervently he had tried to paint for her, twelve years before.

She entered, wiping a dish, and he saw again the bright, kernel-white beauty of her arms.

"You are quite splendid here," he said, and their eyes met.

"Do you like it?" she asked. It was the old, low, husky tone of intimacy. He felt a quick change beginning in his blood. It was the old, delicious sublimation, the thinning, almost the vaporising of himself, as if his spirit were to be liberated.

"Aye," he nodded, smiling at her like a boy again. She bowed her head.

"This was the countess's chair," she said in low tones. "I found her scissors down here between the padding."

"Did you? Where are they?"

Quickly, with a lilt in her movement, she fetched her work-basket, and together they examined the long-shanked old scissors.

"What a ballad of dead ladies!" he said, laughing, as he fitted his fingers into the round loops of the countess's scissors.

"I knew you could use them," she said, with certainty. He looked at his fingers, and at the scissors. She meant his fingers were fine enough for the small-looped scissors.

"That is something to be said for me," he laughed, putting the scissors aside. She turned to the window. He noticed the fine, fair down on her cheeks and her upper lip, and her soft, white neck, like the throat of a nettle flower, and her fore-arms, bright as newly blanched kernels. He was looking at at her with new eyes, and she was a different person to him. He did not know her. But he could regard her objectively now.

"Shall we go out awhile?" she asked.

"Yes!" he answered. But the predominant emotion, that troubled the excitement and perplexity of his heart, was fear, fear of that which he saw. There was about her the same manner, the same intonation in her voice, now as then, but she was not what he had known her to be. He knew quite well what she had been for him. And gradually he was realising that she was something quite other, and always had been.

She put no covering on her head, merely took off her apron, saying: "We will go by the larches." As they passed the old

orchard, she called him in to show him a blue-tit's nest in one
of the apple trees, and a sycock's in the hedge. He rather
wondered at her surety, at a certain hardness like arrogance
hidden under her humility.

"Look at the apple buds," she said, and he then perceived
myriads of little scarlet balls among the drooping boughs.
Watching his face, her eyes went hard. She saw the scales
were fallen from him, and at last he was going to see her as she
was. It was the thing she had most dreaded in the past, and
most needed, for her soul's sake. Now he was going to see her
as she was. He would not love her, and he would know he
never could have loved her. The old illusion gone, they were
strangers, crude and entire. But he would give her her due—
she would have her due from him.

She was brilliant as he had not known her. She showed him
nests: a jenny wren's in a low bush.

"See this jinty's!" she exclaimed.

He was surprised to hear her use the local name. She
reached carefully through the thorns, and put her finger in
the nest's round door.

"Five!" she said. "Tiny little things."

She showed him nests of robins, and chaffinches, and linnets,
and buntings; of a wagtail beside the water.

"And if we go down, nearer the lake, I will show you a kingfisher's. . . ."

"Among the young fir trees," she said, "there's a throstle's
or a blackie's on nearly every bough, every ledge. The first
day, when I had seen them all, I felt as if I mustn't go in the
wood. It seemed a city of birds: and in the morning, hearing
them all, I thought of the noisy early markets. I was afraid
to go in my own wood."

She was using the language they had both of them invented.
Now it was all her own. He had done with it. She did not
mind his silence, but was always dominant, letting him see her
wood. As they came along a marshy path where forget-me-nots
were opening in a rich blue drift: "We know all the birds, but
there are many flowers we can't find out," she said. It was
half an appeal to him, who had known the names of things.

She looked dreamily across to the open fields that slept in
the sun.

"I have a lover as well, you know," she said, with assurance,
yet dropping again almost into the intimate tone.

This woke in him the spirit to fight her.

"I think I met him. He is good-looking—also in Arcady."

Without answering, she turned into a dark path that led up-hill, where the trees and undergrowth were very thick.

"They did well," she said at length, "to have various altars to various gods, in old days."

"Ah yes!" he agreed. "To whom is the new one?"

"There are no old ones," she said. "I was always looking for this."

"And whose is it?" he asked.

"I don't know," she said, looking full at him.

"I'm very glad, for your sake," he said, "that you are satisfied."

"Aye—but the man doesn't matter so much," she said. There was a pause.

"No!" he exclaimed, astonished, yet recognising her as her real self.

"It is one's self that matters," she said. "Whether one is being one's own self and serving one's own God."

There was silence, during which he pondered. The path was almost flowerless, gloomy. At the side, his heels sank into soft clay.

III

"I," she said, very slowly, "I was married the same night as you."

He looked at her.

"Not legally, of course," she replied. "But—actually."

"To the keeper?" he said, not knowing what else to say.

She turned to him.

"You thought I could not?" she said. But the flush was deep in her cheek and throat, for all her assurance.

Still he would not say anything.

"You see"—she was making an effort to explain—"*I* had to understand also."

"And what does it amount to, this *understanding*?" he asked.

"A very great deal—does it not to you?" she replied. "One is free."

"And you are not disappointed?"

"Far from it!" Her tone was deep and sincere.

"You love him?"

"Yes, I love him."

"Good!" he said.

This silenced her for a while.

"Here, among his things, I love him," she said.

His conceit would not let him be silent.

"It needs this setting?" he asked.

"It does," she cried. "You were always making me to be not myself."

He laughed shortly.

"But is it a matter of surroundings?" he said. He had considered her all spirit.

"I am like a plant," she replied. "I can only grow in my own soil."

They came to a place where the undergrowth shrank away, leaving a bare, brown space, pillared with the brick-red and purplish trunks of pine trees. On the fringe, hung the sombre green of elder trees, with flat flowers in bud, and below were bright, unfurling pennons of fern. In the midst of the bare space stood a keeper's log hut. Pheasant-coops were lying about, some occupied by a clucking hen, some empty.

Hilda walked over the brown pine-needles to the hut, took a key from among the eaves, and opened the door. It was a bare wooden place with a carpenter's bench and form, carpenter's tools, an axe, snares, traps, some skins pegged down, everything in order. Hilda closed the door. Syson examined the weird flat coats of wild animals, that were pegged down to be cured. She turned some knotch in the side wall, and disclosed a second, small apartment.

"How romantic!" said Syson.

"Yes. He is very curious—he has some of a wild animal's cunning—in a nice sense—and he is inventive, and thoughtful —but not beyond a certain point."

She pulled back a dark green curtain. The apartment was occupied almost entirely by a large couch of heather and bracken, on which was spread an ample rabbit-skin rug. On the floor were patchwork rugs of cat-skin, and a red calf-skin, while hanging from the wall were other furs. Hilda took down one, which she put on. It was a cloak of rabbit-skin and of white fur. with a hood, apparently of the skins of stoats. She laughed at Syson from out of this barbaric mantle, saying:

"What do you think of it?"

"Ah——! I congratulate you on your man," he replied.

"And look!" she said.

In a little jar on a shelf were some sprays, frail and white, of the first honeysuckle.

"They will scent the place at night,"

He looked round curiously.

"Where does he come short, then?" he asked. She gazed at him for a few moments. Then, turning aside:

"The stars aren't the same with him," she said. "You could make them flash and quiver, and the forget-me-nots come up at me like phosphorescence. You could make things *wonderful*. I have found it out—it is true. But I have them all for myself, now."

He laughed, saying:

"After all, stars and forget-me-nots are only luxuries. You ought to make poetry."

"Aye," she assented. "But I have them all now."

Again he laughed bitterly at her.

She turned swiftly. He was leaning against the small window of the tiny, obscure room, and was watching her, who stood in the doorway, still cloaked in her mantle. His cap was removed, so she saw his face and head distinctly in the dim room. His black, straight, glossy hair was brushed clean back from his brow. His black eyes were watching her, and his face, that was clear and cream, and perfectly smooth, was flickering.

"We are very different," she said bitterly.

Again he laughed.

"I see you disapprove of me," he said.

"I disapprove of what you have become," she said.

"You think we might"—he glanced at the hut—"have been like this—you and I?"

She shook her head.

"You! No; never! You plucked a thing and looked at it till you had found out all you wanted to know about it, then you threw it away," she said.

"Did I?" he asked. "And could your way never have been my way? I suppose not."

"Why should it?" she said. "I am a separate being."

"But surely two people sometimes go the same way," he said.

"You took me away from myself," she said.

He knew he had mistaken her, had taken her for something she was not. That was his fault, not hers.

"And did you always know?" he asked.

"No—you never let me know. You bullied me. I couldn't help myself. I was glad when you left me, really."

"I know you were," he said. But his face went paler, almost deathly luminous.

"Yet," he said, "it was you who sent me the way I have gone."

"I!" she exclaimed, in pride.

"You *would* have me take the Grammar School scholarship—and you would have me foster poor little Botell's fervent attachment to me, till he couldn't live without me—and because Botell was rich and influential. You triumphed in the wine-merchant's offer to send me to Cambridge, to befriend his only child. You wanted me to rise in the world. And all the time you were sending me away from you—every new success of mine put a separation between us, and more for you than for me. You never wanted to come with me: you wanted just to send me to see what it was like. I believe you even wanted me to marry a lady. You wanted to triumph over society in me."

"And I am responsible," she said, with sarcasm.

"I distinguished myself to satisfy you," he replied.

"Ah!" she cried, "you always wanted change, change, like a child."

"Very well! And I am a success, and I know it, and I do some good work. But—I thought you were different. What right have you to a man?"

"What do you want?" she said, looking at him with wide, fearful eyes.

He looked back at her, his eyes pointed, like weapons.

"Why, nothing," he laughed shortly.

There was a rattling at the outer latch, and the keeper entered. The woman glanced round, but remained standing, fur-cloaked, in the inner doorway. Syson did not move.

The other man entered, saw, and turned away without speaking. The two also were silent.

Pilbeam attended to his skins.

"I must go," said Syson.

"Yes," she replied.

"Then I give you 'To our vast and varying fortunes.' " He lifted his hand in pledge.

" 'To our vast and varying fortunes,' " she answered gravely, and speaking in cold tones.

"Arthur!" she said.

The keeper pretended not to hear. Syson, watching keenly, began to smile. The woman drew herself up.

"Arthur!" she said again, with a curious upward inflection, which warned the two men that her soul was trembling on a dangerous crisis.

The keeper slowly put down his tool and came to her.

"Yes," he said.

"I wanted to introduce you," she said, trembling.

"I've met him a'ready," said the keeper.

"Have you? It is Addy, Mr. Syson, whom you know about. —This is Arthur, Mr. Pilbeam," she added, turning to Syson. The latter held out his hand to the keeper, and they shook hands in silence.

"I'm glad to have met you," said Syson. "We drop our correspondence, Hilda?"

"Why need we?" she asked.

The two men stood at a loss.

"*Is* there no need?" said Syson.

Still she was silent.

"It is as you will," she said.

They went all three together down the gloomy path.

" 'Qu'il était bleu, le ciel, et grand l'espoir,' " quoted Syson, not knowing what to say.

"What do you mean?" she said. "Besides, *we* can't walk in *our* wild oats—we never sowed any."

Syson looked at her. He was startled to see his young love, his nun, his Botticelli angel, so revealed. It was he who had been the fool. He and she were more separate than any two strangers could be. She only wanted to keep up a correspondence with him -and he, of course, wanted it kept up, so that he could write to her, like Dante to some Beatrice who had never existed save in the man's own brain.

At the bottom of the path she left him. He went along with the keeper, towards the open, towards the gate that closed on the wood. The two men walked almost like friends. They did not broach the subject of their thoughts.

.   .   .   .   .

Instead of going straight to the high-road gate, Syson went along the woods' edge, where the brook spread out in a little bog, and under the alder trees, among the reeds, great yellow stools and bosses of marigolds shone. Threads of brown water trickled by, touched with gold from the flowers. Suddenly there was a blue flash in the air, as a kingfisher passed.

Syson was extraordinarily moved. He climbed the bank to the gorse bushes, whose sparks of blossom had not yet gathered into a flame. Lying on the dry brown turf, he discovered sprigs of tiny purple milkwort and pink spots of louse-wort. What a wonderful world it was—marvellous, for ever new. He felt as if it were underground, like the fields of mono-tone hell, notwithstanding. Inside his breast was a pain like a wound. He remembered the poem of William Morris, where in the Chapel of Lyonesse a knight lay wounded, with the truncheon of a spear deep in his breast, lying always as dead, yet did not die, while day after day the coloured sunlight dipped from the painted window across the chancel, and passed away. He knew now it never had been true, that which was between him and her, not for a moment. The truth had stood apart all the time.

Syson turned over. The air was full of the sound of larks, as if the sunshine above were condensing and falling in a shower. Amid this bright sound, voices sounded small and distinct.

"But if he's married, an' quite willing to drop it off, what has ter against it?" said the man's voice.

"I don't want to talk about it now. I want to be alone."

Syson looked through the bushes. Hilda was standing in the wood, near the gate. The man was in the field, loitering by the hedge, and playing with the bees as they settled on the white bramble flowers.

There was silence for a while, in which Syson imagined her will among the brightness of the larks. Suddenly the keeper exclaimed "Ah!" and swore. He was gripping at the sleeve of his coat, near the shoulder. Then he pulled off his jacket, threw it on the ground, and absorbedly rolled up his shirt-sleeves right to the shoulder.

"Ah!" he said vindictively, as he picked out the bee and flung it away. He twisted his fine, bright arm, peering awkwardly over his shoulder.

"What is it?" asked Hilda.

"A bee—crawled up my sleeve," he answered.

"Come here to me," she said.

The keeper went to her, like a sulky boy. She took his arm in her hands.

"Here it is—and the sting left in—poor bee!"

She picked out the sting, put her mouth to his arm, and sucked away the drop of poison. As she looked at the red mark her mouth had made, and at his arm, she said, laughing:

"That is the reddest kiss you will ever have."

When Syson next looked up, at the sound of voices, he saw in the shadow the keeper with his mouth on the throat of his beloved, whose head was thrown back, and whose hair had fallen, so that one rough rope of dark brown hair hung across his bare arm.

"No," the woman answered. "I am not upset because he's gone. You won't understand. . . ."

Syson could not distinguish what the man said. Hilda replied, clear and distinct:

"You know I love you. He has gone quite out of my life—don't trouble about him. . . ." He kissed her, murmuring. She laughed hollowly.

"Yes," she said, indulgent. "We will be married, we will be married. But not just yet." He spoke to her again. Syson heard nothing for a time. Then she said:

"You must go home now, dear—you will get no sleep."

Again was heard the murmur of the keeper's voice, troubled by fear and passion.

"But why should we be married at once?" she said. "What more would you have, by being married? It is most beautiful as it is."

At last he pulled on his coat and departed. She stood at the gate, not watching him, but looking over the sunny country.

When at last she had gone, Syson also departed, going back to town.

SECOND BEST

"Oh, I'm tired!" Frances exclaimed petulantly, and in the same instant she dropped down on the turf, near the hedge-bottom. Anne stood a moment surprised, then, accustomed to the vagaries of her beloved Frances, said:

"Well, and aren't you always likely to be tired, after travelling that blessed long way from Liverpool yesterday?" and she plumped down beside her sister. Anne was a wise young body of fourteen, very buxom, brimming with common sense. Frances was much older, about twenty-three, and whimsical, spasmodic. She was the beauty and the clever child of the family. She plucked the goose-grass buttons from her dress in a nervous, desperate fashion. Her beautiful profile, looped above with black hair, warm with the dusky-and-scarlet complexion of a pear, was calm as a mask, her thin brown hand plucked nervously.

"It's not the journey," she said, objecting to Anne's obtuseness. Anne looked inquiringly at her darling. The young girl, in her self-confident, practical way, proceeded to reckon up this whimsical creature. But suddenly she found herself full in the eyes of Frances; felt two dark, hectic eyes flaring challenge at her, and she shrank away. Frances was peculiar for these great, exposed looks, which disconcerted people by their violence and their suddenness.

"What's a matter, poor old duck?" asked Anne, as she folded the slight, wilful form of her sister in her arms. Frances laughed shakily, and nestled down for comfort on the budding breasts of the strong girl.

"Oh, I'm only a bit tired," she murmured, on the point of tears.

"Well, of course you are, what do you expect?" soothed Anne. It was a joke to Frances that Anne should play elder, almost mother to her. But then, Anne was in her unvexed teens; men were like big dogs to her: while Frances, at twenty-three, suffered a good deal.

The country was intensely morning-still. On the common everything shone beside its shadow, and the hill-side gave off heat in silence. The brown turf seemed in a low state of combustion, the leaves of the oaks were scorched brown. Among the blackish foliage in the distance shone the small red and orange of the village.

The willows in the brook-course at the foot of the common suddenly shook with a dazzling effect like diamonds. It was a puff of wind. Anne resumed her normal position. She spread her knees, and put in her lap a handful of hazel nuts, whity-green leafy things, whose one check was tanned between brown and pink. These she began to crack and eat. Frances, with bowed head, mused bitterly.

"Eh, you know Tom Smedley?" began the young girl, as she pulled a tight kernel out of its shell.

"I suppose so," replied Frances sarcastically.

"Well, he gave me a wild rabbit what he'd caught, to keep with my tame one—and it's living."

"That's a good thing," said Frances, very detached and ironic.

"Well, it *is!* He reckoned he'd take me to Ollerton Feast, but he never did. Look here, he took a servant from the rectory; I saw him."

"So he ought," said Frances.

"No, he oughtn't! And I told him so. And I told him I should tell you—an' I have done."

Click and snap went a nut between her teeth. She sorted out the kernel, and chewed complacently.

"It doesn't make much difference," said Frances.

"Well, 'appen it doesn't; but I was mad with him all the same."

"Why?"

"Because I was; he's no right to go with a servant."

"He's a perfect right," persisted Frances, very just and cold.

"No, he hasn't, when he'd said he'd take me."

Frances burst into a laugh of amusement and relief.

"Oh no; I'd forgot that," she said, adding, "and what did he say when you promised to tell me?"

"He laughed and said: 'She won't fret her fat over that.' "

"And she won't," sniffed Frances.

There was silence. The common, with its sere, blonde-headed thistles, its heaps of silent bramble, its brown-husked gorse in the glare of sunshine, seemed visionary. Across the brook began the immense pattern of agriculture, white chequering

of barley stubble, brown squares of wheat, khaki patches of
pasture, red stripes of fallow, with the woodland and the tiny
village dark like ornaments, leading away to the distance, right
to the hills, where the check-pattern grew smaller and smaller,
till, in the blackish haze of heat, far off, only the tiny white
squares of barley stubble showed distinct.

"Eh, I say, here's a rabbit-hole!" cried Anne suddenly.
"Should we watch if one comes out? You won't have to
fidget, you know."

The two girls sat perfectly still. Frances watched certain
objects in her surroundings: they had a peculiar, unfriendly
look about them: the weight of greenish elderberries on their
purpling stalks; the twinkling of the yellowing crab-apple that
clustered high up in the hedge, against the sky: the exhausted,
limp leaves of the primroses lying flat in the hedge-bottom:
all looked strange to her. Then her eyes caught a movement.
A mole was moving silently over the warm, red soil, nosing,
shuffling hither and thither, flat, and dark as a shadow, shifting about, and as suddenly brisk, and as silent, like a very
ghost of *joie de vivre*. Frances started, from habit was about
to call on Anne to kill the little pest. But, to-day her lethargy
of unhappiness was too much for her. She watched the little
brute paddling, snuffing, touching things to discover them, running in blindness, delighted to ecstasy by the sunlight and the
hot, strange things that caressed its belly and its nose. She felt
a keen pity for the little creature.

"Eh, our Fran, look there! It's a mole."

Anne was on her feet, standing watching the dark, unconscious beast. Frances frowned with anxiety.

"It doesn't run off, does it?" said the young girl softly. Then
she stealthily approached the creature. The mole paddled
fumblingly away. In an instant Anne put her foot upon it,
not too heavily. Frances could see the struggling, swimming
movement of the little pink hands of the brute, the twisting
and twitching of its pointed nose, as it wrestled under the sole
of the boot.

"It *does* wriggle!" said the bonny girl, knitting her brows in
a frown at the eerie sensation. Then she bent down to look at
her trap. Frances could now see, beyond the edge of the boot-
sole, the heaving of the velvet shoulders, the pitiful turning of
the sightless face, the frantic rowing of the flat, pink hands.

"Kill the thing," she said, turning away her face.

"Oh—I'm not," laughed Anne, shrinking. "You can, if you like."

"I *don't* like," said Frances, with quiet intensity.

After several dabbing attempts, Anne succeeded in picking up the little animal by the scruff of its neck. It threw back its head, flung its long blind snout from side to side, the mouth open in a peculiar oblong, with tiny pinkish teeth at the edge. The blind, frantic mouth gaped and writhed. The body, heavy and clumsy, hung scarcely moving.

"Isn't it a snappy little thing," observed Anne, twisting to avoid the teeth.

"What are you going to do with it?" asked Frances sharply.

"It's got to be killed—look at the damage they do. I s'll take it home and let dadda or somebody kill it. I'm not going to let it go."

She swaddled the creature clumsily in her pocket handkerchief and sat down beside her sister. There was an interval of silence, during which Anne combated the efforts of the mole.

"You've not had much to say about Jimmy this time. Did you see him often in Liverpool?" Anne asked suddenly.

"Once or twice," replied Frances, giving no sign of how the question troubled her.

"And aren't you sweet on him any more, then?"

"I should think I'm not, seeing that he's engaged."

"Engaged? Jimmy Barrass! Well, of all things! I never thought *he'd* get engaged."

"Why not, he's as much right as anybody else?" snapped Frances.

Anne was fumbling with the mole.

" 'Appen so," she said at length; "but I never thought Jimmy would, though."

"Why not?" snapped Frances.

"*I* don't know—this blessed mole, it'll not keep still!—who's he got engaged to?"

"How should I know?"

"I thought you'd ask him; you've known him long enough. I s'd think he thought he'd get engaged now he's a Doctor of Chemistry."

Frances laughed in spite of herself.

"What's that got to do with it?" she asked.

"I'm sure it's got a bit. He'll want to feel *somebody* now, so he's got engaged. Hey, stop it; go in!"

But at this juncture the mole almost succeeded in wriggling clear. It wrestled and twisted frantically, waved its pointed blind head, its mouth standing open like a little shaft, its big, wrinkled hands spread out.

"Go in with you!" urged Anne, poking the little creature with her forefinger, trying to get it back into the handkerchief. Suddenly the mouth turned like a spark on her finger.

"Oh!" she cried, "he's bit me."

She dropped him to the floor. Dazed, the blind creature fumbled round. Frances felt like shrieking. She expected him to dart away in a flash, like a mouse, and there he remained groping; she wanted to cry to him to be gone. Anne, in a sudden decision of wrath, caught up her sister's walking-cane. With one blow the mole was dead. Frances was startled and shocked. One moment the little wretch was fussing in the heat, and the next it lay like a little bag, inert and black—not a struggle, scarce, a quiver.

"It is dead!" Frances said breathlessly. Anne took her finger from her mouth, looked at the tiny pin-pricks, and said:

"Yes, he is, and I'm glad. They're vicious little nuisances, moles are."

With which her wrath vanished. She picked up the dead animal.

"Hasn't it got a beautiful skin," she mused, stroking the fur with her forefinger, then with her cheek.

"Mind," said Frances sharply. "You'll have the blood on your skirt!"

One ruby drop of blood hung on the small snout, ready to fall. Anne shook it off on to some harebells. Frances suddenly became calm; in that moment, grown-up.

"I suppose they have to be killed," she said, and a certain rather dreary indifference succeeded to her grief. The twinkling crab-apples, the glitter of brilliant willows now seemed to her trifling, scarcely worth the notice. Something had died in her, so that things lost their poignancy. She was calm, indifference overlying her quiet sadness. Rising, she walked down to the brook course.

"Here, wait for me," cried Anne, coming tumbling after.

Frances stood on the bridge, looking at the red mud trodden into pockets by the feet of cattle. There was not a drain of water left, but everything smelled green, succulent. Why did she care so little for Anne, who was so fond of her? she asked herself. Why did she care so little for anyone? She did not know, but she felt a rather stubborn pride in her isolation and indifference.

They entered a field where stooks of barley stood in rows, the straight, blonde tresses of the corn streaming on to the ground. The stubble was bleached by the intense summer, so that the expanse glared white. The next field was sweet and soft with a second crop of seeds; thin, straggling clover whose little pink knobs rested prettily in the dark green. The scent was faint and sickly. The girls came up in single file, Frances leading.

Near the gate a young man was mowing with the scythe some fodder for the afternoon feed of the cattle. As he saw the girls he left off working and waited in an aimless kind of way. Frances was dressed in white muslin, and she walked with dignity, detached and forgetful. Her lack of agitation, her simple, unheeding advance made him nervous. She had loved the far-off Jimmy for five years, having had in return his half-measures. This man only affected her slightly.

Tom was of medium stature, energetic in build. His smooth, fair-skinned face was burned red, not brown, by the sun, and this ruddiness enhanced his appearance of good humour and easiness. Being a year older than Frances, he would have courted her long ago had she been so inclined. As it was, he had gone his uneventful way amiably, chatting with many a girl, but remaining unattached, free of trouble for the most part. Only he knew he wanted a woman. He hitched his trousers just a trifle self-consciously as the girls approached. Frances was a rare, delicate kind of being, whom he realised with a queer and delicious stimulation in his veins. She gave him a slight sense of suffocation. Somehow, this morning she affected him more than usual. She was dressed in white. He, however, being matter-of-fact in his mind, did not realise. His feeling had never become conscious, purposive.

Frances knew what she was about. Tom was ready to love her as soon as she would show him. Now that she could not have Jimmy, she did not poignantly care. Still, she would have something. If she could not have the best—Jimmy, whom she knew to be something of a snob—she would have the second best, Tom. She advanced rather indifferently.

"You are back, then!" said Tom. She marked the touch of uncertainty in his voice.

"No," she laughed, "I'm still in Liverpool," and the under-tone of intimacy made him burn.

"This isn't you, then?" he asked.

Her heart leapt up in approval. She looked in his eyes, and for a second was with him.

"Why, what do you think?" she laughed.

He lifted his hat from his head with a distracted little gesture. She liked him, his quaint ways, his humour, his ignorance, and his slow masculinity.

"Here, look here, Tom Smedley," broke in Anne.

"A moudiwarp! Did you find it dead?" he asked.

"No, it bit me," said Anne.

"Oh, aye! An' that got your rag out, did it?"

"No, it didn't!" Anne scolded sharply. "Such language!"

"Oh, what's up wi' it?"

"I can't bear you to talk broad."

"Can't you?"

He glanced at Frances.

"It isn't nice," Frances said. She did not care, really. The vulgar speech jarred on her as a rule; Jimmy was a gentleman. But Tom's manner of speech did not matter to her.

"I like you to talk *nicely*," she added.

"Do you," he replied, tilting his hat, stirred.

"And generally you *do*, you know," she smiled.

"I s'll have to have a try," he said, rather tensely gallant.

"What?" she asked brightly.

"To talk nice to you," he said. Frances coloured furiously, bent her head for a moment, then laughed gaily, as if she liked this clumsy hint.

"Eh now, you mind what you're saying," cried Anne, giving the young man an admonitory pat.

"You wouldn't have to give yon mole many knocks like that," he teased, relieved to get on safe ground, rubbing his arm.

"No, indeed, it died in one blow," said Frances, with a flippancy that was hateful to her.

"You're not so good at knockin' 'em?" he said, turning to her.

"I don't know, if I'm cross," she said decisively.

"No?" he replied, with alert attentiveness.

"I could," she added, harder, "if it was necessary."

He was slow to feel her difference.

"And don't you consider it *is* necessary?" he asked, with misgiving.

"W—ell—is it?" she said, looking at him steadily, coldly.

"I reckon it is," he replied, looking away, but standing stubborn.

She laughed quickly.

"But it isn't necessary for *me*," she said, with slight contempt.

"Yes, that's quite true," he answered.

She laughed in a shaky fashion.

"*I know it is*," she said; and there was an awkward pause.

"Why, would you *like* me to kill moles then?" she asked tentatively, after a while.

"They do us a lot of damage," he said, standing firm on his own ground, angered.

"Well, I'll see the next time I come across one," she promised defiantly. Their eyes met, and she sank before him, her pride troubled. He felt uneasy and triumphant and baffled, as if fate had gripped him. She smiled as she departed.

"Well," said Anne, as the sisters went through the wheat stubble; "I don't know what you two's been jawing about, I'm sure."

"Don't you?" laughed Frances significantly.

"No, I don't. But, at any rate, Tom Smedley's a good deal better to my thinking than Jimmy, so there—and nicer."

"Perhaps he is," said Frances coldly.

And the next day, after a secret, persistent hunt, she found another mole playing in the heat. She killed it, and in the evening, when Tom came to the gate to smoke his pipe after supper, she took him the dead creature.

"Here you are then!" she said.

"Did you catch it?" he replied, taking the velvet corpse into his fingers and examining it minutely. This was to hide his trepidation.

"Did you think I couldn't?" she asked, her face very near his.

"Nay, I didn't know."

She laughed in his face, a strange little laugh that caught her breath, all agitation, and tears, and recklessness of desire. He looked frightened and upset. She put her hand to his arm.

"Shall you go out wi' me?" he asked, in a difficult, troubled tone.

She turned her face away, with a shaky laugh. The blood came up in him, strong, overmastering. He resisted it. But it drove him down, and he was carried away. Seeing the winsome, frail nape of her neck, fierce love came upon him for her, and tenderness.

"We s'll 'ave to tell your mother," he said. And he stood, suffering, resisting his passion for her.

"Yes," she replied, in a dead voice. But there was a thrill of pleasure in this death.

THE SHADOW IN THE ROSE GARDEN

A RATHER small young man sat by the window of a pretty sea-side cottage trying to persuade himself that he was reading the newspaper. It was about half-past eight in the morning. Outside, the glory roses hung in the morning sunshine like little bowls of fire tipped up. The young man looked at the table, then at the clock, then at his own big silver watch. An expression of stiff endurance came on to his face. Then he rose and reflected on the oil-paintings that hung on the walls of the room, giving careful but hostile attention to 'The Stag at Bay'. He tried the lid of the piano, and found it locked. He caught sight of his own face in a little mirror, pulled his brown moustache, and an alert interest sprang into his eyes. He was not ill-favoured. He twisted his moustache. His figure was rather small, but alert and vigorous. As he turned from the mirror a look of self-commiseration mingled with his appreciation of his own physiognomy.

In a state of self-suppression, he went through into the garden. His jacket, however, did not look dejected. It was new, and had a smart and self-confident air, sitting upon a confident body. He contemplated the Tree of Heaven that flourished by the lawn, then sauntered on to the next plant. There was more promise in a crooked apple tree covered with brown-red fruit. Glancing round, he broke off an apple and, with his back to the house, took a clean, sharp bite. To his surprise the fruit was sweet. He took another. Then again he turned to survey the bedroom windows overlooking the garden. He started, seeing a woman's figure; but it was only his wife. She was gazing across to the sea, apparently ignorant of him.

For a moment or two he looked at her, watching her. She was a good-looking woman, who seemed older than he, rather pale, but healthy, her face yearning. Her rich auburn hair was heaped in folds on her forehead. She looked apart from him and his world, gazing away to the sea. It irked her husband that she should continue abstracted and in ignorance of him; he pulled poppy fruits and threw them at the window. She started, glanced at him with a wild smile, and looked away again. Then almost immediately she left the window. He went indoors to meet her. She had a fine carriage, very proud, and wore a dress of soft white muslin.

"I've been waiting long enough," he said.

"For me or for breakfast?" she said lightly. "You know we said nine o'clock. I should have thought you could have slept after the journey."

"You know I'm always up at five, and I couldn't stop in bed after six. You might as well be in pit as in bed, on a morning like this."

"I shouldn't have thought the pit would occur to you, here."

She moved about examining the room, looking at the ornaments under glass covers. He, planted on the hearth-rug, watched her rather uneasily, and grudgingly indulgent. She shrugged her shoulders at the apartment.

"Come," she said, taking his arm, "let us go into the garden till Mrs. Coates brings the tray."

"I hope she'll be quick," he said, pulling his moustache. She gave a short laugh, and leaned on his arm as they went. He had lighted a pipe.

Mrs. Coates entered the room as they went down the steps. The delightful, erect old lady hastened to the window for a good view of her visitors. Her china-blue eyes were bright as she watched the young couple go down the path, he walking in an easy, confident fashion, with his wife on his arm. The landlady began talking to herself in a soft, Yorkshire accent.

"Just of a height they are. She wouldn't ha' married a man less than herself in stature, I think, though he's not her equal otherwise." Here her granddaughter came in, setting a tray on the table. The girl went to the old woman's side.

"He's been eating the apples, Gran'," she said.

"Has he, my pet? Well, if he's happy, why not?"

Outside, the young, well-favoured man listened with impatience to the chink of the tea-cups. At last, with a sigh of relief, the couple came in to breakfast. After he had eaten for some time, he rested a moment and said:

"Do you think it's any better place than Bridlington?"

"I do," she said, "infinitely! Besides, I am at home here—it's not like a strange sea-side place to me."

"How long were you here?"

"Two years."

He ate reflectively.

"I should ha' thought you'd rather go to a fresh place," he said at length.

She sat very silent, and then, delicately, put out a feeler.

"Why?" she said. "Do you think I shan't enjoy myself?"

He laughed comfortably, putting the marmalade thick on his bread.

"I hope so," he said.

She again took no notice of him.

"But don't say anything about it in the village, Frank," she said casually. "Don't say who I am, or that I used to live here. There's nobody I want to meet, particularly, and we should never feel free if they knew me again."

"Why did you come, then?"

" 'Why?' Can't you understand why?"

"Not if you don't want to know anybody."

"I came to see the place, not the people."

He did not say any more.

"Women," she said, "are different from men. I don't know why I wanted to come—but I did."

She helped him to another cup of coffee, solicitously.

"Only," she resumed, "don't talk about me in the village." She laughed shakily. "I don't want my past brought up against me, you know." And she moved the crumbs on the cloth with her finger-tip.

He looked at her as he drank his coffee; he sucked his moustache, and putting down his cup, said phlegmatically:

"I'll bet you've had a lot of past."

She looked with a little guiltiness, that flattered him, down at the table-cloth.

"Well," she said, caressive, "you won't give me away, who I am, will you?"

"No," he said, comforting, laughing, "I won't give you away."

He was pleased.

She remained silent. After a moment or two she lifted her head, saying:

"I've got to arrange with Mrs. Coates, and do various things. So you'd better go out by yourself this morning—and we'll be in to dinner at one."

"But you can't be arranging with Mrs. Coates all morning," he said.

"Oh, well—then I've some letters to write, and I must get

that mark out of my skirt. I've got plenty of little things to do this morning. You'd better go out by yourself."

He perceived that she wanted to be rid of him, so that when she went upstairs, he took his hat and lounged out on to the cliffs, suppressedly angry.

Presently she too came out. She wore a hat with roses, and a long lace scarf hung over her white dress. Rather nervously, she put up her sunshade, and her face was half hidden in its coloured shadow. She went along the narrow track of flag-stones that were worn hollow by the feet of the fishermen. She seemed to be avoiding her surroundings, as if she remained safe in the little obscurity of her parasol.

She passed the church, and went down the lane till she came to a high wall by the wayside. Under this she went slowly, stopping at length by an open doorway, which shone like a picture of light in the dark wall. There in the magic beyond the doorway, patterns of shadow lay on the sunny court, on the blue and white sea-pebbles of its paving, while a green lawn glowed beyond, where a bay tree glittered at the edges. She tiptoed nervously into the courtyard, glancing at the house that stood in shadow. The uncurtained windows looked black and soulless, the kitchen door stood open. Irresolutely she took a step forward, and again forward, leaning, yearning, towards the garden beyond.

She had almost gained the corner of the house when a heavy step came crunching through the trees. A gardener appeared before her. He held a wicker tray on which were rolling great, dark red gooseberries, over-ripe. He moved slowly.

"The garden isn't open to-day," he said quietly to the attractive woman, who was poised for retreat.

For a moment she was silent with surprise. How should it be public at all?

"When is it open?" she asked, quick-witted.

"The rector lets visitors in on Fridays and Tuesdays."

She stood still, reflecting. How strange to think of the rector opening his garden to the public!

"But everybody will be at church," she said coaxingly to the man. "There'll be nobody here, will there?"

He moved, and the big gooseberries rolled.

"The rector lives at the new rectory," he said.

The two stood still. He did not like to ask her to go. At last she turned to him with a winning smile.

"Might I have *one* peep at the roses?" she coaxed, with pretty wilfulness.

"I don't suppose it would matter," he said, moving aside; "you won't stop long——"

She went forward, forgetting the gardener in a moment. Her face became strained, her movements eager. Glancing round, she saw all the windows giving on to the lawn were curtainless and dark. The house had a sterile appearance, as if it were still used, but not inhabited. A shadow seemed to go over her. She went across the lawn towards the garden, through an arch of crimson ramblers, a gate of colour. There beyond lay the soft blue sea within the bay, misty with morning, and the farthest headland of black rock jutting dimly out between blue and blue of the sky and water. Her face began to shine, transfigured with pain and joy. At her feet the garden fell steeply, all a confusion of flowers, and away below was the darkness of tree-tops covering the beck.

She turned to the garden that shone with sunny flowers around her. She knew the little corner where was the seat beneath the yew tree. Then there was the terrace where a great host of flowers shone, and from this, two paths went down, one at each side of the garden. She closed her sunshade and walked slowly among the many flowers. All round were rose bushes, big banks of roses, then roses hanging and tumbling from pillars, or roses balanced on the standard bushes. By the open earth were many other flowers. If she lifted her head, the sea was upraised beyond, and the Cape.

Slowly she went down one path, lingering, like one who has gone back into the past. Suddenly she was touching some heavy crimson roses that were soft as velvet, touching them thoughtfully, without knowing, as a mother sometimes fondles the hand of her child. She leaned slightly forward to catch the scent. Then she wandered on in abstraction. Sometimes a flame-coloured, scentless rose would hold her arrested. She stood gazing at it as if she could not understand it. Again the same softness of intimacy came over her, as she stood before a tumbling heap of pink petals. Then she wondered over the white rose, that was greenish, like ice, in the centre. So, slowly, like a white, pathetic butterfly, she drifted down the path, coming at last to a tiny terrace all full of roses. They seemed to fill the place, a sunny, gay throng. She was shy of them, they were so many and so bright. They seemed to be conversing and laughing. She felt herself in a strange crowd. It exhilarated her, carried her out of herself. She flushed with excitement. The air was pure scent.

Hastily, she went to a little seat among the white roses, and sat down. Her scarlet sunshade made a hard blot of colour. She sat quite still, feeling her own existence lapse. She was no more than a rose, a rose that could not quite come into blossom, but remained tense. A little fly dropped on her knee, on her white dress. She watched it, as if it had fallen on a rose. She was not herself.

Then she started cruelly as a shadow crossed her and a figure moved into her sight. It was a man who had come in slippers, unheard. He wore a linen coat. The morning was shattered, the spell vanished away. She was only afraid of being questioned. He came forward. She rose. Then, seeing him, the strength went from her and she sank on the seat again.

He was a young man, military in appearance, growing slightly stout. His black hair was brushed smooth and bright, his moustache was waxed. But there was something rambling in his gait. She looked up, blanched to the lips, and saw his eyes. They were black, and stared without seeing. They were not a man's eyes. He was coming towards her.

He stared at her fixedly, made an unconscious salute, and sat down beside her on the seat. He moved on the bench, shifted his feet, saying, in a gentlemanly, military voice:

"I don't disturb you—do I?"

She was mute and helpless. He was scrupulously dressed in dark clothes and a linen coat. She could not move. Seeing his hands, with the ring she knew so well upon the little finger, she felt as if she were going dazed. The whole world was deranged. She sat unavailing. For his hands, her symbols of passionate love, filled her with horror as they rested now on his strong thighs.

"May I smoke?" he asked intimately, almost secretly, his hand going to his pocket.

She could not answer, but it did not matter, he was in another world. She wondered, craving, if he recognised her— if he could recognise her. She sat pale with anguish. But she had to go through it.

"I haven't got any tobacco," he said thoughtfully.

But she paid no heed to his words, only she attended to

him. Could he recognise her, or was it all gone? She sat still in a frozen kind of suspense.

"I smoke John Cotton," he said, "and I must economise with it, it is expensive. You know, I'm not very well off while these law-suits are going on."

"No," she said, and her heart was cold, her soul kept rigid.

He moved, made a loose salute, rose, and went away. She sat motionless. She could see his shape, the shape she had loved with all her passion: his compact, soldier's head, his fine figure now slackened. And it was not he. It only filled her with horror too difficult to know.

Suddenly he came again, his hand in his jacket pocket.

"Do you mind if I smoke?" he said. "Perhaps I shall be able to see things more clearly."

He sat down beside her again, filling a pipe. She watched his hands with the fine strong fingers. They had always inclined to tremble slightly. It had surprised her, long ago, in such a healthy man. Now they moved inaccurately, and the tobacco hung raggedly out of the pipe.

"I have legal business to attend to. Legal affairs are always so uncertain. I tell my solicitor exactly, precisely what I want, but I can never get it done."

She sat and heard him talking. But it was not he. Yet those were the hands she had kissed, there were the glistening, strange black eyes that she had loved. Yet it was not he. She sat motionless with horror and silence. He dropped his tobacco-pouch, and groped for it on the ground. Yet she must wait to see if he would recognise her. Why could she not go! In a moment he rose.

"I must go at once," he said. "The owl is coming." Then he added confidentially: "His name isn't really the owl, but I call him that. I must go and see if he has come."

She rose too. He stood before her, uncertain. He was a handsome, soldierly fellow, and a lunatic. Her eyes searched him, and searched him, to see if he would recognise her, if she could discover him.

"You don't know me?" she asked, from the terror of her soul, standing alone.

He looked back at her quizzically. She had to bear his eyes. They gleamed on her, but with no intelligence. He was drawing nearer to her.

"Yes, I do know you," he said, fixed, intent, but mad, drawing his face nearer hers. Her horror was too great. The powerful lunatic was coming too near to her.

A man approached, hastening.

"The garden isn't open this morning," he said.

The deranged man stopped and looked at him. The keeper went to the seat and picked up the tobacco-pouch left lying there.

"Don't leave your tobacco, sir," he said, taking it to the gentleman in the linen coat.

"I was just asking this lady to stay to lunch," the latter said politely. "She is a friend of mine."

The woman turned and walked swiftly, blindly, between the sunny roses, out from the garden, past the house with the blank, dark windows, through the sea-pebbled courtyard to the street. Hastening and blind, she went forward without hesitating, not knowing whither. Directly she came to the house she went upstairs, took off her hat, and sat down on the bed. It was as if some membrane had been torn in two in her, so that she was not an entity that could think and feel. She sat staring across at the window, where an ivy spray waved slowly up and down in the sea wind. There was some of the uncanny luminousness of the sunlit sea in the air. She sat perfectly still, without any being. She only felt she might be sick, and it might be blood that was loose in her torn entrails. She sat perfectly still and passive.

After a time she heard the hard tread of her husband on the floor below, and, without herself changing, she registered his movement. She heard his rather disconsolate footsteps go out again, then his voice speaking, answering, growing cheery, and his solid tread drawing near.

He entered, ruddy, rather pleased, an air of complacency about his alert, sturdy figure. She moved stiffly. He faltered in his approach.

"What's the matter?" he asked, a tinge of impatience in his voice. "Aren't you feeling well?"

This was torture to her.

"Quite," she replied.

His brown eyes became puzzled and angry.

"What is the matter?" he said.

"Nothing."

He took a few strides, and stood obstinately, looking out of the window.

"Have you run up against anybody?" he asked.

"Nobody who knows me," she said.

His hands began to twitch. It exasperated him, that she was no more sensible of him than if he did not exist. Turning on her at length, driven, he asked:

"Something has upset you, hasn't it?"

"No, why?" she said, neutral. He did not exist for her, except as an irritant.

His anger rose, filling the veins of his throat.

"It seems like it," he said, making an effort not to show his anger, because there seemed no reason for it. He went away downstairs. She sat still on the bed, and with the residue of feeling left to her, she disliked him because he tormented her. The time went by. She could smell the dinner being served, the smoke of her husband's pipe from the garden. But she could not move. She had no being. There was a tinkle of the bell. She heard him come indoors. And then he mounted the stairs again. At every step her heart grew tight in her. He opened the door.

"Dinner is on the table," he said.

It was difficult for her to endure his presence, for he would interfere with her. She could not recover her life. She rose stiffly and went down. She could neither eat nor talk during the meal. She sat absent, torn, without any being of her own. He tried to go on as if nothing were the matter. But at last he became silent with fury. As soon as it was possible, she went upstairs again, and locked the bedroom door. She must be alone. He went with his pipe into the garden. All his suppressed anger against her who held herself superior to him filled and blackened his heart. Though he had not known it, yet he had never really won her, she had never loved him. She had taken him on sufferance. This had foiled him. He was only a labouring electrician in the mine, she was superior to him. He had always given way to her. But all the while, the injury and ignominy had been working in his soul because she did not hold him seriously. And now all his rage came up against her.

He turned and went indoors. The third time, she heard him mounting the stairs. Her heart stood still. He turned the catch and pushed the door—it was locked. He tried it again, harder. Her heart was standing still.

"Have you fastened the door?" he asked quietly, because of the landlady.

"Yes. Wait a minute."

She rose and turned the lock, afraid he would burst in. She felt hatred towards him, because he did not leave her free. He entered, his pipe between his teeth, and she returned to her old position on the bed. He closed the door and stood with his back to it.

"What's the matter?" he asked determinedly.

She was sick with him. She could not look at him.

"Can't you leave me alone?" she replied, averting her face from him.

He looked at her quickly, fully, wincing with ignominy. Then he seemed to consider for a moment.

"There's something up with you, isn't there?" he asked definitely.

"Yes," she said, "but that's no reason why you should torment me."

"I don't torment you. What's the matter?"

"Why should you know?" she cried, in hate and desperation.

Something snapped. He started and caught his pipe as it fell from his mouth. Then he pushed forward the bitten-off mouthpiece with his tongue, took it from off his lips, and looked at it. Then he put out his pipe, and brushed the ash from his waistcoat. After which he raised his head.

"I want to know," he said. His face was greyish pale, and set uglily.

Neither looked at the other. She knew he was fired now. His heart was pounding heavily. She hated him, but she could not withstand him. Suddenly she lifted her head and turned on him.

"What right have you to know?" she asked.

He looked at her. She felt a pang of surprise for his tortured eyes and his fixed face. But her heart hardened swiftly. She had never loved him. She did not love him now.

But suddenly she lifted her head again swiftly, like a thing that tries to get free. She wanted to be free of it. It was not him so much, but it, something she had put on herself, that bound her so horribly. And having put the bond on herself, it was hardest to take it off. But now she hated everything and felt destructive. He stood with his back to the door, fixed, as if he would oppose her eternally, till she was extinguished. She looked at him. Her eyes were cold and hostile. His workman's hands spread on the panels of the door behind him.

"You know I used to live here?" she began, in a hard voice, as if wilfully to wound him. He braced himself against her, and nodded.

"Well, I was companion to Miss Birch of Torill Hall—she and the rector were friends, and Archie was the rector's son." There was a pause. He listened without knowing what was happening. He stared at his wife. She was squatted in her white dress on the bed, carefully folding and re-folding the hem of her skirt. Her voice was full of hostility.

"He was an officer—a sub-lieutenant—then he quarrelled with his colonel and came out of the army. At any rate"— she plucked at her skirt hem, her husband stood motionless, watching her movements which filled his veins with madness —"he was awfully fond of me, and I was of him—awfully."

"How old was he?" asked the husband.

"When—when I first knew him? Or when he went away——?"

"When you first knew him."

"When I first knew him, he was twenty-six—he's thirty-one—nearly thirty-two—because I'm twenty-nine, and he is nearly three years older——"

She lifted her head and looked at the opposite wall.

"And what then?" said her husband.

She hardened herself, and said callously :

"We were as good as engaged for nearly a year, though nobody knew—at least—they talked—but—it wasn't open. Then he went away——"

"He chucked you?" said the husband brutally, wanting to hurt her into contact with himself. Her heart rose wildly with rage. Then "Yes," she said, to anger him. He shifted from one foot to the other, giving a "Pah!" of rage. There was silence for a time.

"Then," she resumed, her pain giving a mocking note to her words, "he suddenly went out to fight in Africa, and almost the very day I first met you, I heard from Miss Birch he'd got sunstroke—and two months after, that he was dead——"

"That was before you took on with me?" said the husband.

There was no answer. Neither spoke for a time. He had not understood. His eyes were contracted uglily.

"So you've been looking at your old courting places!" he

said. "That was what you wanted to go out by yourself for this morning."

Still she did not answer him anything. He went away from the door to the window. He stood with his hands behind him, his back to her. She looked at him. His hands seemed gross to her, the back of his head paltry.

At length, almost against his will, he turned round, asking: "How long were you carrying on with him?"

"What do you mean?" she replied coldly.

"I mean how long were you carrying on with him?"

She lifted her head, averting her face from him. She refused to answer. Then she said:

"I don't know what you mean, by carrying on. I loved him from the first days I met him—two months after I went to stay with Miss Birch."

"And do you reckon he loved you?" he jeered.

"I know he did."

"How do you know, if he'd have no more to do with you?"

There was a long silence of hate and suffering.

"And how far did it go between you?" he asked at length, in a frightened, stiff voice.

"I hate your not-straightforward questions," she cried, beside herself with his baiting. "We loved each other, and we *were* lovers—we were. I don't care what *you* think: what have you got to do with it? We were lovers before I knew you——"

"Lovers—lovers," he said, white with fury. "You mean you had your fling with an army man, and then came to me to marry you when you'd done——"

She sat swallowing her bitterness. There was a long pause.

"Do you mean to say you used to go—the whole hogger?" he asked, still incredulous.

"Why, what else do you think I mean?" she cried brutally.

He shrank, and became white, impersonal. There was a long, paralysed silence. He seemed to have gone small.

"You never thought to tell me all this before I married you," he said, with bitter irony, at last.

"You never asked me," she replied.

"I never thought there was any need."

"Well, then, you *should* think."

He stood with expressionless, almost child-like set face, revolving many thoughts, whilst his heart was mad with anguish.

Suddenly she added:

"And I saw him to-day," she said. "He is not dead, he's mad."

"Mad!" he said involuntarily.

"A lunatic," she said. It almost cost her her reason to utter the word. There was a pause.

"Did he know you?" asked the husband, in a small voice.

"No," she said.

He stood and looked at her. At last he had learned the width of the breach between them. She still squatted on the bed. He could not go near her. It would be violation to each of them to be brought into contact with the other. The thing must work itself out. They were both shocked so much, they were impersonal, and no longer hated each other. After some minutes he left her and went out.

GOOSE FAIR

I

THROUGH the gloom of evening, and the flare of torches of the night before the fair, through the still fogs of the succeeding dawn came paddling the weary geese, lifting their poor feet that had been dipped in tar for shoes, and trailing them along the cobble-stones into the town. Last of all, in the afternoon, a country girl drove in her dozen birds, disconsolate because she was so late. She was a heavily-built girl, fair, with regular features, and yet unprepossessing. She needed chiselling down, her contours were brutal. Perhaps it was weariness that hung her eyelids a little lower than was pleasant. When she spoke to her clumsily lagging birds it was in a snarling nasal tone. One of the silly things sat down in the gutter and refused to move. It looked very ridiculous, but also rather pitiful, squat there with its head up, refusing to be urged on by the ungentle toe of the girl. The latter swore heavily, then picked up the great complaining bird, and fronting her road stubbornly, drove on the lamentable eleven.

No one had noticed her. This afternoon the women were not sitting chatting on their doorsteps, seaming up the cotton hose, or swiftly passing through their fingers the piled white lace; and in the high dark house the song of the hosiery frames was hushed: "Shackety-boom, Shackety-shackety-boom, Z—zzz!" As she dragged up Hollow Stone, people returning from the fair chaffed her and asked her what o'clock it was. She did not reply, her look was sullen. The Lace Market was quiet as the Sabbath: even the great brass plates on the doors were dull with neglect. There seemed an afternoon atmosphere of raw discontent. The girl stopped a moment before the dismal prospect of one of the great warehouses that had been gutted with fire. She looked at the lean, threatening walls, and watched her white flock waddling in reckless misery below, and she would have laughed out loud had the wall fallen flat upon them and relieved her of them. But the wall did not fall, so she crossed the road, and walking on the safe side,

234

hurried after her charge. Her look was even more sullen. She remembered the state of trade—Trade, the invidious enemy; Trade, which thrust out its hand and shut the factory doors, and pulled the stockingers off their seats, and left the web half-finished on the frame; Trade, which mysteriously choked up the sources of the rivulets of wealth, and blacker and more secret than a pestilence, starved the town. Through this morose atmosphere of bad trade, in the afternoon of the first day of the fair, the girl strode down to the Poultry with eleven sound geese and one lame one to sell.

The Frenchmen were at the bottom of it! So everybody said, though nobody quite knew how. At any rate, they had gone to war with the Prussians and got beaten, and trade was ruined in Nottingham!

A little fog rose up, and the twilight gathered around. Then they flared abroad their torches in the fair, insulting the night. The girl still sat in the Poultry, and her weary geese unsold on the stones, illuminated by the hissing lamp of a man who sold rabbits and pigeons and such-like assorted livestock.

II

In another part of the town, near Sneinton Church, another girl came to the door to look at the night. She was tall and slender, dressed with the severe accuracy which marks the girl of superior culture. Her hair was arranged with simplicity about the long, pale, cleanly cut face. She leaned forward very slightly to glance down the street, listening. She very carefully preserved the appearance of having come quite casually to the door, yet she lingered and lingered and stood very still to listen when she heard a footstep, but when it proved to be only a common man, she drew herself up proudly and looked with a small smile over his head. He hesitated to glance into the open hall, lighted so spaciously with a scarlet-shaded lamp, and at the slim girl in brown silk lifted up before the light. But she, she looked over his head. He passed on.

Presently she started and hung in suspense. Somebody was crossing the road. She ran down the steps in a pretty welcome, not effuse, saying in quick but accurately articulated words: "Will! I began to think you'd gone to the fair. I came out to listen to it. I felt almost sure you'd gone. You're coming in,

aren't you?" She waited a moment anxiously. "We expect
you to dinner, you know," she added wistfully.

The man, who had a short face and spoke with his lip curl-
ing up on one side, in a drawling speech with ironically
exaggerated intonation, replied after a short hesitation:

"I'm awfully sorry, I am, straight, Lois. It's a shame. I've
got to go round to the biz. Man proposes—the devil disposes."
He turned aside with irony in the darkness.

"But surely, Will!" remonstrated the girl, keenly disappointed.

"Fact, Lois!—I feel wild about it myself. But I've got to
go down to the works. They may be getting a bit warm down
there, you know"—he jerked his head in the direction of the
fair. "If the Lambs get frisky!—they're a bit off about the
work, and they'd just be in their element if they could set a
lighted match to something——"

"Will, you don't think——!" exclaimed the girl, laying her
hand on his arm in the true fashion of romance, and looking
up at him earnestly.

"Dad's not sure," he replied, looking down at her with
gravity. They remained in this attitude for a moment, then
he said:

"I might stop a bit. It's all right for an hour, I should think."

She looked at him earnestly, then said in tones of deep disappointment and of fortitude: "No, Will, you must go. You'd
better go——"

"It's a shame!" he murmured, standing a moment at a loose
end. Then, glancing down the street to see he was alone, he
put his arm round her waist and said in a difficult voice:
"How goes it?"

She let him keep her for a moment, then he kissed her as
if afraid of what he was doing. They were both uncomfortable.

"Well——!" he said at length.

"Good night!" she said, setting him free to go.

He hung a moment near her, as if ashamed. Then "Good
night," he answered, and he broke away. She listened to
his footsteps in the night, before composing herself to turn
indoors.

"Helloa!" said her father, glancing over his paper as she
entered the dining-room. "What's up, then?"

"Oh, nothing," she replied, in her calm tones. "Will won't
be here to dinner to-night."

"What, gone to the fair?"

"No."

"Oh! What's got him then?"

Lois looked at her father, and answered:

"He's gone down to the factory. They are afraid of the hands."

Her father looked at her closely.

"Oh, aye!" he answered, undecided, and they sat down to dinner.

III

Lois retired very early. She had a fire in her bedroom. She drew the curtains and stood holding aside a heavy fold, looking out at the night. She could see only the nothingness of the fog; not even the glare of the fair was evident, though the noise clamoured small in the distance. In front of everything she could see her own faint image. She crossed to the dressing-table, and there leaned her face to the mirror, and looked at herself. She looked a long time, then she rose, changed her dress for a dressing-jacket, and took up *Sesame and Lilies*.

Late in the night she was roused from sleep by a bustle in the house. She sat up and heard a hurrying to and fro and the sound of anxious voices. She put on her dressing-gown and went out to her mother's room. Seeing her mother at the head of the stairs, she said in her quick clean voice:

"Mother, what is it?"

"Oh, child, don't ask me! Go to bed, dear, do! I shall surely be worried out of my life."

"Mother, what is it?" Lois was sharp and emphatic.

"I hope your father won't go. Now I do hope your father won't go. He's got a cold as it is."

"Mother, tell me what it is?" Lois took her mother's arm.

"It's Selby's. I should have thought you would have heard the fire-engine, and Jack isn't in yet. I hope we're safe!" Lois returned to her bedroom and dressed. She coiled her plaited hair, and having put on a cloak, left the house.

She hurried along under the fog-dripping trees towards the meaner part of the town. When she got near, she saw a glare in the fog, and closed her lips tight. She hastened on till she was in the crowd. With peaked, noble face she watched the fire. Then she looked a little wildly over the fire-reddened

faces in the crowd, and catching sight of her father, hurried
to him.

"Oh, Dadda—is he safe? Is Will safe——?"

"Safe, aye, why not? You've no business here. Here, here's
Sampson, he'll take you home. I've enough to bother me;
there's my own place to watch. Go home now, I can't do with
you here."

"Have you seen Will?" she asked.

"Go home—Sampson, just take Miss Lois home—now!"

"You don't really know where he is—father?"

"Go home now—I don't want you here——" her father
ordered peremptorily.

The tears sprang to Lois' eyes. She looked at the fire and
the tears were quickly dried by fear. The flames roared and
struggled upward. The great wonder of the fire made her
forget even her indignation at her father's light treatment of
herself and of her lover. There was a crashing and bursting of
timber, as the first floor fell in a mass into the blazing gulf,
splashing the fire in all directions, to the terror of the crowd.
She saw the steel of the machines growing white-hot and twisting like flaming letters. Piece after piece of the flooring gave
way, and the machines dropped in red ruin as the wooden
framework burned out. The air became unbreathable; the fog
was swallowed up; sparks went rushing up as if they would
burn the dark heavens; sometimes cards of lace went whirling
into the gulf of the sky, waving with wings of fire. It was
dangerous to stand near this great cup of roaring destruction.

Sampson, the grey old manager of Buxton and Co.'s, led her
away as soon as she would turn her face to listen to him. He
was a stout, irritable man. He elbowed his way roughly
through the crowd, and Lois followed him, her head high, her
lips closed. He led her for some distance without speaking,
then at last, unable to contain his garrulous irritability, he
broke out:

"What do they expect? What can they expect? They can't
expect to stand a bad time. They spring up like mushrooms as
big as a house-side, but there's no stability in 'em. I remember
William Selby when he'd run on my errands. Yes, there's some
as can make much out of little, and there's some as can make
much out of nothing, but they find it won't last. William
Selby's sprung up in a day, and he'll vanish in a night. You
can't trust to luck alone. Maybe he thinks it's a lucky thing

this fire has come when things are looking black. But you can't get out of it as easy as that. There's been a few too many of 'em. No, indeed, a fire's the last thing I should hope to come to—the very last!"

Lois hurried and hurried, so that she brought the old manager panting in distress up the steps of her home. She could not bear to hear him talking so. They could get no one to open the door for some time. When at last Lois ran upstairs, she found her mother dressed, but all unbuttoned again, lying back in the chair in her daughter's room, suffering from palpitation of the heart, with *Sesame and Lilies* crushed beneath her. Lois administered brandy, and her decisive words and movements helped largely to bring the good lady to a state of recovery sufficient to allow of her returning to her own bedroom.

Then Lois locked the door. She glanced at her fire-darkened face, and taking the flattened Ruskin out of the chair, sat down and wept. After a while she calmed herself, rose and sponged her face. Then once more on that fatal night she prepared for rest. Instead, however, of retiring, she pulled a silk quilt from her disordered bed and, wrapping it round her, sat miserably to think. It was two o'clock in the morning.

IV

The fire was sunk to cold ashes in the grate, and the grey morning was creeping through the half-opened curtains like a thing ashamed, when Lois awoke. It was painful to move her head: her neck was cramped. The girl awoke in full recollection. She sighed, roused herself and pulled the quilt closer about her. For a little while she sat and mused. A pale, tragic resignation fixed her face like a mask. She remembered her father's irritable answer to her question concerning her lover's safety—"Safe, aye—why not?" She knew that he suspected the factory of having been purposely set on fire. But then, he had never liked Will. And yet—and yet—Lois' heart was heavy as lead. She felt her lover was guilty. And she felt she must hide her secret of his last communication to her. She saw herself being cross-examined—"When did you last see this man?" But she would hide what he had said about watching at the works. How dreary it was—and how dreadful. Her life was ruined now, and nothing mattered any more. She must only behave with dignity, and submit to her own obliteration. For even if Will were never accused, she knew in her heart he was guilty. She knew it was over between them.

It was dawn among the yellow fog outside, and Lois, as she moved mechanically about her toilet, vaguely felt that all her days would arrive slowly struggling through a bleak fog. She felt an intense longing at this uncanny hour to slough the body's trammelled weariness and to issue at once into the new bright warmth of the far Dawn where a lover waited transfigured; it is so easy and pleasant in imagination to step out of the chill grey dampness of another terrestrial daybreak, straight into the sunshine of the eternal morning? And who can escape his hour? So Lois performed the meaningless routine of her toilet, which at last she made meaningful when she took her black dress, and fastened a black jet brooch at her throat.

Then she went downstairs and found her father eating a mutton chop. She quickly approached and kissed him on the forehead. Then she retreated to the other end of the table. Her father looked tired, even haggard.

"You are early," he said, after a while. Lois did not reply. Her father continued to eat for a few moments, then he said:

"Have a chop—here's one! Ring for a hot plate. Eh, what? Why not?"

Lois was insulted, but she gave no sign. She sat down and took a cup of coffee, making no pretence to eat. Her father was absorbed, and had forgotten her.

"Our Jack's not come home yet," he said at last.

Lois stirred faintly. "Hasn't he?" she said.

"No." There was silence for a time. Lois was frightened. Had something happened also to her brother? This fear was closer and more irksome.

"Selby's was cleaned out, gutted. We had a near shave of it——"

"You have no loss, Dadda?"

"Nothing to mention." After another silence, her father said:

"I'd rather be myself than William Selby. Of course it may merely be bad luck—you don't know. But whatever it was, I wouldn't like to add one to the list of fires just now. Selby was at the 'George' when it broke out—I don't know where the lad was——!"

"Father," broke in Lois, "why do you talk like that? Why

do you talk as if Will had done it?" She ended suddenly. Her
father looked at her pale, mute face.

"I don't talk as if Will had done it," he said. "I don't even
think it."

Feeling she was going to cry, Lois rose and left the room.
Her father sighed, and leaning his elbows on his knees,
whistled faintly into the fire. He was not thinking about
her.

Lois went down to the kitchen and asked Lucy, the parlour-
maid, to go out with her. She somehow shrank from going
alone, lest people should stare at her overmuch : and she felt
an overpowering impulse to go to the scene of the tragedy, to
judge for herself.

The churches were chiming half-past eight when the young
lady and the maid set off down the street. Nearer the fair,
swarthy, thin-legged men were pushing barrels of water
towards the market-place, and the gipsy women, with hard
brows, and dressed in tight velvet bodices, hurried along the
pavement with jugs of milk, and great brass water-ewers and
loaves and breakfast parcels. People were just getting up, and
in the poorer streets was a continual splash of tea-leaves, flung
out on to the cobble-stones. A teapot came crashing down
from an upper storey just behind Lois, and she, starting round
and looking up, thought that the trembling, drink-bleared man
at the upper window, who was stupidly staring after his pot,
had had designs on her life; and she went on her way shuddering at the grim tragedy of life.

In the dull October morning the ruined factory was black
and ghastly. The window-frames were all jagged, and the
walls stood gaunt. Inside was a tangle of twisted débris, the
iron, in parts red with bright rust, looking still hot; the charred
wood was black and satiny; from dishevelled heaps, sodden
with water, a faint smoke rose dimly. Lois stood and looked.
If he had done that! He might even be dead there, burned
to ash and lost for ever. It was almost soothing to feel so.
He would be safe in the eternity which now she must hope
in.

At her side the pretty, sympathetic maid chatted plaintively.
Suddenly, from one of her lapses into silences, she exclaimed :
"Why if there isn't Mr. Jack!"

Lois turned suddenly and saw her brother and her lover
approaching her. Both looked soiled, untidy and wan. Will

had a black eye, some ten hours old, well coloured. Lois turned
very pale as they approached. They were looking gloomily at
the factory, and for a moment did not notice the girls.

"I'll be jiggered if there ain't our Lois!" exclaimed Jack, the
reprobate, swearing under his breath.

"Oh, God!" exclaimed the other in disgust.

"Jack, where have you been?" said Lois sharply, in keen
pain, not looking at her lover. Her sharp tone of suffering
drove her lover to defend himself with an affectation of comic
recklessness.

"In quod," replied her brother, smiling sicklily.

"Jack!" cried his sister very sharply.

"Fact."

Will Selby shuffled on his feet and smiled, trying to turn
away his face so that she should not see his black eye. She
glanced at him. He felt her boundless anger and contempt, and
with great courage he looked straight at her, smiling ironically.
Unfortunately his smile would not go over his swollen eye,
which remained grave and lurid.

"Do I look pretty?" he inquired with a hateful twist of his
lip.

"Very!" she replied.

"I thought I did," he replied. And he turned to look at his
father's ruined works, and he felt miserable and stubborn. The
girl standing there so clean and out of it all! Oh, God, he felt
sick. He turned to go home.

The three went together, Lois silent in anger and resentment.
Her brother was tired and overstrung, but not suppressed. He
chattered on, blindly.

"It was a lark we had! We met Bob Osborne and Freddy
Mansell coming down Poultry. There was a girl with some
geese. She looked a tanger sitting there, all like statues, her
and the geese. It was Will who began it. He offered her three-
pence and asked her to begin the show. She called him a—she
called him something, and then somebody poked an old gander
to stir him up, and somebody squirted him in the eye. He
upped and squawked and started off with his neck out. Laugh!
We nearly killed ourselves, keeping back those old birds with
squirts and teasers. Oh, Lum! Those old geese, oh, scrimmy,
they didn't know where to turn, they fairly went off their dots,
coming at us right an' left, and such a row—it was fun, you
never knew? Then the girl she got up and knocked somebody

over the jaw, and we were right in for it. Well, in the end, Billy here got hold of her round the waist——"

"Oh, dry it up!" exclaimed Will bitterly.

Jack looked at him, laughed mirthlessly, and continued: "An' we said we'd buy her birds. So we got hold of one goose apiece—an' they took some holding, I can tell you— and off we set round the fair, Billy leading with the girl. The bloomin' geese squawked an' pecked. Laugh—I thought I should a' died. Well, then we wanted the girl to have her birds back—and then she fired up. She got some other chaps on her side, and there was a proper old row. The girl went tooth and nail for Will there—she was dead set against him. She gave him a black eye, by gum, and we went at it, I can tell you. It was a free fight, a beauty, an' we got run in. I don't know what became of the girl."

Lois surveyed the two men. There was no glimmer of a smile on her face, though the maid behind her was sniggering. Will was very bitter. He glanced at his sweetheart and at the ruined factory.

"How's dad taken it?" he asked, in a biting, almost humble tone.

"I don't know," she replied coldly. "Father's in an awful way. I believe everybody thinks you set the place on fire."

Lois drew herself up. She had delivered her blow. She drew herself up in cold condemnation and for a moment enjoyed her complete revenge. He was despicable, abject in his dishevelled, disfigured, unwashed condition.

"Aye, well, they made a mistake for once," he replied, with a curl of the lip.

Curiously enough, they walked side by side as if they belonged to each other. She was his conscience-keeper. She was far from forgiving him, but she was still farther from letting him go. And he walked at her side like a boy who has to be punished before he can be exonerated. He submitted. But there was a genuine bitter contempt in the curl of his lip.

THE WHITE STOCKING

"I'm getting up, Teddilinks," said Mrs. Whiston, and she sprang out of bed briskly.

"What the Hanover's got you?" asked Whiston.

"Nothing. Can't I get up?" she replied animatedly.

It was about seven o'clock, scarcely light yet in the cold bedroom. Whiston lay still and looked at his wife. She was a pretty little thing, with her fleecy, short black hair all tousled. He watched her as she dressed quickly, flicking her small, delightful limbs, throwing her clothes about her. Her slovenliness and untidiness did not trouble him. When she picked up the edge of her petticoat, ripped off a torn string of white lace, and flung it on the dressing-table, her careless abandon made his spirit glow. She stood before the mirror and roughly scrambled together her profuse little mane of hair. He watched the quickness and softness of her young shoulders, calmly, like a husband, and appreciatively.

"Rise up," she cried, turning to him with a quick wave of her arm—"and shine forth."

They had been married two years. But still, when she had gone out of the room, he felt as if all his light and warmth were taken away, he became aware of the raw, cold morning. So he rose himself, wondering casually what had roused her so early. Usually she lay in bed as late as she could.

Whiston fastened a belt round his loins and went downstairs in shirt and trousers. He heard her singing in her snatchy fashion. The stairs creaked under his weight. He passed down the narrow little passage, which she called a hall, of the seven and sixpenny house which was his first home.

He was a shapely young fellow of about twenty-eight, sleepy now and easy with well-being. He heard the water drumming into the kettle, and she began to whistle. He loved the quick way she dodged the supper cups under the tap to wash them for breakfast. She looked an untidy minx, but she was quick and handy enough.

"Teddilinks," she cried.

"What?"

"Light a fire, quick."

She wore an old, sack-like dressing-jacket of black silk pinned across her breast. But one of the sleeves, coming unfastened, showed some delightful pink upper-arm.

"Why don't you sew your sleeve up?" he said, suffering from the sight of the exposed soft flesh.

"Where?" she cried, peering round. "Nuisance," she said, seeing the gap, then with light fingers went on drying the cups.

The kitchen was of fair size, but gloomy. Whiston poked out the dead ashes.

Suddenly a thud was heard at the door down the passage.

"I'll go," cried Mrs. Whiston, and she was gone down the hall.

The postman was a ruddy-faced man who had been a soldier. He smiled broadly, handing her some packages.

"They've not forgot you," he said impudently.

"No—lucky for them," she said, with a toss of the head. But she was interested only in her envelopes this morning. The postman waited inquisitively, smiling in an ingratiating fashion. She slowly, abstractedly, as if she did not know anyone was there, closed the door in his face, continuing to look at the addresses on her letters.

She tore open the thin envelope. There was a long, hideous, cartoon valentine. She smiled briefly and dropped it on the floor. Struggling with the string of a packet, she opened a white cardboard box, and there lay a white silk handkerchief packed neatly under the paper lace of the box, and her initial, worked in heliotrope, fully displayed. She smiled pleasantly, and gently put the box aside. The third envelope contained another white packet—apparently a cotton handkerchief neatly folded. She shook it out. It was a long white stocking, but there was a little weight in the toe. Quickly, she thrust down her arm, wriggling her fingers into the toe of the stocking, and brought out a small box. She peeped inside the box, then hastily opened a door on her left hand, and went into the little cold sitting-room. She had her lower lip caught earnestly between her teeth.

With a little flash of triumph, she lifted a pair of pearl earrings from the small box, and she went to the mirror. There, earnestly, she began to hook them through her ears, looking at herself sideways in the glass. Curiously concentrated and intent she seemed as she fingered the lobes of her ears, her head bent on one side.

Then the pearl ear-rings dangled under her rosy, small ears. She shook her head sharply, to see the swing of the drops. They went chill against her neck, in little, sharp touches. Then she stood still to look at herself, bridling her head in the dignified fashion. Then she simpered at herself. Catching her own eye, she could not help winking at herself and laughing.

She turned to look at the box. There was a scrap of paper with this posy:

"Pearls may be fair, but thou art fairer.
Wear these for me, and I'll love the wearer."

She made a grimace and a grin. But she was drawn to the mirror again, to look at her ear-rings.

Whiston had made the fire burn, so he came to look for her. When she heard him, she started round quickly, guiltily. She was watching him with intent blue eyes when he appeared.

He did not see much, in his morning-drowsy warmth. He gave her, as ever, a feeling of warmth and slowness. His eyes were very blue, very kind, his manner simple.

"What ha' you got?" he asked.

"Valentines," she said briskly, ostentatiously turning to show him the silk handkerchief. She thrust it under his nose. "Smell how good," she said.

"Who's that from?" he replied, without smelling.

"It's a valentine," she cried. "How do I know who it's from?"

"I'll bet you know," he said.

"Ted!—I don't!" she cried, beginning to shake her head, then stopping because of the ear-rings.

He stood still a moment, displeased.

"They've no right to send you valentines now," he said.

"Ted!—Why not? You're not jealous, are you? I haven't the least idea who it's from. Look—there's my initial"— she pointed with an emphatic finger at the heliotrope embroidery——

"E for Elsie,
Nice little gelsie,"

she sang.

"Get out," he said. "You know who it's from."

"Truth, I don't," she cried.

He looked round, and saw the white stocking lying on a chair.

"Is this another?" he said.

"No, that's a sample," she said. "There's only a comic." And she fetched in the long cartoon.

He stretched it out and looked at it solemnly.

"Fools!" he said, and went out of the room.

She flew upstairs and took off the ear-rings. When she returned, he was crouched before the fire blowing the coals. The skin of his face was flushed, and slightly pitted, as if he had had small-pox. But his neck was white and smooth and goodly. She hung her arms round his neck as he crouched there, and clung to him. He balanced on his toes.

"This fire's a slow-coach," he said.

"And who else is a slow-coach?" she said.

"One of us two, I know," he said, and he rose carefully. She remained clinging round his neck, so that she was lifted off her feet.

"Ha!—swing me," she cried.

He lowered his head, and she hung in the air, swinging from his neck, laughing. Then she slipped off.

"The kettle is singing," she sang, flying for the teapot. He bent down again to blow the fire. The veins in his neck stood out, his shirt collar seemed too tight.

> "Doctor Wyer,
> Blow the fire,
> Puff! puff! puff!"

she sang, laughing.

He smiled at her.

She was so glad because of her pearl ear-rings.

Over the breakfast she grew serious. He did not notice. She became portentous in her gravity. Almost it penetrated through his steady good-humour to irritate him.

"Teddy!" she said at last.

"What?" he asked.

"I told you a lie," she said, humbly tragic.

His soul stirred uneasily.

"Oh aye?" he said casually.

She was not satisfied. He ought to be more moved.

"Yes," she said.

He cut a piece of bread.

"Was it a good one?" he asked.

She was piqued. Then she considered—*was* it a good one? Then she laughed.

"No," she said, "it wasn't up to much."

"Ah!" he said easily, but with a steady strength of fondness for her in his tone. "Get it out then."

It became a little more difficult.

"You know that white stocking," she said earnestly. "I told you a lie. It wasn't a sample. It was a valentine."

A little frown came on his brow.

"Then what did you invent it as a sample for?" he said. But he knew this weakness of hers. The touch of anger in his voice frightened her.

"I was afraid you'd be cross," she said pathetically.

"I'll bet you were vastly afraid," he said.

"I *was*, Teddy."

There was a pause. He was resolving one or two things in his mind.

"And who sent it?" he asked.

"I can guess," she said, "though there wasn't a word with it—except——"

She ran to the sitting-room and returned with a slip of paper.

"Pearls may be fair, but thou art fairer.
Wear these for me, and I'll love the wearer."

He read it twice, then a dull red flush came on his face.

"And *who* do you guess it is?" he asked, with a ringing of anger in his voice.

"I suspect it's Sam Adams," she said, with a little virtuous indignation.

Whiston was silent for a moment.

"Fool!" he said. "An' what's it got to do with pearls?—and how can he say 'wear these for me' when there's only one? He hasn't got the brain to invent a proper verse."

He screwed the slip of paper into a ball and flung it into the fire.

"I suppose he thinks it'll make a pair with the one last year," she said.

"Why, did he send one then?"

"Yes. I thought you'd be wild if you knew."

His jaw set rather sullenly.

Presently he rose, and went to wash himself, rolling back his sleeves and pulling open his shirt at the breast. It was as if his fine, clear-cut temples and steady eyes were degraded by the lower, rather brutal part of his face. But she loved it. As she whisked about, clearing the table, she loved the way in which he stood washing himself. He was such a man. She liked to see his neck glistening with water as he swilled it. It amused her and pleased her and thrilled her. He was so sure, so permanent, he had her so utterly in his power. It gave her a delightful, mischievous sense of liberty. Within his grasp, she could dart about excitingly.

He turned round to her, his face red from the cold water, his eyes fresh and very blue.

"You haven't been seeing anything of him, have you?" he asked roughly.

"Yes," she answered, after a moment, as if caught guilty. "He got into the tram with me, and he asked me to drink a coffee and a Benedictine in the Royal."

"You've got it off fine and glib," he said sullenly. "And did you?"

"Yes," she replied, with the air of a traitor before the rack.

The blood came up into his neck and face, he stood motionless, dangerous.

"It was cold, and it was such fun to go into the Royal," she said.

"You'd go off with a nigger for a packet of chocolate," he said, in anger and contempt, and some bitterness. Queer how he drew away from her, cut her off from him.

"Ted—how beastly!" she cried. "You know quite well——"

She caught her lip, flushed, and the tears came to her eyes.

He turned away, to put on his neck-tie. She went about her work, making a queer pathetic little mouth, down which occasionally dripped a tear.

He was ready to go. With his hat jammed down on his head, and his overcoat buttoned up to his chin, he came to kiss her. He would be miserable all the day if he went without. She allowed herself to be kissed. Her cheek was wet under his lip, and his heart burned. She hurt him so deeply. And she felt aggrieved, and did not quite forgive him.

In a moment she went upstairs to her ear-rings. Sweet they

looked nestling in the little drawer—sweet! She examined them with voluptuous pleasure, she threaded them in her ears, she looked at herself, she posed and postured and smiled and looked sad and tragic and winning and appealing, all in turn before the mirror. And she was happy, and very pretty.

She wore her ear-rings all morning, in the house. She was self-conscious, and quite brilliantly winsome, when the baker came, wondering if he would notice. All the tradesmen left her door with a glow in them, feeling elated, and unconsciously favouring the delightful little creature, though there had been nothing to notice in her behaviour.

She was stimulated all the day. She did not think about her husband. He was the permanent basis from which she took these giddly little flights into nowhere. At night, like chickens and curses, she would come home to him, to roost.

Meanwhile Whiston, a traveller and confidential support of a small firm, hastened about his work, his heart all the while anxious for her, yearning for surety, and kept tense by not getting it.

II

She had been a warehouse girl in Adams's lace factory before she was married. Sam Adams was her employer. He was a bachelor of forty, growing stout, a man well dressed and florid, with a large brown moustache and thin hair. From the rest of his well-groomed, showy appearance, it was evident his baldness was a chagrin to him. He had a good presence, and some Irish blood in his veins.

His fondness for the girls, or the fondness of the girls for him, was notorious. And Elsie, quick, pretty, almost witty little thing—she *seemed* witty, although, when her sayings were repeated, they were entirely trivial—she had a great attraction for him. He would come into the warehouse dressed in a rather sporting reefer coat, of fawn colour, and trousers of fine black-and-white check, a cap with a big peak and scarlet carnation in his button-hole, to impress her. She was only half impressed. He was too loud for her good taste. Instinctively perceiving this, he sobered down to navy blue. Then a well-built man, florid, with large brown whiskers, smart navy blue suit, fashionable boots, and manly hat, he was the irreproachable. Elsie was impressed.

But meanwhile Whiston was courting her, and she made splendid little gestures, before her bedroom mirror, of the constant-and-true sort.

"True, true till death——"

That was her song. Whiston was made that way, so there was no need to take thought for him.

Every Christmas Sam Adams gave a party at his house, to which he invited his superior work-people—not factory hands and labourers, but those above. He was a generous man in his way, with a real warm feeling for giving pleasure.

Two years ago Elsie had attended this Christmas-party for the last time. Whiston had accompanied her. At that time he worked for Sam Adams.

She had been very proud of herself, in her close-fitting, full-skirted dress of blue silk. Whiston called for her. Then she tripped beside him, holding her large cashmere shawl across her breast. He strode with long strides, his trousers handsomely strapped under his boots, and her silk shoes bulging the pocket of his full-skirted overcoat.

They passed through the park gates, and her spirits rose. Above them the Castle Rock loomed grandly in the night, the naked trees stood still and dark in the frost, along the boulevard.

They were rather late. Agitated with anticipation, in the cloak-room she gave up her shawl, donned her silk shoes, and looked at herself in the mirror. The loose bunches of curls on either side her face danced prettily, her mouth smiled.

She hung a moment in the door of the brilliantly lighted room. Many people were moving within the blaze of lamps, under the crystal chandeliers, the full skirts of the women balancing and floating, the side-whiskers and white cravats of the men bowing above. Then she entered the light.

In an instant Sam Adams was coming forward, lifting both his arms in boisterous welcome. There was a constant red laugh on his face.

"Come late, would you," he shouted, "like royalty."

He seized her hands and led her forward. He opened his mouth wide when he spoke, and the effect of the warm, dark opening behind the brown whiskers was disturbing. But she was floating into the throng on his arm. He was very gallant.

"Now then," he said, taking her card to write down the dances, "I've got *carte blanche*, haven't I?"

"Mr. Whiston doesn't dance," she said.

"I am a lucky man!" he said, scribbling his initials. "I was born with an *amourette* in my mouth."

He wrote on, quietly. She blushed and laughed, not knowing what it meant.

"Why, what is that?" she said.

"It's you, even littler than you are, dressed in little wings," he said.

"I should have to be pretty small to get in your mouth," she said.

"You think you're too big, do you!" he said easily.

He handed her her card, with a bow.

"Now I'm set up, my darling, for this evening," he said.

Then, quick, always at his ease, he looked over the room. She waited in front of him. He was ready. Catching the eye of the band, he nodded. In a moment, the music began. He seemed to relax, giving himself up.

"Now then, Elsie," he said, with a curious caress in his voice that seemed to lap the outside of her body in a warm glow, delicious. She gave herself to it. She liked it.

He was an excellent dancer. He seemed to draw her close in to him by some male warmth of attraction, so that she became all soft and pliant to him, flowing to his form, whilst he united her with him and they lapsed along in one movement. She was just carried in a kind of strong, warm flood, her feet moved of themselves, and only the music threw her away from him, threw her back to him, to his clasp, in his strong form moving against her, rhythmically, deliciously.

When it was over, he was pleased and his eyes had a curious gleam which thrilled her and yet had nothing to do with her. Yet it held her. He did not speak to her. He only looked straight into her eyes with a curious, gleaming look that disturbed her fearfully and deliciously. But also there was in his look some of the automatic irony of the *roué*. It left her partly cold. She was not carried away.

She went, driven by an opposite, heavier impulse, to Whiston. He stood looking gloomy, trying to admit that she had a perfect right to enjoy herself apart from him. He received her with rather grudging kindliness.

"Aren't you going to play whist?" she asked.

"Aye," he said. "Directly."

"I do wish you could dance."

"Well, I can't," he said. "So you enjoy yourself."

"But I should enjoy it better if I could dance with you."

"Nay, you're all right," he said. "I'm not made that way."

"Then you ought to be!" she cried.

"Well, it's my fault, not yours. You enjoy yourself," he bade her. Which she proceeded to do, a little bit irked.

She went with anticipation to the arms of Sam Adams, when the time came to dance with him. It *was* so gratifying, irrespective of the man. And she felt a little grudge against Whiston, soon forgotten when her host was holding her near to him, in a delicious embrace. And she watched his eyes, to meet the gleam in them, which gratified her.

She was getting warmed right through, the glow was penetrating into her, driving away everything else. Only in her heart was a little tightness, like conscience.

When she got a chance, she escaped from the dancing-room to the card-room. There, in a cloud of smoke, she found Whiston playing cribbage. Radiant, roused, animated, she came up to him and greeted him. She was too strong, too vibrant a note in the quiet room. He lifted his head, and a frown knitted his gloomy forehead.

"Are you playing cribbage? Is it exciting? How are you getting on?" she chattered.

He looked at her. None of these questions needed answering, and he did not feel in touch with her. She turned to the cribbage-board.

"Are you white or red?" she asked.

"He's red," replied the partner.

"Then you're losing," she said, still to Whiston. And she lifted the red peg from the board. "One—two—three—four—five—six—seven—eight—— Right up there you ought to jump——"

"Now put it back in its right place," said Whiston.

"Where was it?" she asked gaily, knowing her transgression. He took the little red peg away from her and stuck it in its hole.

The cards were shuffled.

"What a shame you're losing," said Elsie.

"You'd better cut for him," said the partner.

She did so hastily. The cards were dealt. She put her hand on his shoulder, looking at his cards.

"It's good," she cried, "isn't it?"

He did not answer, but threw down two cards. It moved him more strongly than was comfortable, to have her hand on his shoulder, her curls dangling and touching his ears, whilst she was roused to another man. It made the blood flame over him.

At that moment Sam Adams appeared, florid and boisterous, intoxicated more with himself, with the dancing, than with wine. In his eye the curious, impersonal light gleamed.

"I thought I should find you here, Elsie," he cried boisterously, a disturbing, high note in his voice.

"What made you think so?" she replied, the mischief rousing in her.

The florid, well-built man narrowed his eyes to a smile.

"I should never look for you among the ladies," he said, with a kind of intimate, animal call to her. He laughed, bowed, and offered her his arm.

"Madam, the music waits."

She went almost helplessly, carried along with him, unwilling, yet delighted.

That dance was an intoxication to her. After the first few steps, she felt herself slipping away from herself. She almost knew she was going, she did not even want to go. Yet she must have chosen to go. She lay in the arm of the steady, close man with whom she was dancing, and she seemed to swim away out of contact with the room, into him. She had passed into another, denser element of him, an essential privacy. The room was all vague around her, like an atmosphere, like under sea, with a flow of ghostly, dumb movements. But she herself was held real against her partner, and it seemed she was connected with him, as if the movements of his body and limbs were her own movements, yet not her own movements—and oh, delicious! He also was given up, oblivious, concentrated, into the dance. His eye was unseeing. Only his large, voluptuous body gave off a subtle activity. His fingers seemed to search into her flesh. Every moment, and every moment, she felt she would give way utterly, and sink molten: the fusion point was coming when she would fuse down into perfect unconsciousness at his feet and knees. But he bore her round the room in the dance, and he seemed to sustain all her body with his limbs, his body, and his warmth seemed to come closer into her, nearer, till it would fuse right through her, and she would be as liquid to him as an intoxication only.

It was exquisite. When it was over, she was dazed, and was scarcely breathing. She stood with him in the middle of the room as if she were alone in a remote place. He bent over her. She expected his lips on her bare shoulder, and waited. Yet they were not alone, they were not alone. It was cruel.

" 'Twas good, wasn't it, my darling?" he said to her, low and delighted. There was a strange impersonality about his low, exultant call that appealed to her irresistibly. Yet why was she aware of some part shut off in her? She pressed his arm, and he led her towards the door.

She was not aware of what she was doing, only a little grain of resistant trouble was in her. The man, possessed, yet with a superficial presence of mind, made way to the dining-room, as if to give her refreshment, cunningly working to his own escape with her. He was molten hot, filmed over with presence of mind, and bottomed with cold disbelief. In the dining-room was Whiston, carrying coffee to the plain, neglected ladies. Elsie saw him, but felt as if he could not see her. She was beyond his reach and ken. A sort of fusion existed between her and the large man at her side. She ate her custard, but an incomplete fusion all the while sustained and contained within the being of her employer.

But she was growing cooler. Whiston came up. She looked at him, and saw him with different eyes. She saw his slim, young man's figure real and enduring before her. That was he. But she was in the spell with the other man, fused with him, and she could not be taken away.

"Have you finished your cribbage?" she asked, with hasty evasion of him.

"Yes," he replied. "Aren't you getting tired of dancing?"

"Not a bit," she said.

"Not she," said Adams heartily. "No girl with any spirit gets tired of dancing. Have something else, Elsie. Come—sherry. Have a glass of sherry with us, Whiston."

Whilst they sipped the wine, Adams watched Whiston almost cunningly, to find his advantage.

"We'd better be getting back—there's the music," he said.

"See the women get something to eat, Whiston, will you, there's a good chap."

And he began to draw away. Elsie was drifting helplessly with him. But Whiston put himself beside them, and went along with them. In silence they passed through to the dancing-room. There Adams hesitated, and looked round the room. It was as if he could not see.

A man came hurrying forward, claiming Elsie, and Adams went to his other partner. Whiston stood watching during the dance. She was conscious of him standing there observant of her, like a ghost, or a judgment, or a guardian angel. She was also conscious, much more intimately and impersonally, of the body of the other man moving somewhere in the room. She still belonged to him, but a feeling of distraction possessed her, and helplessness. Adams danced on, adhering to Elsie, waiting his time, with the persistence of cynicism.

The dance was over. Adams was detained. Elsie found herself beside Whiston. There was something shapely about him as he sat, about his knees and his distinct figure, that she clung to. It was as if he had enduring form. She put her hand on his knee.

"Are you enjoying yourself?" he asked.

"*Ever* so," she replied, with a fervent, yet detached tone.

"It's going on for one o'clock," he said.

"Is it?" she answered. It meant nothing to her.

"Should we be going?" he said.

She was silent. For the first time for an hour or more an inkling of her normal consciousness returned. She resented it.

"What for?" she said.

"I thought you might have had enough," he said.

A slight soberness came over her, an irritation at being frustrated of her illusion.

"Why?" she said.

"We've been here since nine," he said.

That was no answer, no reason. It conveyed nothing to her. She sat detached from him. Across the room Sam Adams glanced at her. She sat there exposed for him.

"You don't want to be too free with Sam Adams," said Whiston cautiously, suffering. "You know what he is."

"How, free?" she asked.

"Why—you don't want to have too much to do with him."

She sat silent. He was forcing her into consciousness of her position. But he could not get hold of her feelings, to change them. She had a curious, perverse desire that he should not.

"I like him," she said.

"What do you find to like in him?" he said, with a hot heart.

"I don't know—but I like him," she said.

She was immutable. He sat feeling heavy and dulled with rage. He was not clear as to what he felt. He sat there un-living whilst she danced. And she, distracted, lost to herself between the opposing forces of the two men, drifted. Between the dances, Whiston kept near to her. She was scarcely conscious. She glanced repeatedly at her card, to see when she would dance again with Adams, half in desire, half in dread. Sometimes she met his steady, glaucous eye as she passed him in the dance. Sometimes she saw the steadiness of his flank as he danced. And it was always as if she rested on his arm, were borne along, up-borne by him, away from herself. And always there was present the other's antagonism. She was divided.

The time came for her to dance with Adams. Oh, the delicious closing of contact with him, of his limbs touching her limbs, his arm supporting her. She seemed to resolve. Whiston had not made himself real to her. He was only a heavy place in her consciousness.

But she breathed heavily, beginning to suffer from the closeness of strain. She was nervous. Adams also was constrained. A tightness, a tension was coming over them all. And he was exasperated, feeling something counteracting physical magnetism, feeling a will stronger with her than his own, intervening in what was becoming a vital necesity to him.

Elsie was almost lost to her own control. As she went forward with him to take her place at the dance, she stooped for her pocket handkerchief. The music sounded for quadrilles. Everybody was ready. Adams stood with his body near her, exerting his attraction over her. He was tense and fighting. She stooped for her pocket handkerchief, and shook it as she rose. It shook out and fell from her hand. With agony, she saw she had taken a white stocking instead of a handkerchief. For a second it lay on the floor, a twist of white stocking. Then, in an instant, Adams picked it up, with a little, surprised laugh of triumph.

"That'll do for me," he whispered—seeming to take possession of her. And he stuffed the stocking in his trousers pocket, and quickly offered her his handkerchief.

The dance began. She felt weak and faint, as if her will were turned to water. A heavy sense of loss came over her. She could not help herself any more. But it was peace.

When the dance was over, Adams yielded her up. Whiston came to her.

"What was it as you dropped?" Whiston asked.

"I thought it was my handkerchief—I'd taken a stocking by mistake," she said, detached and muted.

"And he's got it?"

"Yes."

"What does he mean by that?"

She lifted her shoulders.

"Are you going to let him keep it?" he asked.

"I don't let him."

There was a long pause.

"Am I to go and have it out with him?" he asked, his face flushed, his blue eyes going hard with opposition.

"No," she said, pale.

"Why?"

"No—I don't want you to say anything about it."

He sat exasperated and nonplussed.

"You'll let him keep it, then?" he asked.

She sat silent and made no form of answer.

"What do you mean by it?" he said, dark with fury. And he started up.

"No!" she cried. "Ted!" And she caught hold of him, sharply detaining him.

It made him black with rage.

"Why?" he said.

The something about her mouth was pitiful to him. He did not understand, but he felt she must have her reasons.

"Then I'm not stopping here," he said. "Are you coming with me?"

She rose mutely, and they went out of the room. Adams had not noticed.

In a few moments they were in the street.

"What the hell do you mean?" he said, in a black fury.

She went at his side, in silence, neutral.

"That great hog, an' all," he added.

Then they went a long time in silence through the frozen,

deserted darkness of the town. She felt she could not go in-doors. They were drawing near her house.

"I don't want to go home," she suddenly cried in distress and anguish. "I don't want to go home."

He looked at her.

"Why don't you?" he said.

"I don't want to go home," was all she could sob.

He heard somebody coming.

"Well, we can walk a bit farther," he said.

She was silent again. They passed out of the town into the fields. He held her by the arm—they could not speak.

"What's a-matter?" he asked at length, puzzled.

She began to cry again.

At last he took her in his arms, to soothe her. She sobbed by herself, almost unaware of him.

"Tell me what's a-matter, Elsie," he said. "Tell me what's a-matter—my dear—tell me, then——"

He kissed her wet face, and caressed her. She made no response. He was puzzled and tender and miserable.

At length she became quiet. Then he kissed her, and she put her arms round him, and clung to him very tight, as if for fear and anguish. He held her in his arms, wondering.

"Ted!" she whispered, frantic. "Ted!"

"What, my love?" he answered, becoming also afraid.

"Be good to me," she cried. "Don't be cruel to me."

"No, my pet," he said, amazed and grieved. "Why?"

"Oh, be good to me," she sobbed.

And he held her very safe, and his heart was white-hot with love for her. His mind was amazed. He could only hold her against his chest that was white-hot with love and belief in her. So she was restored at last.

III

She refused to go to her work at Adams's any more. Her father had to submit and she sent in her notice—she was not well. Sam Adams was ironical. But he had a curious patience. He did not fight.

In a few weeks, she and Whiston were married. She loved him with passion and worship, a fierce little abandon of love that moved him to the depths of his being, and gave him a permanent surety and sense of realness in himself. He did not

trouble about himself any more: he felt he was fulfilled and
now he had only the many things in the world to busy himself about. Whatever troubled him, at the bottom was surety.
He had found himself in this love.

They spoke once or twice of the white stocking.

"Ah!" Whiston exclaimed. "What does it matter?"

He was impatient and angry, and could not bear to consider
the matter. So it was left unresolved.

She was quite happy at first, carried away by her adoration
of her husband. Then gradually she got used to him. He
always was the ground of her happiness, but she got used to
him, as to the air she breathed. He never got used to her in
the same way.

Inside of marriage she found her liberty. She was rid of the
responsibility of herself. Her husband must look after that.
She was free to get what she could out of her time.

So that, when, after some months, she met Sam Adams, she
was not quite as unkind to him as she might have been. With
a young wife's new and exciting knowledge of men, she perceived he was in love with her, she knew he had always kept
an unsatisfied desire for her. And, sportive, she could not help
playing a little with this, though she cared not one jot for
the man himself.

When Valentine's day came, which was near the first anni-
versary of her wedding day, there arrived a white stocking
with a little amethyst brooch. Luckily Whiston did not see it,
so she said nothing of it to him. She had not the faintest
intention of having anything to do with Sam Adams, but once
a little brooch was in her possession, it was hers, and she did
not trouble her head for a moment how she had come by it.
She kept it.

Now she had the pearl ear-rings. They were a more valuable
and a more conspicuous present. She would have to ask her
mother to give them to her, to explain their presence. She
made a little plan in her head. And she was extraordinarily
pleased. As for Sam Adams, even if he saw her wearing them,
he would not give her away. What fun, if he saw her wearing
his ear-rings! She would pretend she had inherited them from
her grandmother, her mother's mother. She laughed to herself
as she went down-town in the afternoon, the pretty drops
dangling in front of her curls. But she saw no one of
importance.

Whiston came home tired and depressed. All day the male
in him had been uneasy, and this had fatigued him. She was
curiously against him, inclined, as she sometimes was nowa-
days, to make mock of him and jeer at him and cut him off.
He did not understand this, and it angered him deeply. She
was uneasy before him.

She knew he was in a state of suppressed irritation. The
veins stood out on the backs of his hands, his brow was drawn
stiffly. Yet she could not help goading him.

"What did you do wi' that white stocking?" he asked, out
of a gloomy silence, his voice strong and brutal.

"I put it in a drawer—why?" she replied flippantly.

"Why didn't you put it on the fire-back?" he said harshly.
"What are you hoarding it up for?"

"I'm not hoarding it up," she said. "I've got a pair."

He relapsed into gloomy silence. She, unable to move him,
ran away upstairs, leaving him smoking by the fire. Again she
tried on the ear-rings. Then another little inspiration came to
her. She drew on the white stockings, both of them.

Presently she came down in them. Her husband still sat
immovable and glowering by the fire.

"Look!" she said. "They'll do beautifully."

And she picked up her skirts to her knees, and twisted round,
looking at her pretty legs in the neat stockings.

He filled with unreasonable rage, and took the pipe from his
mouth.

"Don't they look nice?" she said. "One from last year and
one from this, they just do. Save you buying a pair."

And she looked over her shoulders at her pretty calves, and
at the dangling frills of her knickers.

"Put your skirts down and don't make a fool of yourself,"
he said.

"Why a fool of myself?" she asked.

And she began to dance slowly round the room, kicking up
her feet half reckless, half jeering, in ballet-dancer's fashion.
Almost fearful, yet in defiance, she kicked up her legs at him,
singing as she did so. She resented him.

"You little fool, ha' done with it," he said. "And you'll
backfire them stockings, I'm telling you." He was angry.
His face flushed dark, he kept his head bent. She ceased to
dance.

"I shan't," she said. "They'll come in very useful."

He lifted his head and watched her, with lighted, dangerous eyes.

"You'll put 'em on the fire-back, I tell you," he said.

It was a war now. She bent forward, in a ballet-dancer's fashion, and put her tongue between her teeth.

"I shan't back-fire them stockings," she sang, repeating his words, "I shan't, I shan't, I shan't."

And she danced round the room doing a high kick to the tune of her words. There was a real biting indifference in her behaviour.

"We'll see whether you will or not," he said, "trollops! You'd like Sam Adams to know you was wearing 'em, wouldn't you? That's what would please you."

"Yes, I'd like him to see how nicely they fit me, he might give me some more then."

And she looked down at her pretty legs.

He knew somehow that she *would* like Sam Adams to see how pretty her legs looked in the white stockings. It made his anger go deep, almost to hatred.

"Yer nasty trolley," he cried. "Put yer petticoats down, and stop being so foul-minded."

"I'm not foul-minded," she said. "My legs are my own. And why shouldn't Sam Adams think they're nice?"

There was a pause. He watched her with eyes glittering to a point.

"Have you been havin' owt to do with him?" he asked.

"I've just spoken to him when I've seen him," she said. "He's not as bad as you would make out."

"Isn't he?" he cried, a certain wakefulness in his voice. "Them who has anything to do wi' him is too bad for me, I tell you."

"Why, what are you frightened of him for?" she mocked.

She was rousing all his uncontrollable anger. He sat glowering. Every one of her sentences stirred him up like a red-hot iron. Soon it would be too much. And she was afraid herself; but she was neither conquered nor convinced.

A curious little grin of hate came on his face. He had a long score against her.

"What am I frightened of him for?" he repeated automatically. "What am I frightened of him for? Why, for you, you stray-running little bitch."

She flushed. The insult went deep into her, right home.

"Well, if you're so dull——" she said, lowering her eyelids, and speaking coldly, haughtily.

"If I'm so dull I'll break your neck the first word you speak to him," he said, tense.

"Pf!" she sneered. "Do you think I'm frightened of you?" She spoke coldly, detached.

She was frightened, for all that, white round the mouth.

His heart was getting hotter.

"You *will* be frightened of me, the next time you have anything to do with him," he said.

"Do you think *you'd* ever be told—ha!"

Her jeering scorn made him go white-hot, molten. He knew he was incoherent, scarcely responsible for what he might do. Slowly, unseeing, he rose and went out of doors, stifled, moved to kill her.

He stood leaning against the garden fence, unable either to see or hear. Below him, far off, fumed the lights of the town. He stood still, unconscious with a black storm of rage, his face lifted to the night.

Presently, still unconscious of what he was doing, he went indoors again. She stood, a small, stubborn figure with tight-pressed lips and big, sullen, childish eyes, watching him, white with fear. He went heavily across the floor and dropped into his chair.

There was a silence.

"*You're* not going to tell me everything I shall do, and everything I shan't," she broke out at last.

He lifted his head.

"I tell you *this*," he said, low and intense. "Have anything to do with Sam Adams, and I'll break your neck."

She laughed, shrill and false.

"How I hate your word 'break your neck'," she said, with a grimace of the mouth. "It sounds so common and beastly. Can't you say something else——"

There was a dead silence.

"And besides," she said, with a queer chirrup of mocking laughter, "what do you know about anything? He sent me an amethyst brooch and a pair of pearl ear-rings."

"He what?" said Whiston, in a suddenly normal voice. His eyes were fixed on her.

"Sent me a pair of pearl ear-rings, and an amethyst brooch," she repeated, mechanically, pale to the lips.

And her big, black, childish eyes watched him, fascinated, held in her spell.

He seemed to thrust his face and his eyes forward at her, as he rose slowly and came to her. She watched transfixed in terror. Her throat made a small sound, as she tried to scream.

Then, quick as lightning, the back of his hand struck her with a crash across the mouth, and she was flung black blinded against the wall. The shock shook a queer sound out of her. And then she saw him still coming on, his eyes holding her, his fist drawn back, advancing slowly. At any instant the blow might crash into her.

Mad with terror, she raised her hands with a queer clawing movement to cover her eyes and her temples, opening her mouth in a dumb shriek. There was no sound. But the sight of her slowly arrested him. He hung before her, looking at her fixedly, as she stood crouched against the wall with open, bleeding mouth, and wide-staring eyes, and two hands clawing over her temples. And his lust to see her bleed, to break her and destroy her, rose from an old source against her. It carried him. He wanted satisfaction.

But he had seen her standing there, a piteous, horrified thing, and he turned his face aside in shame and nausea. He went and sat heavily in his chair, and a curious ease, almost like sleep, came over his brain.

She walked away from the wall towards the fire, dizzy, white to the lips, mechanically wiping her small, bleeding mouth. He sat motionless. Then, gradually, her breath began to hiss, she shook, and was sobbing silently, in grief for herself. Without looking, he saw. It made his mad desire to destroy her come back.

At length he lifted his head. His eyes were glowing again, fixed on her.

"And what did he give them you for?" he asked, in a steady, unyielding voice.

Her crying dried up in a second. She also was tense.

"They came as valentines," she replied, still not subjugated. even if beaten.

"When, to-day?"

"The pearl ear-rings to-day—the amethyst brooch last year."

"You've had it a year?"

"Yes."

She felt that now nothing would prevent him if he rose to

kill her. She could not prevent him any more. She was yielded
up to him. They both trembled in the balance, unconscious.

"What have you had to do with him?" he asked, in a barren
voice.

"I've not had anything to do with him," she quavered.

"You just kept 'em because they were jewellery?" he said.

A weariness came over him. What was the worth of speaking any more of it? He did not care any more. He was dreary
and sick.

She began to cry again, but he took no notice. She kept
wiping her mouth on her handkerchief. He could see it, the
blood-mark. It made him only more sick and tired of the
responsibility of it, the violence, the shame.

When she began to move about again, he raised his head
once more from his dead, motionless position.

"Where are the things?" he said.

"They are upstairs," she quavered. She knew the passion
had gone down in him.

"Bring them down," he said.

"I won't," she wept, with rage. "You're not going to bully
me and hit me like that on the mouth."

And she sobbed again. He looked at her in contempt and
compassion and in rising anger.

"Where are they?" he said.

"They're in the little drawer under the looking-glass," she
sobbed.

He went slowly upstairs, struck a match, and found the
trinkets. He brought them downstairs in his hand.

"These?" he said, looking at them as they lay in his palm.

She looked at them without answering. She was not
interested in them any more.

He looked at the little jewels. They were pretty.

"It's none of their fault," he said to himself.

And he searched round slowly, persistently, for a box. He
tied the things up and addressed them to Sam Adams. Then
he went out in his slippers to post the little package.

When he came back she was still sitting crying.

"You'd better go to bed," he said.

She paid no attention. He sat by the fire. She still cried.

"I'm sleeping down here," he said. "Go you to bed."

In a few moments she lifted her tear-stained, swollen face
and looked at him with eyes all forlorn and pathetic. A great

flash of anguish went over his body. He went over, slowly, and very gently took her in his hands. She let herself be taken. Then as she lay against his shoulder, she sobbed aloud:

"I never meant——"

"My love—my little love——" he cried, in anguish of spirit, holding her in his arms.

A SICK COLLIER

She was too good for him, everybody said. Yet still she did not regret marrying him. He had come courting her when he was only nineteen, and she twenty. He was in build what they call a tight little fellow; short, dark, with a warm colour, and that upright set of the head and chest, that flaunting way in movement recalling a mating bird, which denotes a body taut and compact with life. Being a good worker he had earned decent money in the mine, and having a good home had saved a little.

She was a cook at "Uplands", a tall, fair girl, very quiet. Having seen her walk down the street, Horsepool had followed her from a distance. He was taken with her, he did not drink, and he was not lazy. So, although he seemed a bit simple, without much intelligence, but having a sort of physical brightness, she considered, and accepted him.

When they were married they went to live in Scargill Street, in a highly respectable six-roomed house which they had furnished between them. The street was built up the side of a long, steep hill. It was narrow and rather tunnel-like. Nevertheless, the back looked out over the adjoining pasture, across a wide valley of fields and woods, in the bottom of which the mine lay snugly.

He made himself gaffer in his own house. She was unacquainted with a collier's mode of life. They were married on a Saturday. On the Sunday night he said:

"Set th' table for my breakfast, an' put my pit-things afront o' th' fire. I s'll be gettin' up at ha'ef pas' five. Tha nedna shift thysen not till when ter likes."

He showed her how to put a newspaper on the table for a cloth. When she demurred:

"I want none o' your white cloths i' th' mornin'. I like ter be able to slobber if I feel like it," he said.

He put before the fire his moleskin trousers, a clean singlet, or sleeveless vest of thick flannel, a pair of stockings and his pit-boots, arranging them all to be warm and ready for morning.

"Now tha sees. That wants doin' ivery night."

Punctually at half-past five he left her, without any form of leave-taking, going downstairs in his shirt.

When he arrived home at four o'clock in the afternoon his dinner was ready to be dished up. She was startled when he came in, a short, sturdy figure, with a face indescribably black and streaked. She stood before the fire in her white blouse and white apron, a fair girl, the picture of beautiful cleanliness. He "clommaxed" in, in his heavy boots.

"Well, how 'as ter gone on?" he asked.

"I was ready for you to come home," she replied tenderly. In his black face the whites of his brown eyes flashed at her.

"An' I wor ready for comin'," he said. He planked his tin bottle and snap-bag on the dresser, took off his coat and scarf and waistcoat, dragged his arm-chair nearer the fire and sat down.

"Let's ha'e a bit o' dinner, then—I'm about clammed," he said.

"Aren't you goin' to wash yourself first?"

"What am I to wesh mysen for?"

"Well, you can't eat your dinner——"

"Oh, strike a daisy, Missis! Dunna I eat my snap i' th' pit wi'out weshin'?—forced to."

She served the dinner and sat opposite him. His small bullet head was quite black, save for the whites of his eyes and his scarlet lips. It gave her a queer sensation to see him open his red mouth and bare his white teeth as he ate. His arms and hands were mottled black; his bare, strong neck got a little fairer as it settled towards his shoulders, reassuring her. There was the faint indescribable odour of the pit in the room, an odour of damp, exhausted air.

"Why is your vest so black on the shoulders?" she asked.

"My singlet? That's wi' th' watter droppin' on us from th' roof. This is a dry un as I put on afore I come up. They ha'e gre't clothes-'osses, an' as we change us things, we put 'em on theer ter dry."

When he washed himself, kneeling on the hearth-rug stripped to the waist, she felt afraid of him again. He was so muscular, he seemed so intent on what he was doing, so intensely himself, like a vigorous animal. And as he stood wiping himself, with his naked breast towards her, she felt rather sick, seeing his thick arms bulge their muscles.

They were nevertheless very happy. He was at a great pitch

of pride because of her. The men in the pit might chaff him, they might try to entice him away, but nothing could reduce his self-assured pride because of her, nothing could unsettle his almost infantile satisfaction. In the evening he sat in his arm-chair chattering to her, or listening as she read the newspaper to him. When it was fine, he would go into the street, squat on his heels as colliers do, with his back against the wall of his parlour, and call to the passers-by, in greeting, one after another. If no one were passing, he was content just to squat and smoke, having such a fund of sufficiency and satisfaction in his heart. He was well married.

They had not been wed a year when all Brent and Wellwood's men came out on strike. Willy was in the Union, so with a pinch they scrambled through. The furniture was not all paid for, and other debts were incurred. She worried and contrived, he left it to her. But he was a good husband; he gave her all he had.

The men were out fifteen weeks. They had been back just over a year when Willy had an accident in the mine, tearing his bladder. At the pit head the doctor talked of the hospital. Losing his head entirely, the young collier raved like a madman, what with pain and fear of hospital.

"Tha s'lt go whoam, Willy, tha s'lt go whoam," the deputy said.

A lad warned the wife to have the bed ready. Without speaking or hesitating she prepared. But when the ambulance came, and she heard him shout with pain at being moved, she was afraid lest she should sink down. They carried him in.

"Yo' should 'a' had a bed i' th' parlour, Missis," said the deputy, "then we shouldna' ha' had to hawkse 'im upstairs, an' it 'ud 'a' saved your legs."

But it was too late now. They got him upstairs.

"They let me lie, Lucy," he was crying, "they let me lie two mortal hours on th' sleck afore they took me outer th' stall. Th' peen, Lucy, th' peen; oh, Lucy, th' peen, th' peen!"

"I know th' pain's bad, Willy, I know. But you must try an' bear it a bit."

"Tha manna carry on in that form, lad, thy missis'll niver be able ter stan' it," said the deputy.

"I canna 'elp it, it's th' peen, it's th' peen," he cried again. He had never been ill in his life. When he had smashed a finger he could look at the wound. But this pain came from inside, and terrified him. At last he was soothed and exhausted.

It was some time before she could undress him and wash him. He would let no other woman do for him, having that savage modesty usual in such men.

For six weeks he was in bed, suffering much pain. The doctors were not quite sure what was the matter with him, and scarcely knew what to do. He could eat, he did not lose flesh, nor strength, yet the pain continued, and he could hardly walk at all.

In the sixth week the men came out in the national strike. He would get up quite early in the morning and sit by the window. On Wednesday, the second week of the strike, he sat gazing out on the street as usual, a bullet-headed young man, still vigorous-looking, but with a peculiar expression of hunted fear in his face.

"Lucy," he called, "Lucy!"

She, pale and worn, ran upstairs at his bidding.

"Gi'e me a han'kercher," he said.

"Why, you've got one," she replied, coming near.

"Tha nedna touch me," he cried. Feeling his pocket, he produced a white handkerchief.

"I non want a white un, gi'e me a red un," he said.

"An' if anybody comes to see you," she answered, giving him a red handkerchief.

"Besides," she continued, "you needn't ha' brought me upstairs for that."

"I b'lieve th' peen's commin' on again," he said, with a little horror in his voice.

"It isn't, you know it isn't," she replied. "The doctor says you imagine it's there when it isn't."

"Canna I feel what's inside me?" he shouted.

"There's a traction-engine coming downhill," she said. "That'll scatter them.—I'll just go an' finish your pudding."

She left him. The traction-engine went by, shaking the houses. Then the street was quiet, save for the men. A gang of youths from fifteen to twenty-five years old were playing marbles in the middle of the road. Other little groups of men were playing on the pavement. The street was gloomy. Willy could hear the endless calling and shouting of men's voices.

"Tha'rt skinchin'!"

"I arena!"

"Come 'ere with that blood-alley."

"Swop us four for't."

"Shonna, gie's hold on't."

He wanted to be out, he wanted to be playing marbles. The pain had weakened his mind, so that he hardly knew any self-control.

Presently another gang of men lounged up the street. It was pay morning. The Union was paying the men in the Primitive Chapel. They were returning with their half-sovereigns.

"Sorry!" bawled a voice. "Sorry!"

The word is a form of address, corruption probably of "Sirrah". Willy started almost out of his chair.

"Sorry!" again bawled a great voice. "Art goin' wi' me to see Notts play Villa?"

Many of the marble-players started up.

"What time is it? There's no treens, we s'll ha'e ter walk."

The street was alive with men.

"Who's goin' ter Nottingham ter see th' match?" shouted the same big voice. A very large, tipsy man, with his cap over his eye, was calling.

"Com' on—aye, com' on!" came many voices. The street was full of the shouting of men. They split up in excited cliques and groups.

"Play up, Notts!" the big man shouted.

"Plee up, Notts!" shouted the youths and men. They were at kindling pitch. It only needed a shout to rouse them. Of this the careful authorities were aware.

"I'm goin', I'm goin'!" shouted the sick man at his window.

Lucy came running upstairs.

"I'm goin' ter see Notts play Villa on th' Meadows ground," he declared.

"You—*you* can't go. There are no trains. You can't walk nine miles."

"I'm goin' ter see th' match," he declared, rising.

"You know you can't. Sit down now an' be quiet."

She put her hand on him. He shook it off.

"Leave me alone, leave me alone. It's thee as ma'es th' peen come, it's thee. I'm goin' ter Nottingham to see th' football match."

"Sit down—folks'll hear you, and what will they think?"

"Come off'n me. Com' off. It's her, it's her as does it. Com' off."

He seized hold of her. His little head was bristling with madness, and he was strong as a lion.

"Oh, Willy!" she cried.

"It's 'er, it's 'er. Kill her!" he shouted, "kill her."

"Willy, folks'll hear you."

"Th' peen's commin' on again, I tell yer. I'll kill her for it."

He was completely out of his mind. She struggled with him to prevent his going to the stairs. When she escaped from him, who was shouting and raving, she beckoned to her neighbour, a girl of twenty-four, who was cleaning the window across the road.

Ethel Mellor was the daughter of a well-to-do check-weighman. She ran across in fear to Mrs. Horsepool. Hearing the man raving, people were running out in the street and listening. Ethel hurried upstairs. Everything was clean and pretty in the young home.

Willy was staggering round the room, after the slowly retreating Lucy, shouting:

"Kill her! Kill her!"

"Mr. Horsepool!" cried Ethel, leaning against the bed, white as the sheets, and trembling. "Whatever are you saying?"

"I tell yer it's 'er fault as th' pain comes on—I tell yer it is! Kill 'er—kill 'er!"

"Kill Mrs. Horsepool!" cried the trembling girl. "Why, you're ever so fond of her, you know you are."

"The peen—I ha'e such a lot o' peen—I want to kill 'er."

He was subsiding. When he sat down his wife collapsed in a chair, weeping noiselessly. The tears ran down Ethel's face. He sat staring out of the window; then the old, hurt look came on his face.

"What 'ave I been sayin'?" he asked, looking piteously at his wife.

"Why!" said Ethel, "you've been carrying on something awful, saying: 'Kill her, kill her!'"

"Have I, Lucy?" he faltered.

"You didn't know what you were saying," said his young wife gently but coldly.

His face puckered up. He bit his lips, then broke into tears, sobbing uncontrollaby, with his face to the window.

There was no sound in the room but of three people crying bitterly, breath caught in sobs. Suddenly Lucy put away her tears and went over to him.

"You didn't know what you was sayin', Willy, I know you didn't. I knew you didn't, all the time. It doesn't matter, Willy. Only don't do it again."

In a little while, when they were calmer, she went downstairs with Ethel.

"See if anybody is looking in the street," she said.

Ethel went into the parlour and peeped through the curtains.

"Aye!" she said. "You may back your life Lena an' Mrs. Severn'll be out gorping, and that clat-fartin' Mrs. Allsop."

"Oh, I hope they haven't heard anything! If it gets about as he's out of his mind, they'll stop his compensation, I know they will."

"They'd never stop his compensation for *that*," protested Ethel.

"Well, they *have* been stopping some——"

"It'll not get about. I s'll tell nobody."

"Oh, but if it does, whatever shall we do. . . ?"

THE CHRISTENING

THE mistress of the British School stepped down from her school gate, and instead of turning to the left as usual, she turned to the right. Two women who were hastening home to scramble their husbands' dinners together—it was five minutes to four—stopped to look at her. They stood gazing after her for a moment; then they glanced at each other with a woman's little grimace.

To be sure, the retreating figure was ridiculous: small and thin, with a black straw hat, and a rusty cashmere dress hanging full all round the skirt. For so small and frail and rusty a creature to sail with slow, deliberate stride was also absurd. Hilda Rowbotham was less than thirty, so it was not years that set the measure of her pace; she had heart disease. Keeping her face, that was small with sickness, but not uncomely, firmly lifted and fronting ahead, the young woman sailed on past the market-place, like a black swan of mournful disreputable plumage.

She turned into Berryman's, the bakers. The shop displayed bread and cakes, sacks of flour and oatmeal, flitches of bacon, hams, lard and sausages. The combination of scents was not unpleasing. Hilda Rowbotham stood for some minutes nervously tapping and pushing a large knife that lay on the counter, and looking at the tall, glittering brass scales. At last a morose man with sandy whiskers came down the step from the house-place.

"What is it?" he asked, not apologising for his delay.

"Will you give me sixpennyworth of assorted cakes and pastries—and put in some macaroons, please?" she asked, in remarkably rapid and nervous speech. Her lips fluttered like two leaves in a wind, and her words crowded and rushed like a flock of sheep at a gate.

"We've got no macaroons," said the man churlishly.

He had evidently caught that word. He stood waiting.

"Then I can't have any, Mr. Berryman. Now I do feel disappointed. I like those macaroons, you know, and it's not often I treat myself. One gets so tired of trying to spoil oneself, don't you think? It's less profitable even than trying to spoil somebody else." She laughed a quick little nervous laugh, putting her hand to her face.

"Then what'll you have?" asked the man, without the ghost of an answering smile. He evidently had not followed, so he looked more glum than ever.

"Oh, anything you've got," replied the schoolmistress, flushing slightly. The man moved slowly about, dropping the cakes from various dishes one by one into a paper bag.

"How's that sister o' yours getting on?" he asked, as if he were talking to the flour-scoop.

"Whom do you mean?" snapped the schoolmistress.

"The youngest," answered the stooping, pale-faced man, with a note of sarcasm.

"Emma! Oh, she's very well, thank you!" The schoolmistress was very red, but she spoke with sharp, ironical defiance. The man grunted. Then he handed her the bag, and watched her out of the shop without bidding her "Good afternoon".

She had the whole length of the main street to traverse, a half-mile of slow-stepping torture, with shame flushing over her neck. But she carried her white bag with an appearance of steadfast unconcern. When she turned into the field she seemed to droop a little. The wide valley opened out from her, with the far woods withdrawing into twilight, and away in the centre the great pit steaming its white smoke and chuffing as the men were being turned up. A full rose-coloured moon, like a flamingo flying low under the far, dusky east, drew out of the mist. It was beautiful, and it made her irritable sadness soften, diffuse.

Across the field, and she was at home. It was a new, substantial cottage, built with unstinted hand, such a house as an old miner could build himself out of his savings. In the rather small kitchen a woman of dark, saturnine complexion sat nursing a baby in a long white gown; a young woman of heavy, brutal cast stood at the table, cutting bread and butter. She had a downcast, humble mien that sat unnaturally on her, and was strangely irritating. She did not look round when her sister entered. Hilda put down the bag of cakes and left the room, not having spoken to Emma, nor to the baby, nor to Mrs. Carlin, who had come in to help for the afternoon.

Almost immediately the father entered from the yard with a dust-pan full of coals. He was a large man, but he was

going to pieces. As he passed through, he gripped the door
with his free hand to steady himself, but turning, he lurched
and swayed. He began putting the coals on the fire, piece by
piece. One lump fell from his hands and smashed on the white
hearth. Emma Rowbotham looked round, and began in a
rough, loud voice of anger: "Look at you!" Then she con-
sciously moderated her tones. "I'll sweep it up in a minute
—don't you bother; you'll only be going head-first into the
fire."

Her father bent down nevertheless to clear up the mess he
had made, saying, articulating his words loosely and slavering
in his speech:

"The lousy bit of a thing, it slipped between my fingers like
a fish."

As he spoke he went tilting towards the fire. The dark-
browed woman cried out; he put his hand on the hot stove to
save himself; Emma swung round and dragged him off.

"Didn't I tell you!" she cried roughly. "Now, have you
burnt yourself?"

She held tight hold of the big man, and pushed him into
his chair.

"What's the matter?" cried a sharp voice from the other
room. The speaker appeared, a hard well-favoured woman of
twenty-eight. "Emma, don't speak like that to father." Then,
in a tone not so cold, but just as sharp: "Now, father, what
have you been doing?"

Emma withdrew to her table sullenly.

"It's nöwt," said the old man, vainly protesting. "It's nöwt
at a'. Get on wi' what you're doin'."

"I'm afraid 'e's burnt 'is 'and," said the black-browed
woman, speaking of him with a kind of hard pity, as if he were
a cumbersome child. Bertha took the old man's hand and
looked at it, making a quick tut-tutting noise of impatience.

"Emma, get that zinc ointment—and some white rag," she
commanded sharply. The younger sister put down her loaf
with the knife in it, and went. To a sensitive observer, this
obedience was more intolerable than the most hateful discord.
The dark woman bent over the baby and made silent, gentle
movements of motherliness to it. The little one smiled and
moved on her lap. It continued to move and twist.

"I believe this child's hungry," she said. "How long is it
since he had anything?"

"Just afore dinner," said Emma dully.

"Good gracious!" exclaimed Bertha. "You needn't starve the child now you've got it. Once every two hours it ought to be fed, as I've told you; and now it's three. Take him, poor little mite—I'll cut the bread." She bent and looked at the bonny baby. She could not help herself: she smiled, and pressed its cheek with her finger, and nodded to it, making little noises. Then she turned and took the loaf from her sister. The woman rose and gave the child to its mother. Emma bent over the little sucking mite. She hated it when she looked at it, and saw it as a symbol, but when she felt it, her love was like fire in her blood.

"I should think 'e canna be comin'," said the father uneasily, looking up at the clock.

"Nonsense, father—the clock's fast! It's but half-past four! Don't figet!" Bertha continued to cut the bread and butter.

"Open a tin of pears," she said to the woman, in a much milder tone. Then she went into the next room. As soon as she was gone, the old man said again: "I should ha'e thought he'd 'a' been 'ere by now, if he means comin'."

Emma, engrossed, did not answer. The father had ceased to consider her, since she had become humbled.

" 'E'll come—'e'll come!" assured the stranger.

A few minutes later Bertha hurried into the kitchen, taking off her apron. The dog barked furiously. She opened the door, commanded the dog to silence, and said: "He will be quiet now, Mr. Kendal."

"Thank you," said a sonorous voice, and there was the sound of a bicycle being propped against a wall. A clergyman entered, a big-boned, thin, ugly man of nervous manner. He went straight to the father.

"Ah—how are you—" he asked musically, peering down on the great frame of the miner, ruined by locomotor ataxy.

His voice was full of gentleness, but he seemed as if he could not see distinctly, could not get things clear.

"Have you hurt your hand?" he said comfortingly, seeing the white rag.

"It wor nöwt but a pestered bit o' coal as dropped, an' I put my hand on th' hub. I thought tha worna commin'."

The familiar "tha", and the reproach, were unconscious retaliation on the old man's part. The minister smiled, half wistfully, half indulgently. He was full of vague tenderness. Then he turned to the young mother, who flushed sullenly because her dishonoured breast was uncovered.

"How are *you*?" he asked, very softly and gently, as if she were ill and he were mindful of her.

"I'm all right," she replied, awkwardly taking his hand without rising, hiding her face and the anger that rose in her.

"Yes—yes"—he peered down at the baby, which sucked with distended mouth upon the firm breast. "Yes, yes." He seemed lost in a dim musing.

Coming to, he shook hands unseeingly with the woman.

Presently they all went into the next room, the minister hesitating to help his crippled old deacon.

"I can go by myself, thank yer," testily replied the father.

Soon all were seated. Everybody was separated in feeling and isolated at table. High tea was spread in the middle kitchen, a large, ugly room kept for special occasions.

Hilda appeared last, and the clumsy, raw-boned clergyman rose to meet her. He was afraid of this family, the well-to-do old collier, and the brutal, self-willed children. But Hilda was queen among them. She was the clever one, and had been to college. She felt responsible for the keeping up of a high standard of conduct in all the members of the family. There *was* a difference between the Rowbothams and the common collier folk. Woodbine Cottage was a superior house to most— and was built in pride by the old man. She, Hilda, was a college-trained schoolmistress; she meant to keep up the prestige of her house in spite of blows.

She had put on a dress of green voile for this special occasion. But she was very thin; her neck protruded painfully. The clergyman, however, greeted her almost with reverence, and, with some assumption of dignity, she sat down before the tray. At the far end of the table sat the broken, massive frame of her father. Next to him was the youngest daughter, nursing the restless boy. The minister sat between Hilda and Bertha, hulking his bony frame uncomfortably.

There was a great spread on the table of tinned fruits and tinned salmon, ham and cakes. Miss Rowbotham kept a keen eye on everything: she felt the importance of the occasion. The young mother who had given rise to all this solemnity ate in sulky discomfort, snatching sullen little smiles at her child, smiles which came, in spite of her, when she felt its little limbs stirring vigorously on her lap. Bertha, sharp and abrupt, was chiefly concerned with the baby. She scorned her sister, and treated her like dirt. But the infant was a streak of light to her. Miss Rowbotham concerned herself with the function and the conversation. Her hands fluttered; she talked in little volleys, exceedingly nervous. Towards the end of the meal, there came a pause. The old man wiped his mouth with his red handkerchief, then, his blue eyes going fixed and staring, he began to speak, in a loose, slobbering fashion, charging his words at the clergyman.

"Well, mester—we'n axed you to come here ter christen this childt, an' you'n come, an' I'm sure we're very thankful. I can't see lettin' the poor blessed childt miss baptizing, an' they aren't for goin' to church wi't——" He seemed to lapse into a muse. "So," he resumed, "we'n axed you to come here to do the job. I'm not sayin' as it's not 'ard on us, it is. I'm breakin' up, an' mother's gone. I don't like leavin' a girl o' mine in a situation like 'ers is, but what the Lord's done, He's done, an' it's no matter murmuring. . . . There's one thing to be thankful for, an' we *are* thankful for it: they never need know the want of bread."

Miss Rowbotham, the lady of the family, sat very stiff and pained during this discourse. She was sensitive to so many things that she was bewildered. She felt her young sister's shame, then a kind of swift protecting love for the baby, a feeling that included the mother; she was at a loss before her father's religious sentiment, and she felt and resented bitterly the mark upon the family, against which the common folk could lift their fingers. Still she winced from the sound of her father's words. It was a painful ordeal.

"It is hard for you," began the clergyman in his soft, lingering, unworldly voice. "It is hard for you to-day, but the Lord gives comfort in His time. A man child is born unto us, therefore let us rejoice and be glad. If sin has entered in among us, let us purify our hearts before the Lord. . . ."

He went on with his discourse. The young mother lifted the whimpering infant, till its face was hid in her loose hair. She was hurt, and a little glowering anger shone in her face. But nevertheless her fingers clasped the body of the child beautifully. She was stupefied with anger against this emotion let loose on her account.

Miss Bertha rose and went to the little kitchen, returning

with water in a china bowl. She placed it there among the tea-things.

"Well, we're all ready," said the old man, and the clergyman began to read the service. Miss Bertha was godmother, the two men godfathers. The old man sat with bent head. The scene became impressive. At last Miss Bertha took the child and put it in the arms of the clergyman. He, big and ugly, shone with a kind of unreal love. He had never mixed with life, and women were all unliving, Bibical things to him. When he asked for the name, the old man lifted his head fiercely. "Joseph William, after me," he said, almost out of breath.

"Joseph William, I baptize thee . . ." resounded the strange, full, chanting voice of the clergyman. The baby was quite still.

"Let us pray!" It came with relief to them all. They knelt before their chairs, all but the young mother, who bent and hid herself over her baby. The clergyman began his hesitating, struggling prayer.

Just then heavy footsteps were heard coming up the path, ceasing at the window. The young mother, glancing up, saw her brother, black in his pit dirt, grinning in through the panes. His red mouth curved in a sneer; his fair hair shone above his blackened skin. He caught the eye of his sister and grinned. Then his black face disappeared. He had gone on into the kitchen. The girl with the child sat still and anger filled her heart. She herself hated now the praying clergyman and the whole emotional business; she hated her brother bitterly. In anger and bondage she sat and listened.

Suddenly her father began to pray. His familiar, loud, rambling voice made her shut herself up and become even insentient. Folks said his mind was weakening. She believed it to be true, and kept herself always disconnected from him.

"We ask Thee, Lord," the old man cried, "to look after this childt. Fatherless he is. But what does the earthly father matter before Thee? The childt is Thine, he is Thy childt. Lord, what father has a man but Thee? Lord, when a man says he is a father, he is wrong from the first word. For Thou art the Father, Lord. Lord, take away from us the conceit that our children are ours. Lord, Thou art Father of this childt as is fatherless here. O God, Thou bring him up. For I have stood between Thee and my children; I've had *my* way with them, Lord; I've stood between Thee and my children; I've cut 'em off from Thee because they were mine. And they've grown

twisted, because of me. Who is their father, Lord, but Thee?
But I put myself in the way, they've been plants under a
stone, because of me. Lord, if it hadn't been for me, they
might ha' been trees in the sunshine. Let me own it, Lord,
I've done 'em mischief. It would ha' been better if they'd never
known no father. No man is a father, Lord: only Thou art.
They can never grow beyond Thee, but I hampered them. Lift
'em up again, and undo what I've done to my children. And
let this young childt be like a willow tree beside the waters,
with no father but Thee, O God. Aye, an' I wish it had been
so with my children, that they'd had no father but Thee. For
I've been like a stone upon them, and they rise up and curse
me in their wickedness. But let me go, an' lift Thou them up,
Lord . . ."

The minister, unaware of the feelings of a father, knelt in
trouble, hearing without understanding the special language of
fatherhood. Miss Rowbotham alone felt and understood a
little. Her heart began to flutter; she was in pain. The two
younger daughters kneeled unhearing, stiffened and impervious.
Bertha was thinking of the baby; and the young mother thought
of the father of her child, whom she hated. There was a clatter
outside in the scullery. There the youngest son made as much
noise as he could, pouring out the water for his wash, muttering in deep anger:

"Blortin', slaverin' old fool!"

And while the praying of his father continued, his heart was
burning with rage. On the table was a paper bag. He picked
it up and read: "John Berryman—Bread, Pastries, etc." Then
he grinned with a grimace. The father of the baby was baker's
man at Berryman's. The prayer went on in the middle kitchen.
Laurie Rowbotham gathered together the mouth of the bag,
inflated it, and burst it with his fist. There was a loud report.
He grinned to himself. But he writhed at the same time with
shame and fear of his father.

The father broke off from his prayer; the party shuffled to
their feet. The young mother went into the scullery.

"What art doin', fool?" she said.

The collier youth tipped the baby under the chin, singing:

> "Pat-a-cake, pat-a-cake, baker's man,
>   Bake me a cake as fast as you can. . . ."

The mother snatched the child away. "Shut thy mouth," she said, the colour coming into her cheek.

> "Prick it and stick it and mark it with P,
> And put it i' th' oven for baby an' me. . . ."

He grinned, showing a grimy, and jeering and unpleasant red mouth and white teeth.

"I s'll gi'e thee a dab ower th' mouth," said the mother of the baby grimly. He began to sing again, and she struck out at him.

"Now what's to do?" said the father, staggering in.

The youth began to sing again. His sister stood sullen and furious.

"Why does *that* upset you?" asked the eldest Miss Rowbotham, sharply, of Emma the mother. "Good gracious, it hasn't improved your temper."

Miss Bertha came in, and took the bonny baby.

The father sat big and unheeding in his chair, his eyes vacant, his physique wrecked. He let them do as they would, he fell to pieces. And yet some power, involuntary, like a curse, remained in him. The very ruin of him was like a lodestone that held them in its control. The wreck of him still dominanted the house, in his dissolution even he compelled their being. They had never lived; his life, his will had always been upon them and contained them. They were only half-individuals.

The day after the christening he staggered in at the doorway declaring, in a loud voice, with joy in life still : "The daisies light up the earth, they clap their hands in multitudes, in praise of the morning." And his daughters shrank, sullen.

The Complete
SHORT STORIES
of D. H. Lawrence

VOLUME ONE

In the judgment of many, Lawrence's expansive genius found its happiest expression within disciplined limits, for in his short stories and short novels his powers are never weakened by the repetitions which mar some of his longer works. As a short-story writer, Lawrence at his best was unexcelled.

This first volume contains the following stories:

THE VIKING PRESS • 625 Madison Ave. • New York 10022
Cover design by Jeanyee Wong